BETRAYAL

and the

CAMBRIDGE BLUE

Alex Anvik

FriesenPress

One Printers Way
Altona, MB R0G 0B0
Canada

www.friesenpress.com

Copyright © 2025 by Alex Anvik
First Edition — 2025

Edited by Laura Apgar & Miranda Summers-Pritchard

ISBN
978-1-03-832312-5 (Hardcover)
978-1-03-832311-8 (Paperback)
978-1-03-832313-2 (eBook)

1. FICTION, THRILLERS, ESPIONAGE

Distributed to the trade by The Ingram Book Company

Special thanks to

Who would have thought
this is how the adventure would end

I am walking on a cement pathway, looking down at my feet. I can see grass on either side of the smooth and unblemished concrete pathway, bathed in sunlight. I am wearing brown brogues, jeans, and a pale blue shirt. As I look up, I realise I am walking through a quintessential English city park. There is a large green space to my right, and in the distance, I see a few people playing football or lying on a blanket.

The sun is setting ahead of me, making it a little difficult to see, but I can feel its warmth on my face.

Despite being in a city park, all I can hear are the sounds of my foot steps. The pathway leads to the end of the large central green space and some interconnected flower beds in full bloom. As I approach, I notice five benches overlooking the central green space.

All the benches are empty except for the one in the middle, where my father is sitting. He sees me and smiles. I walk up to the bench and sit next to him. My father doesn't look at me, and we don't speak.

I feel somewhat detached and disconnected from the moment, anxious and alone despite my father's presence. After a few moments, my father pats me on the knee without looking at me and says, "Don't worry, everything is going to be okay".

As he pats me on the knee, I notice his watch, a present from me. My father then gets up and walks away. I don't watch him leave but look out onto the park. Sitting there, looking out over the green space, I take a deep breath, and a sense of calm eases through me.

Inevitably, I wake up. This was a recurring dream I had after my father passed away. I had this dream almost every night for three months, and even now, it sometimes recurs. Not a day goes by without me thinking of him. This book was written because my father was right; everything is going to be alright. It is easy to find excuses for why your life isn't the way you want it to be.

You are the reason your life isn't working, and only you can fix that.

I wear my father's watch every day, as a reminder, that I am the maker of my own destiny and one day I shall pass this on to my nephew.

CHAPTER 1

ALGERIA, RN 49 HIGHWAY, NORTH AFRICA

Peter Cartwright had been on the move for about twelve hours, and he was exhausted. Even the Audi R6 he was pushing to the limits sounded like it needed a break. All around him, the mountainous region of northern Algeria demanded his attention, but he sped the car with relentless intent through the breathtaking wilderness.

He had left Gharyan, Libya in a blaze of gunfire and confusion and hadn't looked back, knowing he had to get out of Africa and back into southern Europe as soon as possible. He could have roared away from the safe house to Tripoli and got on the first ferry. He knew however that Dominic, the team leader at the house, would have figured that out and alerted the authorities. He would give some fabricated but plausible story that Peter had attacked his team and kidnapped and tortured Chloe. He would have announced that Peter was a threat to Libya's national security, and Peter also knew that, plausible stories aside, the authorities in Tripoli weren't the most honest of chaps.

Chloe lay on the back seat under Peter's jacket, making only the occasional whimper to remind him she was there. Peter tried to keep the Audi level as he tore round the mountain bends, but he knew the ride was causing her pain as she lapsed in and out of consciousness. He would need to stop soon and assess both himself and her, but for now, he had to press on.

He'd been amazed to find her alive—he knew how relentless interrogators could be. He felt bad for not trying harder to stop her from going to the safe house, when he'd had a pretty good idea of what she was facing. He tried to convince himself that even if he had, she'd still have gone, but he still couldn't shake off his sense of guilt. She looked awful—a few more hours of that and she might have died.

They'd really worked her over in that squalid little room.

Peter couldn't believe the sight that had met him as he entered the eight-by-eight-foot concrete cell. It was easily forty degrees in there, and Chloe was sat in the middle. He'd secured his handgun in the rear of his jeans and removed his jacket as sweat beaded off him. She was barefoot and wore only a pair of torn jeans and her black bra. Her long red hair was blood-soaked and lay matted against her skin.

She was tied with wire at the ankles to a metal chair, which was bolted to the floor. Her waist was strapped into a leather harness. Chloe's five-foot-six, toned, athletic frame looked almost childlike in the dismal little room. Her left hand had been cuffed to the chair, but her right arm was outstretched and attached to a wire cable that was bolted to the wall, giving the half-mirror-image of what Peter imagined someone being crucified would look like. Her shoulders were almost separating under the pressure, and her muscles strained to the point of breaking. He could see that the wire bindings had sliced through her skin during her struggles. There was also a strong smell of urine, and he saw a puddle beneath her.

As he figured out how to cut her free, he could see the punch and kick marks, the electrical burns on her body, and the car battery in the corner with its obligatory cables attached. *Electric shock treatment, Jesus. What had Dominic done?*

Peter didn't want to say her name in case she called out, but as soon as he touched her, she went rigid as if receiving another shock. She instantly started to fight. Even after all she'd been through, she wasn't going to let them have it easy. He leaned in towards her ear, cradled her head, and whispered, "It's okay, Chloe. I'm here to save you."

He lifted her head back and tasted the bile in the back of his throat. She was a battered and bloodied mess. He wanted to storm out of the room and kill them all.

He'd been a police officer for a long time and had seen some appalling sights, but he was not prepared for what he felt when he looked at Chloe. But he needed to move quickly now—it wouldn't be long before they found the body of the guard he'd killed, and then all hell would break loose.

Peter looked around and found some tools he could use to cut Chloe free. He was sure these men would have a sinister toolkit for cutting and slicing limbs from those shackled to "The Chair." He knew that he'd be rescuing a pain-ravaged body, so he had brought morphine. He tried to remember what they had taught him in his training about administering it. *Too little and it won't be effective. Too much and it could kill them. Look for signs of rejection by the body.*

His adrenalin was through the roof. He cut the wire to the first wrist, assessing her as he worked and thinking, *You are going to need a couple of hits.* He gave the first to the thigh—not much of a change—so he took another syringe and drove it into her shoulder. Safe to say, he saw a reaction. She went completely limp, and he immediately heard her breathing go shallow, almost inaudible. The morphine, thankfully, hadn't stopped Chloe's breathing. Peter continued to cut her free, and as he laid her on the floor, she resembled a rag doll.

He took off his jacket and pulled it around her, securing her arms inside and zipping it up. He then took the arms of the jacket and tied them around her, making her a secure bundle. He needed to get up a flight of stairs, along a narrow corridor, and into the garage where the car was parked.

He knew taking Dominic's Audi would infuriate him, but killing his guard, rescuing Chloe, and thwarting his operation was already sure to drive him up the wall. In Peter's mind, he had already thrown caution to the wind, so why not steal Dominic's beloved car? He also knew it was equipped with a few weapons, comms, and more importantly, a medical kit.

He lifted Chloe over his shoulder, and she didn't make a sound. Thankfully, she only weighed a mighty 120 lbs, so he wasn't going to struggle. He drew the Glock, silencer attached, from his waistband and made his way out of the dungeon.

It was hard to concentrate with his heart going like a pneumatic drill. Plus, shooting one-handed wasn't exactly his forte. This was stuff out of a Jason Bourne movie, and Jason Bourne he was not. He was just some cop who, only six months earlier, had been sitting behind his desk as a Special Branch Intelligence Officer, contemplating his tedious life.

He'd been selected for this whole affair because he was the only single guy in the office, was ten years younger than all his counterparts, and most importantly, had shown a modicum of enthusiasm.

He'd always wondered what it would be like to be part of a world he'd read so many books about. He had read a lot of autobiographies of SEAL operators, CIA agents, and rogue MI6 sources and also devoured popular espionage fiction. He found the subject endlessly fascinating. But now here he was, in his own adventure and finding it a whole different ball game. Even if he didn't make it out alive, he had to get Chloe out.

They moved along the hallway, and he could hear distant voices as guards watched television and smoked. Thankfully, that created quite a bit of noise, so his movement wasn't heard.

Halfway down the corridor, he found the door that led to the garage. He eased it open and slowly moved inside, handgun raised in case he had to dispatch another guard. As he entered the room he managed to smash Chloe's head into the door frame with a resounding thump.

He froze for a heart-stopping moment, waiting for the sound of raised voices and running feet. But all he heard was Chloe mumble, "Put me back in the chair, why don't you? It would be safer."

Chuckling, he opened the back door to the Audi, rolled her off his shoulder, and laid her inside, behind the passenger's seat. This meant that from the driver's seat, with a slight turn of the head, he could see her face while driving. Predictably, the black key fob for the ignition was resting on the front tyre. If you didn't know it was there, you would never spot it. He got in and put his gun on the passenger seat.

He exhaled. *I've done it. I can't believe I've done it!*

His moment of triumph was smashed as the driver's-side door burst open and a punch landed across his jaw. Then a scream. "Dominic, they're escaping!"

Then fists flew in, and he immediately reverted to police mode. *Fight. Come on, fight!*

This guy was big and all set to win, but he knew that winning wasn't his strategy. He just needed to keep hold of him until Dominic and his team arrived, which was sure to be only seconds from now. Peter could hear the pounding of feet along the corridor.

Bollocks to this noble police stuff. He didn't have to let some guy keep beating on him until his back-up arrived. He grabbed his gun, brought it up, and with one contact-shot to the chest, his attacker flew back against the wall, retracting in pain.

As Peter leaned out to shut the door, he failed to see the small pistol in his assailant's hand. *Clack!* The round hit his right shoulder. In panic, Peter shot again, and the guard went limp against the wall.

Another burst of gunfire littered the inside of the driver's door as Peter pulled it shut and hit the garage remote. The door opened quickly, and as he fumbled to get the car into gear, he made out Dominic in the rearview mirror, standing with his carbine in hand. He accelerated into the street and sped off—in no real direction, just away from Dominic and the house.

*

Dominic stood in the garage, watching his Audi weave its way along the dusty road as pedestrians dived for cover. He told his men not to shoot, as there were too many people, then ordered them to get the garage door closed before anyone saw the guard's corpse.

"Shall we go after them?" one of his men asked.

"No," Dominic replied. "I need to make a phone call, and we need to get out of here. Get this place cleaned up. I don't want to see a single trace of our presence here. We leave in thirty minutes. Now move."

His team moved with the consummate efficiency expected of such a professional outfit.

Once his men were occupied, Dominic reached for his cell phone, punched in a code, waited for the encrypted tone, and dialled. A female voice answered. "Speak."

"Papa One has Charlie One. He rescued her from the safe house in Awbari moments ago."

"What do you mean he rescued her? I thought you took him out of the equation," came the rather terse response.

"Maybe we underestimated him," Dominic replied defensively.

"What do you mean 'we?' You are leading a team of trained professionals from Special Forces, or maybe 'special' doesn't quite mean what I thought anymore. What about Charlie One? Did you get the information out of her?"

"No, we didn't." Dominic was angry now and didn't appreciate the way she was speaking to him.

"Alert all those we have in North Africa. They are both to be captured alive. Keep me posted. Let's get this cleared up as soon as possible," said the woman.

Dominic replied with a simple, "Okay," and hung up. He'd been in counter-intelligence his entire career and wasn't used to being caught out like this.

The audacious rescue and unexpected violence displayed by Peter had surprised Dominic, but it did provide him with valuable intelligence. Dominic realised that Peter wouldn't have acted in such a manner if he didn't care for, or perhaps even love, Chloe. This vulnerability could be exploited. It was a weakness common to all men, making them sloppy and careless.

CHAPTER 2

ALGERIA, RN 49 HIGHWAY, WEST OF MAISON VERTE

Peter had taken a round to the right shoulder, but it had been a glancing effort. It had only penetrated a few millimetres under his skin and had travelled about an inch upon entry to exit, but it felt as if a hot poker had been driven through his entire shoulder. Even though he told himself to drive on, he desperately wanted to stop for a little morphine and take a moment to recover. He'd placed Chloe on the back seat in the recovery position, facing him, so he could reach back and check her pulse as he drove, as well as see that she was still breathing via the rearview mirror.

After an hour or so, he decided he had to stop to properly assess his wounds and check on Chloe. Glancing at the map, he saw a town called Ouargla. It seemed to be small and off the beaten track; he hoped it wouldn't be overly populated. He was aiming for little or no police presence, which would allow him to keep a low profile. With his Libyan plates, he hoped he would look like a tourist who'd just lost his way.

As he cruised his way through the town, he saw the usual stores and coffee shops, but he needed somewhere a little quieter. He made two circuits of the town, thinking if there were nowhere suitable, he'd move on. Then, on the outskirts, near a gas station, stood a coffee shop with parking in the rear. There, he could keep the Audi out of sight of the main highway and do what he needed to, away from prying eyes.

He parked the car, nose facing out, and turned off the engine, which ticked softly as it wound down from its long drive. He sat for a moment, watching and waiting, hand on the gear stick.

When he felt it was okay, he opened the door and tried to get out. The adrenalin had certainly worn off, and he ached from head to toe. His upper body was ravaged with muscle pain, and as he swung his legs out of the car, he had to vomit from the pain. Regaining composure, he used his left arm to lever himself to standing. *Mate, you really are in bad shape.*

Feeling a little better and somewhat more human and in control, he took in some fresh air. Surveying his shoulder through the hole in his T-shirt, it didn't look too bad, but as he moved his arm, it stung, bringing further waves of nausea. He moved round to the boot and, searching inside, found the medical kit.

It contained all sorts of goodies, including a bottle of 30 mg codeine tablets. He didn't want to take morphine as he knew it would put him out of action, but he'd taken codeine tablets before and was sure he'd still be able to operate on them.

He also found a large duffle bag and, on opening it, discovered random clothes—coveralls, jackets, T-shirts, trousers, hats, and wigs. Peter assumed this must be Dominic's changes of clothes for surveillance. He found a T-shirt and placed two codeine tablets in his pocket. He grabbed some antiseptic liquid and two large dressings and slid them inside one of the jacket pockets.

First, he needed to check on Chloe. The Audi's windows were blacked out, so he climbed inside and shut the door behind him. Chloe was petite enough that Peter was able to lower one of the seats to gain access to the first aid kit while still keeping her comfortable.

Chloe needed an I.V. to replace lost fluids. He broke open some of the antiseptic solutions and, with a sterile swab, started to clean her up. Once he'd cleaned her face, she didn't look too bad. She had clearly been punched, as her eyes had some minor swelling, and there was a slight cut on her upper lip. He cleaned and bandaged the cuts the cables had caused on her right wrist. Thirty minutes later, he slid a clean T-shirt on her and laid her back down on the rear seat.

He crouched down and whispered in her ear, "I'm so sorry, Chloe. We will make this right. I promise."

Chloe reached out, and he took her hand. She softly said, "Don't worry. I knew what I was doing." Then she turned and kissed him, leaving Peter overwhelmed.

He couldn't contain himself, and as he held her head, he kissed her more passionately. He felt the tears beneath his thumbs as they grazed her face. The world disappeared, and all he saw, all he felt, all he wanted, was her. He knew then that all of this had been for her. His decision, the carnage, the nightmare had been nothing more than a process for making her a part of his life.

He didn't want to admit it, but he'd become emotionally

attached to this red-headed creature that lay before him. The moment was brief and intense, and he knew he needed to let her sleep while he focused on their escape.

She fell silent, and Peter exited the car and composed himself, wiping tears from his own eyes. He couldn't determine if the anger he felt was towards the men who had tortured her or if he was livid at his own cowardice for leading her into that terrible room.

He pondered her response. *Don't worry, I knew what I was doing.* It made him cringe because it meant she had entered that arena of torture knowing he had betrayed her. He got out of the car, slid on his jacket, and zipped it up. He checked his face in the mirror for blood flecks, and after making sure the car was secure, he headed for the coffee shop.

The coffee shop was modern and well-decorated in that trendy bohemian style. It was designed to make you want to pull up a bean bag and stay for a while. There were a few people enjoying coffee and oversized muffins. As he made his way to order, he felt their eyes assess him before returning to their conversations or laptops. He got the impression they didn't get many tourists through town and didn't really care either. The young girl behind the counter asked Peter something in Algerian, and he asked if she spoke English, which of course she did.

Peter was always amazed that so few of his friends spoke another language, yet here in this random town in Algeria, this young girl, who was probably nineteen or twenty, spoke English with ease. She was wearing traditional Muslim headwear that covered her hair but left her face exposed, revealing the deep, dark, opal eyes you might expect to see in those of Arab descent.

Peter smiled and asked for a double-shot espresso. There was some dark, rich, Algerian chocolate for sale, and he threw a bar of it onto the counter. The girl slid his espresso over, which seemed to have been made in the blink of an eye. Peter paid with cash and, having grabbed his coffee, headed off to the washroom. The whole time, he was careful to try to look as relaxed as possible. It was amazing how paranoia can set in as you think everyone who looks at you is about to call the authorities.

He entered the men's washroom, a large room with the obligatory baby-changing table for the modern man. Peter smiled—these tables always gave him somewhere to dump his stuff when he needed to park his breakfast. He pulled down the table and laid down his coffee, the surgical dressing, the antiseptic wash, and the new T-shirt. Then his silenced handgun. He took off his jacket as carefully and painlessly as he could, and then slid off his T-shirt.

As he examined himself in the mirror, he drew out the painkillers, placed them in his mouth, and began to crunch them up. They tasted vile, but he knew that it was a quicker way for him to get them into his system. He took a swig of his espresso to drain away the remaining grainy substance, knowing also that the caffeine would expedite the relief.

He wasn't sure if it was because he hadn't drunk anything in almost ten hours, but the espresso tasted amazing and gave him a tingle through his face.

He stood with his head resting on the mirror, enjoying the moment of euphoria. He also wanted to give the painkillers a little time to work their magic. He then took the antiseptic wash and poured it onto one of the dressings. It was a clear orange liquid, and as he held it in his left hand, it felt somewhat cool against his palm.

He stood in front of the mirror and gripped the frame with his right hand—so tightly you could see the muscles flexing through his arm and shoulder. He heard his respiration quicken and did a little "combat breathing" as he tried to calm down. With a fast inhale, he placed the dressing on top of the wound. It probably took a second or two before it dawned on him that it didn't sting as much as he'd expected. Instead, it just felt cold, and he could feel his shoulder going numb.

He opened his eyes and breathed normally again. He saw the beads of sweat on his forehead and let go of the mirror, noticing how white his hand had become from his tight grip. He chuckled to himself at his ingrained fear. He'd convinced himself that cleaning the wound was going to be agonising. He left the dressing on his shoulder, and the liquid ran down his arm and back. He picked up the bar of chocolate and snapped off a couple of chunks. As he crunched through the dark, sweet delight, he took the final sip of his espresso and remembered how much he enjoyed the taste combination.

Then he cleaned the wound as best he could before removing the adhesive strips of a new dressing and placing it on his shoulder. He wrapped the first dressing and all the other garbage into the damaged T-shirt and bundled it all together. He slid on the fresh T-shirt, and as he looked at himself in the mirror, he thought he looked almost respectable.

The dressing didn't stand out too much, so he carried the jacket over his arm, with the old, soiled T-shirt slid into its sleeve. He removed the silencer from the gun and stored that in a zipped pocket of the jacket. Then he slid the gun into the rear of his waistband, checking in the mirror that it didn't stand out too much.

He walked out of the washroom, and as he left the café,

the girl wished him a good day. It was then, for the first time, that he felt a little more relaxed and began to enjoy the warm summer evening. Maybe it was the painkillers or the fusion of chocolate and espresso, but he didn't feel too bad. And his shoulder certainly wasn't throbbing as it had before.

A quick check on Chloe reassured him she would be comfortable enough for the drive to the ferry port in Morocco. He ensured the I.V. was in place. Although tempted by another coffee, he decided he needed to press on. After fuelling the vehicle, he headed back to his route. He managed to find a classical music channel, eased into the leather seat, dialled in the air conditioning, and set off, trying as he drove to process everything that had happened.

CHAPTER 3

THE VENUE, THE COTSWOLDS, ENGLAND

The woman Dominic had called was Abigail West, and she stood in her office looking out onto the rolling hills of the Cotswolds.

It was early morning, and the mist was lingering across the open fields. She crossed over to one of the four large sash windows that looked out onto the gently undulating hills beyond. Her office, although large, was furnished elegantly, with a tasteful sofa set and a leather-gilded desk. Refined rather than ostentatious, it spoke of history in reverent tones.

The office was part of a stately home located in a very secluded, quintessential English hamlet. But on closer inspection, one might see that the glass in the authentic-looking windows was bulletproof and observe that the groundsmen had the manner of serving military personnel. Or one might notice the well-placed cameras that tracked every movement in and outside the house.

Those who lived in the shadowy world of this imposing woman knew the stately home as "The Venue."

It was not somewhere you stumbled across by chance, and if you did, it might not be the most pleasant encounter. The Venue was the home of MI6, and Abigail West, known the world over as "C," was the head of this secretive organisation.

Most people believed that Sir Mark Goodlove, in his London office, was the head of MI6, but in the current climate, it had been prudent to move the operational work to another location, appointing Sir Goodlove as the visible presence of MI6.

Sir Goodlove had a lot of power and sway in the political arena, but he was not bred in her world. In fact, he was too liberal for Abigail's taste, and following his appointment, he was well-positioned to assess what should and shouldn't be passed to The Venue, thus steering MI6 away from the more aggressive tactics that Abigail preferred. He also wasn't representing them enough at the cabinet level, which she found frustrating. All Abigail's actions now had to be sanctioned by the cabinet, and these decisions were passed through Sir Goodlove, who often questioned and challenged them.

Sir Goodlove was moving more operations on to their sister agency, MI5. Abigail felt that this was a move to prevent him from having to answer awkward questions, especially since their operations upset a few people. Yet Sir Goodlove was still getting all the accolades for the work of those she sent out there to keep Great Britain, and the world, safe.

Abigail was in her late forties with a willowy build and fine blonde hair that she kept drawn back into a ponytail, putting her elegant features on display. She held herself with a subtle presence that demanded respect. She was well dressed, today wearing a dark navy, skirted business suit with a white shirt, pearls, and a delicate, gold-rimmed Omega watch.

She sipped her first coffee of the day contemplatively, gently tapping the toe of her high-heeled shoes. A door opened behind her, but she did not turn to see who had entered.

"Ma'am, you wanted to see me," said the man as he intruded on her morning-coffee ritual.

Still not turning, she lowered her cup and said, "Yes, take a seat, Andrew."

Andrew was tall, in his early thirties, lean, fit, and clean-cut. He wore jeans, brown brogues, a navy-blue shirt, and a tweed sports blazer. He carried himself well, with a commanding presence and a manner that spoke of experience, of being a part of the world rather than a spectator.

Still facing out the window, Abigail began. "Andrew, do you remember that training exercise? The one where we were using that Special Branch man, Peter, and our new agent, Chloe?"

"Yes, ma'am. They're in Algeria, being tested on their tradecraft and agent-handling, while carrying out Operation Erebus. We were worried about using Special Branch for the first time with one of our agents. Understandable, as 'P.C. Plod' can be a little tiresome and can be seen as . . ." He hesitated before saying, "blunt-force trauma." He chuckled at his word choice.

There was no emotion from Abigail. In fact, she just shifted her posture and continued to stare out the window. Andrew realised this was not the time for flippancy.

Abigail turned abruptly to face him and said, "It would appear that Chloe and Peter have overstated their brief and acted out of the operation parameters. I have received intelligence that Chloe met the source alone. Following the meeting, she sent me a message giving information from the source that implicates a high-ranking member of the intelligence community. Don't ask me how, but I know this to be a fabrication, a diversion on her part, to send us in the wrong direction.

"I sent orders for Chloe to be picked up and questioned in a safe house and for Peter to head home by his own means. However, Peter went rogue on us, and while Chloe was being held and interrogated, he entered the house, killed two of our men, and left with Chloe in a blaze of gunfire. They have been off the radar for twenty hours now, and their whereabouts are currently unknown."

Abigail paused, allowing Andrew to take in this information.

"This is incredible, ma'am," Andrew interjected dramatically. "Why wasn't this information forwarded to my operations team? I'm Peter's point of contact, his handler, and the head of his department. I should have been made aware of this immediately."

Abigail continued, her tone a little terse and irritated. "Yes, I know all that, but look at it this way. Would you want all and sundry to learn that your newest agent—who we now suspect may be a traitor—and a member of Special Branch have committed a double homicide on foreign soil? One takes steps to confirm or refute intelligence before one picks up the phone to call the Home Secretary. Peter and Chloe are responsible for two homicides on foreign soil, and it is safe to say that Chloe, possibly Peter too, have shown their allegiance to another power.

"And to answer your earlier comment, I am informing you now, as *head of department*. Is that okay with you?"

Andrew shifted in his seat, feeling a little chastised. "Yes, of course, ma'am. I understand the rationale. So, what are we doing, and what do you need from me? Who did Chloe adversely implicate in her message?"

Abigail moved from the window and sat opposite him. "She implicated me, Andrew. She was there to extract the name of a mole within the intelligence community. The source she was meeting would provide her with this name, and she was to send me a coded message identifying the mole. But she identified me."

Abigail allowed that to sink in before speaking again. "I have activated all assets in North Africa with a capture order for both of them." She knew that this information would shock Andrew, but she continued before he could respond. "I need you to mobilise your people and networks to be prepared to act when and if we get intelligence as to their whereabouts. All actions are to be placed through me, and not through the official channels. I am concerned there may be those simpatico to Chloe and Peter. Any assistance those two might get could hinder our efforts. Your networks, I know, are well-trained and should be able to deal with them. I am, however, worried about who's helping them. They're not that good, but they have made some of our finest operators look a little silly."

Abigail paused, allowing Andrew to compose his thoughts. She knew what she had suggested was against all protocols and standard operating procedures. Andrew's mind would be racing as to how he should answer.

Andrew, however, sat calmly, looking at her while he sipped his coffee. He had gone through the elite path of those in this odd little world. Eton, Cambridge, officer training at Sandhurst, before deploying to Afghanistan with an "interviewing team" that was affiliated with a combined Special Forces group. He was a trained operator with Special Forces but had found himself in the lead interrogator role for those who needed a more persuasive hand. Abigail had read some of the debriefing notes and seen video footage of Andrew pulling men and women alike to pieces, both physically and mentally.

She noticed the trademark pinky ring he wore glinting in the morning sun and wondered if his Sandhurst training had prepared him for a day like this. It had been the scandal of the Americans photographed with naked prisoners and the infamous man on the box, who had been hooded, with electrodes attached to his hands, that had brought Andrew into the world of MI6.

She wasn't at all phased by these methods. She just got irritated with those who needed to photograph them and tell the world. Andrew had saved the lives of hundreds or maybe thousands of innocent people. He had most definitely infringed on some civil liberties, but as she put it, if those individuals wanted to come to her doorstep for a fight, then they would damn well get one.

Andrew sighed and said, "Ma'am, my team will be ready to go within the hour. They are currently training in Wales, and I will have them prepped at our jump-off location there. Might I suggest we make contact with the Chief Constable of Kent Police in case Peter tries to contact anyone in their domain? I know him quite well, and they can have covert markers placed to only notify the chief constable if triggered. I will research this Peter and see what his background is. Even with help, it's pretty impressive to enter a safe house, kill two, and escape with a detainee. To me, that indicates previous training, and not just the stuff he got from us in Wales."

"I want to be quite clear." Abigail was calm, but her tone spoke of her resolve. "We have been side-swiped here, and now we're playing catch-up from a long way back. These two didn't just falsely implicate a high-ranking member of the intelligence community, they escaped from a safe house and committed what could be viewed as an act of war on foreign soil. Do your research, but do it quietly. There's more to this, and I feel we're being manipulated. We do not tolerate that. I am speaking with my American counterpart in an hour to bring him up to speed."

Andrew said, "Do you think that's wise, bringing in the Americans so soon? That could make our job even more challenging."

Abigail grinned and sighed. "Unfortunately, the second man Peter killed was one of theirs. He was a covert operator and had been undercover for some years. So, as you can imagine, they are a little ticked that Peter killed him. I have no choice but to bring them in, and I hope we get to Peter and Chloe before they do—they will take great pleasure in debriefing them in their own special way."

Abigail and Andrew both knew it was going to be difficult enough to track Peter and Chloe down, but with the Americans moving pieces into play, it would make the whole world a lot more dangerous.

CHAPTER 4

Peter sat in a plain-looking transit van with badly tinted windows and a poorly kept interior. No creature comforts and a smell of cigarettes. The van rolled up the ramp and swung out of the underground parking lot located at Thames House—MI5 headquarters—before taking its place in the slow-moving traffic, somehow avoiding raising the eyebrows of any onlookers.

He'd been dropped off there by his teammate, Claire. As he got his kit out of the car, she leaned across and said, "Good luck, mate. I think you are going to need it."

Peter squatted down, looking through the passenger window, smiling back at her. "I think you're right. It seemed like a great idea at the time, but I feel it's going to be quite the challenge."

Claire and Peter had been partners for a couple of years,

and she had been outstanding. She had worked in one of the toughest areas in their county, Gravesend, and even though she had only a few years left to serve, she was as keen to get the work done as she'd been on her first day.

"I'll let you know how it goes—if they don't kill me," he joked.

She smiled, gave him that all-knowing wink, and roared off, leaving him standing alone.

He grabbed his backpack and his two North Face duffle bags and headed inside. He entered a large atrium, decorated with a marble floor, thick wooden furniture, and the obligatory security desk. He laid down his duffle bags and grabbed his ID and paperwork from his pocket.

As he stood waiting, he looked down at the two duffle bags and smiled, recalling how, a few years before, he'd helped out on an operation where he was to hike to a rural location and fit some bugging material. He'd turned up, adorned head-to-foot in North Face attire, and an instructor from an outside agency had called across the room with a booming voice, "Holy shit. It's the North Face Man!"

The nickname had stuck, and even his personal-issue radio had a sticker on the side that read, *"The North Face Man."*

Peter's office was no different from any other police area he had worked. It was a place where tough love was born, and if you rode it out, you gained respect. One time, on an overseas climbing trip, he'd ordered a Suunto Core mountaineering watch to be delivered to the office. When he got back, it was sitting on his desk in the nice, new box, but on closer inspection, he found that his colleagues had gone to the trouble of making a new label, switching the "C" and the "S". Thankfully, that nickname didn't stick.

Back in the atrium, Peter presented himself at security, and they ran the name on his ID. They checked the paperwork and made a call that he couldn't hear because of the ballistic-proof glass. After a few minutes, an MI5 officer dressed in jeans, hiking boots, and a T-shirt came out of the adjacent elevators and introduced himself. Peter couldn't remember the guy's name, which he knew wasn't good. He had come to realise that this outfit would put you through some of the most rigorous training and then without warning, they'd turn to you and say, "What was the guy's name who met you at Thames House?" Peter's nerves had set in with a vengeance, and he was trying everything he could to relax and take it all in. This wasn't the first time he'd been on selection courses with the police or training courses with MI5, so what was it that had him pretty much shaking, with zero ability to concentrate? He had only felt this way once before and that was during his first arrest. So, he asked to use the washroom and took a few minutes to give himself a little pep talk. Peter looked at himself in the mirror and said, "Get a grip. Focus on the task at hand." After saying this a few times, he left the washroom, joined the MI5 officer and asked him his name. The MI5 officer smiled and said, "You can call me Mike." Peter was then led away to the basement of Thames House and the unremarkable transit van.

Now, the van was meandering its way through the streets of London, and Peter asked the driver and Mike where they were going. They both ignored him, and Mike leaned across and turned up the radio. Peter decided to lie down on the empty seats, and as Capital Radio played, his thoughts went to the moment he had walked into his inspector's office a month earlier.

CHAPTER 5

KENT POLICE SPECIAL BRANCH, KENT, ENGLAND

Peter had come in early as usual to work out, and he selected a session from a book written by a New York firefighter. There was a large section on stair-running workouts, so Peter took great delight in running the stairs in his office building, much to the annoyance of those using them to go about their daily business.

This morning's workout had been swimming, air squats, and push-ups. There was an underground, twenty-five-metre pool at his office, so he would swim a width, climb out and do ten air squats, dive in, swim across and do ten push-ups. This would be repeated for twenty minutes without rest. In the final minute, he was to do the width underwater. He tried but almost blacked out so decided to leave that for another day. As he dragged himself out of the pool for the last time, he looked up to see, standing in the viewing gallery, his inspector and another man in a grey suit. He gave them a cursory wave but didn't look to see if they reciprocated. He sucked in the oxygen then headed to the changing room, dried off, and proceeded to part B of his workout—strength training. Once fuelled with a protein shake and some oats, he headed upstairs, where he ran into Claire, who told him as she glided past, "Boss wants you in his office."

"Oh, yeah? What have I done now?"

Claire laughed. "Who knows, but there were a few stern-looking suits with him."

"Better get a move on then."

Peter went to his office and grabbed himself a cup of tea. As he stood drinking it from his favourite Stormtrooper mug, the inspector stepped out and shouted across the office, "Peter, got a minute?

"Absolutely, boss. On my way."

He returned to his desk and grabbed his notebook. He was met with the usual banter from the rest of his team.

"Naughty, naughty, Peter. Off to see the headmaster."

"Bugger off . . . he probably has another wonderful trip to Belfast for me."

"Chop-chop, Peter, or you will get double detention."

He walked into the inspector's office, a large conference room with an ornate round table in the centre. He scanned the other men and women, and other than the expected regimental ties—the whiff of MI5, MI6, and probably GCHQ in the air—he didn't know anyone.

The inspector's office was, in essence, a fully functional operations room with multiple screens, interactive whiteboards, and a myriad of phones with differing encryptions.

"Ah, Peter, grab a seat," said the inspector, indicating where he wanted him to sit. "I would offer you tea, but I see you have one. Need a top-up?"

"No, I'm good. Thanks, boss."

"I thought you'd be drinking one of those protein shakes or something equally awful-looking after that workout."

"I've already had one. But you can't beat a cup of tea after all that running around. So, how can I help?"

"Peter, do you know anyone here?"

"No, sir, all strangers to me."

"Well, I won't do the usual introductions. I'll let those present speak for themselves if they choose to. However, I must emphasise that schoolyard rules apply. Anything discussed in this room must remain confidential, and no note-taking is allowed. Is that clear?"

"Understood, sir."

"Peter, the British Government has decided it needs a more effective response to the threat of in-country terrorism. Now, I know we have MI5 and the Metropolitan Police Anti-Terrorism Branch, who are supported by Special Branch, GCHQ, and MI6, but this coverage is deemed to be fragmented in some respects. It has been agreed that a number of people from the intelligence agencies and the police are to be trained and deployed to address internal threats and support the local Special Branch.

"We have been asked to choose someone from our Special Branch to go on a six-month selection course, starting next month. They are to be trained by all the main agencies—MI5, MI6, etc. The course will train you on all the up-to-date tactics and techniques needed to operate in the field. It will also deliver first-on-scene responder training, teaching you the vital manoeuvres that are immediately put into play in a crisis before back-up assets can be mobilised, as it were. I would like you to be our representative. You will still be a police officer, but you'll be working under the direction of MI6. This whole affair has been named Project Genesis."

"Sorry, sir, but I thought our response to terrorist events was effective as it is. Isn't that why I've been on mutual aid to London and elsewhere?" asked Peter.

One of the men sitting at the end of the table in a rather unremarkable suit with an army tie leaned forward and said, "If I may, Inspector?"

"Of course," replied Peter's boss.

"My name is Devon, and I represent the Service, more commonly known as the SAS. We have determined that our response isn't always timely, certainly not outside the capital. I mean, we're dealing with real-time intelligence, and mobilising takes time. We need support from those able to deploy locally, prior to our arrival. Having said that, I have to add that I'm not a supporter of this Project Genesis. Working with the police is not an effective solution, but the Home Office feels differently. In my mind, this program has been created to win votes."

"Thank you, Captain," said a grey-haired man from the centre of the group as he leaned back into his chair. "My name is Colonel Aran Grieves. I am the head of the Joint Intelligence Committee and oversee all Special Forces and military intelligence deployments in the country. It's my signature you see on the final proofs, but we are a collective group who try to safeguard our little island. My friend, the captain, is a very proud man and sees this . . . 'initiative' as something of a slight on his regiment's reputation and efforts to date. I agree with the Home Office's initiative to have a more developed response, however, like the captain here, I don't agree with who they want to select. By that, I mean I don't feel the police and staff within MI6 are the greatest choice. We have extremely well-trained members of the military and operational staff within our existing agencies, but the Home Office is insisting on police involvement, as it gives an immediate law enforcement presence in the event of a terrorist situation."

Peter sipped from his Stormtrooper mug and sat back casually, crossing his legs and looking at the assembled people. "I do understand the Home Office's point, and it certainly sounds intriguing."

"It definitely will be," said the colonel. "The selection and training takes six months, and you will be based primarily in London, in a house we have secured for you. Interviewing and psychological testing will be delivered by MI6 and MI5. Technical training will be conducted by GCHQ and all physical and scenario training will be delivered by Special Forces. All four groups will contribute to your training and preparation. If you are successful, you will be deployed back to your home county, where you will keep up with regular training and be ready to deploy in cycles with other trained officers."

"Why me?" asked Peter.

His inspector decided to answer that one. "We discussed this and agreed the selected officer should be from Special Branch, due to their security clearance, knowledge of counter-terrorism, existing low profile in the service and, importantly, physical fitness."

"I suppose it has nothing to do with me being the only unmarried officer in the department and the youngest by at least a decade," Peter said glibly.

Without looking up from his notebook, Devon, replied, "Peter, surname irrelevant, thirty-two, single, wife deceased due to cancer four years ago, no children or pets. Known as a dedicated and hard-working officer who spent most of his time on the beat until moving to the service's Armed Response Unit.

"After your wife passed away, you punched a detective during a briefing—sounds like an interesting story—and it pretty much ended your firearms career. However, thanks to a friendly inspector whom you had worked with before, you moved to Special Branch, where you have been for the last four years. The death of your wife, according to psychologists and your colleagues, has made you withdrawn and isolated from society. Your team tell us you're a hard worker with a somewhat overly dedicated mentality for the force. You rarely socialise, are not a big drinker, and live for fitness. Did I miss anything?"

Peter didn't like the way his life had just been laid out among all these strangers, but he felt it may be some sort of test to get him riled up. Despite this awareness, he was a little irked and replied, "Pretty close, but it was a detective inspector I punched."

The captain looked rather smug and said, "Can I ask why?"

"Sure, you can ask. But it's none of your business."

"Thank you, Peter," his inspector cut in.

"Maybe the force has become the replacement for your dead wife. Not very wise," said the SAS officer.

Peter felt a surge of emotion and replied, "I wouldn't say that. Your wife keeps me satisfied when you're away, pretending to be a soldier."

The colonel leaned in and said, "Yes, thank you, gentlemen. That will be quite enough."

Peter and the SAS officer looked at each other but not

with anger. Theirs was a shared look that said, *This could be interesting.*

The colonel spoke again. "Peter, you were selected because you are a former Royal Marine Commando, you have weapons training, you are single—as you say—with no children, and from what I can see, very fit. But I am sure the captain will put that to the test. Project Genesis is being looked at from the highest level, and we want it to succeed. Your inspector and I know each other of old, and he speaks highly of you."

Peter sighed. "It does sound like good fun. Why not?"

"Good," said the colonel. "We shall send you the details in the next few weeks."

This was the signal for everyone to grab their belongings and get back to their respective jobs. Nodding to Peter, the colonel made his way for the door, accompanied by the inspector, who turned back to say, "Back in a minute, Peter. Don't go anywhere."

Devon, the SAS officer, approached Peter and stood facing him for a few seconds before putting out his hand. "Don't let me down, P.C. Plod."

"Oh, don't worry. I won't, Mr. Action Man," replied Peter.

He wasn't alone long before his inspector returned. "So, Peter, I want you to get all your files up to date and handed over. I want you to have a clear two-week window before you leave, understand? As you know, I'm retiring in a few months, so I shall wish you good luck now."

Although still wondering what on earth he had let himself in for, Peter appreciated his inspector's support. "Thank you, sir. No doubt you'll be kept informed."

The inspector hoped the last decision of his career had been the right one.

CHAPTER 6

TRAINING CAMP, SOUTH WALES, UK

It was only the stillness of the van that made Peter realise they had arrived. He had woken up a few times during the journey and thought perhaps that they might be in Wales, but if honest, he could have been anywhere. He sat up, rubbing the sleep from his eyes. He could see a nondescript set of buildings, a gravel car park, and roaming hills in the distance.

"Out you get," said the man who had greeted him.

"Grab your bags and throw them in Room A. Pick any bunk you want and meet me outside in ten minutes."

"Sounds good to me," said Peter. He slid off the seat and, once out of the van, had a good stretch. As he took in his surroundings, he could see a few people milling around who looked like training staff. They were moving equipment from one vehicle to another or to another unremarkable building. They would look in his direction and, without acknowledging him, carry on with what they were doing.

Peter picked up his bags and headed for Room A. It was clearly a large former office. There was one set of bunk beds in the middle, so Peter threw his bags on the bottom bunk.

The building seemed to be made up entirely of windows. There were no blinds. It was going to be a nightmare trying to get some sleep during the day.

He stepped outside, and the helpful greeter was there to meet him. "So, you will be the only one using this building, but keep the place clean and tidy." The man smiled.

"Okay, at least it won't get too cramped or noisy," Peter replied.

"Don't worry. You won't be getting a lot of sleep—the beds here are shit. I would recommend using the army cot they will provide you."

"Great. This keeps getting better," said Peter.

They walked a short distance and stopped in the middle of a large concrete square which had several paths leading off to the various buildings. Peter was given the whistle-stop tour.

"That is where you will eat, when you are told. Those are the stores, that is the general office, and that is the NAAFI. That's the bar, which you will not use while you are here, and that over there is the shower block. Understood?"

"Sure. I think I have it."

"Good. Now, head to the general office, where you will get more direction." With this, the man walked away.

Peter stood for a moment, hoping to remember which building was which as he tried to find something that distinguished one from the other. Every building was made up of a metre-high brick base upon which stood a modified hut in brilliant white. There were metal stairs leading up to the main entrance, and they were painted in galvanised, shiny black paint. Each window and door seemed to have reflective silver screens, making it impossible to see inside.

He headed for the general office, cracked open the door, and peered inside to find several women and one chap busy at work.

One of the women, who appeared older than the others, stood up and walked over. "You must be Peter," she said in a friendly tone.

"I suppose I must be," replied Peter as he shook her hand.

"So, we need to get some admin done, and you can be on your way. I need you to read this document. It is the Official Secrets Act, and you are signing that you won't tell anyone about this project. If you do, you will be subject to prosecution. This next form says that you are here voluntarily and that you are willing to partake in the training, regardless of what they throw at you. Lastly, this is the next-of-kin form. Please fill it out and identify to whom you want us to send your personal belongings, which you will place in this bag. Also, it will identify who will be the benefactor, in case of demise. Sorry to be morbid."

Peter wasn't overly phased with the paperwork, as he'd done it before. He read and signed it and placed his personal belongings in the bag provided.

What Peter did have trouble with was whose name to put on the next-of-kin form.

Previously, it would have been his wife, but her death, of course, had changed that. His parents had passed away, he had no siblings, and he didn't really have any friends who he thought should have his things.

His wife's death had hit him hard, and he'd spent the best

part of two years in a very dark place before the depression began to lose its grip. At that point, he decided a few months of travelling would do him good, so he packed his bags and headed for Europe.

After several weeks, he found himself in Venice, Italy. One particular day, after sightseeing, riding the water taxis, and taking photos from the Rialto Bridge, he decided to find a place to have a coffee and a much-deserved sit-down.

The café he found was just off St. Mark's Square and it was buzzing with tourists. As he entered the seating area, he realised he'd have to ask to share a table with a woman who was thumbing her way through her *Lonely Planet* guide to Venice. She looked a few years younger than him, and he took in her athletic frame, piercing blue eyes, and smile that lit up her face.

"Sure, you can join me," she said as she slid her professional-looking camera out of the way.

"Thanks very much," Peter replied, taking a seat. "This place is certainly popular."

"I know. It's been like this for the last hour," said the lady.

"I'm Peter, by the way." He shook her hand.

"And my name is Sophie. Pleasure to meet you."

Peter ordered himself a black coffee, and Sophie ordered something very fancy-sounding.

"So, are you travelling alone, or am I about to get punched by a large, jealous boyfriend?"

Sophie laughed and said, "No, you're quite safe. I'm here by myself."

"Phew, I wasn't in the mood for a fight today."

She laughed. "What about you? Am I going to have some lady come over here and hockey-jersey me without warning?"

"No, you are quite safe. I am also flying solo."

Their coffees arrived, and Peter felt compelled to tease Sophie about hers. It was the most elaborate coffee concoction he'd ever seen, with an equally elaborate name. All served in a glass, which to Peter, seemed at odds with it being a hot drink. They shared stories, laughed, and compared cameras and the photos they'd taken, chatting comfortably as if they'd known each other for years.

When the waiter came over and told them they were closing, they both looked a little taken aback. Peter had learned that Sophie had been divorced for a year and laughed that she was doing her own version of *Eat, Pray, Love.* She was Canadian, hence the hockey-jersey reference, and this was her first trip to Europe. She had no kids and sounded as if she had weathered a painful marriage and an equally unpleasant divorce.

Peter had told her about his wife and was pleasantly surprised that her response hadn't been the usual patronising platitudes, *That must have been awful* and, *Don't worry, everything will be all right.* Most people wanted to hear every private detail. Instead, she had leaned forward, touched his hand, and looked him in the eye as she said, "She must have been quite a woman. I can only imagine you are a better man for having been married to her. I'm sure she's up there, hoping that you enjoy your life and honour her memory by actively participating in the world."

Peter had never heard that before; her words moved him. He felt suddenly vulnerable and safe at the same time. She was captivating.

Over their coffees, they had talked about everything from where she lived in Canada to where they both wanted to travel in the world. They even discussed their favourite animal, both agreeing on the elephant.

Peter had told her about being a police officer and learned that she was the chief cardiovascular surgeon at a hospital in Victoria on Vancouver Island, Canada.

Suddenly, he found himself asking if she had plans for the following day.

"No," she replied. "Why?"

"I've rented a motorbike and am heading to Ferrara. Would you like to join me? It'll take just over an hour to get there. I was going to take a few pictures in the city, then have lunch."

She sat quietly, then asked, "Have you been riding long?"

Peter smiled, "Yes, I have ridden bikes all my life. I wouldn't ask you to come if I didn't feel confident we'd be safe. We can rent everything we need from the bike shop, but if you don't feel comfortable, we can always just get a car."

After a brief pause, Sophie said, "Okay, that sounds great. But if I don't like it, will you bring me back?"

"Of course, and if you change your mind overnight, that's fine too. Bikes aren't for everyone, and I don't want you to feel uncomfortable."

"I appreciate that. Okay, what do I need to bring?"

"I'll have bags added to the bike, so bring something cool to change into. Wear jeans that don't have any holes in them. We'll rent everything else. I'll drive us to the same store in Ferrara and leave the bike and our stuff there so we can wander around—there should be somewhere for you to change. Can you meet me at eight in the morning at my hotel? We can head off from there."

"Sounds like a good plan to me," said Sophie.

They decided to indulge their shared passion for

photography and wander the streets, taking all types of night-time photographs in the cooler evening air. They left the café and walked around the city, watching the night-time crowd travel from bistro to bistro for dinner. As they stood on one of the small, ornate bridges over a canal, Peter invited her to his hotel for supper.

Sophie turned to him and said, "Peter, that is really sweet of you, but we've only just met. I don't want to be swept up in the moment and for you to think I am a girl who goes back to a man's hotel on the first night."

With a wry smile, he said, "I wouldn't think any less of you if you did. I promise it will be supper in the dining room, and then I'll put you in a water taxi to your hotel. I'd like the company, and I won't try any old moves, promise."

"Promise?" she said, smiling over her shoulder as she walked away.

"Promise," Peter replied. "I have all-new cheap moves to try."

She laughed and said, "Okay, let's have supper and see these moves of yours."

They continued to walk the canal-lined streets, talking and laughing, stopping to take pictures of beautiful antique build-ings or someone dressed all carnivalesque. They crossed the final bridge leading to Peter's hotel, and as the sun set, it cast a mirroring light across the water and along the buildings.

They both took pictures of this stunning scene, and Peter found himself standing very close to her. She looked up, smiling coyly, with her perfect upper teeth biting down on her full, lower lip. Peter felt a flutter he barely recognised, so long it had been since he'd last felt it. Light-headed, his legs trembled slightly, and he felt like he was floating, disconnected from reality. And then, almost as if observing himself, he leaned towards her and softly found her mouth with his own. Immediately, the electric rush of desire burned through him, and his hands explored her firm waist and exciting body. Then he realised they had stopped and all he could do was look at the ground. He took a deep breath. This was the first woman he had kissed since his wife, and he felt guilty.

Sophie lifted his head and looked at him as if she understood. She kissed him again and said, "Come on, show me this hotel of yours."

Peter managed to find a balcony table overlooking one of the many waterways of Venice. They enjoyed a delightful meal with a fine wine. After dinner, he ordered her a water taxi and accompanied her to make sure she got to her hotel safely. They sat in the back of the open-air boat, taking in Venice and the night air.

Back at her hotel, she kissed him and walked towards the entrance. She turned to see that Peter had asked the taxi to wait to make sure she got inside okay. It was only after the hotel doorman had ushered Sophie in, and she had turned to catch a last glimpse of him, that Peter turned to his driver to ask him to leave.

Peter got up early to have breakfast and confirm the booking at the motorbike store. He was standing outside the hotel, drinking coffee as the taxi carrying Sophie floated into view.

As she disembarked, he said, "You came back. My cheap moves couldn't have been that bad."

She smiled and leaned in to kiss him, but yesterday's spontaneity was suddenly gone. Now, it all felt very awkward. They were like fumbling teenagers, trying to figure out how this was all supposed to happen. Laughing, Peter said, "Oh my word, that was terrible. Let's try that again."

They kissed again and, giggling, both agreed that was a better effort.

They got to the motorbike store, and Peter dealt with the staff to rent all the boots, jackets, gloves, and helmets. While he was busy talking to the owner, Sophie spotted a vintage blue leather jacket and decided to try it on. As they chatted, Peter noticed the owner's attention had drifted and turned to see what he was looking at. The jacket seemed to have been made for Sophie, fitting her curves perfectly, bringing out the blue of her eyes—she looked amazing. The breath caught in Peter's throat.

Sophie wanted to pay, but Peter insisted it was his treat. Eventually, they agreed that Sophie would buy lunch.

Peter rented a brand new V7 Stone Centenario E5, which he considered a beauty. He then explained to her how she should hold onto him and lean with him when they turned. He also instructed her that if she didn't like the speed or wanted to stop, she should tap his thigh.

Once they were kitted up and ready, Peter took the route to Ferrara, ever mindful of his nervous passenger.

They stopped twice along the way to admire the scenery, Peter checking each time that Sophie was okay. Sophie was aware that it had taken much longer to get there than it should have, and that Peter had done this so as not to scare her, which she thought was sweet. When they arrived at the bike shop in Ferrara, Sophie disappeared into the changing room, reappearing a few minutes later in a blue-and-white polka dot summer dress.

The owner of the motorbike store looked up. "Molto bella," he murmured, smiling broadly. For the second time that day,

Peter was astounded. She was stunning.

They wandered the streets, taking pictures of the busy and vibrant city, then sat in the square, enjoying some people-watching and sampling some of the amazing food, once again, feeling relaxed in each other's company.

As the afternoon came to a close, they found a park, busy with families enjoying the warm start to the early evening. Peter pulled a blanket from his camera bag.

Sophie smiled, "Smooth. Do you also have a bottle of wine in there?"

"Thank you, and no, sorry, there's no wine. We both need to be sharp for the ride back, but I promise you a glass later."

He threw out the blanket, and Sophie wandered off, quickly returning with two gelatos. They sat on the blanket, watching life bustle around them. Peter glanced at her, taking in her windswept hair and sun-kissed skin.

Suddenly, he said, "You've got ice cream on your nose."

As she raised her hand to wipe it away, Peter took it and pulled her close to him, lowering her to the ground. For a moment, they stared at each other. "Is this one of your moves?" she asked.

He lowered himself closer. "I think it might be." He smiled, and their lips met tentatively at first, neither wanting to be the first to deepen the kiss, then surrendering.

Sophie was the first to pull away. "God, Peter, remember where we are!"

They sat up, looking at the families and children playing in the park. "True." He grinned. "I guess I'll have to rein it in until we can be properly alone."

Sophie raised an eyebrow, "Properly alone? On a second date? We'll have to see about that."

Eventually, they decided it was time to head back to Venice. They packed up their belongings and returned to the bike store to prepare for the ride home. Sophie mounted the bike behind Peter, but just as they were setting off, she tapped his thigh.

Peter pulled up his visor and turned to look at her.

Smiling, she pulled up her own visor. "Perhaps you can go a little faster this time?"

Peter nodded and, revving the bike, headed out of the city. Sophie held on tightly to his waist and felt the thrill as he pushed the bike hard to get back.

Back at the Venice bike store, Sophie ruefully placed the lovely blue jacket on the counter.

"Something wrong?" asked the shop owner. "You want to return?" Then seeing her confusion, he added, "He not say? Your boyfriend, he buy it for you."

She turned to Peter, who looked a little shy. "Well, I thought you'd like a little souvenir, you know. Besides, it might inspire you to get into bikes."

Hand in hand, they returned to Peter's hotel and dined—along with the promised wine—before going up to his room. Peter opened the large balcony doors, allowing in the night air and city sounds. The opaque linen curtains fluttered in the breeze, and the night closed in.

Standing in the near darkness, they slowly undressed each other, relying on touch to guide them. Once again, Peter's breath hitched as he made out Sophie's toned form, and she, in turn, leaned into his warm, strong hands as they roved her smooth skin.

Peter stopped hearing the noise of the city floating in through the window. He'd spent the last two years finding excuses to stay distracted, but this felt good and right. The evening was so warm that after they undressed, Peter simply lowered her onto the bed. Almost on top of her, he held himself up with one arm and with the other hand, traced his fingers across her body, taking in her naked beauty, not wanting to lower himself onto her yet, not wanting the moment to end, not wanting this night to end. But when Sophie smiled up at him and pulled him down into a kiss, he could hold out no longer and became lost in her.

When he awoke, she was gone.

The night had seemed like a dream, but Peter woke, for the first time, feeling he had exorcised some demons. He made an espresso and stood in the open window, feeling euphoric and calm. He then noticed a note on the desk.

"I had to go before you woke. It was an unforgettable evening, but I thought it better I leave. You have no idea the effect you've had on me, but I feel Venice, the wine, and the moment may have caused me to get carried away. I am heading home today, and if, one day, you are ever on Vancouver Island, maybe you could come and say hi. Maybe then I can buy you dinner this time. Thank you for being an experience I will never forget. Sophie."

On more than one occasion, Peter had thought about travelling to Vancouver Island to see Sophie, but the pain of losing his wife had been so hard, and he didn't want to go through losing a romantic connection again.

When he returned to work, he'd used a few resources and managed to find out Sophie's last name. Now, staring at the next-of-kin form, he decided to put her name down. There was no one else in his life, and she'd been the only person who had renewed some resilience and given hope that the world wouldn't beat him.

Peter filled in Sophie's name and the address of the hospital where she worked and returned the paperwork. The older lady quickly reviewed it and confirmed that everything was in order. "Peter," she continued, "you now need to go to the stores and get your equipment and clothing. It's two buildings down from here with the attached C-cans behind."

*

QUARTERMASTERS, TRAINING CAMP

He entered the building and was met with a long desk that ran the length of the building. It had rows and rows of shelving units with all sorts of kit laid upon them. As he closed the door, he heard, from somewhere inside, the dulcet tones of a Scotsman. "Be with you in a wee minute, sir. Take a seat."

"Okay," replied Peter. He stood for about ten minutes or so, taking in his surroundings, before the man with the Scottish accent came into view.

"My name is Peter. I'm here for a training course, and I've been sent to pick up my kit."

"Aye, I knew you were coming in sometime today. We have quite a few things to give you, so shall we get started?"

"Absolutely, but I'm really parched. Is there anywhere I can get a cup of tea? How about the NAAFI?" asked Peter.

"Och, dinne go there. It costs a fortune. I will make us a tea here, and we can drink it as we get going."

Peter watched as the little grey-haired man busied himself making tea. He must have been only five-foot-four. He had a slight build and what must have once been an athletic frame under his uniform. He was immaculately dressed, with creases in his shirtsleeves, bulled shoes, and a tie pin.

"What's on that?" asked Peter, pointing to the pin.

"It's the cap badge of the Argyll and Sutherland Highlanders, Ninety-first and Ninety-third. Twenty-three years, man and boy, sir," said the man, who had almost stood to attention. It was clear this guy had a real sense of duty and even after leaving the army, was still that proud wee soldier.

Peter's father had died at the young age of sixty-five, and this man reminded him of him. He'd had that quiet dignity right until the end.

Peter spent about two hours with this man, trading war stories and drinking far too much tea. There were all sorts of articles of kit he would need for his six-month training course, and it took him two trips to get everything back to his room. As he had the place to himself, he decided to lay it all out and group it into categories to make life easier.

After getting organised, he wandered over to the NAAFI, where he bought a cup of tea. The store man was right—it did cost a fortune. Even Starbucks would be embarrassed to charge those prices.

*

The sun was setting, and Peter was sitting on the concrete steps outside his building, sipping his expensive and not-very-good tea when he spotted a man striding across the quadrangle towards him. He had, as his old training corporals would say, a sense of purpose about his gait.

"Peter, yes?"

"Yes, sir."'

"Good. Grab a notebook and follow me. Bring your tea."

Peter picked up the pad in its fancy camouflage holder, and off they went, exiting the quadrangle and heading for another building at the bottom of a steep, craggy hill. As Peter approached, he could see a well-defined path leading to the top. He wondered how many men and women had run up it to "learn a valuable lesson." He had a strong feeling he would be doing the same.

He entered the classroom, which was adorned with the usual military maps and the odd crest of a regiment, but nonetheless immaculately tidy. There was a central aisle with chairs on either side—those wide, comfortable chairs with a somewhat seventies pattern you only find in military bases around the world.

He was told to sit on the left at the front, and as he did, he noticed a female sitting on the right. He nodded and said hello, and she returned the greeting.

Red hair, around twenty-five. She looked just as Peter did: nervous.

They sat in silence for ten to fifteen minutes, when finally the doors at the back flew open. In marched six people, led by Devon and the colonel from his inspector's office.

They gathered at the front, and each sat on a single desk or stood to one side of it. Apart from the colonel, they wore a mix of Gore-Tex and half-camouflage clothing. They had a quiet, unassuming look about them, which Peter knew meant they were probably very good at what they did. Every single person before him was someone to be wary of. The colonel droned on about mutual partnership and interoperability, while the others looked on stoically. Finally, the colonel left, and Devon stepped forward.

"Peter, this is Chloe. Chloe, this is Peter," Devon said, gesturing between the two.

"You'll get to know each other very well over the next six

months. This first week will be Basic Assessments. Your tasks will relate to fitness, mental aptitude, and tactical skills, so we can get a baseline read on you. Chloe, you will be called Charlie One from now on, and Peter, you will be Papa One. You will not use your names again until the course is complete. Right now, get yourself acquainted. Remember, you can't go to the bar, so perhaps hang out here. You will be going for a run tomorrow morning at zero four hundred hours with our medic." He pointed at one of the women in Gore-Tex.

At this point, they all left, making no further introductions.

When the door closed, Peter got up and shook Chloe's hand. "I'm Papa One. Nice to meet you."

"It's nice to meet you too," said Chloe.

"Why don't we go grab a drink at the NAAFI and bring it back here before we get some sleep? I think this is going to be a long week," said Peter.

"Agreed," said Chloe.

After grabbing a couple of beers each, they spent a couple of hours chatting back in the classroom. They didn't reveal anything about their families, sticking to discussions about work, the course, and how they thought this might proceed. They parted company at around 10:00 p.m. and headed to their accommodations.

The medic, Jen—they later found out everyone called her the Matron—was probably the fittest person Peter had the misfortune to meet. That first run turned out to be a most unpleasant nightmare. As instructed, they met at 0400 hours—they knew it was stupidly early, but away they went. Matron had turned up wearing army boots; green, army-style trousers; a black T-shirt; and a reasonably sized backpack.

Oh, they're breaking us in easy with her.

But Peter quickly realised the arrogance of his assessment. She went off like a ferret on acid, and he and Chloe were at their limits to keep up. This was disheartening, as Peter was under the impression that he was in good condition from playing rugby and doing CrossFit. It turned out that the Matron was one of five women who deployed and supported Special Forces as medical cover. She had been a recipient of the Afghanistan and Iraq Medals six times cumulatively, and she had received royal recognition for her recovery of a downed operator in a foreign country under heavy enemy fire.

Peter was politely told that if he asked too many questions, he would find himself in the boot of a car being driven to an open field with a sack over his head for a quiet chat.

Point taken.

They did a five-mile cross-country run, which concluded at the bottom of the large, craggy hill with the well-worn path. They didn't have time to catch their breath as the Matron took off up the incline. It was steep and rocky, and it seemed to go on and on. At the top, she stood waiting. She patted a clearly placed large rock and said, "When you don't pay attention, you will be told to run the hill. You will run up here and touch this stone. Understood?"

"Understood," said Chloe and Peter through gasps of breath.

And with that, she took off back down the hill, shouting, "Come on, it's breakfast time."

Chloe and Peter smiled at each other, and Peter gestured for her to go first. She curtsied sarcastically then took off.

They were given thirty minutes to shower and get to the mess hall, which was further down the hill and away from the drab-looking huts. Peter acknowledged wryly that every military training location he went to had to be reached by going up or down a hill. The mess hall could easily fit two hundred people, but he and Chloe sat at one end, while the instructors gathered at the other.

The schedule for the first week was comprised of fitness every morning with some kind of run thrown in. They would then head to the range and practise shooting—very basic stuff to start, with their sessions soon progressing to more complex shoots involving elements of timing and accuracy.

The course wasn't what Peter imagined it to be. They were tested to the limits, but there was no shouting and no unnecessary punishment. There were what would be described as corrective training methods, but they seemed measured and in line with clear errors either Chloe or he had made. Peter found himself struggling with the finesse of the agent-handling scenarios, but Chloe was a natural. She, on the other hand, during tactical firearms training, found it hard to gauge a natural pace, whereas Peter's experience served him well, and he simply glided through. They came from very different worlds and had developed unique skill sets to suit their environments. Chloe was incredibly intelligent, a talented linguist, and without a doubt the subtle half of their team. Peter, with his policing and military experience, was far more able to navigate dynamic and unfolding events effectively.

They came to understand that only together did they stand a chance of passing the course. When they were finished for the day, they would agree to meet in the training room. Chloe would act as the agent and push Peter to the limit. One evening, she acted as a double agent and played the role of femme fatale to seduce him, which he found most discombobulating, causing Chloe to break into fits of laughter. Hugging him, she said, "I can see why you're single. That was terrible. We might need to practise that one again."

Peter was embarrassed, but Chloe just winked and said, "Come on, let's do some weapons handling to cheer you up."

They gradually became acquainted, Chloe telling of her life at university and direct recruitment into MI6, her passion for travel, and her love for anything chocolate. She also shared that she had only had one boyfriend in the last three years— that hadn't lasted.

During one of their nights off together, Peter let her in on the story of his wife and her illness, becoming emotional. Chloe's mind flashed back to the seductress role-play, and things made more sense. On impulse, she wrapped her arms around him, "I'm so sorry, that must have been hard for you." Those old words, he'd heard from well-meaning people so many times before, but coming from her, they seemed to quell some of the ache in his heart.

The night after, they were up very early for a lengthy map-reading exercise. They had been given separate routes to follow from their training camp, taking them through nearby villages with the goal of arriving at the next training location at the same time. Peter, however, had used what he thought was his initiative and diverted from the planned route. This had caused him to be late to the meeting place, thus delaying a training exercise, which then affected a number of instructors. His smugness at having reached the location soon dissipated as he was met with a less-than-amused bunch of people. One of the instructors, Hugo, explained, in a way that only the military can, why deviating from instruction is a poor choice.

"Papa One and Charlie One, come with me, please," he ordered.

Peter and Chloe were walked over to the bottom of a large, grassy bank. "Okay," Hugo barked. "Strip off. Get naked."

Peter paused for a moment. "Sorry, what?"

"Strip off. Come on. It's your time we're wasting."

They removed their clothes and stood for a moment until Hugo said, "Excellent. Now just go onto the other side of this bank, and we can discuss your lateness. Double away."

They climbed the eight-foot bank, feeling the cold wind whistle between their arse cheeks. Peter grimaced. *It's gonna be naked star jumps for us.*

As they cleared the bank, they were faced with a dark and swirling river. Hugo joined them, saying, "Don't hang about. Straight in, please. Don't worry, it isn't cold." He dusted a nonexistent piece of fluff from his jacket. "It's just freezing."

Peter and Chloe slid themselves into the river. Hugo was quite right: It was ice-cold and fast-flowing.

"That's it. Keep moving. The water in the middle is a little warmer. Make sure you're chest-deep, and then turn to face each other."

Peter stood facing Chloe. He could see the goosebumps on her skin.

Hugo, enjoying a hot drink from an army-style kidney mug, explained that Peter needed to listen to instruction, and he would, in time, be able to demonstrate his ingenuity. He spoke quietly, never raising his voice. "So, sir, I just want to make sure that we are clear."

Peter looked at Hugo, trying to regulate his breathing. "Yes, I understand." Hugo had squatted down on the bank. Peter could see the steam rising from the drink as it met with the cold, frosty morning air.

"Glad to hear it," said Hugo. "What about you, ma'am, do

we understand each other?" he asked.

Chloe never took her gaze away from Peter, and as she said, "Yes, I understand," he heard the shivering in her voice.

When Hugo felt they had been in the river long enough, he told Peter and Chloe to get out. They had to help each other back to the riverbank and out of the water, their hands and feet having started to go numb. As they cleared the bank, they saw the other instructors had placed their clothes on a blanket near the river. Hugo ushered them onto it.

As Peter stood on the blanket, Hugo handed him the mug. "Share this between you. Dry yourselves off, get dressed, and don't be a clever bastard next time. Got it?"

Peter shivered, nodded, and took a sip before handing the mug to Chloe.

"Good man. You both have twenty minutes," said Hugo as he wandered away.

After Hugo had left, Chloe, who was trying to get herself dressed, said, "Not that I didn't enjoy that, but where the fuck did you go?"

Peter reached down for his backpack and produced a box of Belgian chocolates.

He handed them to Chloe and said, "This morning, I Googled that there was a store in one of the villages that sold these chocolates. I wanted to say thank you for listening to me talk about my wife last night. I didn't mean for us to get put in the river. Sorry."

"That is very sweet of you, Peter," she replied, handing him back the mug and kissing him on the cheek. "Now, come on, let's get ourselves dressed."

Hugo seemed to be a fairly permanent fixture in the training group, and Peter enjoyed having him teach the classes. He was a short man and about as broad as he was tall. Heavily tattooed, he sported a thick, full black beard, which blended in with his full head of hair. Peter thought he looked like the ghost characters from a video game he used to play.

Hugo was a good instructor; he never shouted or lost his temper. He explained what he needed, and when you messed up, it was simple: He would introduce a learning phase, which never felt like a punishment.

As the days, weeks, and months passed, the testing became more complex. There were daylong interrogations with role actors playing foreign agents. There was night navigation, the setting up of dead-letter drops, surveillance training, and weapons handling. They would work with Special Forces to set up explosives to affect an escape if compromised and in the event of a hot extraction.

As with every course Peter had taken, there was always a final-selection test. They had been told that they would, as one of their final assessments, be made to complete a thirty-mile march. It wasn't explained when this would be, if it would be timed, or if they would need certain equipment. They were in their final two weeks, so Peter thought, as did Chloe, that it had to occur soon.

CHAPTER 7

A SMALL VILLAGE, FIVE MILES FROM THE TRAINING CAMP

One evening, they were instructed to practise an agent-meet in the local town. As they were doing their reconnaissance in preparation, they were on their way from the local pub to a small cottage that was to be used for the later meeting. From nowhere, a white-panelled van glided silently up alongside them, and before they knew it, they were met with violence as their attackers apprehended them.

Peter fought against them, but this only caused him to receive a decent series of blows. He was thrown into one van and Chloe into another. They were driven for what seemed like hours, presumably to disorientate them. Peter had been hooded and forced to wear a pair of blacked-out ski goggles and a set of ear defenders.

Peter knew this was a test, but he had no clue as to where he was or for how long he'd been travelling. For a brief moment, he began to doubt and wondered if he really had been taken by a foreign agency. But his mystery tour finally came to an end, and he was dragged from the van into some kind of building, where he was stripped naked and plastic-tied to a wooden chair. There he sat for hours, and he had almost fallen asleep when the hood and ski goggles were ripped off. He was in a square, concrete room with a door behind him. It was cold, and the light above seemed to be the brightest in the world. His face was covered in blood, his left eye had closed, and his top lip wasn't feeling the greatest.

Men and women would come in, wearing balaclavas and asking questions in heavy Middle Eastern accents. They would talk to each other in Arabic, then ask more questions. When they didn't get the answers they wanted, he would get punched or kicked.

"What is Operation Genesis?"

"Tell me who you work for."

"Who is your friend?"

"What is your name?"

"Why are you here?"

"Who is with you? Tell us now."

The questions went on and on for what seemed like days. The only thing that changed was that he would be routinely placed in a stress position and asked the same questions again and again while they used a water hose on him.

At one point during the questioning, they sent in a female, who said she was a medic, to examine him. Since he was naked, Peter knew this was being done to humiliate him. The cold had turned his penis into something resembling a button mushroom, which the medic took time to comment on. He was feeling like quite the broken unit, and he guessed this had been going for about five days. As he pondered this, he was hooded and marched from the room to another location, where he was told to remove the hood.

He slid it off and found himself standing three feet in front of Chloe, who was also naked and looking worse for wear. There were tables on either side and a door at each end but no windows. They looked at each other, and Peter gave her a little wink, which she didn't seem to acknowledge. She looked on the verge of tears, and it was clear her ordeal had been as intense as his.

They stood there gathering their thoughts when one of the balaclava-wearing interrogators spoke. "You have managed to escape your interrogators, and you are now on the run. You are in hostile territory and need to get to a border region thirty miles from here. You have stolen a map, some clothing, and some footwear. You will grab the items that are on the tables, get out of this room, and make your way to the border town marked on your map. In one hour, a company of soldiers will be tasked with tracking you down. If you are captured, you will fail. If you don't reach the border village, you will fail. And if you separate, you will fail. Now get out of here!"

The other interrogators started shouting and screaming at them as they grabbed their items off the table and ran out the door. They had to cover their eyes from the harsh daylight while orienting themselves. Barefoot and naked, they ran in no purposeful direction, purely to find cover. After ten minutes, they turned to establish that they were out of sight. Finding a poorly maintained wall, they hunkered behind it, searched the clothing they had been given, and slid on the footwear. Peter never thought putting socks and boots on would feel so good.

The clothes were old army-style, and the boots were

crappy. The jackets came down to their ankles. They'd been given a water bottle each, a compass, and a watch—no strap.

Once dressed, they discovered they'd been supplied rations, so they ate as they studied the map of a region of Wales, but with the names changed to mirror an area of Iraq or Afghanistan. They knew they had to move since the hunter team would be on-site soon and coming for them. Peter also realised he couldn't cover the thirty miles in one go and needed to sleep. Chloe agreed they needed some recovery time before they could move on.

Peter ventured an option, "Okay, this is my thought. There's a dam six miles from here, and it's not a direct route to our destination. We hike there and rest up for the night. In the morning, we follow the route of the river and get to this bridge." He indicated the bridge on the map. "This should take us within a mile or so of our target. They will be expecting us to head there as fast as possible, so let's take time to recover and plan."

Chloe was quiet for a short while, then said, "Okay, let's do it."

They used back bearings to determine where they were and where they needed to go. They filled their water bottles in a nearby stream and drank the entire amount, which almost caused them to vomit, and then filled the bottles to the brim again.

They set off at a steady but not record-breaking pace. They allowed their aching limbs to recover after being in stress positions and crappy wooden chairs. It must have been mid-morning, and they'd made good progress, only having to stop occasionally to catch their breath or take cover from passing vehicles.

They reached the dam and sat, watching it for at least an hour to ensure it wasn't occupied. They had gone at least six miles in what Peter considered was not a direct route to the village. He felt confident they would be safe here, so they made their way to a small building that looked like a maintenance hut near the base of the dam. The door was padlocked, so Peter found a decent-sized rock, and after a few good strikes at the latch, it came away from the wood. The padlock had held firm, but Welsh rain had degraded the wood, and the screws fell out easily.

Inside, they found a sparse room, which was attached to the dam itself, allowing you to walk down into its internal workings. They looked around—no signs of anyone. Peter then secured the door to conceal the forced entry.

The dam workers had made themselves a makeshift staff room with a sofa and comfortable chairs. Peter and Chloe laid out the food and water and assessed the map again. Peter decided he and Chloe needed to also check themselves over and discovered they'd received quite the beating over the last few days.

They agreed to take turns getting some sleep—three hours each—and decided that Chloe would go first. Choosing the sofa, she disappeared under her large army coat and was out. Peter went for a wander and found that the only way out, other than the door they'd come in, was to head to the top of the dam and exit somewhere up there. However, he and Chloe were in no shape for that.

Peter did, however, find a rickety old boathouse, and inside, a dilapidated rowing boat with no oars and a barely functional rudder.

At the three-hour mark, he woke Chloe, who, on Peter's

assessment, looked worse than before. Peter then took his turn, after which they ate. He then showed her the boat.

"You have to be kidding. It looks like a death trap," said Chloe.

"We're not looking to circumnavigate the globe here. We just need to let it take us downriver until we get to the bridge. After that, it's only a short hike to the border town. I say we wait until dark and then head off. We should be there by dawn."

"I want it known that I think this is a terrible idea. However, I am so wrecked from the last few days that I'm in. We need to go tonight. They'll widen their search as of tomorrow morning if they haven't found us."

"Agreed. Let's rest up and wait until dark."

When darkness had fallen, they sat outside and listened to the night. They could hear the echo of dogs barking through the valleys, and they even thought they could hear men's voices, but they put that down to imagination. There was a slight current, so Peter found a long pole, probably from a washing line used by the dam workers. Using it as a punt, he moved them between the slower sections.

The plan was to pull themselves to the bank if they thought they heard their trackers. There were even one or two occasions when they thought they heard helicopters.

It was maybe four in the morning when they reached the bridge that told them they were about three miles from the village. Utterly frozen, it was a joy to get off the boat and feel the blood moving again.

As they approached the little town, they sought out and found a good observation point. They hunkered down and huddled together for warmth while they waited for sunrise. They had planned to keep watch in rotation, but Peter fell asleep on his watch. As the sun rose, they woke to find themselves nestled together. He agreed with Chloe that it felt surreal but peaceful.

They could see the border town in the distance. It looked like a small Welsh town, busy with people going about their lives. As they skirted the village, they saw Devon and the Matron in a car park, sitting on the tailgate of a Land Rover. They were drinking tea and chatting.

Peter and Chloe decided that this must be the rendezvous point and strolled into the parking lot, approaching their trainers.

"About time," said Devon, pointedly looking at his watch.

"I thought you had gotten lost or died of hypothermia." The Matron laughed.

"Probably found a hayloft and been screwing this whole time," said Devon, handing them hot cups of tea.

"What happened to the hunter group who were after us?" Chloe asked.

Devon patted her on the shoulder. "There was no one hunting you, apart from your own paranoia."

"Get in the Landy, and we will take you back to your accommodation. It's only ten minutes away," said the Matron, ushering them into the vehicle. They clambered in, and before they knew it, they were at the barracks and headed towards their accommodation. But suddenly, the Land Rover swerved along a road to an area known as the Hangar. It was as it sounds—a large, open area resembling an aircraft hangar. They had started many hikes, night navigations, and training exercises from there.

They drove through the large doors that were pulled almost shut behind them by two members of the training team.

"Oh, God, here we go again," said Peter, sitting himself up.

The Land Rover stopped, and they were ordered to get out. They shuffled out the rear and were ushered round to the front of the vehicle. There, waiting for them, was the colonel and the other suits Peter had seen in his boss's office, including his inspector and some unknowns.

The colonel strode forward and shook both their hands, "Well done. Well done, indeed."

He did, however, look a little annoyed, and he beckoned Devon over. "Captain, come here."

Devon walked over to face the colonel, who said, "I thought I made it quite clear that there was to be no excessive use of coercion."

Before Devon could answer, Peter said, "I took a tumble when I was on the run, sir. That's how I got these injuries."

The colonel looked a little perturbed. "How many tumbles did you take, Peter? I suppose you were carrying Chloe when you fell, and that's how she got all her injuries? Your inspector didn't mention your propensity for being accident-prone."

Devon smiled, and the colonel wandered off to speak with the other guests.

"There is some food over there and a few drinks," said Devon, and he followed the colonel.

Peter and Chloe moved over to the food and started to eat and drink some water.

"Good lord, Peter. You look like me after my first marriage," said Peter's inspector, laughing as they greeted each other.

"Thanks, boss," said Peter.

"Anyway, I am retiring tomorrow and wanted to come and say goodbye. Please don't try to reach me. You won't get a postcard either."

"Okay, boss. Enjoy retirement."

"Don't you worry. I will love every minute of it. Take care."

Chloe and Peter smirked at each other as Peter's inspector gave them a knowing wink and sauntered off.

Chloe headed off to see some of her work people, who congratulated her and showed sympathy for her beaten and bloody face.

Peter drifted from the crowd and was enjoying the view from the hangar doors. After a while, Devon appeared next to him, and they silently looked out, shoulder to shoulder.

"I like being wrong, Peter."

"Oh, and what were you wrong about?"

"You. I thought you'd have broken a long time ago."

"Sorry to disappoint."

"Not at all. You won't be getting some medal or beret at the end of all this, but I wanted to say well done." He turned to Peter and reached out his hand.

As Peter shook it, he felt something being placed into it. He then walked away. Looking down, Peter recognised an SAS metal cap badge glinting back at him.

As he looked up, he could see that Devon had joined the men and women from the Special Forces team who had been with him through the course. They all looked in his direction and gave a slight nod before leaving the hangar.

Peter stared at the cap badge, then up at the clouds skittering along in the sky. His dad would have been proud.

Chloe joined him, and Peter saw her discreetly pocket the cap badge she had been given. They headed off to their respective accommodations where the Matron visited, dressed their wounds, and prescribed pain medication. She also advised them that tomorrow's training would start later, at 1300 hours, and that this evening was "theirs." They were even permitted to have a few drinks in the bar that night. But being too tired, they skipped that and were in bed by 1900 hours, soon after dinner, and remained comatose until morning.

At breakfast, they both admitted they didn't look or feel any better.

"How's the eye?" asked Chloe.

"Good, thanks. How are you feeling? You look a little beat-up yourself."

"Oh, I'm good, just a little battle-weary."

As they drank their tea and spoke of their individual debriefs, Devon joined them. "Good morning. How we doing? You look like a couple of rock stars," he smiled.

"Yeah, we're just discussing how great we both feel," said Peter.

"Good, glad to hear it. Peter, we need to cover off on some of your training, and we need you to do another night navigation tomorrow," Devon instructed. "And Chloe, you're needed back in London tomorrow afternoon for some paperwork."

"Oh, okay. Did I not do what was required?" Peter asked.

"Good lord, yes. This is a training package, and for some reason, we didn't sign you off on one of the modules, so we need one fairly straightforward night navex to sign you off. Remember that cottage where you were going to meet the agent a few days ago? We need you to head there. It should take about an hour, and then you'll head back."

"Don't I need to cover off on that?" asked Chloe.

"Er, no, I am told you did some night navex in your training to get into the service. Is that wrong?" said Devon.

"No, that's right. But we've done everything together, so it seems a little strange," said Chloe.

"Feel free not to go to London to get the paperwork signed off and join young Peter here. Makes no difference to me."

"No, no, that's fine. As long as I've done everything I need to do to complete the training," replied Chloe.

"Oh, you have. Don't worry about that," said the captain.

"I'd take that as a lucky break," Peter said to Chloe with a wry smile. "Just make sure you spare me a thought as I'm crawling about in the dark and you're pushing your pen around."

CHAPTER 8

THE COTTAGE

After navigating his way to the cottage, Peter was led into the kitchen. He'd hiked on his own through the night, and on arrival was greeted by his military and non-government agency trainers. He'd been given a certain route to follow and hadn't found it that challenging.

But there was something different about this that Peter couldn't put his finger on. He just had a sense, on arrival at the cottage, that this wasn't a normal evolution. It had been a much easier route than previous ones, and for the first time, he hadn't been paired with Chloe. The instructors were also not talkative and seemed preoccupied. They ushered him into the kitchen, told him to sit down, and placed a steaming mug of tea in front of him.

It was probably twenty minutes before he saw the headlights of a vehicle coming up the drive. That's when the instructors moved. He hadn't noticed until now, but they were all carrying sidearms, and the military instructors had discreetly slung carbines.

Peter felt the atmosphere change as the vehicle approached and the instructors all headed in different directions to either greet it or set up a secure perimeter. He heard the engine cut out and three doors open and close. Then through the open door, the sounds of footsteps on the gravel driveway. A pause at the door, voices, but he couldn't catch what they were saying.

An elegant, blonde-haired lady entered, shadowed in the front and rear by one ordinary-looking male and another man identified later as Andrew, a Special Forces captain working with MI6, respectively. It was clear she had garnered all the activity from the instructors. All three were dressed in Barbour jackets, jeans, brogues, and flat caps.

The men positioned themselves in the room, and the lady who had led them in stood at the opposite end of the table to Peter. She eyed him contemplatively, then said, "Are you Peter?"

Suspecting this was another test, he opted for caution. "I might be. Who are you?"

She smiled and, looking around, noticed the food. Turning to her bodyguard, she said, "I haven't eaten yet today. Can you bring me something? Oh, and a cup of tea would be great, thank you." She unzipped her jacket, revealing a plain blue wool sweater, and sat down. As the bodyguard moved around the kitchen, she and Andrew sat in silence, observing Peter, who sat quietly, looking back at them. He wondered if this was an attempt to intimidate him. He remembered his interview training with the police. If you just sit quietly, there will be an overwhelming need to speak, and if you hold your nerve, your suspect may spill all.

The tea and a sandwich were placed in front of the woman. Her bodyguard asked, "Will there be anything else, ma'am?"

With her gaze still fixed on Peter, she replied, "No, I'm good. Thank you. You can leave."

The bodyguard exited, and after waiting a few seconds, the woman spoke. "I am Abigail. This is my lead operational intelligence officer, Andrew. He will stay while we talk."

"And are you going to tell me who you are and why I am here?" asked Peter.

"Peter, I'm the one who orchestrated this coalition between our two agencies. I, through the Home Office, put in motion this little charade. And now, I am going to tell you a story.

"About a year ago, we captured some men who were rather supportive of the ISIS cause, if you get my meaning. Before we 'dealt' with them, one of them thought we might treat him more leniently if he gave us a little information. I'm always wary of this kind of single-source intelligence—in my opinion, until it's corroborated, it's just hearsay."

Peter cut in, "Again I am going to ask, who are you, and what was the information?"

"Patience, Peter, please. I am the official head of the Secret Intelligence Service, or as most people know it, MI6. And most people believe that the big building in London is the headquarters. You probably think that, too. But it's not. It's just a front for the public, and so is the guy who most people, probably including you, believe is the boss. Sir Mark Goodlove, head of MI6, is simply a figurehead, an avatar, if you like, the safe face of MI6. He's not supposed to be any more than that, but in the last year or so, for reasons I can't quite fathom, he's become more engaged in the goings-on, including my operations. Now, back to our ISIS friend. He told us that we, the intelligence community, had a mole who was busy leaking information to them. Can I go on now?'

Peter took a swig of tea. "That certainly is interesting, but yes, please, go on."

"Now, one of our known and trusted sources has reached out to us, saying they have information that may identify the leak. But as you can imagine, they're somewhat on edge. The last thing they want is to get caught by their people—we all know that would not go down well for them. So . . . it's been decided that in what will appear to be the final part of your training, you and Chloe will deploy to Algeria for a covert meet with this source. The operation is highly classified, and for most people, it really is just a final training exercise for you two. You will, I hope, be given the name of the mole.

"I know this must be something of a shock to you. It was a hard pill for me to swallow when the report came across my desk, I can tell you. I liken it to the Cambridge spies in the middle of the twentieth century who fooled everyone, masquerading as patriots, while cleverly and masterfully destroying networks and placing our people at risk. Things are different now. We're not worried about communism and the threat of another Cuban missile crisis. We're looking at an ideology that, without compunction, will kill and maim as many as they can in the name of Allah. I can't imagine the suffering they'll be able to inflict if one of their agents is placed on the inside."

Peter did feel rather shocked, but more for himself if he were honest. Things had moved fast from being a straightforward training exercise into something else entirely. Something very unnerving.

"So, why me, and why send a police officer? Isn't this your forte?"

"I wish it was that easy. It has been agreed by your chief constable that you will continue to work with us. You will be deployed immediately on active duty. But the 'why you' of it all is an interesting question. That was my doing. Not you in particular, but the idea to use a police officer. You see, you're 'vanilla,' Peter—we know for sure that you have no involvement and know nothing because until now, you haven't been a part of the intelligence community. Therefore, you are low risk of being under suspicion or corrupting the process. But . . . you can keep an eye on Chloe."

"Is she under suspicion?" asked Peter.

"Until the mole is caught, yes," replied Abigail. "We need her to contact this source of ours. She is one of our brightest and most quickly ascending handlers and has solid knowledge of North Africa, as she travelled there during her university years. I expect you already know she's an accomplished linguist, too. You will both go to Algeria. On arrival, you'll be met by one of our counterparts, Dominic, who will act as a liaison. Remember, very few people know this is not just a training exercise, and you don't know who those people are, so say nothing about it to anyone. Once you're positioned, we will signal the source and arrange the meet. When we know you have the name, we'll decide how to handle the source and whether to bring you both home effective immediately or issue you further orders. As I say, Dominic is your point of contact, and he will advise you."

Stunned by all this information, Peter said, "So to be clear, this entire narrative of joint, multi-agency cooperation to improve response to domestic terrorist attacks has been nothing but a charade to flush out a mole within the intelligence services? It all seems a little extravagant. Why can't you guys just pick up the source and extract the information yourselves? Save us all the hassle."

"We want to know who recruited the mole, who their contacts are, and if there are any others they can identify. If we remove the source, the mole may become suspicious and simply disappear. We also want these Islamist extremists to know we have them in our sights and hopefully, send them back to their damn caves."

"So, am I to assume that Chloe and I might have to use force to acquire this information?" asked Peter.

"Peter, I don't have time for you to be squeamish or noble P.C. Plod. Your boss told us you were one of his better officers and that you wouldn't mind getting your hands dirty. We are, for all intents and purposes, at war. Our people are being run over by trucks and cars as they shop for their families. Police officers are being stabbed to death because cowardly politicians refuse to allow them to carry guns. Poppy wreaths are being burned at Remembrance Day parades, and we just stand by and watch. Our soldiers are being slaughtered because we don't want to be seen as racist for attacking those who attack us. We have children at a concert having their limbs blown off because a little Muslim boy, who couldn't get pussy in the real world, hopes he will have seventy-two virgins waiting for him when he commits martyrdom. So, yes, Peter, I am going to force the information out of whomever I have to, and if it means they will have fewer fingernails and teeth when we're done, then so be it."

The passion and fire in Abigail's eyes was so savage, it unsettled Peter. Was this lady just being patriotic, or had lines become blurred from all her years in this murky world? Peter didn't mind someone getting a slap if it got the result they needed. He'd been a police officer long enough to see a long line of offenders be protected by the system while their victims were humiliated, embarrassed, and belittled in the courtroom. Had he given a dig to the ribs of the husband who said that his wife deserved to be burned on the face with a hot iron as he struggled against being arrested? Maybe. Had he perhaps banged a rapist's head off the door frame of his police car as he explained to Peter that the little whore deserved it? Quite possibly. Peter had never really been in Abigail's arena, and perhaps in their world, this was seen as proportionate. But as he considered her words, he knew this was something he'd previously only ever read about.

"Peter, your role is really quite simple. You will, by any means possible, ensure Chloe meets that source."

"We have scheduled for you to be there for at least two weeks, but it may be longer. The exercise will play out as planned, and you will both be given tasks that you will achieve and debrief with each other."

"I would like to talk to my chief constable before I make my decision on all this," he said.

"I've already cleared it with him, so you can take my word, and that's sufficient," said Abigail.

Peter smiled—he'd heard that before. From every promotion-eager inspector and sergeant, who at the critical moment, would evaporate in the face of being challenged, leaving you standing alone. "I don't know you," he said. "And trust is earned. I will speak with my chief constable in private, and then we can move forward."

"Andrew, give me my phone," ordered Abigail.

Andrew hadn't taken his gaze off Peter, and that didn't change as he pulled the phone out of his pocket and handed it to Abigail.

Abigail accessed the phone and was clearly looking for the number. She pressed dial and slid it across the table. It stopped in front of Peter.

Peter could see it ringing, and the contact just read "CC Kent"—Chief Constable Kent.

Then he heard his chief's voice. "Hello?"

Peter looked at Andrew and Abigail and said, "In private."

An irritated-looking Abigail stood up, grabbed her tea, and left, with Andrew following behind.

"Sir, it's Detective Peter—"

"I know who this is. This line isn't secure, so don't use your last name."

"So, you know why I'm calling?"

"Yes, I do, and I'm in full agreement with Abigail as to your immediate deployment with them."

"Did she tell you why I am being deployed and what my objective will be?"

"She did, so I called your inspector, as I didn't know if you were the kind of officer who could manage this type of assignment. He assured me you could." There was a pause, and then he continued, "Peter, are you still there?"

"Yes, sir, I am still here."

"Peter, this is really important stuff. It will be without a shadow of a doubt the most significant event in your career. However, if you decide not to do it, there'll be no questions asked, and you can head back to Special Branch and pick up where you left off. I'll leave it up to you."

The phone then went dead.

Peter sat for a while, deep in thought, then took a breath and strolled outside to find Abigail and Andrew standing in front of their vehicles. As he approached, they turned to look, and he handed Abigail her phone.

"So, now you have spoken with your surrogate father, feel brave enough to take this on?" she asked as she pocketed her phone.

"You really are quite an obnoxious person," Peter replied. He'd been in the force long enough that his patience was exhausted by prickly and hostile people with over-inflated egos. "You must be a delight to work for. I understand that this is your brainchild, but I feel it only prudent that you should not be my point of contact for this operation."

"I don't think you're in any position to negotiate," snapped Abigail.

"I think I am," said Peter. "If I head home now, your plan will stall and you will have to devise another elaborate scheme. So, Andrew here will be my handler, and he, in turn, can update you. That's my deal, take it or leave it."

"Fine," Abigail huffed.

After she'd gone, leaving a cloud of dust as her car roared away, Andrew and Peter went back inside.

Andrew spoke first. "She really isn't that hard to work for. She fought tooth and nail to get where she is, earning her stripes in the trenches after being spotted at a fairly medio-cre university. She's tough and gets pushback because she's not afraid to tell the Old School Tie they aren't making the right decision."

Peter sighed and sat back in his chair. "Thank you for that speech. I'm not diminishing her achievements, but her people skills are awful. I am not trained for this—it's the sort of thing you people get up to and I read about in the paper."

Andrew slid his jacket off and laid it on the chair next to him. "I appreciate the confidence, but we all think that at the start. I was a beer-drinking, rugby-playing man who was going to work with my father in the city. Then one day, I watched an interview with Robert O'Neill, the guy who killed bin Laden. He spoke about why they'd gone on the mission to kill him. He said it was for the mum who dropped her kids off at school and, forty-five minutes later, chose to jump out of the World Trade Centre rather than burn to death. And when she jumped, she held her skirt down to maintain her dignity before she hit the pavement."

Andrew was gazing past Peter. "I felt a desire burning within me and thought that if there was a chance I could stop something like 9/11 from happening again, I would try my utmost to do so. So, here I am."

Peter liked this guy, though he was sure he was just doing his job as the handler and reassuring him as the agent. But he didn't really care; it was good to talk to him and shoot the shit while he let his nerves settle.

"So, Peter, here's what's going to happen and how we will communicate with each other. I want you to know that I will be available for you at any time, and that means 24-7. You're going to be fine, and when all of this is over, we shall sup a beer together in a quaint English pub, maybe watch a game of rugby. Now, let's get this started."

The two men sat for an hour or so as they determined how Peter would call or message Andrew and when tasks could or should be done. Peter really drilled it down to basics and then went over what to do in a scenario in which he felt he had been compromised.

Andrew smiled, "If you're compromised and the world is collapsing around you, take no prisoners and run for home."

Peter sighed. "Big Boys' Rules."

Andrew nodded. "Indeed. Big Boys' Rules."

Peter made ready to start his hike back to the training centre, and Andrew accompanied him outside to see him off. It was deserted now—the other trainers and assessors seemed to have disappeared. Peter checked the night navigation route, reversing it for the 'homeward' leg. By his reckoning, it would take an hour or so to get back, giving plenty of time to clear his head. And then he could sleep.

It was 0100 hours, so he would see Chloe over a late breakfast at say, 1000 hours. Peter trusted his memory and walked into the gloom to start his journey back to camp. He allowed the darkness to envelop him. *This is going to be an interesting day, indeed.*

CHAPTER 9

PRESENT DAY, LANGLEY, VIRGINIA, USA

Jessica was on her thirtieth lap of the pool at the underground training centre for the CIA, more commonly known as The Farm. After the events in the Netherlands three years before, she had been passed from one training exercise and notional operation to the next. She had progressed in promotion within the regular channels, but she was bored shitless, and physical exercise was her only real release. She'd been placed onto a team that was responsible for Special Forces integration. She, in essence, trained those Velcro-wearing, camouflage-adorned gentlemen about the methodical world of intelligence-gathering.

It wasn't the most exciting job, but she had certainly taken advantage of the situation. Her weapons-handling was outstanding, her appreciation of operational tactics was second to none, and she had enjoyed, on occasion, the masculine presence. These men, like her, had no need for commitment or even dinner with refined conversation. She had by no means been overactive, but she did have a captain who was more than just a useful training partner.

Back in the pool, Jessica reflected on the events in the Netherlands that had brought her so swiftly to The Farm. She had been the team leader on what was considered a straightforward arrest-and-extraction operation. The target was a South African member of Special Forces who had killed a member of the CIA during an operation in Turkey. When she instructed the team to move in, a CIA operator had gone off-script, causing the South African to react and a gunfight to ensue. By the time she'd regained control, the target was dead, and so was the off-script CIA operator. And then, as Jessica was trying to regroup, the sound of screaming rang out. During the gunfight, a stray bullet had struck a baby in the head as it lay in its stroller, killing it instantly. The fallout had been monumental, and as team leader, she had borne the brunt of the CIA director's wrath.

She came to a stop and rested her head on the edge of the pool, allowing her breathing to ease and the ache in her shoulders to calm. It was 0500 hours, and the place was like a ghost town. It disappointed Jessica that the amazing gymnasium was always empty, considering all the staff who worked at Langley, but she had grown to understand that no matter where you were in the world, those assigned to headquarters always seemed to become somewhat detached from real life. There were too many meetings involving coffees and nice lunches.

She heard the footsteps first before she saw the well-dressed man. She didn't recognise him, and from her position in the pool, she couldn't really make a fair assessment.

He didn't introduce himself, but instead opened with, "The director of operations wants to see you. Get dressed and meet him in his ready room in an hour."

"Good morning to you, too. What's the order of dress, and what do I need to bring?"

The gentleman shifted slightly on his feet as he stood on the edge of the pool, looking directly down at her. "I would suggest something other than that bathing suit, but casual is fine. You are to be briefed on a series of events, and the director feels you may be able to offer something."

As the gentleman walked away, she called out to her suited man, "And I suppose you don't?"

The man didn't stop or turn, but she heard him shout, "No, no I don't."

She dressed in jeans and a plain black T-shirt, pulled on her tactical, sand-coloured boots, grabbed her notebook, and made her way to the director's ready room. En route, she met up with one of her Special Forces liaison officers who was on a yearlong rotation to Langley.

He also looked as if he'd been rushed into the briefing. He mentioned he'd been in the services gym when his phone shrilled, and he was commanded to get his arse upstairs.

"Any idea what is going on?" Jessica asked.

"Not a clue," he replied.

The operator was of medium height, with a large, muscular build and the Navy SEAL beard, as she called it. Like her, he was wearing a T-shirt and jeans. He had full-sleeve tattoos on each arm and looked as if he should be in a rock band. She'd worked with him before, and he'd taught her some refined handgun skills.

Both of them carried their sidearms. Even though many at

Langley felt it unnecessary, both Jessica and those she had to deal with believed it kept your head in the game.

As they approached the ready room, they could see lots of activity both inside and outside the door.

There were men and women in business suits having those conversations that were probably irrelevant, or at least, blatant attempts to make them look important to observing eyes. She also spotted a few visitors' passes, which informed her that whatever this was about, they hadn't managed to keep it in-house. She recognised a few faces and spotted her friend Helena Miller, who worked for the NSA. She was a few years older than Jessica, but she was as sharp as a tack and a solid professional.

Helena was a deputy director and the NSA's number-one advisor on the rising trends of ISIS. They had done a joint training exercise in the Middle East when ISIS were rearing their ugly heads. They had become friends and tried to meet for coffee between their demanding work commitments.

Helena came over and said hello, and they embraced, smiling. Helena was fairly tall, with a modest build, olive skin, and long dark hair. She was probably the most intelligent person Jessica had ever met. Her mother was Egyptian and her father American, a former member of the CIA who had been posted to the Middle East for most of his career.

She spoke fluent Farsi, and as a student training for the NSA, she had written a paper about the threat from al Qaeda. At the time, nobody took note of her dissertation, even though it scored exemplary marks. When al Qaeda and then ISIS came over the horizon, the NSA director was looking for those who could come to those meetings and answer that always asked question: "What's the NSA's position on all this?" It was clear that Helena was the best-informed, and the NSA director liked her blunt and forthright attitude. He needed her, as even in the worst situation, she would tell him what he needed to know, not what he might want to hear.

"So, it must be something big if they're bringing you in, Helena," said Jessica.

Helena laughed. "Oh, yes. I'm here again, holding my director's hand. Whatever's going on, he called me and was not a happy camper. Whatever's happened is in Europe and North Africa, and a lot of people have been mobilised. When we were heading over, my boss took a call from the president's security advisor, and it was quite a guarded conversation. He's briefing in the Oval Office in two hours."

Jessica looked a little bemused. "What am I doing here then? I am a training legend, and my knowledge of ISIS is only as good as those tedious briefing documents that float around the office every week."

Helena suddenly put on her game face and said, "You were, before that mess in the Netherlands, the best operational agent in Europe. I know what happened wasn't your fault. It was a heavy-handed gunslinger who couldn't control himself that landed you here. I'm tired of seeing good people being punished for something beyond their control. You could have told the team to do a hot extraction, but you didn't, and the team came home safe. That's why when my boss asked who we should have in Europe as our liaison with the CIA, I asked for you."

It dawned on Jessica now why the man at the pool this morning had been pithy with her. But still, she was a little taken aback. "Look, my experience out there is historical and not even relevant now. It's going to upset a lot of people that

I'm even in the room, let alone being asked by the head of the NSA to be part of whatever this is."

Helena smiled, and as she placed her hand on Jessica's shoulder, she said, "It's not the first time we've pissed off the male bastion here, so why should we stop now? Anyway, if it irritates a few stiff-collared dickheads, then it's been a good day indeed. Come on, it looks like it's all going to kick off."

As they walked towards the room, Jessica noticed the familiar, worn leather briefcase that Helena always carried with her. It seemed out of place with her smart outfit and looked like something an archaeologist would carry his books in.

"I can't believe you still have that bag. It looks like it has seen some action," Jessica smiled.

Helena patted it. "It used to be my father's, and it's brought me good luck. I'd be lost without it. I can't believe it's still going strong."

They entered the room, and there was a large oak table in the centre. Everyone had grabbed a coffee from the little buffet area, so Jessica followed suit. It tasted great. The first coffee of the day is always a treat, and she felt that this morning, in particular, needed a little joy. The atmosphere in the room was incredibly tense, and there were a lot of concerned faces.

They all took their seats and waited for their directors to enter. Jessica and her Special Forces liaison looked out of place. They chatted quietly, wondering what the hell this was about.

The office was fairly plain, with three sixty-inch screens on one wall and the rest glass. Lastly, the director of the NSA entered, followed by the director of the CIA. They were also accompanied by Jessica's pithy man from the pool. As the directors took their seats, the suited man walked to the front of the screens. Before turning them on, he pressed a button that immediately frosted the glass walls.

The suited man began, "My name is Michael, and I am the director's advisor here with the CIA. The glass, as you can see, is frosted, and the room is now soundproofed. If you would like to check your phones, all the signals are now blocked. This meeting is being videoed and transcribed, so be mindful of that and don't say anything stupid. Please remember that this might make its way to a congressional hearing, and you don't want to impeach yourself. Does anyone have anything they want to say before we start?" Without waiting for long, he continued, "No? Good, then we shall begin."

The screens flickered on, showing on one a map, and on another, the pictures of Peter and Chloe and the man Peter shot in the garage. On the last screen was a live feed to Sir Mark Goodlove, the public face of MI6.

Jessica watched as Michael commanded the audience. She hadn't had the chance to take him in at the pool, but he was tall, with a muscular build, clear features and short blond hair. He had the air of an operator, and Jessica could see under his suit jacket that he was carrying a sidearm, which, as she knew, was a rare entity in this world. It wasn't until afterwards that she found out he had been with the US Rangers as an intelligence officer and had been brought over to the CIA only a year before to advise the director of operations.

"So, yesterday evening our time and early morning Libya time, a British police officer from Special Branch named Peter and an MI6 intelligence officer named Chloe, who were on a routine training exercise in North Africa, broke out of a British safe house in a hail of gunfire. During this escape, this man"—Michael pointed to the man on the screen—"was shot and killed. He is one of ours and had been working for us for the last two years, infiltrating an ISIS network within North Africa and Southern Europe. He was in a cell that we believe is planning a large-scale attack on multiple targets across America, Canada, and Europe.

"The operation was deemed at the highest level to be allowed to progress as planned. If timed correctly, we would have been able to cripple ISIS outside of the Middle East for good. The plan was that when it was time to act, multiple insertions by Special Forces in key locations would move in and crush ISIS. Then we could have supported the establishment and security of their governments, which would, in turn, have allowed for greater stability in the region.

"Sir Mark Goodlove from MI6 has joined us this morning as he has an update for this training exercise. Good morning, Sir Goodlove. I'll hand over to you now."

Sir Goodlove shifted in his seat and sipped tea from what looked like a china cup. Jessica smiled inwardly, as he reminded her of a classic British sitcom character.

Sir Goodlove began, "Good morning, everyone. Approximately six months ago, MI6 decided that there was a need for greater cooperation between ourselves and local law enforcement. As you know, for us to operate on home soil, we need to be supported by local law enforcement. A dash annoying, as one can imagine, but needs must.

"As their final exercise was coming to a conclusion, intelligence was received that one of our verified sources had some urgent information. It was agreed they would travel to Algeria and meet the source. This they did, and afterwards, the intelligence given was passed to our head office. Peter was instructed to return to the UK for his debriefing with his people, but we needed to talk to Chloe, so she was instructed to go to a safe house in Algeria for her debriefing, which, for reasons that will become clear, was more of an interrogation. While being held at the safe house, Peter took it upon himself to enter with force and determination, killing two guards—one being one of yours—and taking Chloe. They left in a hail of gunfire and have not been seen or heard of since. That's about the sum of it. All our assets are on standby with a capture order in place."

The room was quiet, and the suited man stood again and asked if there were any questions.

Helena broke the silence. "Who was this source that warranted the deployment of newly qualified staff?"

Sir Goodlove replied, "It is a reliable and credible source who's been used by several agencies around the world. For various reasons, we felt Peter and Chloe were best-suited."

Helena spoke, "Okay. Then why separate them and take them to alternate locations for debriefing?"

Sir Goodlove replied, "To interrogate a police officer on foreign soil would not go down well, as you can imagine. Sorry, I didn't feel I needed to point that out."

Helena enjoyed the moment of having Sir Goodlove on the defensive. "Sir Goodlove, I am going to assume that the intelligence was good enough to warrant your training exercise being halted and your assets interrogating Chloe. Peter would have known that Chloe would be 'tortured,' so he went in there to rescue her. My question is, if you thought the intelligence was good enough to pull the fingernails off Chloe, why did you allow Peter to travel back to the UK on his own? I have a hypothesis, if you'd like to hear it."

Sir Mark Goodlove sipped his tea, but he looked irritated. "Oh, please. I am intrigued."

Helena sat back in her seat and took a moment. "I think

you sent Chloe and Peter to Algeria to meet this designated source. The source must have had some intelligence that you desperately needed, I'm guessing something like a leak in your organisation or maybe someone else's, which is why you dressed it up as a run-of-the-mill training exercise, so as not to rattle the leak. You could even have hidden in plain sight and come right out saying the objective was to obtain the name of a leak—or shall we say, *mole*—because it was 'just a training exercise.'"

She paused for a moment, then said, "Or perhaps you had doubts about Chloe and her loyalty?

"It seems she was not fully briefed or at least not given the full story. I assume the police officer was, which is why he could head home on his own. Perhaps you felt that Chloe had betrayed you, or perhaps you suspected she was the mole and decided to move in.

"There is more to this situation, as a police officer wouldn't act in this manner in order to rescue someone who is supposedly being held by a friendly party. He must have acted out of honour, love, or duty to her, or your security checks failed to identify his vulnerability. They must be located and debriefed. Additionally, you must provide us with the identity of your source so they can be discreetly approached. Is that all, Sir Goodlove?"

Jessica took a sip of her coffee and inwardly smiled to herself. *Christ, Helena, you really are just a delight to watch.*

Sir Goodlove looked unimpressed with the blunt assessment. "Yes, that would be a fairly winning overview," he said, "although, to suggest that Chloe betrayed us is a little over the mark. Chloe is one of our newest and brightest agent handlers, and she was sent because of her reliability."

Sir Goodlove glanced at his notes, then said, "One last thing. The source—the one Peter and Chloe were sent to meet—was found dead soon after. It looked like a sloppy mugging."

Helena put down her pen and, looking at the screen, said, "What a fuck-up. No wonder people ended up dead. This seems like a real mess. But you can count on us to bail you out."

Before she could start again, Michael rose. "Look, this is the situation we find ourselves in and the direction we intend to move. Multiple agencies are coming together to track these two down. We have Special Forces assets on the ground standing by to move in. Our listening stations across Europe are monitoring all telecommunications traffic. There will be three twenty-four-hour cells—one here at Langley, one at the MI6 head office in London, and the third in one of our undisclosed locations in Germany. I would now like to introduce Jessica, who is this young lady to my right."

Jessica sat up and raised a hand to identify herself.

"Jessica was," Michael began, "one of our most prolific and successful agent handlers in Europe. She's been teaching here at Langley and working with our Special Forces liaison team for the last three years on joint operations. Jessica will head up our operations team in Germany. With her knowledge and training, we feel she would be best-suited. These intelligence cells will mobilise immediately."

Jessica looked a little bemused and the room could sense her surprise.

Michael continued, "So, that's what we know so far, and there are further briefings to follow. Thanks for your time, and please break into your respective teams for further detailed tasking. Jessica, come with me."

CHAPTER 10

CIA BRIEFING ROOM, LANGLEY

Jessica got to her feet and navigated through the moving bodies, taking the discreetly hidden door. She found herself with Michael, the director of the NSA, Helena, and the director of operations for the CIA.

The director of the NSA spoke first. "We have to get to the White House. I will leave you to brief Jessica, Michael."

As they left, Helena said goodbye to Jessica. As Helena left the very ornate office with the directors of the NSA and CIA, she smiled and said, "Keep me posted and let me know if you need anything."

She nodded towards Michael and left.

"Just to make life easy, you shall call me Michael." He was looking out the window and spoke to her without facing her.

"On the desk is a non-disclosure document I need you to read and sign. If you refuse, then you will sign the regular non-disclosure document next to it regarding the meeting we just had before going back to swimming and training the keyboard legends who work here."

Jessica looked at the document, emblazoned "TOP SECRET." There was also the phrase "eyes only" on there, which meant that it was highly classified. On the front was the title of the document, *Operation Renegade*. Then came the usual mantra, "I solemnly swear that I will not disclose or discuss the details of Operation Renegade beyond those authorised by the White House National Security Advisor and to do so would blah blah blah . . ." She had signed a number of these, but not so many from the White House. She added her signature.

Michael turned to face her, his outline somewhat blurred by the light coming through the window, which gave him an angelic halo. "I've been with the director for sixteen months and was brought here from the Rangers. It has been rumoured that I left the Rangers to come here, but that isn't true. I was brought in because ISIS have conducted a number of operations around the world that have unexpectedly resulted in a considerable loss of life. It seems ISIS know we're coming and have no qualms about demonstrating their effectiveness at slaughtering people. It has been concluded that there must be a carefully placed mole, or moles, within our intelligence community who are passing information to ISIS.

"Sure, we get the odd ISIS leader or intelligence officer killed by a drone, but that is small in the grand scale of things. We seem only to be picking off one or two at a time, while they're carrying off mass killings. To give you an example, the Paris attacks happened to occur on the date of a major training exercise for the French police. This meant many officers, including their anti-terrorist team, were at a training exercise miles away, leaving the city under-protected. When we looked at it, there were too many factors that allowed ISIS members to move into Paris and slaughter over a hundred and eighty people. So, a few questions were asked.

"Chloe was indeed an intelligence officer for MI6, and even though she was junior in service, Sir Mark Goodlove deemed her suitable. She was sent to North Africa, ostensibly on a training operation—only a select few knew it was a live operation to meet with a source.

"She was there to hopefully find out who the mole or moles might be. We think that she decided to confide in Peter for reasons we can't quite determine. Perhaps a sense of loyalty or even because she sensed danger and felt there was strength in numbers. There are other factors at play currently, and even I am only aware of certain elements. Keep your head on a swivel with this one."

Jessica spoke for the first time since the meeting had started. "But why did she not just give the name over? She would have had them exposed, arrested, or even fed false intelligence to help our efforts."

Michael sighed. "We haven't been given the full story, but my theory is not dissimilar to Helena's. Chloe either did give them a name and they didn't like what they heard, or she didn't even get the name or meet the source. I believe her people are so on edge that they can't see their enemies from their friends. If they'd failed to get anything, Chloe and Peter probably knew that not having the intelligence was more dangerous than having it. Chloe knew what would happen to her if she followed orders and went to the safe house, and I think Peter realised that after she'd gone. That's why he went in and extracted her. Jessica, there are some huge stakes at play here, and you need to realise that."

"Okay, then why me? This is some serious stuff, and to say I am a little ring-rusty would be an understatement."

There was a brief silence, and then Jessica spoke again. "It's because I am not known out there. Due to my absence, I'm not considered a security risk."

Michael smiled. "Helena said you were good, and when I read your file, overlooking the Netherlands incident, it was outstanding."

Jessica smiled nervously. "So, I'm to go out there and see if I can get hold of these two and bring them in? Is that it?"

Michael sat down and spoke quietly. "No, not quite. We think there's more than one asset feeding intelligence to ISIS. They may or may not be aware of each other, but we feel they're only a few in number. We want you, while doing the obvious, to make plays, and through me feed intelligence into the arena to see what actions or reactions take place. I want to draw out these sources and, as you put it, deal with them or use them to our advantage."

Jessica looked at Micheal contemplatively.

Michael understood her reservations. She'd been persona non grata for some years now and probably didn't want to step into another shit show.

After a brief period, she asked, "Who's going to be my team?"

Michael took a swig of his coffee. "We have a standardised operations team waiting for you in Germany. It's the usual crowd of intelligence bods, analysts, logistics, and Special Forces. However, you know you can have anyone else you want."

Jessica thought for a moment, then said, "I want a guy called Andrew from MI6. He was there in the Netherlands, and I've dealt with him a few times over the years. He seems pretty good."

"No outsiders. All in-house, I'm afraid."

"You can be afraid all you like. I want Andrew exactly for the fact he isn't in-house. He has no allegiance to anyone in this building or the agency. I want him or I will go back to filing operations reports."

"Fine. I'll make a few calls and see what can be arranged. You can reach me by the usual channels. Now, I suggest you get yourself together and off to Germany."

With that, he brought the meeting to an abrupt end, leaving Jessica in a whirlwind of excitement and apprehension, with a lot to do.

CHAPTER 11

TWO WEEKS BEFORE LEAVING FOR ALGERIA, ABIGAIL'S OFFICE, THE VENUE

Chloe took the train to The Venue and arrived at Abigail's office. Abigail was relaxing in a chair, reading the newspaper, when Chloe knocked and entered.

"Don't you look charming with all your bumps and bruises," Abigail said. "You look like you should have said yes a little more. I'm assuming the training course was . . . diverse, shall we say? Come in, grab a tea, and we can talk."

Without speaking, Chloe made herself a tea, then slumped in a chair opposite Abigail. "How's it all going?"

Abigail smiled. "It's going okay for the moment. We've managed to convince the source to meet with you in Algeria. They insist they have the name, and everyone thinks it's imperative we know it for the 'safeguarding of the nation'—Sir Goodlove's words, not mine. I'm assuming Peter is unaware of the true nature of this meeting, and that you were only made aware of it a month ago?"

"No, I don't think he has a clue. The story they gave for his extra training didn't raise an eyebrow. Out of curiosity, how do you know this isn't a ruse just to get us out there so they can execute us on national TV?" asked Chloe.

"I don't, so you better pay attention," said Abigail.

"This all seems a little laborious, don't you think? If the source knows the name of the mole, then why don't we just get them to tell us?" asked Chloe.

"Chloe, you have been patient. We are close to finding who the leak is. When they give you the name, you must get that name to me and only me. If Sir Goodlove gets involved, he'll just get more nervous, if that's even possible. You will send me a flash message, which will start with 'This message is for,' and then you'll add the name you were given. I would have suggested using code words, but we haven't got any idea of who it could be, so this system will have to suffice."

"Do we know where the source got the name or if it's even reliable? And what has Peter been told?" asked Chloe.

Abigail took a second to think. "The source has previously provided information that's been corroborated and deemed credible. They claim to have been a teenager when being used as a messenger for the mole, but they have never met face to face. They tell us the mole is known as Benjamin, which is a cover name. As for Peter, he knows nothing and thinks this is merely a training operation."

"Okay, but that does sound a little weak. How do we know our source can be trusted?"

"Because they've been nothing but reliable in the past. They've been the closest we've come to getting any kind of information."

"Okay, do we know if it's a man or a woman at least? So, I get the name then get it to you as soon as I can. What happens after the meeting? Do I let the source leave?"

"Ok, we don't have any information on gender yet, and yes, once you have the name, you will let the source leave, so as not to raise any suspicion. If anything happens to them, Benjamin will know and will certainly disappear."

"What about Peter? If he gets nervous or overzealous, he may become a hindrance or fuck it all up."

"Don't worry about him. My man, Dominic, will order him to follow your lead. Peter will see you meet the source and then he'll report back to Dominic. Dominic will then tell Peter he's been instructed to head home for an urgent matter, and you're to be directed to a safe house. We will supply the address when needed. You will telegraph the name to me, and I will meet you at the safe house. All clear?"

"Yes, it all sounds good to me."

"Chloe, this has been a tough game of chess, so to speak, and we've played our best moves to get close to winning. It requires patience and discipline to knock out the queen and main pieces, let alone get checkmate, but we will get there."

Chloe rose from her chair and headed out, saying over her shoulder, "I'll be in touch."

As she strolled down the corridor, she sighed to herself. *That was quite the metaphor. I'm surprised she didn't give me a polo analogy.*

She made her way out of the building and was driven back to the station. Once on board the train, she walked through the carriages until she came to one that was relatively empty and sat in the most isolated seat she could find. The other passengers seemed oblivious and engrossed in their own worlds.

Placing her handbag on her lap, she took out her compact mirror and, after checking her makeup, manipulated the glass to pop it out. Taped behind it was a SIM card. She took out an old-looking phone, powered it up, and inserted the SIM, then waited for it to gain a signal.

There was only one contact number on the card, which she selected, and then listened to the ringing tone. It rang for what seemed like an age before the voice at the other end spoke. "Do they know?"

"If they do, they aren't telling me."

"When do you leave?"

"Next week. I just need to heal up a little."

"What about the SB man? What does he know?"

"Very little, I think. He is good, however, so who knows. Don't worry, I can handle him. I'll suck his cock, tell him I love him, putty in my hands."

"Yes, indeed. When this is done, we shall be united. We'll be somewhere safe, warm, and together."

"Yes, we will. Forward as One," ended Chloe.

"Forward as One," came the reply from the end of the line.

The phone clicked off, and Chloe immediately removed the SIM card. She got up from her seat and moved to the area between the carriages. She snapped the card and cell phone in half and threw it out of the moving train.

She then took a seat in another carriage, rested her eyes, and waited for her stop to come.

CHAPTER 12

THE AUDI, ALGERIA

Peter had settled himself in for the long drive to Morocco. The Audi was comfortable, and the painkillers and coffee had done their jobs. The car was fitted with SiriusXM radio, so he found Classic FM, dialled in Myleene Klass, and allowed her soothing tones to help the journey glide by. Chloe lay on the back seat, and with the morphine and saline solution feeding in, she seemed relaxed. The GPS said seventeen hours and eleven minutes to Casablanca, so he had a little time to think and figure out what on earth he was going to do next. He knew that it was Dominic's car, so they were probably being tracked. Even if it hadn't been, Peter had to be aware that they'd have every seaport and airport on alert for him and Chloe.

He thought he would let the dust settle and let them make their plans, and when he was on the ferry to England, he'd make some calls to figure things out. He probably thought through a million different scenarios, from being killed or put in prison, to fleeing the country and trying to live off-grid. He then realised he wasn't James Bond and didn't have the intelligence or the resources to disappear.

His only realistic option was to try to call those he trusted, hand himself in, and then let the process take its course. In his mind, he'd done everything with reasonable cause and justification. He hadn't acted beyond what would be expected of a reasonable person. He'd almost convinced himself, then he shook his head. *Don't be an idiot. They'll make you disappear or send you to prison for the rest of your life.*

He forced himself to relax and watch the road glide by. He stopped only once to fuel up and grab water, and eventually, he managed to get himself to the ferry terminal. It was pretty quiet and seemed to be mainly for freight rather than passengers. He parked the car in a quiet spot and went for a walk to get the lay of the land. Everything made him nervous; he expected Dominic or his team to appear from the shadows and grab him. Deciding not to even enter the terminal building, he found a coffee shop and used their Wi-Fi to book tickets to England.

On his way back to the car, he found a souvenir shop. He bought some cheap kids' costume rings that looked the part without close inspection, beach towels, sun hats, sun cream, crappy T-shirts, and some travel luggage.

Back at the car, he emptied out half the sun cream, kicked the sun hats and luggage around the parking lot to get them dusty, and pulled on the crappy, touristy T-shirt. On Chloe's wedding finger, he slid the fake kids' costume ring, then put one on his own.

After booking the tickets, he drove into the port, his heart beating like a jackhammer. He had checked on Chloe, who was still pretty much out for the count, and made sure her drips were all in place. He also wanted to ensure they looked neat and tidy, as if someone with medical training had put them in, not him in a panic.

When they arrived at passport control, the officials wanted to speak with them. Peter had no doubt that when they looked in the back and saw Chloe, they would realise he needed to be a little more thorough and make sure she wasn't being kidnapped. Pulling up to the booth, he handed over the two passports with a strained smile. The official asked in broken English where Chloe was. Peter indicated the back seat, and the official told him to pull forward. When he saw her, he told Peter to pull into Bay 2 and stay there.

Peter sat in Bay 2, and in the rearview mirror, saw the passport official exit his office. He'd been joined by a female colleague. Standing by the car, with the back door wide open so they could see Chloe, they questioned him.

"What was the nature of your visit to Morocco?"

"We were on our honeymoon, but my wife here had a fall. She's been treated, and I've been advised to take her home."

"How did she fall?"

"Slightly embarrassing. We'd been out eating and drinking when we decided to head down to the beach. She took a tumble down a flight of concrete stairs before hitting the sand at the bottom. We were taken to the hospital and then to the consulate, where the resident doctor patched her up, ready for travel."

The female official pulled back the jacket and spoke to Chloe.

"How is your honeymoon going? Hello, can you hear me?"

Peter watched Chloe and wondered what she might say or if she was even conscious enough to say anything. Chloe reached up, brushing her hair back and said, "Delightful, thank you for asking. I am hoping to visit again and see more of the interesting concrete stair work you have here."

She then pulled the jacket away from the female official and covered herself up, ducking her head back inside.

"Sorry about that. She's had a rough old journey. I think she just wants to go home," Peter said, trying to sound glib.

He was told to wait while the officials pondered a moment. After an agonising wait, they returned their passports and told them they could leave. Once past passport control, things got much easier. He joined the queue of stationary cars waiting for the ferry, switched off the engine, and went into the back of the car.

Peter pulled back the jacket, saying, "Chloe, we need to go for a little walk. I need you to get up and come with me."

Without a word, she pulled the jacket back, and Peter helped her to sit up. She fixed her hair, and Peter gave her one of the tourist hats. It had a large, drooping brim that hid her face. He also slid onto her a pair of Jackie Onassis–style sunglasses. Chloe caught herself in the mirror. "Hell, I look like an accident-prone recovering drug addict."

Peter helped her out of the car, pulled her jacket on properly, then slid the IV bag into the inside pocket. Finally, he put some shoes on her, and off they went.

They walked together, with Peter supporting her. As gently as he could, he guided her to a flight of steps that led to the pedestrian gantry. As they slowly moved away from the car, they could see the other passengers watching them as they navigated their way across the lanes of lined-up cars. They made it to the ship and were met with a slightly concerned-looking ship staff. They asked if everything was okay, and after some reassurance, they checked their online tickets. Peter led Chloe to their room and made her comfortable again.

Then, as fast as he could without standing out, he headed back to the car, exited the lanes of queuing vehicles, and joined a different group of moving vehicles. He was ushered with the other cars onto a ferry, and the official checked his ticket, which was to get him to South Africa. He drove onto the ferry and casually but quickly walked upstairs, making his way to the back of the ferry.

As he headed down the gantry, the official shouted after him, "Sir, the ferry is leaving!"

Peter shouted over his shoulder, "I've changed my mind. I'm going to stay here and get drunk with the locals."

Standing on the dock, he watched the ferry pull up its anchor and slowly make its way out of port. Once satisfied it was on its way, he ran back to his ferry. With minutes to spare, he found himself standing at the stern, watching Morocco disappear into the distance. Knowing Chloe was safe and comfortable, he headed to the bar and ordered a beer. The air conditioning was good and the beer even better. He felt the engine rumble increase and decrease in power as they left the harbour. Then, with a steady hum, they headed out to sea.

CHAPTER 13

LANGLEY, VIRGINIA

Jessica went to her office, grabbed her to-go bag and battle folder, and headed out the door.

After a quick trip home to pack, she headed for the airport, where she drove up to an obscure, unmanned gate. Using her swipe card, she was granted access. She drove another five minutes, then swung into a hangar, where a private jet was being loaded and prepped for take-off.

She stayed in her vehicle for a moment, taking in the view.

It was good to feel engaged again as she headed out for an assignment. This one seemed particularly interesting and would hopefully get her out of Langley for a little while. As she boarded, chatting with the team loading the plane, she realised she was the only one with a shitload of kit. She found herself a space, laid out a sleeping bag, and tried to get some sleep. As the plane entered German airspace, the co-pilot woke her, and she hit the washroom, made herself respectable in fresh clothes, and waited for them to land.

One thing about being in the CIA is that you don't have to worry about passport control or wait to get your bags. The plane landed and taxied to a remote hangar that looked very similar to the one she'd left in the U.S, where she was met by the usual suspects—all sorts of official-looking people from the European field office, and all the other personnel she'd been told to expect. The Special Forces guys were easy to spot with their haircuts and T-shirts in boys' size large, which only served to make them look like they were trying too hard to blend in.

Jessica was told that these particular men were from Delta Force. She also knew they were useful to have around when the world got out of hand.

A CIA officer from the European office greeted her and told her she could dump her gear in the office. Once the plane was unloaded, she could then meet and brief the team.

"Will you be joining us for the briefing?" asked Jessica.

He paused from checking off and organising equipment. "That would be a no. I've been advised to welcome you to Site B and provide you assistance. I was given an overview of why you're here, but the rest is classified."

"Right. Sounds good." Jessica then walked into an office, dumped her kit, and waited for the rest of the team to get ready.

About twenty minutes later, Jessica came out of the office to find the room had been transformed into a fully equipped base of operations, with every piece of up-to-date technology imaginable at their disposal.

She cleared her throat and shouted, "Everyone ready for a briefing in two minutes."

There was an instant silence as the team listened to the instruction before the activity resumed. Jessica went to the refreshments table and made a large pot of coffee. As she was pouring the water into the machine, one of the Special Forces chaps wandered over to grab a cup. "So, you're the team leader they had to fly in from Langley to look after us all?"

"I wouldn't quite say that. The boss was fed up with me sitting around Langley and annoying him, so here I am. My name is Jessica."

"Yes, I heard you've been doing a fair bit of sitting around, since the Netherlands anyway. Let's hope we are not planning an ambush, because I hear you're a legend when it comes to those. Oh, and you can call me Shaukey—most people do." At this, he smirked and moved away.

Jessica sighed. *This is going to be fun.*

She poured herself a piping-hot black coffee and secured it in a travel flask so she could take her time drinking it. The flask was a favourite of hers—it had an ample cup on one end and a detachable section where you could store things, such as sugar, on the other. However, on this occasion she switched them around. She got her battle folder ready for the briefing and placed the flask on top of it as she walked over to the team, now assembled in a semi-circle.

"Good evening, everyone. My name is Jessica, and I am the designated team lead for this operation."

Shaukey and the Special Forces boys shifted in their chairs, giving each other knowing smiles. Shaukey was sat in an army-green camping chair and seemed to be the self-appointed leader of this little gang. Before Jessica could continue, he piped up, "Before we move on, I think it's only fair that we know what to call you. I was thinking 'Dutch' would be appropriate."

This seemed to amuse the Special Forces team. The rest of the group was smirking and looking away awkwardly. But the Special Forces chap wasn't finished. "I understand that this is a capture-and-extraction operation. As I said to you earlier, let's hope it's not an ambush, as I quite like my career. I haven't practised my infant first aid in a while."

Jessica felt the colour drain from her cheeks as she gritted her teeth. Then she took a deep breath, mustering all her confidence. "I am sorry to tell you that this is not the case. We are here to secure some intelligence that is being passed from a high-level asset. I'm here because I know the asset historically, and this will make the trade, we hope, easier."

Jessica didn't wait for a reaction. "The source will be in Berlin in two days, and we have to scout out a suitable drop location, identify a plausible cover story for them, and ensure I am the point of contact. The source, due to the nature of their work, has advised us that the swap will be done using one of these." She held up the flask she had on her battle folder. "It's a simple Thermos for hot or cold drinks. What we need to do is get their Thermos, swap it for ours, scan the intelligence within, and then make the swap back again. The source has a two-hour window for getting the intelligence back to its origins."

Shaukey sat up and gave a look of surprise to the onlooking group.

Jessica had clearly gotten their attention, so she carried on in earnest. She walked over to Shaukey and handed him the flask for inspection. "The intelligence will be hidden in the bottom of a flask just like the one Shaukey is holding now. It will be in the compartment where you would normally find sugar."

Shaukey held the flask the right way up and unscrewed the bottom of it, where the intelligence would be hidden. The boiling-hot black coffee poured out into his lap. He reacted immediately as the scalding coffee engulfed his groin. "Holy shit!" he exclaimed.

Jessica flew at Shaukey and drove her heeled boot into his groin, causing him to lurch forward. Then she punched him in the windpipe, making him reel backwards. She used the momentum to push him over while travelling with him. Landing with her knees on his chest, she punched him as hard as she could, square on the nose. In one swift movement, she knelt across his throat and drew her sidearm from her waistband, then levelled it on the other Special Forces members who were moving in to help their colleague.

She fixed her gaze on each of them, ensuring they didn't advance or make any stupid moves. Neither operator moved towards her, but instead, silently eased back in their stances. Shaukey was still trying to figure out what had just happened when Jessica spun him over and secured him using a set of plastic handcuffs she had tucked away in the cargo pocket of her trousers.

Once secured, she stood up and grabbed a bottle of water. Cracking the seal, she poured the entire bottle onto Shaukey's groin. He was now reasonably orientated and not best pleased. He rolled around and sat up, saying, "Who the hell do you think you are, bitch?"

Jessica shot forward again, kicking him in the chest and again kneeling across his throat, using her shin to control the pressure. "I am the bitch who ambushed *you* with a cup of coffee. I am in charge here, Shaukey. Or should I call you 'Starbucks' from now on?"

She stood and faced the group, who had either hidden behind equipment or carefully placed themselves with a weapon of choice in defendable positions. "Right, forget about everything I said about assets and Berlin and listen carefully. This is a capture-and-extraction operation, and I am the team lead. If anyone else wants to call me 'Dutch' or make further reference to my previous work, then please feel free to leave. My name to you from now on is 'ma'am' or 'boss.' This operation is being watched at a very high level by a lot of people, and I am not going to let anyone mess it up. So, if any of you want to work at an embassy in the middle of nowhere, checking visas or giving the ambassador hand-jobs for a few extra privileges, just piss me off, and I will throw you on a plane myself if I don't shoot you first. Am I clear?"

The silence permeated the room.

"AM I CLEAR?"

There was a ripple of "yes, ma'am" and "yes, boss" around the room.

"Good. I was beginning to wonder," said Jessica. She picked up her flask, walked back to the table, and poured herself a new coffee, sipping it slowly and allowing her breathing to return to normal. *Thank God I pulled that off.*

"Starbucks" was helped from the ground, and the handcuffs were removed. He composed himself, then approached the coffee table and stood behind Jessica. "I'll get my gear together and arrange transport out of here within the hour."

She turned to face him and, holding her coffee in front of her, making Shaukey move back slightly, said, "Don't be foolish. Clean yourself up and get ready for deployment. You know this team better than I do, and you've been on active duty in Europe for the last two years. I am going to need you on this."

Shaukey stood for a moment before speaking. "Yes, ma'am. I'll get my gear together, and we can discuss your plan," he said, then walked away.

She blew on her coffee and smiled to herself. *Christ, why are these things never straightforward?*

CHAPTER 14

FERRY, OFF THE COAST OF NORTH AFRICA

Peter had made his way back from the bar to the cabin where Chloe lay asleep. It was fairly spacious, with its own bathroom, a mini fridge, and everything one might need for morning tea or coffee.

He'd made a trip to duty-free and purchased a bottle of gin and some tonic. He found a glass, added some ice, and poured himself a healthy measure. He would like to say he added tonic, but it was more like he showed the tonic to the gin. He took a sip and headed for the shower. He peeled off the dressing on his shoulder and checked his wound—it looked okay. He sipped the gin as the water poured over him.

He had bought some new clothes from the ferry shop for himself and for Chloe. He put his out to wear after his shower. As he let the water cascade over his body, he leaned his head on the side of the shower and breathed. When he had cleaned what he could reach, he decided to let the gunshot wound breathe in the open air before bandaging it up again. He wasn't sure if that was a good or a bad thing, but he remembered that his mother would always say, "Let it breathe, son. It will do it good." And she always made him wash it out with salt water.

He decided the saline treatment could wait, as the shower had already made his eyes stream. He went into the bedroom and gently woke Chloe, placing a glass of water on the table next to her.

"How long have I been asleep?" she asked.

"About four hours," Peter replied. "Since we got on the ship."

She sat up and drank from the glass. Peter thought she didn't look too bad, just a little out of sorts.

"I'm going to take a shower and freshen up," she said, sliding her legs around so her feet touched the floor.

I've got you some new clothes over there. I hope they're okay. I'm going to get some first aid supplies too, as we're nearly out. There are painkillers on the desk, so help yourself. Oh, and there's a G and T on the table if that takes your fancy," said Peter.

"Thanks. Gin does sound nice," said Chloe.

Peter got up and exited the cabin, leaving Chloe to gather her thoughts. She checked the spyhole and watched Peter disappear down the ship's corridor. She then grabbed the cabin's phone and asked for an outside line. She dialled a number and spoke. "We're on our way to England."

"Where are you?"

"That's not important."

"Okay, how long till you get there?"

"A few days, I think."

"Is it done?"

"Yes, it is done."

"You dealt with our problem and got the message out?"

"Yes."

"Good. Well done."

"Must go. Forward as One."

"Forward as One."

She hung up, made herself a drink, and walked into the shower.

Peter took his time on his shopping quest, allowing Chloe space to decompress. When he returned, she was standing, looking out the cabin window, drink in hand. Her hair was still wet, and she was wearing the clothes he'd bought her.

"They fit okay?" he asked, gesturing at the jeans and T-shirt.

"Yes, they're good. Thank you," she replied, turning to face him.

"You don't look too bad at all."

"I'll take that as a compliment. I'm aching to say the least, but the gin and painkillers are doing their part. I suppose we need to talk." She sighed.

"Yes, I suppose we do." He made himself a gin and sat down. "Why don't I start? Why did you go to the safe house if you knew they would interrogate you? After you sent that message, you must have known what they were going to do."

"I went there to try to get you out of North Africa." She smiled ruefully. "Didn't work, though, did it? I wanted you out of the picture so they didn't drag you into all of this. They suspect me, you see. I know you know that—your face gave you away when I told you the source gave Abigail's name. She told you, didn't she? Perhaps you've been doubting me, too? Anyway, I knew this would create a storm and I didn't want you involved with that, so I went, hoping you'd follow orders and go home. I knew I was in for a tough time, but they wouldn't kill me. If I could ride my way through the interrogation, I might have been able to get someone to take me seriously and they'd look at Abigail a little more closely. I know it seemed an insane thing to do, but I didn't really have a choice. They already thought I was someone of concern. If I'd not gone to the safe house, I think it would have been a lot worse. It was the lesser of two evils, I guess."

Peter felt another wave of guilt for not trying harder to stop her from going to the safe house. He should have told her what Abigail had told him in the cottage.

"After you left, I knew that they were going to hurt you, and I thought they might even kill you," Peter said, shifting uncomfortably. "I always thought there would be a time in my life when I would be able to take a stand and do something noble. I made the decision to come and get you, no matter what the cost. We would figure out what to do."

"I am grateful for the rescue, but we are probably both wanted people in the eyes of the law. I expect there's a capture order on us."

Peter drank his gin. "I'm thinking that we contact the Matron, ask for help, and make a plan. If Abigail is the source, then she'll be doing everything she can to find us. If she isn't, she'll think that you're trying to implicate her. Either way, life is going to be difficult indeed."

Chloe poured herself another drink. "I agree with calling the Matron to see if she can help us when we dock. All I know is the source was terrified when he passed me the name. He almost ran from the café after telling me. I went after him but lost him in the streets. I'd only been back at the café a few minutes when you arrived. Let's get back to England and figure this out."

"Maybe we should have gone there together," said Peter.

"No, the staggered arrival was definitely better. It looked more natural, him joining me, and then you just-so-happening to turn up later. Anyway, it's done now."

They chatted as they enjoyed the gin, Chloe telling Peter about what she'd endured in the interrogation, and Peter explaining how he'd rescued her and the men he'd killed. There were a few hours before dinner, so they pulled down the blackout blinds, crawled into bed, and fell into a coma.

CHAPTER 15

BUENOS AIRES, ARGENTINA

Carl sat in his large, tastefully decorated apartment in his usual leather armchair, enjoying the early evening. It was summertime, and Buenos Aires was sweltering, but as the evening drew closer, the air became cooler and less draining.

Carl was well-dressed in a fine blue shirt, linen trousers, and a pair of green, crocodile-patterned slip-on shoes. He was well known in Buenos Aires and would, most evenings, stroll through the city, enjoying a martini at his favourite places. He was never seen drunk and he held the respect of those who knew him.

His family, for reasons beyond their control, had become infamous in the city due to his grandfather, who had owned a gentlemen's tailor in the heart of the city. Everyone from the president to the head of the city's banks to the everyday businessman would come to his grandfather to be fitted for a suit.

Carl's grandfather was known for his perfectionism and ability to cater to everyone, regardless of how wealthy they were. Carl had never gotten the chance to meet his grandfather, as he had died before he was born. He would, however, listen intently as his mother talked of her admiration, devotion, and love for her father. She would talk of how, before and after school, she would visit him at his store. Even though she had been very young, she would remember fondly the advice her father would bestow upon her. She would often recount their conversations together and of course, more than once, told Carl about the day that changed everything.

Carl could close his eyes and hear his mother's voice telling him about that day.

My father would explain that when you are alone with someone and they trust you, they will often bare their souls. He would often say, "I am counsellor, advisor, therapist, and tailor, all rolled into one."

It was well known that foreign intelligence agencies had tried to recruit Carl's grandfather, but on each occasion, he had declined. The spies of Buenos Aires were better known than the movie stars. If anyone had agreed to work for them, it would have been known to those who lived in the city. The family business would have ended overnight, and the family would have needed to leave the country.

It was in May 1960 that the world changed for Carl's mother and their family. As usual, she had been to visit her father before school. They sat in the front window of the tailor's shop in two chairs that looked out at the world—deep-green leather chairs with dark wooden legs that looked like they belonged in a gentlemen's club where old men slept off heavy lunches.

When she was very little, and visited along with her mother, she would need to be lifted into the chair. Her father would sit in the other. She would always be given a lollipop, and her father would sip coffee. As she grew, she would visit on her own, but they still always sat in those chairs together.

One morning, as they watched out the window, they saw a man dressed in an Argentinian soldier's uniform walking along the pavement.

"Were you in the army?" she asked.

"I was, yes," replied her father.

"Did you have to kill anyone?" she asked.

"Good lord, no. I made the uniforms for all the soldiers."

Carl's grandfather wasn't technically lying. He had indeed been a tailor when the war started and did make uniforms at first. However, it was identified early on that his skills were misplaced.

During some remedial training, he was selected for the Brandenburgers. This was an elite German Special Forces unit. He excelled in this unit, and although he would never admit it, he had killed a lot of people, both German and allied forces, in the name of the Führer and the new Germany.

But more than a year before Germany surrendered, he came to understand the full horror of what he was fighting for and decided to take his family to Argentina to start a new life.

He re-established his tailoring business, and it became hugely successful.

"They tell us in school that everybody doesn't like us because we let some people called the Nazis come and live here. Is that true, Lieber Vater?" she asked.

Her father sighed and said, "Now, you listen to me. True Germans are an amazingly warm and generous group of people. During the war, we all wanted a better Germany, and we thought that a man called Adolf Hitler and the Nazi party would be that future. However, a year before the end of the war, I saw something called a concentration camp."

"What is that?" she asked.

"It is a place where Nazis of pure evil worked. They were certainly not part of the Germany we wanted. I was and still am a proud Nazi, but I knew then and there that I needed to get your mother and our family out of Germany, so we came here."

"Shouldn't the bad people get told off?" she asked.

"I don't disagree, and there are some people here who are hiding from what they have done. If I get asked by the right person, at the right time, I might nudge them in the right direction." Her father smiled, looking down at her.

She was then helped from her chair and told that she should be getting off to school. She hugged her father, who murmured, "I killed who I had to, my young angel, so you would never have to face such horror yourself." Then he released her and watched her walk down the road.

A few hours later, when she had finished school, she stopped, as always, at her father's shop. As she approached, she saw a lot of police officers standing in the street, talking. The area had been cordoned off. As she came closer, she saw her mother outside, crying. On seeing her, her mother ran up and swept her into her arms. She told her that her father had died. Then, hand in hand, they walked past the police officers— who seemed unconcerned with protecting the scene—and went inside the shop.

Carl's mother would describe that her father was lying on the floor in the middle of the store, still holding a piece of marking chalk. She said that it looked like he had simply lain down to sleep. Her mother was beside herself with grief. She stood, listening to her mother weep as she stared at her motionless father. The afternoon sun flooded through the glass-fronted building, and she felt detached from everything, as if frozen in time.

Her father's body was carefully removed, and at his funeral the following week, nearly four thousand people came to say their goodbyes.

Carl's mother said that the loss of her father was overshadowed by the trial of Adolf Eichmann, which was broadcast around the world for all to see. It was the talk of Buenos Aires. What happened next has been forged in rumour, myth, conspiracy, and gossip. Carl's family were convinced that members of Mossad had killed his grandfather after he had refused to work with them, as they had tried to catch Adolf Eichmann in the same month. Whether he helped them or not was not Carl's concern. It was ensuring that the legacy of his grandfather didn't die with him. Carl had listened to the stories told of his grandfather, that he was a proud man and only wanted what was best for his family. Carl's grandfather had devoted his time to his work, ensuring his family wanted for nothing.

Carl became angry and resentful of his family and their relentless ambition to prove that Mossad agents had killed their family patriarch. He could see the pain it caused his mother, who was a shattered soul after the death of her father. Carl's mother would take him to the tailor shop and they would both sit in the same chairs in the window and look out onto the world. Whether Mossad had or hadn't killed his grandfather was irrelevant and wouldn't bring him back. After the death of Carl's grandfather, family members and friends had taken on the business, but it was feared the store might close. Carl decided that this would never happen. As soon as he was able, he started working at his grandfather's store after school and learning the tailor's craft. Now it was one of the most renowned tailors in Argentina, and because of Carl's work, he was able to support his family comfortably, along with several charities.

CHAPTER 16

CARL'S APARTMENT, EARLY EVENING

Carl left his apartment and joined the evening throng of people making their way through the streets. He strolled along the sidewalks, nodding at those he knew and to those who wanted to be acknowledged by him. Like his grandfather, he had the ear of the president, powerful organised crime bosses, successful businessmen, and every important man and woman who came to his store. It was well known that foreign spy agencies had approached Carl, and like his grandfather, he had declined their offer, so his standing in the community was unrivalled.

Carl had a forty-five-minute walk to the hotel Alvear Palace. This was the regular place for him and his friends to meet, and tonight was a special evening. He strolled casually, watching the nightlife of the bustling city, and pondered the weeks to come.

As he entered the main doors, the concierge nodded and,

smiling, pointed down the corridor. Carl followed his direction, then stopped at a door and pressed his ear to it but heard nothing. He knocked, then entered the beautifully decorated meeting room, one of several in the hotel. Inside sat four people, who nodded at his arrival but didn't utter a word.

Carl slid off his jacket and removed a small device from his pocket. After switching it on, he proceeded around the room, using the device to scan certain items—lamps, the phone, the unstaffed bar, and the hot-serving food platters. He even climbed onto the table to sweep the large chandelier that illuminated the room.

"All is clear, my friends," he said, switching off the device and putting it into his jacket pocket.

"Are you sure?" asked one man, walking towards his friend.

"I like to be safe. You know that."

"I know, but if your oldest friend can't make fun of you, then who can?" said the man, hugging Carl. This was Johannes, Carl's oldest and dearest friend and business partner.

The others present were Alicia, Augustus, and Hanna.

Now that the room was deemed safe, they greeted one another, served themselves food and a drink, and sat around the table. These five people had been friends since high school and were known in the city via their friendship with Carl. Due to people's opinions of the Germans who had arrived in Argentina after the war, they were not always met with open arms. It was true that where his people had a strong presence, like Bariloche, they were well accepted, but in Buenos Aires, they were resented, hated even. These five friends had learned from their families the brilliance and power of the Nazi party before the war ended, before Adolf Hitler was betrayed. There were rumours and stories that Hitler had been betrayed by one of his generals, Heinrich Müller. These rumours had even suggested that Müller had told Mossad where Adolf Eichmann had been hiding. This particular group of friends hated the fact that Müller's betrayal had precipitated the fall of the Nazi party and resulted in the murder of one of their grandfathers. These five friends forged an inseparable bond together that only grew stronger with the anti-German and anti-Nazi sentiment and discrimination they faced growing up.

It had been one particular incident when they were in high school that had cemented their allegiances to each other.

Augustus had joined the school later than the others when his father was transferred from Austria. His father worked for a chemical engineering company based in Austria and had come to Argentina for work. Augustus's mother was a nurse and worked in the intensive care unit of the local hospital. Augustus didn't speak great English or indeed Argentinian Spanish, so his father held him back a year so he could acclimate and catch up. Augustus was incredibly intelligent, and it didn't take long for him to pick up the languages he needed. It was thought that he may become a doctor, as his knowledge of the sciences was well beyond that of anyone else at his school.

Augustus, Hanna, Alicia, Johannes, and Carl all joined the school chess club and were pretty good players. Augustus, however, was exceptional and a brilliant tactician.

The group participated in regular sports, were all academically bright, and enjoyed a reasonable social life. One day, Augustus was approached by a girl who seemed to have taken a shine to him. He later found out she was the girlfriend of a large, brutish student called Santiago, the captain of the football team. Santiago told Augustus to leave his girlfriend alone. Augustus immediately apologised and told the girl to stay away from him. But she decided to embarrass Santiago in the large communal lunchroom by shouting that he had no right to tell her who she could or could not talk to. Santiago was enraged at being spoken to like this and decided the whole thing was Augustus's fault.

That same afternoon, Santiago, with some of the football team, confronted Augustus and proceeded to throw him over a railing into a stairwell. He fell twenty feet, landing on and dislocating his shoulder, and breaking his clavicle.

Everyone in school knew what had happened, but Augustus refused to tell anyone who had done it. Carl wanted to seek revenge, but Augustus said no. He just wanted to get on with high school without further drama. He returned to class about a month later with his arm in a sling.

Santiago and his football team friends would tease Augustus, and when Carl threatened Santiago, Augustus would drag him away. Santiago would find this amusing, and he shouted after Carl that he should be careful or he might fall into the stairwell.

It was agreed, for safety reasons, that they should stick together at school. They made sure they were always in pairs in case the football thugs decided to dish out further punishment.

Augustus's shoulder healed, but it was never quite the same again. On colder evenings, it would ache, and he was told he would probably suffer from the injury all his life.

It was probably six months after the attack that they were all at Carl's house, playing chess, when the doorbell rang.

Carl's mother answered and spoke to whoever was at the door.

A police officer then entered and, on seeing the friends, said, "There has been a very serious incident, and I need to talk with Augustus."

"Okay. How can I help, Officer?" asked Augustus.

"I would like you to come with me to the police station," the officer replied.

"Am I under arrest?"

"No, you are not."

"Then I am not going anywhere. Anything you want to say to me, you can say in front of my friends. There are no secrets between us," said Augustus.

"Fine. What time did you get here?" asked the officer.

Augustus stood up and said, "We came here together, straight after school. And we haven't been anywhere else."

The group didn't blink at this last statement, even though they knew it was a lie.

"Is that true?" asked the officer.

All four friends nodded it was.

The police officer turned to Carl's mother and asked if that was true.

Carl's mother said she'd been home for about an hour. When she got home, all the friends were at the house.

"A boy from your school has been attacked and seriously injured this evening," said the officer.

"And what does that have to do with us?" asked Carl.

"The young man's name is Santiago, and he goes to your school," replied the officer.

"Yes, we know him from school. What does him being attacked have to do with us?" asked Johannes.

"We know that he hurt you, Augustus, and that you, Carl, have almost come to blows over this."

Carl's mother looked at Carl. "Is this true, Carl? Did you hurt this boy?"

"No, Mother, I didn't hurt him. Anyway, Officer, if you

knew that he hurt my friend here, why didn't you do anything about that? Or maybe it's because Santiago's father is the chief inspector of police, and you wouldn't want his son to get into trouble? But now his son has been hurt, you're pulling out the stops," said Carl.

Augustus stepped forward and, placing his hand on Carl's shoulder, said, "It's okay, Carl. What happened to Santiago, Officer? Is he okay?"

The officer looked irritated and, staring at Augustus, said, "Tonight, when Santiago was heading for football training, he was attacked. The attacker held him down and sliced through both his buttocks. Whoever it was knew what they were doing, as they severed the nerves quite accurately."

"That's terrible, Officer. Santiago was a talented footballer, and I heard he was being considered for the national team. But do you really think I could have restrained someone his size and hurt him like that?" Augustus asked.

"No, I don't think you could, but the five of you might," said the officer.

Carl's mother asked, "Excuse me, Officer, but when did this take place?"

"About two hours ago."

"Well, I called the house before I came home—it was around that time. Johannes answered, and when I asked for Carl, he went and got him. And I could hear Hanna in the background, too."

"Did you hear Augustus and the other young lady here?" asked the officer.

"No, I didn't, but if you think it would have needed all five of them to hold the boy down, then it must have been someone else."

The officer looked at the group, who were all staring back at him. "You all understand that it is a criminal offence to lie to the police. So, I am going to ask one last time. Have you been here, together, all evening?"

The friends, without taking their gaze off the officer, answered, "Yes."

The officer thanked Carl's mother for her time and, looking very irritated indeed, left the house.

Carl turned to Augustus, "Remind me never to get on your bad side."

Augustus smiled, "I don't know what you mean. But now, it is done."

A wave of relief drifted over the group. Navigating Santiago at school had become dangerous and tiresome.

The friends were interviewed repeatedly, but they held to their story, and no one was ever charged.

The story was later released that Santiago had been on his way to football training when he had been attacked in a darkened alleyway. The attacker had injected him with something that rendered him unconscious. Then his buttocks were sliced and the wounds dressed to stop him from bleeding to death. Santiago had come to, lying in the alleyway, to find his trousers pulled down, his buttocks exposed, and blood on his legs. He was unable to move.

His football career was over, and he never returned to school.

The rumours about the attack were rampant, and Carl and his friends were feared by everyone, including the football team.

The friends never spoke of that night again, but the resultant bond that had formed between them was now unbreakable.

CHAPTER 17

ALVEAR PALACE, BUENOS AIRES

The friends sat down to eat and drink—good food and fine wine always a precursor to discussion. Not wishing to be intruded upon, they cleared their own plates before returning to the table.

"Ladies and gentlemen, we are very close to the end of our long journey. I have spoken with Benjamin, and they are very pleased with our progress. Everything is falling into place as we had hoped. There's the target's security detail to deal with, but at the moment, local police know nothing of their upcoming visit. As you know, the Oilman came to see us, and he is ready. Now let's go around the room and get an update, starting with Alicia," said Carl.

Alicia put down her coffee. "I have researched and sourced the weaponry used by the Calgary Police Service. We should be able to move around without drawing attention to ourselves. I have also acquired some other items—hand grenades that include fragmentation, smoke, and incendiary. I have purchased the couple of additional handguns you asked for that can be secreted in your body armour. Please don't use them when we are deployed, as they aren't standard-issue. You're likely to stand out if you do."

She took another drink of her coffee, then continued, "As an added touch, I have purchased some Claymore mines that might come in handy. The M134 Miniguns are also en route to us from our contact in Alaska. They will arrive in the city a few days before the parade. I'll meet the couriers and then have them installed."

"Excellent. Thank you, Alicia. I know we have already offered, but do you need assistance when you collect the Miniguns?" said Carl.

Alicia smiled, "No, I am good. Thank you. If for some reason I am betrayed, it would be better that only I get arrested or killed."

Carl then laid his eyes on Johannes, who began to speak. "I have secured a subterranean floor of an office building in the centre of the city. Rental prices during the Stampede are out-rageous, but that has worked to our advantage, as owners don't tend to ask questions. As long as they get their money, they don't seem to be interested in what you want it for. The area is large enough that we can camp out there, thus reducing our footprint. We can also make use of this 'Plus Fifteen' system they have there. In case you don't know, it's a walkway network that connects all the main parts of the city. It was built so citi-zens didn't have to go outside too much in the harsh winters."

Looking around at his friends, he could tell they'd done their research. He moved on, "I told the management agency that we are a security company coming in for the parade. There are shower facilities, a kitchen, a conference room, and the usual logistics, tables, chairs, phones, and so on. The room also is a communications nightmare—it's almost impossible to get a signal. I have established repeaters in the basement area, so we won't be affected, but it will certainly hinder any trespassers coming down from street level, as they would need to be on our channel to use the repeaters.

"Lastly, the uniforms have also been secured. I organised a break-in at a local shopping mall and acquired a number of them. It surprised me that these people used an external provider, but it made my job a little easier. We also have EMS, bylaw, and fire uniforms, so we can use them if needed."

Hanna sensed Johannes was finished and, without being prompted, launched into her update. "I have secured our fake identities for when we leave Argentina and head to our respective destinations. I have blindly given us all different routes to get to Vancouver, and you are not to disclose those routes to each other. I have used Canadian passports, which shouldn't raise suspicion with the authorities. When we arrive in Vancouver, I will provide everyone with another identity.

"After the mission is complete, we shall separate and head to vehicles I will have placed in the city. Only I know the location of each vehicle. You will not disclose where your vehicles are to anyone in the group. In the vehicles are fresh clothes, new identities, weaponry, food, and water."

She paused, checking she had everyone's attention, then added, "One last thing. When you arrive at each destination, please destroy the identities before assuming the new ones. If someone finds the old identity, it creates a trail. I would recommend burning them. Don't be stupid and keep the old one with you. No souvenirs. Once you are done with it, get rid of it."

Augustus waited to see if anyone had any questions. Knowing he would be last, he finished off his coffee and spoke. "Okay, it has been confirmed that the parade is going ahead as scheduled, and from what our sources tell me, our target will be there. Carl is correct—there will be a protection detail with him, and the police are not aware he's coming. Apparently, his security team feels that support from local police is not necessary, which is good news for us. On the morning of the parade, law enforcement will do a sweep of the route but then leave it lightly guarded until assigned officers arrive on scene. As for specialty units, they have their tactical unit, and that's about it, so it's not really an issue for us. There are a lot of police at the parade, but for them, it is a real public relations event, so they won't be on high alert. There will be dignitaries present, too, but once the attack starts, their protection people will take their charge and get out. Again, not an issue for us."

"How did you get this information, Augustus?" asked Hanna.

Augustus smiled. "I would like to take the credit, but the rank-and-file are so disenfranchised, it was easy to get one or two talking. That's how we found out about the uniform store, the security at the parade, the weapons they use, their radio frequencies, all that insider stuff."

"Do we have any loose ends?" asked Carl.

"No, not at all. I am not worried at this point," said Augustus.

There was a pregnant pause before Augustus spoke again. "The only concern I have is your fondness for Caeli."

Carl sighed and said, "I told you, Augustus, that it would not be a problem. I will manage the situation."

"So you have said, Carl. I appreciate that she has helped us, certainly unknowingly, but when we all disappear, she is going to be questioned. It would be unfortunate if this whole thing came crashing down around us because of her," said Augustus, rather pointedly.

Carl placed his coffee cup back into his saucer without taking his eyes off Augustus. "I told you and the group that I shall deal with Caeli. I have been committed to this operation from the outset, and I shall not falter now. I don't expect to be questioned when I have given my word. Is that clear, Augustus?"

"Yes, perfectly," said Augustus, who hadn't let his gaze leave Carl's.

"Friends, we are on the eve of greatness. I spoke with Benjamin, and they are pleased with our progress and have promised to meet us after this is done," said Carl.

The group looked a little surprised, as Benjamin had only ever been seen in person and spoken to by Carl. They had been the supporter of the operation and provided them with finances and help where they could. The group was eager to meet Benjamin, who had become to them almost like a figure from folklore.

Carl stood and, raising his coffee cup, gestured for the group to stand. He looked at each friend. "After we leave here, the next time we see each other will be in Canada. I wouldn't want to do this with any other people, and we shall be victorious in the face of evil. A new dawn is coming, and we shall be the ones to ignite the touchpaper and bring forward the revolution. Forward as One."

"Forward as One," said the friends in unison.

The group then gathered their belongings and spent a good

while thoroughly wiping down everything they had touched before embracing each other and departing.

Except for Hanna and Carl, who stayed behind.

"I'll pick you up at the lake tonight," said Hanna.

"Sounds good," said Carl.

Then he made his way home. When he arrived, he called out for Caeli, who emerged from the bathroom. It was clear she had just had a shower. Caeli was a petite woman with a slender frame, long blonde hair, and striking blue eyes. She had been a promising athlete, and her body reflected that hard work and dedication. She was also a nurse at the largest hospital in Buenos Aires. Her father was a well-known surgeon and public figure in the city. She enjoyed the parties she attended with Carl and her father.

As she stood with the small bath towel shrouding her figure, Carl admired her beauty. He sat on one of the bar stools, and she stood between his legs. They embraced and kissed. Carl's hand wandered around her waist, and she made no effort to stop him.

She smiled and between the now frantic kissing, said, "Someone missed me on night shift."

She then took a step back and pulled off her towel, letting it drop to the floor. With a small smile, she turned and walked to the bedroom.

Sometime later, they lay, naked and breathless. Carl turned to her, "Why don't we head up to your family's cabin tonight? Didn't you say it would be empty this weekend?"

"That's a great idea. Yes, everyone's away on holiday."

"I have some work to do, so why don't you drive up there tonight, and I will come up later? We can have a late supper. And we can do this again."

Caeli rolled over onto her side. Carl wondered if he'd ever get used to her body. "Sounds perfect. I'll go and pack."

"Oh, and text your friends this time and let them know—you know how terrible the service is up there. We don't want a repeat performance of last time, where they went into a flat spin because they couldn't get hold of you."

Caeli pulled a face. "It was hardly a flat spin. They were just a bit concerned, that's all. But thank you, darling, you think of everything. I am one lucky lady." She grabbed her phone and disappeared into the bathroom, fingers working furiously on the keypad.

Carl got dressed and made himself a coffee.

About thirty minutes later, Caeli emerged from the bedroom with a small case packed and ready to go.

"All ready? And your friends all know?" asked Carl.

Caeli rolled her eyes. "Yes, I've messaged them all, and they've all replied. They said you're amazing and asked if they could come, too."

Caeli was once again standing between Carl's legs as he sat sipping his coffee. She was wearing a light summer dress that hung gently on her frame.

"Sorry, baby, I don't share very well," Carl replied. "Only you get me."

"Aren't I the lucky one?" said Caeli.

They kissed, and Carl turned Caeli around, pulling her close and brushing her hair to the side. As she relaxed into him, he pushed a needle into the base of her neck. Before she even had time to realise something was wrong, she had gone limp. Carl let her body fall against his, then lowered her to the ground.

He removed a large, wheeled suitcase from the bedroom

closet and brought it into the living room. He kissed her on the forehead and, making sure she was still breathing, placed her unconscious body into it. He laid her on her side and brought her knees up to her chest. She fit inside quite comfortably, but he made sure her head was upright, so as not to restrict her airway, then placed an oxygen mask over her face.

After cleaning up, he wheeled the suitcase to the parking garage and placed Caeli into the trunk of her Mercedes. He drove out of the city, and then about two miles from the city limits, arrived on the shores of a large lake. In the height of summer, it was a real tourist attraction, but at this time of year, and this time of night, it was deserted.

Carl parked the vehicle, then took Caeli out of the suitcase and placed her in the driver's seat. He had her cell phone, which he threw onto the passenger seat. He paused a moment—she looked peaceful. He kissed her again and released the parking brake, then closed the door, and with a gentle push, the car slowly rolled forward. Gradually, it gained momentum. It tipped over the edge and dropped into the dark water of the lake.

Carl walked to the bank and watched as the vehicle headlights disappeared into the darkness. Then he returned to the road, and after a short wait, Hanna pulled up and he climbed in. Without a word, they drove to the airport. He retrieved his bags and entered the terminal.

CHAPTER 18

FERRY CABIN, HEADING TO SOUTHAMPTON

Peter awoke first, feeling like he couldn't open his eyes. His body was a dead weight, clearly telling him how exhausted he was. He slowly came to and found he was still curled up behind Chloe. She wasn't stirring either. Without thinking, he pulled her closer and kissed the back of her head. She moved and with what seemed like a Herculean effort, turned herself round to face him. She kissed him back and nestled her head into his chest.

"What would I do without you?" she whispered.

Peter sighed and kissed the top of her head. "Don't worry, we'll figure this out."

After a few minutes, they both got up, and Peter realised it was almost dinner time, making him feel hungry. They chuckled as they assisted each other in getting off the bed, resembling an elderly couple. The effects of the drugs had worn off, and lactic acid had taken its toll on their bodies. Peter stood in front of a large mirror in his shorts, examining himself. "Just look at me," he remarked as he noticed bruises he hadn't been aware of, the wound on his shoulder, and various scrapes and scratches.

Chloe, also not fully dressed, took her place beside him. "If this is a who-looks-the-most messed-up contest, then I've definitely won."

She stood in front of him and turned slowly, looking at her battered, small frame in the mirror. Peter looked at her reflection and shook his head. As she finished her circle and faced him again, she took a step forward and pressed herself against him, enjoying the skin-on-skin contact. Peter returned the pressure as he bent to meet her upturned face and gently kissed her bruised forehead, neck, and then lips. The aches and pains melted away as they explored each other, and their kiss became more urgent.

"How long until dinner?" murmured Chloe.

"About an hour or so."

Smiling, she said, "So . . . let's have a shower—take the edge off a little. Then we can go for dinner."

Peter grinned back and, taking her hand, led her to the bathroom, closing the door behind them.

The shower was large enough to accommodate them both. Without waiting, they slid each other's underwear off and stepped under the cascading water. The hot water was painful and exhilarating in equal measure, every open wound, cut, and graze stinging fiercely and making them feel alive. They allowed their dressings to get a little wet before removing them, each working on the other, gently easing the tape away, massaging the remains of the adhesive, taking care to avoid touching the wounds, until the skin was clean. Once done, Chloe faced him, looking him up and down. "You'll do, soldier."

The sound of the water centred Peter's focus as they kissed. Their skin felt rejuvenated and soothed by water running over their bodies.

Peter eventually stepped out of the shower, allowing Chloe some time to gather her thoughts. "I am going to fire up those cell phones, see if they work. When you come out, we can call the Matron."

"What if that isn't her number anymore? Maybe it was only for training. Also, what makes you think she'll help us?"

"I'd thought of that. If that's the case, then I propose we head to the training area and see if we can find her. I don't know if she'll help us, but I do know she isn't connected to any of our groups. My instinct tells me we can trust her."

He went to the bedroom and set up the two phones—they worked fine. They agreed to go and have dinner, then come back and make the call. Peter suggested keeping the phones powered down at all times, only powering up if and when needed.

Chloe asked what the duct tape, sealable sandwich bags, and black bags were for.

Peter smiled, "That is in preparation for us getting off this ship—you know, if we need to in a hurry."

She looked a little concerned. "I was wondering what the plan was for that. But I want to get some food inside me first before I hear any more of your plans."

"Deal."

They redressed their wounds, Chloe artfully covering up the most obvious of their bruises with make-up, and made their way to dinner.

CHAPTER 19

RAF BRIZE NORTON, ENGLAND

Andrew had protested about being sent to Germany but was politely told he was going whether he liked it or not. The conversation had centred around where he would like to check passport applications at foreign embassies for the rest of his career. After consideration, Germany didn't seem too bad.

He had travelled to his home and collected some clothing and the usual items he needed for a trip of this nature. Although he knew that if he simply asked, he could get anything he wanted shipped to the nearest friendly embassy.

It was the dead of night when he arrived at the RAF base, and all seemed quiet, apart from the guard, who was clearly expecting him and was waiting, along with a vehicle, to show him to his hangar.

He swung into the large, vacuous building, and the escorting vehicle drove away. Andrew's car door sprang open, and there stood one of the flight crew.

"Hello, sir. We've been expecting you. Put your vehicle to the side and leave the keys on the dash so it can be moved if needed. Get your bags and wait for me over there." He pointed to a large table against the wall. "We are preparing the Puma Eurostar for the flight and should be good to go in about twenty minutes. There are toilets over there, so take a piss—and a shit if you need it—as the flight will be about three hours. I'll be back shortly."

The airman slammed the door shut and then disappeared. Andrew moved his vehicle as instructed, taking note of his waiting point on the way. He grabbed his bags and wandered over to the table.

The airman returned, and Andrew could see that he was wearing a military shirt and trousers, not your usual airman flight suit. He approached and looked Andrew up and down in his three-piece suit. "Mr. Bond, let's get this briefing underway, shall we? Due to the urgency of this flight, we've had to strip the helicopter down to make it a flying fuel can to get you where you need to be. So, if we crash on land, we'll create a mushroom cloud that will be seen from space. If we land over water, we'll sink like a depth charge large enough to take out an aircraft carrier. So, keep your fingers crossed that all goes well. Anything for me?"

Andrew stood, looking at the airman. He liked this guy. He glanced at his rank slide but couldn't see a designation. Instead, it bore a crest identifying the Special Boat Squadron (SBS).

"I appreciate the briefing, but any chance of a cup of tea and cake?" asked Andrew glibly.

The SBS operator had seen Andrew look at his unit identification. "Yes, Mr. Bond, sir, thanks to my extensive training in hosting, I'll be able to get right onto that. I can offer you a tea with Biscuits Brown or Biscuits Fruit, and if you ask me nicely, perhaps even a Mars bar."

"A Mars bar and a tea would be great. Thank you."

The SBS operator smiled and said, "Behind you is a kettle and some Thermoses. Get three of them filled with water, a teabag, milk, and sugar. I'm sure the rest of the crew will appreciate your efforts. I'll get something to eat and have it ready on the helicopter. You must be pretty special, as I got dragged off my team to replace the airman for this flight. The whole airbase has been locked down waiting for you."

"I'm flattered, I'm sure. I recognise your badge, so I feel quite safe."

"The only thing you have to remember is if we crash into water, the second splash you'll hear is me coming to save you, 007. The crew hasn't asked any questions, and neither will I. We couldn't give a shit. We'll get you where you need to be, and I'll keep you safe. Now, let's get moving. We leave in ten minutes."

Andrew got the Thermos flasks ready, then headed out to the helicopter. As he exited the hangar, the pilot gave him a brief glance before returning his attention to the cockpit and the pre-flight checks.

Andrew handed the Thermoses to the SBS operator, who passed one to the co-pilot. He nodded at both Andrew and the operator. His bags were then taken, stowed under the seats, and secured with cargo netting. The seats ran along each side of the helicopter, facing each other.

Once Andrew was seated, the operator passed him a helmet, and as he slid it on, the ambient noise disappeared and all became quiet.

The operator put on his own helmet, and as he pulled the door shut, the operator activated the comms channel. "Package aboard, green light. I say again, green light."

There was a perfunctory, "Copy," and the helicopter moved forward a little on its wheels and with a surge of energy, lifted off.

Andrew watched the operator check his gear, which included customised weaponry, fins, a medic kit, and various other baggage. As the helicopter gained elevation, the operator reached into his pocket and threw Andrew a Mars Bar. He caught it, cracked the Thermos, and sat back for the ride.

A short while later, the operator's voice came over the comms, telling Andrew his crew were going to communicate on a different channel to give him some peace. He should try to get some sleep. Andrew loosened his tie and lay on the seats. Pulling down the built-in sun visor on the helmet, he tried to block out the world. Inside the helmet, his mind was in overdrive, wondering what nightmare he was walking into.

CHAPTER 20

ABIGAIL'S MERCEDES, M4 MOTORWAY, ENGLAND

Abigail knew it wasn't good when she'd been asked to go to Sir Goodlove's home in Newquay at this late hour. The events in North Africa with Peter and Chloe had been a disaster, and Abigail was starting to feel the ripple effects. Sir Goodlove was most certainly going to lecture her accordingly.

On arrival, she exited her vehicle and was met by the Special Forces team who protected the house. She was instructed to go through the side gate and enter Sir Goodlove's study through the large patio doors.

The night was warm, and the only noise was that of the ocean. Abigail followed the path through the gate and into a large back garden, bathed in moonlight. The patio doors were open, and although there was no one in sight, she felt the video surveillance watching her.

As she entered the large, ornate study, Sir Goodlove was

sitting at his desk with only a reading lamp to illuminate his newspaper. "You made it, Abigail. Good. Something to drink?"

"Yes, please. A scotch, neat," replied Abigail.

Sir Goodlove got up and walked to his drinks collection. He poured himself a healthy gin and Abigail a scotch.

He walked over to her and gestured to sit on a large leather couch that looked out onto the garden. He switched on another small lamp that gently bathed the sofa in a yellowish light.

"So, tell me, Abigail, what is the update on this operation we are having in North Africa?"

Abigail took a sip of her scotch and collected her thoughts. "As you know, we had scheduled Peter and Chloe's final exercise in Algeria, after receiving information that a tried-and-tested source had valuable intelligence. We had good reason to believe the source would provide the name of a mole within the intelligence community. What particular agency, or even where in the world that mole might be, we had no idea. We just knew someone somewhere was posing as one of us and leaking highly sensitive information. This source seemed to be the key to identifying them, so I decided to act and deploy our new trainees."

"Yes, yes, but why not use the normal measures to get the name of a mole? Why use Peter and Chloe?" asked Goodlove.

"It's possible this entire mole thing was a storm in a teacup, but if it wasn't, we needed to find a way of prising them out without them suspecting and going to ground. So I decided to act on this information, using Peter and Chloe's training exercise as cover for what was actually a live operation."

Sir Goodlove shifted in his seat. "This source was reliable?"

"Yes, indeed. They were the one who tipped us off about the liquid bombs that were going to be placed on flights leaving the UK," said Abigail.

"Oh, yes, I have read some of his other stuff. He's a very interesting asset."

"Yes indeed, they were. Anyway, as you know, the meeting took place, and afterwards, I did receive the message update with the name implicating the mole. That name was mine." She paused to allow Sir Goodlove to process this. "Then, of course the source was later found dead in what was made to look like a botched robbery. We've been keeping an eye on Chloe for some time now, and I felt she may have forwarded false intelligence, possibly even having something to do with the source's death, although I can't fathom how. Something just didn't fit, so I had her picked up and taken to a safe house where our people could subject her to some robust questioning.

"Peter was allowed to travel, as I didn't think he was involved in whatever Chloe may or may not be up to. I was wrong about that. He took it upon himself to invade the safe house, kill two, and leave with Chloe." She took a large swig of her scotch. "That's the abridged version." Sir Goodlove offered her a top-up, which she accepted.

After refilling their glasses, Sir Goodlove sat down. "That's quite the tale. Now, I think it is time for me to tell you a story.

"About two years ago, an operation was launched to disrupt a terror attack being prepared off the coast of Yemen. A bunch of terrorists was going to ram a cruise ship with a large whaling boat. Once it had been rammed, they were going to head on board and kill everyone—the usual stuff."

"Yes, I remember—it was a joint operation between US Navy SEALs and our own SBS. We successfully killed everyone and found a little treasure trove of intelligence, if I recall it correctly."

"Correct, but what didn't come out was that there were three newly enrolled terrorists on guard duty. Special Forces didn't kill them, and we got them into custody pretty much unharmed. They were flown to a black ops site for questioning. After a few days, one of these young and idealistic men, whom I shall call Bob, decided to tell us about his uncle. Bob said that his uncle had a very useful informant who worked high up in Western intelligence. Now, this young man had a few missing teeth and hadn't slept for a while, so we didn't know if he was fabricating it in order to save himself. He told us he didn't know who his uncle got the information from, but he did tell us that this secret informant would sometimes come into town and meet with their lover, who he could identify."

Sir Goodlove sipped his gin and let the information sink in. "Now, Bob was from Yemen, and we confirmed who his uncle was. He was indeed well connected to extremism and had links to terrorism in that region. So we put him under surveillance and did our usual digital forensic sweep, which confirmed he was a legitimate player and had been involved in several high-profile attacks. Bob was kept alive while his two friends were killed. The questioning continued. After a few months, we had no further leads, so one day, while hosting a meeting with his senior command, the uncle had a drone missile parked in his living room. A good result for us. Of course, our people entered the house afterwards and combed through the remains. Inside was a charred photograph of a young woman in an Islamic headdress. We showed it to Bob, who positively identified her as the informant's lover. And then he admitted she had stayed at his uncle's house once, maybe twice.

"We were none too pleased he hadn't mentioned this information before, as had we known that, we'd probably have delayed the drone strike so we could glean more intel, possibly from inside the property, bugs and all that. It was a real missed opportunity. But anyway, we then focused on trying to identify this mystery lover, thinking that if we found her, then that may lead to our mole."

"Yes, exactly," said Abigail.

"All our searches for this mystery woman are negative. We did low-level intelligence searches, downplaying our reason for finding this young lady, who we gauged was perhaps eighteen. We found nothing and were running out of options.

"Then, one day, we had a new batch of trainee intelligence officers who were in their final week before being released into the world. They were being toured through the operations floor at MI6, where, to give the trainees a taste of a day in the life of an intelligence worker, staff had picked the hunt for this informant's lover to present as an example operation. As they're standing in front of the large operations board, one of the new young officers steps out of the group and points at the charred picture and announces to everyone that he knows her. Of course, the staff working on the operation all stop working and laugh. The lead officer tells them to shut up and asks how the young man knows her.

"He tells them that she'd been at Cambridge with him— she was a couple of years below him. Apparently, she had a love of rugby, an honorary Cambridge Blue, if you know what I mean. But more interestingly, if I remember correctly, he told them that she studied foreign languages and was well travelled. But even better than that, this young man then brings out his phone and locates a picture of this young lady on Facebook. Sure enough, she's right there amongst a throng of chaps after a game. Our mystery young lady, our lover, has finally been identified," said Sir Goodlove.

"What are the chances of that?" said Abigail.

"Indeed. We ask what her name is, and he ponders for a moment before telling us her name was Chloe. And yes, before you ask, the young lover was our own Chloe Greene, who is now on the run with Peter Cartwright," finished Sir Goodlove.

"Okay, I don't understand," said Abigail. She knew there was a watch on Chloe, but she'd never known why. This appeared to be a case of departments keeping their secrets.

"Once we had identified Chloe, we reached out to Cambridge. They confirmed her identity. We placed her under surveillance and tracked her around Europe, North Africa, and South America, but she acted completely normally, so we got nothing on her.

"Now, I am going to explain something that may be difficult to hear, Abigail. The reason I was brought in is that just over two years ago, there was credible intelligence suggesting we had a mole. I was not connected to the intelligence community, so I selected a few people who were chosen because they had no prior connections, and we have been working on identifying this mole. I would like to add that up until the operation in Algeria, you were one of those suspects."

"So, to clarify, me being tasked with finding our mole was nothing more than a ruse to discover whether I was that mole? All my efforts have been a waste of time. I've been played," said Abigail, her voice rising.

"Yes, I am afraid so. I would like to remind you that you are in my home, so please keep your voice down."

Abigail, seething with rage, hissed, "Who do you think you are to question my loyalty? I can only imagine the old school tie-and-pinky-ring group have been helping as you hold my sacrifices for this country to account."

Sir Goodlove fixed his gaze on Abigail. "Now you listen to me. I was more than happy working in London before I got dragged into your murky little world. You really are a bunch of schoolchildren playing schoolyard games while trading people's lives and loyalty like playing cards. It really is a seedy environment you work in, and I don't want to be here any longer than I have to. I'm going to tell you the rest of this story so you can go back to your manor house in the Cotswolds. We decided we'd recruit Chloe into the service then watch, wait, and hopefully give her enough rope to hang herself.

"We recruited her quietly, and with our contacts in Cambridge, we made her feel it was her idea. Once recruited, we put surveillance on her, and she never put a foot wrong. We even had her visit the United States and had their people pick her up under the cover of a training exercise. Apart from one random gentleman caller, there was nothing. What is interesting is in the early days after recruitment, she did head into southern Europe and Africa, but the team and our assets couldn't keep with her. She clearly knew unofficial routes and simply disappeared."

Abigail was not happy and again, trying to keep her voice low, said, "What would you and your little cabal want me to do now?" As she spoke, she rose from her chair and stood, drink in hand, looking out over the garden.

Sir Goodlove stood, too. "As far as we're concerned, you're no longer a person we need to concentrate our attention on."

"How kind of you to say. Do you want me to curtsey?"

Sir Goodlove sipped his gin. "Do what you want. Perhaps now, when you're trading people's lives, you'll consider this moment. You are to go back to your office and be the dutiful head of MI6. When this is all over, I can go back to my life, and you can carry on in your murky world. Now please show yourself out."

Without waiting, Sir Goodlove turned and left the room.

Abigail finished her scotch, and as she walked out into the garden, she threw her glass into the bushes. "Damn you, Chloe."

CHAPTER 21

SITE B, GERMANY

Jessica was in her morning briefing with Twyla and Lars, asking for updates or intelligence that might offer a starting point.

There had been the usual chatter. The cruise ship where Dominic's car was being tracked had been followed up on, and it was determined that it was a dead end. Several other cruise ships had left the port that day, and all of them were being looked into.

Twyla and Lars had worked together for a number of years and always seemed to be brought in when things got a little bit "greasy." Jessica knew them both from Langley and had requested them, as she knew they were trustworthy. They were the two lead intelligence officers at Langley for this operation, which consisted of about thirty people. Lars had been given the primacy of European liaison and Twyla the "rest of the world." Lars liked it when he had to head up a team and got to work with Twyla. They had the same mindset and leadership style. It made for a good working environment.

Jessica heard a knock at the door and shouted, "Come in."

The door opened and there stood Shaukey. "We just got word that some Brit is on his way and should be here in about two to three hours. What would you like us to do with him?"

Jessica sat back in her chair. "Can you meet him on the helipad and bring him here? He's our link man to MI6. Nothing's happening, so get your workout in, and we can brief him when he arrives. Sound good?"

Shaukey smiled. "Sounds good to me."

He turned away, leaving the door open enough for Jessica to hear him shout, "Hey, Groovy Gang, it's workout time, then we're on taxi service."

And for her to hear, "Sounds good, ass-muncher. Who we picking up, when, and where?"

"Some legend from the helicopter pad for the boss lady. I want us ready to go in two hours."

"Roger that. The circuit's all set up—let's go. Hooyah!"

Jessica turned back to Twyla and Lars. "Sorry about that."

They discussed that the NSA and GCHQ had been working together and had ears on every connection known to Peter and Chloe in case the pair called for help. They had sent out their images to every intelligence asset and office manageable with an alert-only status. They hadn't gone out to the police agencies as that would potentially make things messy—they were just sticking with the intelligence groups.

"So, we have established our connections here, and we're prepared to move if we get anything. Did you know that Helena paid me a visit?" asked Jessica.

Twyla replied, "No, we didn't. Seems a little odd, don't

you think, to have a deputy director of the NSA dropping in like that?"

"She's put her reputation on the line to vouch for me, and I am sure she's just being cautious. There are a few people who'd like to see me fail. She didn't seem concerned about anything we'd done, and we only spoke for a few minutes. She did say this one is getting a lot of attention, so maybe that's making her edgy. I don't think it's anything to worry about, so let's move on," said Jessica.

CHAPTER 22

TRAINING CAMP, WALES

Devon, the Matron, Hugo, and the rest of the training team had been ordered to an unscheduled briefing by Colonel Grieves.

Colonel Grieves stood to address the assembled personnel. "Ladies and gentlemen, we have a serious and ongoing situation. I was informed this morning that Peter and Chloe, or Papa One and Charlie One, have a capture order placed on them. They are in breach of the Official Secrets Act and are implicated in the homicide of a covert agent on foreign soil. They are to be treated with extreme prejudice."

As the colonel paused to consider elaborating on these basic facts, a suited man at the back audibly exhaled, and everyone turned to see him shaking his head. Grieves simply moved on, raising his voice a little to regain the attention of the room.

But Devon didn't turn back to face the colonel. Instead,

he continued to stare at the suited man, who stared back and nodded slowly with determination. Slowly, Devon turned to face front, holding eye contact until the last moment.

"If anyone is contacted by either party, they are to inform me immediately. Be very clear on this: Anyone seen helping them will be subject to prosecution. All training is being rescheduled, and the units here are being sent back to their operational bases. All present are now on standby. That is all. Carry on."

Devon and the Matron headed back to finish their breakfast. Sitting in the now-empty mess, they finished their food and drank their tea.

Hugo had also disappeared but came to join Devon and the Matron. "So, a little bird tells me there's an operational team staged up in Germany, waiting to go on any intelligence regarding Peter or Chloe. It's headed up by some chick dragged out of Langley. They've got the usual analysts and a team of Delta operators."

The Matron looked surprised. "How did you find that out?"

Hugo grinned. "I've got contacts, too, you know."

"Okay, so changing topics, are you going to tell us who that man you were glaring at before is?" The Matron smiled, looking at Devon.

Devon grinned. "That, ladies and gentlemen, was Major Douglas Smyth, or as I originally knew him, First Lieutenant Smyth. I was a new operator with the regiment, and we were posted in Northern Ireland. One day, I was in the operations room with one of the senior operators. They were mentoring me, and we were monitoring an IRA funeral. The tension was high due to the recent attack at the Milltown cemetery by that idiot Michael Stone. The funeral might have been for someone killed in the attack, but don't quote me on that. As the cortège made its way through the streets, a car drove into the procession, and the crowd thought it was another attack. A very angry and hostile mob surrounded the car and the two male occupants. Then a gun was produced. Initially, the crowd backed off but not for long. It was a frenzy, and these two poor bastards were dragged out of their car. Then someone in the operations room recognised one of them. Turned out they were British army soldiers."

The Matron had a face of hard concentration. "Yes, I saw the helicopter footage of that incident. A hard watch."

Devon continued, "Indeed. The driver of the car had just picked up his replacement and was giving him a little tour of the area. Unfortunately, he took a wrong turn. The gold commander had an aide advising on strategies, and that aide was First Lieutenant Smyth. He advised that sending in a rescue would ignite the situation, cause a riot, and turn the area into a war zone. My mentor and I knew we were just going to see our own be killed, which, as you can imagine, did not make us happy. We watched those lads disappear into the back of a black cab and when they came out, they were half-naked and severely beaten. According to my mentor, they'd have had their eyeballs slit to disorientate them. A favourite trick of the IRA. Then they were shot multiple times, and their bodies left like garbage for us to recover. As per protocol, there was the usual inquiry, and Mr. Smyth, when asked, said he had given the gold commander a 'number of options.' That was bullshit, but ultimately, it had been the gold commander who'd made the decision to leave those boys to their fate. The gold commander, a brigadier, ended up being sent back to the UK. He resigned from the army not long after that."

Hugo sipped his tea. "So, our Mr. Smyth is not to be trusted, it would seem."

Devon was staring past them. "It was rumoured that Margaret Thatcher had issued a shoot-to-kill policy in Northern Ireland. I was never aware of that, but I made a decision there and then. If some IRA Provo stepped up to the plate, I would remove the back of their head and make it into the shape of a canoe. Their families could then sit in some dingy pub, and when they were all drunk, sing some dirge of a song about 'Billy Boy,' who died for the cause. We should have gotten out of Northern Ireland years ago and left them to it."

The Matron, grinning, said, "So to sum up—Smyth is a treacherous arsehole and not to be trusted; Devon has a side business of head readjustment, which probably wasn't referenced in the Good Friday Agreement; and Hugo here is a walking customer service department." Then she got up, telling them she was going for a run before making sure her kit was all squared away. After that, she planned to spend the rest of the day relaxing. Devon told them to have their phones on and be available if needed. If they didn't hear anything by the next morning, they should make plans to head to their London base and stand by for further orders.

CHAPTER 23

VANCOUVER AIRPORT, BRITISH COLUMBIA, CANADA

Carl had travelled first to Cuba and then to Seattle before taking his final flight to Vancouver. He had gone to Cuba under his real name and used his new false identity for the rest of the journey.

Augustus, Alicia, Johannes, and Hanna had all left Argentina in a similar manner, using their real names to travel to a location and then discarding their identities to travel under new names to a random city in the United States before continuing on to Vancouver. Some had travelled almost nonstop, while others had spent a few days in their new cities before proceeding into Canada.

Carl was the last to arrive in the land of the maple leaf, and this was done for a reason. He thought that being Caeli's boyfriend, he would be the one they would be looking for. He wanted a few days to pass to allow airport officials to become distracted by other matters.

He'd passed through without issue and managed to pick up his hire vehicle, a Ford F-150—he'd read about them when researching the trip. When he got to the parking lot, he was quite surprised by the size of it. It wasn't really necessary, but it would be perfect for the Calgary stage of the plan. He left Vancouver and headed for the rental property Augustus had selected, a cabin set in the woods at the base of Rainbow Mountain. It would take him about three hours, so he put it into drive, sat back, and steered through the stunning scenery.

When he arrived, it was indeed a remote location in the heart of the forest at the base of the mountain. He pulled up in front of the large log cabin and saw there were only two other vehicles. Alicia appeared and greeted him, saying she was glad he'd made it safely.

"Come inside, Carl, and I shall show you your room."

"Where are the others?"

"Out for a run. If you are wondering where their cars are, we have two inside the garage. It's connected to the house, so we can load them up in secret when it is time to leave. We agreed one of us should be in the house at all times. I did my run this morning."

They went inside, and Carl was shown to his room on the second floor, with its en-suite bathroom.

Alicia then pulled from under the bed a number of varying-sized pelican cases and opened them up. Inside were weapons ranging from handguns to shotguns and carbines. There were also hand grenades of varying types from HE to smoke, and some flash-bangs.

"Every weapon here has been selected because they're typically carried by the local police agency. They won't look out of place when we're wearing them. If you look at the tactical body armour, there's a few modifications for hiding an additional sidearm and the grenades. So we should be good."

Carl looked at the weapons and took out a handgun. He worked the action, slid in a magazine, loaded it, then put the holster onto his belt and secured the weapon.

"Excellent. Now tell me about this place," he said.

"We're just over two miles away from the nearest town. There are no cameras here, apart from the ones we have put in ourselves. The nearest is a traffic camera about 300 metres down the road. As you can see, the area is heavily wooded. We can get from the cars to the house pretty much under the tree canopy at all times. The rear, where we can have a barbecue, is also covered by trees. When we go running, we have scouted a route that keeps us under the cover of the forest—it's quite testing. When it was just two of us here, we sent the drone out to find the weak points and marked them with those solar-powered garden lamps that you just shove into the earth on a stake. If you see one, draw a five-metre radius around it—it's a vulnerable area. As long as you do that, anyone flying over will see nothing out of place. We even did a drone flight at night. It looked fine."

"You have been busy," said Carl.

"Thank you. I can't take all the credit. Augustus did some fine work finding this place," said Alicia. "But come on, Carl. Let's grab you a traditional British Columbian pale ale, and we can wait for the others."

They went downstairs, and after collecting a beer, wandered outside and enjoyed the afternoon sun. It wasn't long before the others returned and greeted Carl before heading off to clean up.

Once they were all refreshed, more beers were in order, and they gathered on the rear deck as the air cooled with the setting sun.

"We've come a long way, and we're almost there. Augustus, I would like an update on how things are progressing back in Buenos Aires," said Carl.

Augustus took a swig of his beer. "Caeli's death is being treated as a misadventure, due to the drugs found in her system. They think she lost control of her car and crashed into the lake. The police, however, have been looking for you as the primary witness. They've put warnings out at the ports and airports, but only in Argentina, not beyond. Caeli's family is pushing hard that she did not take drugs and that your disappearance is suspicious. I heard from my contact that they searched your apartment, but apart from evidence of recent sexual activity, they found nothing."

"Excellent. Thank you, Augustus. Weapons, Alicia?"

"Our Miniguns are currently en route from Alaska and will be in place the day before the parade. With all the preparations for the Stampede, another large transport vehicle won't look out of place. We'll have them set up, then they can be remotely accessed by me from anywhere using my phone. We've booked two corner rooms in locations on either side of the street. They're at the same height and cover the street in both directions, so we'll be able to target not just the roadway but also the sidewalks. Additionally, I have met with the Oilman and provided him with a sidearm, smoke grenades, and some HE grenades for when he starts his attack. It'll add to the confusion nicely and allow us to carry out our part," said Alicia.

"Johannes and Hanna, I know you have sourced a base. What can you tell me about that?" asked Carl, moving around the group.

Johannes leaned forward, placing his beer on the table. "I've briefly mentioned this before, but I can now give a little more detail. Because Calgary's so cold, most hotel and office parking is underground. Typically, all floors can be accessed from the parking floor, but in some buildings, permission is needed to enter them. Hanna and I have found an office building that will allow us to have all five vehicles parked underground. We can then use an elevator to access the second subterranean level. I've spent time securing communications down there that only we will be able to use. If anyone goes down there, their communications can't reach the outside. We can also access that walkway system, the Plus 15, without having to go outside. We have the entire floor, which has multiple rooms for us to spread out, sleep, and set up. As I said, I told the company we were a security group working for the Stampede, and they didn't seem too interested."

At this natural pause, Hanna started to speak. "We've all rented F-150s, and I suggest we keep them until we leave the city. They have enough storage that we can secure our weapons and keep them concealed. On a cursory inspection, they won't be seen. I also met with the Oilman, and we talked through how to handle his vehicle and secure the doors during the attack, and where he will wait for us to collect him when it's done. I've already secured six additional vehicles in long-term parking in Calgary, and I will provide you and the Oilman with their location when we arrive there. Once the attack is complete, we separate, go to our vehicles, and leave the city. I've placed bags in the trunks of these vehicles with a change of clothing, new identification, and a preprogrammed cell phone so we can communicate. I have not secured any weapons in these vehicles as I think getting stopped carrying a sidearm would be a problem, so if you want one, remember to bring it with you. That's about it for now."

"Well done, everyone," said Carl. "It's only three days until the Stampede parade, so we'll be leaving tomorrow morning. We'll stagger our times of departure and not speak to each other again until we're in our secure location. Oh, I forgot to ask, do we have the uniforms?"

"Yes, sorry, I should have said that. The uniforms are all ready and upstairs in my room, so make sure you pick them up before you go," said Hanna.

"Good. I wanted to let you know that I spoke with Benjamin this morning and they are pleased with our progress. They told me the attack will spark a new revolution, and a new order will prevail. They have also confirmed that our target will be there, and because of his arrogance, they still haven't informed the local police or intelligence agencies of their movements. Upon our success, we will strike a blow for all the injustice he and his country have hailed in the name of 'peace' around the world. I will have my revenge, and we shall all be part of the new Reich."

Carl raised his beer aloft and said, "Forward as One, my friends."

They raised their beers. "Forward as One."

CHAPTER 24

GRANT MACEWAN UNIVERSITY, EDMONTON, CANADA

Professor Alice Huber loved the early mornings at the university campus. She would sit in the large central quadrangle and enjoy her green tea. There weren't usually many students around, and it was her time to collect her thoughts before embarking on a day of lecturing.

The world always seemed to move at a more elegant pace at this time of the day. It had been a fiercely hot summer, and the early mornings gave a little respite before having to retreat into the air-conditioned buildings. As she sat, deep in thought, she spotted Khaleed coming towards her. She raised a hand to get his attention, and he nodded that he'd seen her.

He put his phone away and went over to her.

The professor liked Khaleed. He was dedicated to his work, personable, and disciplined, and he always seemed to have time for people. He was open to learning—an easy mind to shape, having come to Canada as a young immigrant after his family fled Syria due to persecution, although his family was originally from Algeria.

Khaleed was exceptionally intelligent, and the professor had no doubt he would get a first in his chemical engineering degree.

"Morning, Professor. You're early."

"I could say the same to you, Khaleed." She gestured for him to sit.

Khaleed obliged, and they sat side by side, looking out at the world. The quadrangle was surrounded by grassed areas and well-kept flowerbeds. The sprinklers were on, and as the sun rose, it created a reflective rainbow that fractured colour around them.

"How was your trip to Argentina? Did you meet the friends I told you about?" asked the professor.

"I did, thank you. I am ready to go now. I learned so much when I was there."

"Excellent. Buenos Aires is such a wonderful city. Are you still able to drive the truck for us in the parade?"

"Yes, I had my training, and I am good to go," replied Khaleed.

"Good. We need someone reliable to drive it—I have absolute faith in you."

"Thank you, Professor. I won't let you down."

"I know you won't." She briefly looked down at her hands, then said, "Edmonton Special Branch was looking for you again when you were away."

Khaleed looked annoyed. "Why can't they leave me alone? Just because Abdulahi was in my class and I happen to be Middle Eastern doesn't mean I know him, and it doesn't make me a terrorist."

The professor smiled. "Unfortunately when young Mr. Abdulahi Sharif decided to try to run over a few people in Edmonton, that's exactly the conclusion they drew. Counterterrorism policing in this country is laughable, and as you are the only other Muslim in a five-kilometre radius of a known terrorist, they're focusing all their attention on you. Try not to let them get to you, they're petty functionaries with badges—you know you're bigger than that. I know they're just fishing—they didn't even know you were out of the country. They asked why you were in Argentina, and I told them it was part of your thesis and that you were there on a cultural exchange. Let them ask their questions. They'll eventually leave you alone."

"What if they don't, Professor?" asked Khaleed.

"Then I shall file a complaint under the Human Rights Act for harassment. Scare the chief into putting his dogs on a shorter leash. If there's anything a chief of police hates more than a suspected terrorist in their community, it's press about their organisation being accused of racism. But try not to dwell on it, it will distract you—just focus on your studies, Khaleed, and the parade."

"Yes, Professor. I will. Thank you." Khaleed got up and stood, facing the professor. "I should get to class."

"Yes, you should. Forward as One, young Khaleed—or should I say, Oilman—Forward as One," said the professor, a smile growing on her face.

Khaleed smiled back. "Forward as One."

Calling him the Oilman had been her idea. The local hockey team was called the Edmonton Oilers, so if the name was picked up, it wouldn't raise any real suspicion.

Khaleed was a good student with impeccable grades and a

drama-free life. However, Abdulahi Sharif's attack had brought unnecessary turmoil into his life. The professor's observation was accurate; the police seemed clueless and their clumsy handling of the situation was almost comical. It was evident that they had been given advice on how to handle such incidents but chose to ignore it. They had placed surveillance on mosques and community police officers were attempting to engage with the imams. They were interrogating every classmate of Abdulahi and trying to establish connections with a community that was resistant to their presence, using heavy-handed tactics. Khaleed had only one class with Abdulahi and had never spoken to him. They were not friends and had no mutual contacts or social media connections. Despite this, the police repeatedly questioned Khaleed on five separate occasions, asking the same questions each time.

Khaleed resented this intrusion and felt marginalised by the country he loved. The fallout of the Abdulahi Sharif incident had merely been the catalyst that led him to his true and higher purpose.

Khaleed needed to stay focused. He would be reunited with his Benjamin, in this life or the next.

CHAPTER 25

THE FERRY CABIN

Peter and Chloe enjoyed a good dinner, then headed back to the room. There, Peter fired up one of the cell phones and called the Matron's number.

It rang, giving Peter some hope that it was still being used. Just when they thought it was going to voicemail, someone answered.

"Hello?"

"Is this the Matron?" asked Peter.

"Who is this?"

Peter hesitated for a moment and then said, "It's Papa One."

The Matron had been walking through the barracks. She stopped dead in her tracks. It was getting dark in the camp, and even though she knew she was alone, she still checked her surroundings. "Call me on this number in five minutes," she ordered.

The call ended, and Peter powered down the phone. He checked his watch and told Chloe the plan to call the Matron back.

Chloe looked at him. "Why do you think she asked you to do that?"

"Not sure. Maybe she needs to get to a safe location to talk. Or maybe she wants to track the call. Who knows? Let's see how it goes."

He powered up the phone again and redialled the number. It was answered immediately.

The Matron had run through the camp and up the hill upon which Peter and Chloe had received many punishments during their course.

She looked out over the city as it started to glow from the fluorescent lighting against the setting sun.

Peter spoke first. "Matron, is that you?"

"Yes, it's me. Is Charlie One with you?"

He had the phone on speaker and looked at Chloe, who nodded in response.

"Yes, she's with me."

"What do you want?"

"We need help and a chance to explain ourselves before we're either killed or thrown in jail."

"Everyone is looking for you. The man you killed was an American asset, and they want to get hold of you."

"I didn't know that, and he attacked me. I just defended myself. We need you to put us in contact with someone who'll let us explain. Will you help us?"

The Matron looked out over the city and contemplated the question before saying, "What are you asking for?"

"There's a beach southwest of the Southampton ferry

terminals. South of Marchwood Port. I need you to be there at 0400 hours tomorrow. When you get to the beach, use a red-filtered flashlight to signal three times every two minutes towards the ships. We'll meet you there, and you can ask us any questions you like."

"If you're coming by ferry, then you should understand that every port is being watched."

"I understand. Leave that to me. We'll be there, but if you decide it's a bad idea and we don't see you by 0500 hours, you'll never hear from us again."

There was again a long pause, and the Matron said, "Don't worry, I will be there." The line went dead.

"Do you think she'll help us, or will there be a welcoming committee?" asked Chloe.

"I don't know, but at the moment, I have no other ideas."

Peter powered down the phone, then instructed Chloe to bag up and waterproof everything.

"I'm not liking the thought, but I'm assuming we're going for a swim."

"Hopefully not, but when have any of our plans gone the way we wanted?"

CHAPTER 26

TRAINING CAMP, WALES

The Matron contemplated the universe for a moment, then sought out Devon. She found him in his room, reading, and marched him up the hill so they couldn't be overheard.

Once there, she told him about the communication from Peter.

"You know they're probably listening in to our calls," said Devon.

"Oh, I have no doubt, but this is a training cell number. I was walking back to the storeroom when they called me. If they'd called five minutes later, the phone would have been powered down in the storeroom, and we never would have spoken. I only ever use it for training."

Devon looked out at the glowing city. "Okay, we're going to do this by the numbers to hopefully avoid jail time. Go and get Hugo, and tell him to be ready. Then get one of the extraction vans with blacked-out windows—get the one we use to secure a high-value-asset transfer. I'm going to make a call and get a safe house, some inquisitors, and a small security detail."

"How on earth are you going to keep this quiet with that amount of logistics?"

"I know the operations officer at MI6. I'll tell him that we'll send up a flare when we have them secure. Remember this could be a set-up, ambush, or diversion. They'll be treated with prejudice until proven otherwise. Understand?"

"Understood."

"Okay, let's get moving. I want to be in place at least an hour before. Pick me up at my accommodation when you're set."

The Matron ran down the hill, and Devon pulled up his contact at MI6 and called the number.

The Matron had advised Hugo of what was happening, and as she pulled up in front of his accommodation, he hung up his phone and threw his bags in the back.

"Who are you calling at this hour?"

"There is a firefighter I've gotten to know, and after she finishes night shift, I go round and cook her breakfast. I was telling her I won't be available this morning."

"How very chivalrous of you. I'm sure she's going to miss her breakfast," said the Matron, smiling.

"Yes, I'm a regular knight in shining armour," replied Hugo, grinning to himself.

They picked up Devon who, after dumping his bags in the back, climbed up front with Hugo. He asked the Matron to wait a moment before they set off.

"Okay, we are about to break a few rules here with some big consequences. If you don't want to be a part of this, then you need to hold your hand up now."

"It wasn't as if I was going to win Instructor of the Month. Besides, with these gorgeous looks, I should do quite well in prison," said Hugo.

"I'm in, and I fully support making Hugo the scapegoat," said the Matron, smiling.

"Okay, it's settled. Let's go. I've secured Safe House Orange. We're being sent two inquisitors, and a small security detail will meet us there. My friend at MI6 agrees that until we have them secured, we keep this low-key. When we have them, I will call the colonel and tell everyone to meet us at the house used by Quick Reaction Force, which is known as Location Orange Alpha. Everyone can monitor the interviews, and if they decide to go to the house itself, it's just a five-minute drive. This should give us a few hours to speak with them and get some answers. Let's get going, Matron, time's against us."

They left the barracks and headed towards the port. It was a three-hour drive at normal speed, so they expected to arrive at 0230 hours, well ahead of the time stipulated by Peter.

As they drove, the Matron said, "I called one of my Special Branch contacts, and they're going to meet us in the village near the port to give us the gate access code. He said that once inside, we don't need a code to get out. You just drive up to the gate. He said the port is swarming with police and firearms teams, so he won't be able to help us. If any calls come in about us being there, he'll respond and deal with it."

"How do you know this Special Branch guy? On second thought, I don't want to know," said Devon.

The Matron smiled and concentrated on the road ahead.

They arrived in Pooksgreen close to 0230 hours, and the Matron called her Special Branch man. After hanging up, she said, "He's on his way."

Fifteen minutes later, the sound of a fast-approaching diesel car was heard, followed by the sight of a car flying past at high speed. Then silence before the Matron, looking in her side mirror, said to Devon, "He is coming up your side."

Devon spotted the Special Branch man approaching in civilian clothing and a bright, reflective coat.

"Good evening. I didn't want to pull up next to you, as my car sounds like a tank. Here's the code. The section of the port where you're going is empty tonight. If a call comes in, I'll respond and do a little drive around and, of course, 'fail' to report anything I see you doing. All I ask is that you keep a low profile, please."

"Excellent. We appreciate the help," said Devon.

"No problem. Always happy to help. Hey, good seeing you again, Jen. When you're back in town, give me a shout and we'll catch up." Then he disappeared.

Hugo couldn't hide his grin, "So . . . does he keep the reflective jacket on when you guys"— he used air quotes for the next part—"'Catch up?' And if so, do you need to wear sunglasses because of the glare?"

Both Hugo and Devon were laughing uncontrollably. The Matron replied, "Only if we keep the lights on. Bugger off you bastards, or I'll give you a vasectomy with a spoon."

They drove through the coded gate, and Devon advised the Matron to have the vehicle ready while he and Hugo headed to the beach for the meet-up.

"Soft armour only and concealed sidearms," commanded Devon. "Hugo, bring your carbine in case we need it. Matron, kill the lights on the vehicle. I want everything done by night vision from here on out. We shall recce the beach and let you know if anything changes. Meet back here in an hour for a final brief and tea. I brought flasks and food. Everybody clear?"

Both the Matron and Hugo nodded, and they set about their preparations.

CHAPTER 27

FERRY CABIN, SOUTHAMPTON PORT

They had waterproofed what they needed and as they readied to leave, Chloe asked about the plan.

Without stopping his own dressing and packing, Peter replied, "On all trips like these, the ship will have one or two people who'll pass away. We joined this ferry, which I suppose technically is a cruise ship, on its final leg returning to the UK. I quietly spoke with staff, and they've had two people die on this trip. Just old age, nothing sinister, of course."

"Okay, how does that help us?" asked Chloe.

"The bodies are never taken off via the main door. They use a loading door or, in this case, a pontoon, which is accessed from the rear of the ship. We're going to collect the bodies, leave with them, and hopefully avoid the police."

"What do you mean, leave with the bodies? You're not suggesting we get in the bags with them?" said Chloe, looking alarmed.

"No, of course not. That would be mental." Peter laughed. "You've probably noticed staff jackets hanging up around the ship. We're going to grab a couple, then head down to the freezer room to carry the bodies out."

Chloe's alarm turned to concern. "Don't you think someone will say something? They might not recognise us."

Peter indicated that they should leave the room, so they headed out the door, navigating their way through the other passengers who were heading to disembark. Once Peter had found some staff jackets on the wall, just as he'd said, they hung back, waiting for the corridor to clear before he grabbed them, handing one to Chloe and telling her to put it on. There was a pair of matching trousers, too, which Peter put on.

"Jesus. With those on, you could be seen from space," said Chloe, laughing.

He smiled back. "Overt to be covert, as they say."

He then found a real staff member and asked where the freezer was, as they had been told to help move the two deceased passengers, and was directed without a second thought. On reaching it, they discovered it was a large walk-in room with eight doors, like something you'd see in a morgue set of a movie.

"What are you two doing in here?" asked a booming voice behind them.

They turned to see a very tall, heavy-set man wearing head-to-foot reflective clothing. Large and loud, he went one step further with a reflective yellow baseball hat. He looked radioactive, almost glowing.

"What part of the ship do you two work in? I don't recognise you," he barked.

Peter answered, "Oh, we're from the terminal. There's

a lot of police up there, checking the staff, so we were asked to come on and get the bodies ready. Didn't they tell you we were coming?"

"They don't tell me anything. I'm like a mushroom down here, kept in the dark and fed on shit."

When Peter viewed this man's clothing again, it was easy to tell that it hadn't done a day's work in its life. It was certainly a management outfit, as it looked as though it still had the creases from being taken out of the packaging.

"Are you going to give us a hand?" asked Peter.

"Do I look like the help? The bodies are in freezers one and two. Take them out to the pontoon, then wait for the boat. Come on, hurry up. I want to get off this fucking tub and go for a drink."

Peter was impressed, as it was just coming up to four in the morning, but who knew what this genius got up to? But as well as the condition of his attire, it hadn't escaped Peter's notice that the man had been continuously gazing at Chloe, his height giving advantage to leer down at her. It was clearly making Chloe uncomfortable. As he left, passing between the two of them, he pressed himself against her, then looked back at her, chuckling lasciviously.

"Two minutes. That's all I'd need. Just two minutes," said Chloe.

"Not our fight. Another time, Chloe."

Peter checked where they needed to go. Their exit was a large doorway at the rear of the ship that led to a flat, one-metre-wide walkway parallel to the stern. There was then a steady-incline ramp that ran the length of the ship, which rested on a floating pontoon. There were two floodlights at the back of the ship that crossed over each other, illuminating most of the walkway, ramp, and pontoon. There were railings at the port and starboard side of the walkway and the ramp; however, the pontoon was unprotected.

They got the first body out, and as they laid it down on the walkway, they heard, "Not that way, you idiots. Turn it the other way, so it's easier to get off."

They turned to see that the fat man had returned and was standing on the port side of the walkway, leaning on the railings and smoking. The harbour wall was on the starboard side, and Peter could see that the police were there, ready to check the staff leaving from the pontoon. As he and Chloe began up the ramp, he said, "We're going to have to go for that swim."

Chloe merely nodded.

"What was that?" asked the fat man. "Never mind, doesn't matter. Hey sweetheart, you okay? You look all tense. Maybe you can come over here and I'll make you all better."

Chloe turned to go back out the door, but Peter grabbed her arm. "No, Chloe. Come on."

The fat man laughed and shouted after them, "Go on, let her go. I like them feisty."

As they walked out with the second body, the fat man was not close to relenting, "Come on, darling. We could have some fun together, whether you like it or not."

As they put the second body down, Peter said, "Did I hear him correctly? Did that talking traffic cone say what I think he said?"

"I think he might have," said Chloe.

"We aren't going to get very far with that mouthpiece up there. Perhaps quietly, and I mean quietly, you could go and explain to him that his choice of words isn't respectful," said Peter.

"With pleasure," said Chloe.

They had taken off their jackets, and Peter was sitting on the floor, taking off his trousers.

"What are you two doing?" asked the fat man, but he got distracted as he saw Chloe coming towards him. She was wearing a tight-fitting, long-sleeved shirt and jeans and walking with a little sass as she approached.

"Aren't you a tight little package," the man continued. "I'm definitely going to have fun with you."

She stopped in front of the obese man, as close as she could. Her head just about reached his chest, so she indicated for him to bend down. She slid her hand between his legs, and somewhere under his overhanging belly, found his cock and squeezed it gently. She brought his head down onto her shoulder so their cheeks were touching. She could smell the nicotine on his breath, the cheap aftershave, and the Brylcreem on his slicked-back hair.

She massaged his cock a little harder and could hear his breath quicken, almost panting. She slid her hand behind the back of his head, and after finding a nice roll of neck fat, gripped it hard. It was sweaty and difficult to hold, but she managed to pull his mouth into her shoulder to whisper into his ear.

"This is for all the women you've had fun with, you slimy piece of shit."

There was then a quick flick of the wrist between his legs, and the fat man went rigid. He screamed into her shoulder as she gripped hard onto the roll of fat.

She then took a step back, and the man pulled his hand away from his groin. Even in the dim light, Peter could see blood. The fat man's pain then turned to rage, and he angled towards Chloe. She moved towards him, and with a solid kick to his stomach, sent him over the railing and into the water with a resounding splash.

She darted inside and reappeared with a fire extinguisher. Peter wanted to get moving. *What the hell is she going to do to him now?* She swung the fire extinguisher upwards, smashing one light then the other, shrouding the entire area in darkness. She then leaned inside and with a little volume shouted, "Man overboard!" and hit the alarm.

Finally, she returned to Peter on the pontoon and took her flotation bundle from him. "Shall we?"

"It wasn't the diversion I expected, but it'll certainly keep everyone busy while we slip away. I bet that cold, salty water feels delightful," said Peter.

"I bet it does. I'm not even sure that was his penis I cut. I could have been squeezing a roll of fat for all I know. It did the trick, though. Come on, we'd better get going. Which way we heading?"

"Towards the beach over there. Look for the red flashing lights," he said, and they slowly swam away from the mooring bay.

CHAPTER 28

BEACH NEAR MARCHWOOD, SOUTHAMPTON FERRY PORT

Devon and Hugo made their way onto the beach and started the signalling sequence with the red-filtered flashlight.

"Hugo, get your carbine and see if you can pick them up with the scope."

"Sure, sounds good," said Hugo. Using the scope's night vision, he scanned the area, making the ship's stern the centre of axis. As he scanned back and forth, he saw a body bag being brought down onto the pontoon. "That's one way to end the cruise."

"What do you mean?" asked Devon.

Hugo shifted his stance slightly, brought the scope down from his eye, and said, "They're bringing a dead body onto the pontoon. Apparently, at least three or four of these old buggers die when on a cruise. Not a bad way to go, I suppose." He pulled on an extra layer to combat the bracing wind. "So, do you reckon we can keep this under wraps once we have them?"

"As soon as they're in the safe house, I'm making the calls. I plan to meet everyone at the QRF jump-off location. I'm hoping they'll be happy to watch the interviews from there. If not, they should wait until the briefing is done before heading to the safe house. I'll leave you with the security detail and the inquisitors. The Matron and I can go and give everyone an update."

"Sounds like a reasonable plan. I'm sure we can get a few questions in before the big team comes rolling in," said Hugo, who had put the scope back to his eye and was once again scanning the area. "I'm not sure what's happening, but there's a lot of activity at the back of the ship. The whole stern's gone completely dark. They seem to be looking at something in the water. Oddly, there seem to be staff members' jackets covering the two bodies on the pontoon. I'm going to switch to thermal imaging and see if I can pick something out."

A few moments later, he handed Devon the rifle. "I think you should look at this, Devon."

Devon looked through the scope, and after getting some direction from Hugo, he saw two very dark blobs against the light grey seawater heading towards them. The wind was up, and with the choppy waves, it was proving a little challenging to keep them in sight.

"Hugo, I want you to move up onto higher ground and radio to me where they are. The current will be taking them, so we'll need to move up the beach. I need to talk to the Matron. Now, move."

Without a word, Hugo secured his backpack and was off. He headed up and quickly radioed when he had them again.

"Matron, this is Devon. Do you copy?"

"Yes, go ahead," said The Matron.

"I need you to prepare for two hypothermic patients who will be with us in about twenty to thirty minutes. Also, move the vehicle closer to the end of the beach, as they may have difficulty walking, copy."

"Copy that."

CHAPTER 29

FIGHTING THE CURRENT, MIDDLE OF THE RIVER TEST

"This is fun," said Chloe. "You doing okay over there? You sound like an asthmatic St. Bernard."

"Speak for yourself, Darth. We might need to turn ourselves a little—the current's pushing us towards the harbour. I can see the red light flashing, so the Matron must be over there," replied Peter.

With every stroke, freezing water rushed over their bodies. They could feel their fingertips going numb and their feet losing mobility. Every time Peter checked for the flashing light, it never seemed any closer. It was about a kilometre swim, but he felt like they had been swimming for an age.

Eventually, he looked and saw a figure on the beach, and even though he was exhausted and the lighting poor, he said to Chloe, "I don't think that's the Matron."

"Never mind, let's just get on the beach, and we can figure

it out," gasped Chloe, her voice now shuddering.

Peter's mind went back to the advice he had been given about open-water swimming while training for a triathlon. *Wait until your hand hits the floor, and then stand up. If the water's really clear, it's easy to get a false perspective and stand up too early, wasting time and energy.*

A few minutes later, his hand hit the floor, but on the next stroke, nothing. The next time, it hit the ground hard, and they steadied themselves to stand. They had to help each other, as they were now exhausted and freezing, and their feet didn't seem to be functioning.

On the beach, they hugged and were about to kiss when black sacks were thrust roughly over their heads. The bags were pulled tightly to their faces, and using that momentum, they were pulled onto the ground. Peter felt a couple of blows to the ribs.

"I thought you were here to help us," he shouted.

"If I wasn't here to help you, I'd have just shot you. Or worse, I'd hand you over to the Americans. Now, do not resist," said Devon.

Peter could hear Chloe being spoken to but had no idea what was being said. Their hands were plastic-cuffed and then they were marched up the beach and pushed into a vehicle.

Once in their seats, Peter felt himself being checked over as he heard the Matron say, "Just stay still."

"Is that you, Matron?" asked Peter.

"Shut up," commanded Devon. Blacked-out ski goggles were put over Peter's eyes and then a set of ear defenders. He was now in complete auditory and visual exclusion. His clothes were cut off, leaving him in his underwear. He then felt the crinkling of a space blanket being placed over him, and his feet being wrapped in what felt like a wool blanket.

He assumed the same had been done to Chloe, as she had been a little worse off than him. The van stayed motionless for a short period, then Peter felt a seatbelt being buckled across him, and they started moving.

Hugo was driving as the Matron sat in the back, assessing both Peter and Chloe. Using their comms system, Devon asked the Matron if they'd both be ready for interview on arrival at the safe house.

It was clear they'd both been quite badly injured and probably needed some decent rest and good medical attention, but the Matron said they should both be good to go for at least three to four hours.

Devon then made a call to the operations officer at MI6, after which he told Hugo and the Matron that the safe house was ready to go, the security detail was in place, and the inquisitors were standing by.

It would take them roughly thirty-five minutes to get to the safe house and another twenty-five minutes or so before they could commence interviews.

CHAPTER 30

SAFE HOUSE ORANGE, UNDISCLOSED LOCATION, ENGLAND

The vehicle came to a stop. Both Peter and Chloe had drifted off to sleep in their seats.

With the blankets securely fastened, Peter was incredibly hot. When they moved him from his seat, his muscles didn't seem to work at all. The blanket was readjusted, and the cold air rushed in. He knew this was a tactic to unsettle him, and he needed to stay focused.

He stepped out of the van and covered a short walk on gravel before his feet reached a harder surface. They sat him in a chair that he could tell was bolted to the floor. Then he was left alone—he assumed Chloe was getting the same treatment, while their captors met in the operations room, along with the security lead, who'd been waiting for them.

Also in the room were Marcus and Sarah, the two inquisitors from MI6. They'd already obtained some briefing notes.

They were given the rundown on their detention on the beach, what they had said on the phones, and the briefing at the training centre.

Marcus and Sarah seemed young to Devon, although everyone was beginning to look young to Devon these days. But when they spoke, it was with an air of proficiency and professionalism that reassured him a little. They both wore jeans and dress shirts. Marcus wore a jacket with elbow pads and Sarah, some outdoor Gore-Tex number.

Marcus decided he would take Chloe and Sarah would interview Peter.

"So what's the plan?" asked Marcus.

"As promised, we were waiting until we had them secured. Now, I am going to make the call to the colonel, which will set off an unstoppable chain of events. I will ask them to meet at the QRF jump-off location, which is about five minutes from here. If they decide to come straight here, then so be it. The Matron is coming with me, and Hugo is going to work with the security people."

Sarah and Marcus nodded to the group and then went back to preparing their notes. The spacious operations hub had a wall of monitors that covered almost every inch of the place, including the interview rooms, the corridors, the small gym, and the exterior perimeter fencing.

There was a fridge to keep those on camera duty supplied. Also, there were controls for the gates to get in and out. If the building was put into lockdown, the control room doubled as a safe room.

The security lead said he had four of his group on perimeter watch, and he would remain in the control centre.

Devon had gone outside to make the call, and when he

returned, he said, "That went better than I thought. The colonel was very happy and was going to inform Abigail, so I suggest you two get in there and start interviewing."

"Roger, I think we're almost there," said Sarah.

"Good," said Devon. "Come on, Matron, we better get going."

"Perhaps we can grab a tea on the way. I'm parched," said the Matron.

They left, and the interviewers finalised their preparations, part of which was requesting Hugo and the security lead provide a full set of clothing each for Chloe and Peter. The place was fully stocked, and they were provided with great-looking grey cotton tracksuits, along with fairly standard underwear, socks, and army-issue sneakers in their sizes.

The interviewers had the clothing placed in the room on the table, then entered with two coffees and sat down.

First, they took off the ear defenders, then they told Peter and Chloe they were going to free their wrists. Then they were invited to remove their ski masks and hoods when they were ready.

The first thing Peter saw was Sarah sitting opposite him. She smiled and pointed out the fresh clothing and coffee, saying she wasn't sure how he took it and offering to get milk and sugar if he wanted it.

"The coffee's perfect, thank you, and I assume these clothes are for me?" he replied.

"Yes, Peter. Would you like me to leave while you get changed?"

"No, thank you. It's fine."

He turned his back, and Sarah noted the cuts and bruises that littered almost every part of his body.

"You certainly seem to have been through the wars, Peter."

"You could say that. It's been something of an interesting journey," he said as he pulled on the clothes. They felt wonderful. He threw his wet underwear into the trash and was surprised they didn't run off on their own.

He sipped the coffee—mediocre but most welcome nonetheless—and allowed the warm, dry clothes and comfortable environment to envelop him.

"So Peter, what can you tell me about your adventure before getting here?"

"Nice try, but you'll have to be a little more specific. I know how much trouble I am in, and I want to speak to someone in charge, or at least a lawyer. No free-flowing information until then."

"Fair enough," said Sarah. "How about we start with the journey from the UK to North Africa? What was your route?"

She already knew most of this information, but she wanted to see if Peter would tell her the truth about the basic elements, at least.

In another room, Chloe was getting acquainted with Marcus. When he offered to leave so she could get changed, she said she didn't mind, but she did say she wanted milk in her coffee.

He went to find the milk—the security supervisor took him, ensuring Hugo kept an eye on the two rooms until he got back. Hugo watched the monitors, Chloe glancing at the camera before undressing, putting on the new clothes, and sitting down.

Marcus returned with the milk, noticing Chloe's bra was in the trash can.

"I am not sure if we have spare bras here. However, I am sure if you give us the details of your size, we could arrange for a few new ones to be purchased," said Marcus.

"That's kind of you, and yes, perhaps we can sort that out later," said Chloe.

"Chloe, we know things didn't go well in Algeria, and we need to establish the chain of events that got you to this point. I'd like you to explain what happened when you arrived in North Africa. Please don't skip any details. I can help jog your memory if you need any information from the operations reports you submitted."

Chloe leaned back in her chair. "God, I don't really know where to start. I've had time to think about all of this, and it still makes no sense to me. Can you tell me if Peter is here?"

Marcus smiled, "I think you already know the answer to that. Yes, he is here, and he's doing the same thing as you are right now."

"How do I know I can trust you? The last time I was interviewed, I was lashed to a chair that was bolted to the floor, and I was beaten, electrocuted, and tortured." To demonstrate her point, she raised her shirt to show her injuries and in doing so, exposed her ample breasts. Marcus seemed more unsettled by seeing Chloe's breasts than the injuries and looked away.

"So let's start with your arrival in Algeria. Who was your contact, and what was the mission statement?"

The interviews continued, to determine a baseline and gain a basic rapport. It wouldn't be long before they were led to describe the meeting with the source, but Sarah and Marcus would allow for natural pauses and washroom breaks, which security facilitated. Hopefully, they would have some answers before everyone else showed up.

Hugo watched intently, and when he was confident that Peter and Chloe weren't going to misbehave, he left the security supervisor to it and checked the perimeter.

CHAPTER 31

ABIGAIL'S OFFICE, THE VENUE

Abigail was in her office when her assistant buzzed through that Major Douglas Smyth was outside and waiting to come in.

"Thank you. Send him in, please," said Abigail.

She was still reeling from the meeting with Sir Goodlove. Her mind was turning at a hundred miles an hour. She didn't like to feel she'd been played, let alone been under suspicion for the very same crime she was investigating, but having time to simmer had allowed her to refocus her irritation onto Chloe.

Major Douglas Smyth glided in and was directed to sit on the leather sofa and help himself to coffee. "Morning, ma'am, how are we doing today?" he asked.

"Fine, thank you, Major. I have brought you here to give you an update on the events surrounding Chloe and Peter. I just received a call from Colonel Grieves that we have them in custody at Safe House Orange. Devon, the Special Forces team leader, has requested we meet at the QRF jump-off Location Orange Alpha, where we'll be briefed and can observe the interviews. As you know, an American contingent will be arriving, and they're rather keen to speak with Peter and Chloe. It is hoped that our presence will mitigate the intensity of their handling of them, if you get my drift. I want you to head there, and I will follow shortly. I need to call Sir Goodlove and Helena from the NSA. Questions?"

"No, ma'am. I'm glad we have them, and I'll head there as soon as possible." He knew this operation was being viewed at the highest level, and he'd never miss an opportunity to get his name out in the right places. "Perhaps I should go straight to the safe house and supervise the interviews with the inquisitors. I can be that direct liaison for you."

Abigail smiled internally—she knew exactly what the major wanted. "No, that's fine, Major. Go straight to Orange Alpha and make sure we're prepared for the Americans' arrival. Leave the inquisitors to work their magic in drawing the information out of Peter and Chloe."

"Yes, ma'am. I'll get going." At this, he left the room. He returned to his office and, closing the door, pulled out his cell phone.

Abigail pressed a button on her desk, and a wooden wall panel slid open to reveal a large screen. Then she made two calls simultaneously and waited for the recipients to connect.

Helena was first, and it was clear she was in her vehicle. "Hello, Abigail. How are we today? I hope you're calling with news on our two fugitives."

"I am, Helena, and I'm just waiting for Sir Goodlove to come online . . . Oh, stand by, he's connecting."

Sir Goodlove was still at his home, behind his desk. "Good

morning, ladies. How can I help you?"

Helena smiled. "Dinner at the expense of MI6 when I am next in town, Sir Goodlove."

"It's a deal. Now what do you need, Abigail?"

She took a deep breath and said, "I received a call twenty minutes ago from Colonel Grieves that Peter and Chloe were apprehended early this morning near Southampton port. They were transported to a safe house for interrogation."

"Why weren't we informed the moment they were captured?" asked Helena, as she instructed her driver to head straight to the airfield.

"It was decided by the Special Forces team that they wouldn't put up the flare until they'd confirmed they had them. The call to the colonel was made, as per the instructions, thirty-five minutes after apprehension," replied Abigail.

Sir Goodlove huffed. "It's not their decision to make. We stated very clearly that we needed to be advised straight away. Helena, I assume you are heading to us now, and you'll be directing your Germany team to come to us, correct?"

"Damn right, I am. I'll be at the airfield in twenty minutes and will touch down in the UK within an hour of that. The team will pack up and follow me after. And I don't want any bullshit about jurisdiction or 'the good of British interests' with this. I want to be kept updated on the interviews and the information that Peter and Chloe provide. Remember Peter killed one of ours, and we want him. Understood?" said Helena.

"Yes, of course," said Abigail.

There was a pause, and Abigail said to Goodlove, "Should we bring Helena up to speed on our recent conversation? We're on a secure connection here."

Sir Goodlove paused then said, "Yes, I think so. As long as you are happy with it, Abigail, please go ahead."

"Helena, Sir Mark Goodlove was brought into the service as MI6 had concerns that they had a mole in their midst. It should be noted that until recently, I was one of those under suspicion and was suspected of orchestrating this Peter-and-Chloe operation as a cover for my own nefarious activities. We've been keeping an eye on Chloe for quite some time since receiving intelligence surrounding her loyalties, or lack thereof. It's possible she's in regular contact with those sympathetic to the Islamic Extremist cause. I know you may be questioning why we sent a suspected traitor in, but that was deliberate. We'd been trying for a while to give her tasks that might give her enough rope to hang herself, but nothing worked. The hope was this operation would be close enough to home to draw her out. I realise it was a big risk, but we felt it necessary. Chloe was to message me with the name of the mole. This she did, naming *me* as the mole. As I am not, and since our source is reliable and trusted, it could only be assumed that Chloe is our bad apple. As a consequence, I ordered for her to be arrested. Peter then acted autonomously, entering the safe house to extract Chloe and killing your man in the process."

Helena sat quietly, then said, "Holy shit. What a mess. I'm glad I wasn't completely off the mark, when you briefed us the other day. I would like to apologise if I came across a little terse—that was more for my director's benefit than an attack on you. Speaking with Chloe and Peter is most certainly a priority. I'm going to update Michael in Langley and my director."

"I never take anything personally, and I know tensions are running high," said Sir Goodlove.

"I think that's wise, too," said Abigail.

Helena spoke. "Oh, before I make these calls, do we have any clue as to who the mole actually is? And has anything been said by Peter or Chloe? I'm going to suggest that the mole could be from either of our camps or another foreign intelligence agency."

Abigail replied, "No, Helena, we have nothing, and nothing from the interview yet. I also agree that the source could be from someone outside British intelligence, but we think that unlikely at this stage."

"I'm going to brief my people but not mention this mole hypothesis. I think we need to get together soon and determine what our options are. I'm going to direct my team to bolster the security at the safe house, and I'd appreciate a location as a base for them. Jessica, my operation leader, is exceptional and would be invaluable in working on the interviews. I suggest we meet at the safe house, Abigail, when I arrive. Agreed?" said Helena.

Abigail replied, "We shall meet at the safe house QRF location first. I'll send you the details. I think that would be best."

"Great. I'm going to leave you both to it. Keep me updated," said Sir Goodlove, and he disconnected.

CHAPTER 32

SITE B, GERMANY

Andrew arrived in Germany, and the SBS operator helped him from the helicopter. Then he handed him over to the Delta team reception committee.

Shaukey explained to the SBS operator that they'd informed the military on base to tow the helicopter to a nearby hangar for refuelling, while they grabbed a bite and reorganised before heading back to the UK.

The SBS operator thanked them and went off to inform the rest of the crew.

Andrew's bags were thrown into the back seat of the car, and Andrew joined them. Shaukey explained that they were going to head to their base of operation, where he could meet Jessica.

On arrival, Jessica was in her room. As Shaukey entered, all eyes turned to Andrew in his suit.

"Jessica, here's your guy," said Shaukey, pointing Andrew inside. He was about to leave when Jessica told him to stay.

"Hello, Andrew, how are you? Long time no see," said Jessica.

"Yes, I think it's been three years since the Netherlands. Our paths have crossed briefly a few times when I found myself in Langley at those awkward inter-agency training operations," said Andrew.

They shook hands and Jessica said, "I assume you've met Shaukey here? He heads up my Special Forces group here."

"Yes, we met when I landed," said Andrew.

"Okay, good. Let me bring you up to speed, then you can let me know what you know. Peter and Chloe go to Algeria on what most people are told is a training exercise, which in reality is a live operation. They plan to meet a source, and somehow this meeting goes wrong. I say this because after the meeting, the source is found dead. The feet on the ground are saying it was a botched robbery, but that's yet to be confirmed. Since the operation went pear-shaped, and Chloe is the one with all the answers, she is detained in a local safe house for questioning. Peter, it seems, is quite the knight in shining armour and decides to rescue Chloe. He enters the house and gets her out, killing one of our people in the process. So, now they're both wanted pretty much everywhere in the world. Did I miss anything?"

Andrew nodded and said, "No, that's about it. Our people have a capture-and-extraction order on the two of them, and communications are being channelled through Abigail, which is again, a little strange. The last update we had was that they were in Morocco and boarded a ferry out of Casablanca. The vehicle they used to escape the safe house and drive to the port was found on a ferry bound for South Africa, but we believe that's a false lead. And that's about it."

"Okay, well, there isn't a huge difference between what we know. Looks like we have to wait for further solid intelligence before we can make any decisions," said Jessica. She didn't want to disclose what Michael had said to her when they had met in Langley, about Chloe and Peter being sent to Algeria to get the identity of a potential mole. She wasn't sure who may or may not be included in the concerns the director of the CIA had.

Shaukey, who had remained silent, now spoke to Andrew. "Let me show you your quarters. I assumed you'd want a separate operations room to Jessica, so we have you in an office at the other end of the hangar."

Andrew turned to Jessica. "I think it might be better if we share an office."

Jessica paused a moment, then said, "I appreciate the effort, Shaukey, but I am happy to have Andrew set up in here. In fact, you can find a space to set yourself up too. We need to work together on this—having separate offices doesn't make sense."

Shaukey showed Andrew where to put his bags, and Andrew took the opportunity to freshen up. As he was brushing his teeth, his phone started to ring.

"Hello, how can I help?"

"This is Abigail. We have them, and they're currently in Safe House Orange. I need you to get back over here and meet me at Orange Alpha. Understood?"

"Yes, ma'am. Do the Americans know?"

"Yes, they do, so you need to get there as quickly as possible. I suggest you travel back with Jessica. That'll be the fastest way to catch a ride," she said, and hung up.

As Andrew bent over and spat into the sink, Shaukey came to the door and said, "We just got word that they have them, and we're going to London."

"Yes, thank you. I just got the call, too. I've been told to travel with you guys. I'll get ready."

As Shaukey walked away, he shouted, "Hey Jessica! Andrew already got a call, and he's coming with us."

"Roger that. Let's get this packed up. I want to be out of here in under an hour," shouted Jessica.

It was impressive to watch them strip everything down. Even though Andrew offered to help, he knew he'd just be a hindrance. In fact, when the plane arrived, he was politely told to get out of the way.

CHAPTER 33

STARBUCKS DRIVE-THROUGH, NEAR SAFE HOUSE ORANGE

Devon and the Matron sat in their nondescript, unmarked van, watching the world go by and quietly contemplating what might happen next. It had certainly been an interesting day so far, and with the circus turning up, it was going to get a lot more entertaining.

When they got to the speaker, the voice on the other end snapped them out of their daze.

"Hello, welcome to Starbucks. What can I get for you today?" said the young girl, who seemed like the cheeriest person on the planet.

The Matron, who was driving, said, "A dark roast coffee with nothing in it and a slice of banana bread."

Devon then leaned across. "I'll have a grande vanilla soy latte with chocolate drizzle and a vanilla scone, please. Thank you."

The Matron looked at Devon, "Interesting choice. Does your boyfriend normally order that for you?"

"Shut up, and for that, you can pay."

They both snorted with laughter.

The order was passed through the window, and when the most pleasant young girl in the world was out of earshot, the Matron piped up innocently. "I think there is something wrong with your order, Devon. I don't see a rainbow sticker on the cup."

"You're gonna wear your coffee in your lap in a minute. Now, let's get going."

"Of course, boss," said the Matron, sniggering to herself.

They travelled the next few minutes in silence, then pulled up to Location Orange Alpha.

When they had parked, a man emerged from the building and asked for their identification. They knew he was a Special Forces operator because he had that air of being able to disappear into the crowd or fold you up like a deck chair with little or no effort.

The Matron and Devon knew he was armed, and they also knew that behind the two-way window to the right of the door stood another operator, gun at the ready.

Once given the all-clear, they were shown inside to find two more heavily armed gentlemen waiting to support their colleague if needed.

"Sir, please follow me," said the operator who had met them outside.

They were shown to a large operations room that had the usual wall of screens displaying CCTV footage, including the ongoing interviews with Chloe and Peter.

It had only taken ten to fifteen minutes for them to get to

Safe House Orange Alpha, so they'd arrived in time to watch as Peter and Chloe got changed and enjoyed their hot drinks.

As Devon sipped his vanilla latte, he saw Hugo walk the perimeter and interact with the other guards. There were spots when Hugo was out of sight, but he would quickly appear on another camera feed. Devon felt quite happy with the coverage.

The Matron returned to say the QRF was all set to go and that the briefing they'd been given was accurate.

"Okay, now we wait," said Devon.

CHAPTER 34

THE VENUE, THE COTSWOLDS

Major Smyth had decided to leave his office and take a walk on the grounds of the Cotswolds estate. Once he'd reached a secluded spot, he dialled a number on his cell, and the male voice on the other end said, "Yes?"

"Hello, this is Major Smyth. I wanted to call you as I feel that Abigail isn't, in my opinion, making smart decisions. Papa One and Charlie One have been located, and when I suggested that I head to the safe house to supervise, she refused. She wants me to go to the QRF location and meet her there. I don't think this is a wise move, and I know you would want someone with my abilities there to make sure it all goes smoothly."

The voice on the other end said, "Yes, I know they've been detained. Do you think it necessary for you to attend?"

"I do think a steady hand on the tiller would be wise.

Abigail, like most women, allows emotion to guide her judgement. Sometimes, we need to be that steadying element."

"You may be right. But going straight to the safe house may anger Abigail and cause her to lose her trust in you. She may not confide in you moving forward," said the voice.

"Don't worry. I know how to manage her, and I'll make sure it doesn't get out of control."

"Okay, keep me posted. I do appreciate the help you have given me during this strange period. I certainly wouldn't have been able to be a step ahead of Abigail without you," said the voice.

"I shall, and thank you. I know it's for a greater cause." He ended the call, with a rather contemptuous grin on his face. The only cause that mattered to Major Smyth was his own, and he had played both sides well.

Sir Goodlove then hung up the phone and, as he leaned back into his chair, murmured, "Abigail, I hope you know what you're doing."

CHAPTER 35

EDMONTON, ALBERTA

Khaleed had been studying hard to complete his course but had still found time to socialise with the people he'd be travelling to Calgary with. He had spoken to the student organiser and explained he would drive the truck down and meet them all there.

He had paid for an extra couple of days at a hotel and had arrived three days before the Stampede. After the parade, which opened the whole event, the group was to have an information stand inside the grounds. And after that, they would hit the bars, which stayed open late for the legendary partying.

All the students were excited about this ten-day trip—it made for a good way to burn off post-exam energy.

Khaleed had been given a map of the parade route and had identified where he needed to be to meet his university friends and staff. He had taken care to read through safety procedures that the Stampede board required him to know. He then walked the route, which wasn't challenging, but he wanted to familiarise himself, especially with the location where he would begin his attack.

Khaleed had met Hanna and Alicia on several occasions. Hanna had refreshed him on the truck-handling dynamics. Alicia had gone through placing the weapons Khaleed would have available in the truck.

She had explained, "I would recommend that when you come onto the sidewalk, you lock the doors and make sure the driver's window is fully up. We have brought some heavy tint that we can add to the windows now. We recommend you keep the passenger window down and throw the grenades out as you drive. It'll create more confusion and panic within the crowd. Once you have thrown them, bring the window back up. I also have some body armour for you. The front will be secured above the seat on the roof. The rear plate will be behind the seat to protect your back."

Alicia showed how Khaleed could pull the front of the vest from the ceiling and over his chest. She also showed how Khaleed could still drive and be mobile. Alicia then demonstrated that the grenades had been secured to a metal frame under the dashboard.

"There are two flash-bangs and two smoke grenades. Deploy all four of them as you drive along the sidewalk. All you need to do is grab the grenade by the body and pull it hard to free it from the ring. The rings are attached to the metal frame, so you can do this one-handed." Alicia had placed a dummy grenade under the dash and showed him how he could pull one out, priming it immediately, and throw it from the window.

"We have looked at the security, and they don't search the vehicles before the parade starts, so we can put everything in place. I assume you're the only one who will have access to the truck before the parade?"

Khaleed nodded. "Yes, and I keep it locked at all times."

"Good," said Alicia.

"Once the truck has reached its endpoint, you must meet one of us in the alley and together, we shall leave the city. I'm not going to tell you any more, for operational safety reasons. You have been provided an emergency number you can call if something changes. Remember, it is not secure, so ask to meet whoever answers and we can arrange something as soon as possible. Text the same number 1, if you have been uncovered; 2, if you believe we have been uncovered; 3, if you are on the run; or 4, if you are unable to proceed with your part of the mission. Questions, Mr. Oilman?" Alicia smiled.

"No, that is good. Thank you. I am ready and prepared. Thank you again," said Khaleed.

"Forward as One," said Alicia.

"Yes, sister. Forward as One," answered Khaleed.

CHAPTER 36

FAIRMONT CHATEAU HOTEL, LAKE LOUISE, CANADA

Yigal Ben-Eliezer heard a knock at his hotel door and, after wiping his mouth, left his breakfast behind to open it.

Standing there was Noya, one of his security detail who had come to brief him on the day's events and the plans for the coming week.

"Morning, sir. I didn't mean to interrupt your breakfast. Do you want me to come back later?" asked the smartly dressed young lady. She was the leader of his security outfit for this particular trip across Canada. There were ten of them, but they would spell each other off, so on a typical day, it was one leader and four others. The risks were deemed low for Yigal, although being a former defence minister for Israel, he needed some protection, particularly when he travelled abroad.

"No, no. Come, eat with me. Please sit."

Noya accepted coffee, but she'd already eaten, so she

declined the food. She liked looking after Yigal Ben-Eliezer—
he was polite and pleasant to be around, and he listened to her
advice. He reminded her of her grandfather, who had passed
away only the year before.

"So, what are we doing today, young Noya?" asked Yigal as
he ate his breakfast.

"Sir, we're going to meet some Jewish families here at
the chateau. These are people who fled to Canada after the
war. Some of them escaped the concentration camps, and
Israel has paid for them to spend a week here. Your role is to
acknowledge them for their sacrifice and bravery," said Noya.

Yigal sat back in his chair and, holding his coffee cup close
to his face, looked over towards Noya. "There are times, Noya,
when I forget about the camps, the genocide, the fighting, and
the hatred our people had to deal with. I also sometimes question the things I did in the pursuit of justice. I pray that when I
leave this mortal world, God will look upon me with kindness,
and I can be with my wife again."

Noya sat for a moment, then said, "Sir, it is because of the
bravery of people like you and my grandfather, who didn't
stop fighting against the Nazis, that has allowed Israel to be a
safe and strong place for our people. God will welcome you
with open arms, and I know your wife will be waiting for you.
She was taken from you too soon, but she would be proud of
what you are doing."

Yigal laughed and said, "She would tell me to stop being
nostalgic and feeling sorry for myself. Even in the final days
before the cancer took her, she was always so positive. She
would say that we did what we did during the war, so that you,
Noya, and people like you, could live as free Jews and have a
life that would never see the horrors that we saw. Okay, now

I really am going to get emotional. Let's talk about the rest of the week."

Noya had a lump in her throat and took a moment to clear it. Then she continued, "On Thursday, we are heading into Calgary. We need to be there the day before, because on Friday, there is a parade that will close the city down until about midday. We will be visiting a Jewish centre, and you are going to unveil a plaque there. It commemorates the Jewish community in Calgary. Some local dignitaries from the Jewish centre will be there. Of course, there will be the usual photo opportunities."

"Sounds good to me. And then we're heading to the airport, yes? And back to Israel?" asked Yigal.

"Yes, that's right, sir. I should mention that because of the parade, we will be walking from the hotel to the unveiling. We have not informed the local police of this visit, as all their resources will be focused on the parade, and once we have finished and the parade clears, we will be leaving. The city has a unique walkway system called the Plus 15. It is used more in the winter so people can move around the city without having to go outside. However, the streets will be busy, so the walkways will be the safest choice—it is a ten-minute walk there and back, sir."

Yigal laughed and said, "I might be as old as the synagogues in Jerusalem, but I can walk for twenty minutes, young Noya. Now, let's go meet these families."

Noya smiled and got up to help Yigal put his jacket on.

"Thank you, Noya. I am a little sad our trip is almost over."

"Why is that, sir?"

"Because, Noya, if the Nazis hadn't made it impossible for my wife to have children, I would have loved to have had a girl just like you."

Noya felt a wave of emotion as she slid Yigal's jacket over his shoulders and watched him stand in front of the mirror, making sure he looked presentable. She, too, felt sad because she cared about this tiny little white-haired man who seemed to have all the time in the world for everyone. She also felt a huge sense of sadness for what the Nazis must have done to his poor wife in the camp, which rendered her infertile.

Yigal saw her expression and with his usual big smile said, "Come, Noya. Get those boys of yours ready to go."

"Yes, of course, sir," and she snapped back into her professional demeanour. After giving a quick update on the radio, the door opened, and off they went.

CHAPTER 37

SAFE HOUSE ORANGE, ENGLAND

The security supervisor was in the operations room, watching the interviews, which were still in their early stages. Hugo was present, only intending to leave if he needed to take or make a call.

Sarah and Peter had discussed the training he and Chloe had undertaken, their initial arrival in Algeria, and the meetings they'd had with Dominic. They were just getting to the arrangements for meeting the source.

As the morning wore on, Peter decided that he might as well tell them everything. He knew that holding things back and being found out later would not be good for him. He knew he'd acted in good faith and was sure if he told the whole truth, it would fall his way.

He'd taken time to tell Sarah about his meeting with Abigail in the cottage and explained why he'd been chosen.

Sarah was exceptional at her work—if she hadn't known about that meeting, she didn't let on.

"So, Peter, tell me what the plan was for meeting the source," she said.

"It was orchestrated by Chloe, primarily, and Dominic. It was well and truly in their wheelhouse, and I just did what I was told. Chloe decided she would meet the source at the arranged time and I would arrive fifteen minutes later. Her thinking was that if the source was jumpy, she'd be able to build a rapport better by herself—she's good at that—and then I could come along a bit later and support the dynamic. Dominic wasn't directly involved—he was back-up support via phone. We were going to use his base of operation, the safe house, to send any information we got from the source."

Sarah was taking notes here and there, but she asked Peter to go on.

"Dominic had contacted the source and arranged for them to meet Chloe at a local café. Chloe was to be wearing a pale-blue headscarf, and the source would ask if she had a light for a cigarette. Chloe would then say, 'I do,' and produce a silver lighter, a lighter that belonged to and had come from the source, signalling that the meeting was genuine. The source would then take his lighter back, and the meeting would start."

He paused, and Sarah gestured for him to continue. "So, on the night we'd planned the meet-up, Chloe left, and I went to another café nearby but well out of sight. When fifteen minutes had passed and I hadn't been given the abort signal, I headed to her café. But as I approached, Chloe was leaving, looking really concerned.

"I asked her what had happened, and she told me we mustn't speak in the street, and we needed to go back to the hotel. We walked for about twenty minutes in silence—it was clear she didn't feel safe to speak. Finally, she said that she didn't think the hotel room was safe, so we walked to a local park, which was busy with children and families.

"Chloe then told me that the source had arrived, but they were like a cat on a hot tin roof. They were scared and Chloe said she had to do everything she could to get them to sit down and relax. She had to produce the lighter and ask for a cigarette just to get them focused. She said that it took all of her persuasion to get them to talk, but they just told her the name of the mole and left. She said she tried to follow them, but after a short distance, lost sight of them. She looked around for a little longer, but then came back to the café, where she found me."

"Okay, so did she pass on any information to you?" asked Sarah.

"She told me that the source had named Abigail as the mole. I was a little taken aback, and Chloe looked genuinely worried. I think she knew that if she sent the name back the way she'd been instructed, it would warn Abigail, and Abigail would come after her."

Sarah had placed her pen down. "So what did you do?"

"I suggested that we call Dominic and tell him. The phones we had were encrypted, and I knew we couldn't deal with this on our own. Chloe was in panic mode, and after some discussion, she agreed to call him. I made the call and told him what the source had said. He went quiet, then said he'd call me back. About, maybe five minutes later, he called, saying I was to direct Chloe to the safe house, and I must return to the hotel."

Peter went quiet at this point and his head went down. "I knew what this meant—you know, that Chloe was going to face an unpleasant interrogation. After all, we'd just implicated the head of MI6, and I knew MI6 didn't entirely trust Chloe and would be suspicious of the information she'd given. The whole thing scared me. Selfishly, I just wanted to go back to the UK and get away from it all. So, I gave Chloe Dominic's instructions."

He seemed to well up, and Sarah could see the emotion in his face.

"Take your time, Peter. There's no rush."

"Chloe knew what it all meant too. She hugged me and said it was going to be all right. She said she'd see me soon. Then she kissed me on the cheek and left."

Sarah could see Peter needed a break and offered to get him another coffee. They could start again later. She headed off to the control room.

*

"How is it going?" asked Hugo.

"Good, thank you."

She then texted Marcus, watching him on the screen as he received and read the message before leaving the interview room to join her.

Marcus entered and asked how it was going for her.

"I need to tell you about a meeting Abigail had with Peter before they went to Algeria. Have you got to the point where Chloe meets the source?"

"No, not yet. We spent some time talking about the training and a conversation she had with Abigail before she left. She seems quite drained. I was going to give her thirty minutes, then go on to the source meeting."

"That's a good idea—keep it structured."

She turned to Hugo. "I know Devon wanted answers, but

I don't want to push this. Can you let him know that we're having a thirty-minute break?"

"No problem at all. You're the experts. So, to be clear, Peter has discussed the source meeting and Chloe will be asked about it when you go back in, Marcus? I'm not sure if they've been monitoring from Orange Alpha, so I want to give them a quick update," said Hugo.

"Yes, that's right," Marcus replied.

Hugo left, pulling out his phone.

About five minutes later, he came back, saying that Devon had no issues with the way things were going, and he had been monitoring the interviews. "Our group and the Americans have been advised and should be at Orange Alpha soon. I suggest you two enjoy the break, as the next part is going to be a long run."

Sarah and Marcus agreed and headed off to find the kitchen.

CHAPTER 38

SAFE HOUSE ORANGE ALPHA

Colonel Grieves had arrived and was asking for an update. He was more interested in the security arrangements than the interviews, so Devon talked him through it all.

Then Devon and the colonel found somewhere private to talk. The colonel wanted to know the chain of events that had led to Peter and Chloe being apprehended. Clearly, he—and others—were unimpressed with the delay in being apprised of this information, and this would be spoken about again. Devon told the colonel that from the point the Matron had told him about the call, he had taken every decision. Only he should be held accountable for them. Hugo and the Matron had merely followed his orders.

The colonel laughed. "I don't believe that for a second, Devon, but I admire your intent. The good thing is we have them. Now, we have an element of control, which I hope will go a little way to appease the Americans."

"Indeed, sir, and I want to say again that the Matron and Hugo followed my direction. What about my contact in MI6? Are they facing the music?"

"Who knows. That's not my world. I'm only going to go to bat for you three if I have to. If we get what we need from Chloe and Peter and the Americans get their pound of flesh, your delay in informing everyone may well just boil down to a finger-wagging," said the colonel.

The colonel and Devon left the office and placed themselves in front of the screens. The colonel then spoke. "I got a call from Abigail that she's going to be here in a few minutes. Major Smyth will also be joining us."

"Oh, great," said Devon. "Abigail's lapdog. Guard your wallets and your wives, boys."

"Yes, thank you, Devon," said the colonel with a chastening glance in his direction.

The Matron grinned at Devon and said she'd go out and greet Abigail when she arrived.

"Thank you, Matron," said the colonel.

It was only a few minutes later that the chauffeur-driven Range Rover and its escort vehicle glided into the courtyard.

On the cameras, you could see staff opening the door for Abigail. She shook hands with the Matron, and they disappeared out of sight.

Their voices and footsteps could be heard before they appeared in the room, flanked by the security team.

"Hello, Colonel. Nice to see you again," said Abigail, offering her hand.

"Yes, indeed, ma'am. Can I introduce you to Devon, the team leader who got us to where we are now?" said the colonel, signalling towards Devon.

Abigail smiled. "Ah, yes. Nice to meet you, and well done for getting them here unscathed."

"No problem at all, ma'am," said Devon, shooting the colonel a glance.

He only nodded slightly in reassuring approval.

Abigail's protection leader, known as Halifax, came over and asked if it was okay for his people to go on a break while he stayed. Abigail agreed, then said they should have someone replace him shortly so he could swap out. Halifax then found a seat out of the way at the back.

"So, what have they told us so far?" asked Abigail.

"Ma'am, we haven't been listening to the interviews, as we needed to get some reports done and deal with other logistics. Let me bring up the audio. I did notice that both inquisitors came out about fifteen minutes ago and headed towards the operations room."

The audio was turned up, and you could hear Chloe and Peter shuffling around.

"Okay, perhaps I can get a cup of tea while we wait for it to start up again. I got a call from Helena just before I arrived here—she should be with us in about thirty minutes."

"Perhaps you could give Hugo a call, Devon. Please get an update or have one of the inquisitors give us a call before they go back in," said the colonel.

"Yes, of course, sir," answered Devon, and he went off.

Abigail and the colonel continued discussing the next steps but were interrupted only a minute later by Devon. "Strange. I can't reach Hugo. Matron, would you mind giving him a shout? Maybe it's my phone."

"Sure," said the Matron. "In fact, I'll go outside in case

there's a signal issue in the building." She headed out of the room.

When she returned, she was still looking at her phone, confused, and then Abigail said she'd lost the feed to the interview rooms. Abigail stood, watching the security feeds to the safe house as she saw an Audi pull up to the gate. The driver entered the key code. This initiated a camera showing the driver and sole occupant of the vehicle. Major Douglas Smyth. The gate swung open and the car drove inside.

Abigail sighed and said, "What is he doing there? I told him to meet us here."

The Matron returned, reporting that she hadn't been able to reach Hugo and, when she'd texted him, it had come back as undelivered. And then, they stood in disbelief as they watched the security screen feeds go off one by one.

"What the fuck is going on?" asked Abigail, reaching for her cell and dialling a number. "Major Smyth and the inquisitors aren't picking up either."

Then the QRF team leader came in. They had been monitoring from a different location, and when the security feeds went down, they also lost communications with those on-site. He instructed that the group should remain on-site, and he explained that his team was going to deploy to the safe house. This triggered Halifax to rally his staff.

"Yes, go! Go! Go!" shouted Abigail.

The team was already getting into vehicles, and the QRF leader merely jumped into the last car. They had already practised the five-minute drive and now sped away in four Land Rover Defenders with blacked-out windows and supercharged engines. They flew through streets with a presence that forced other cars to get out of the way. When on-site, they broke into pairs, two vehicles entering from the front and two from the back.

Once they had smashed through the security gating, they immediately deployed into the building.

CHAPTER 39

The security supervisor was sitting in the operations room, watching the monitors to ensure that Peter and Chloe didn't try to hurt themselves or deteriorate medically. His four guards were on patrol, and he would check in with them shortly, but for now, he was relaxing and waiting for the new arrival to get to the operations room. He heard the outer door click open. Then the man's well-made shoes echoed as he strode down the corridor.

"Hello, sir. How can we help you?" asked the security supervisor.

"My name is Major Smyth, and I shall be taking overall command of things here. Who is currently in charge?"

"That would be Hugo, who is checking the perimeter. Were you not greeted outside by one of my group when you arrived?"

"No, I was not. Get this Hugo in here so I can get this

shamble of an operation back on track. I will probably have to report to the Home Office directly."

Major Smyth looked down his nose at the security supervisor, who was not impressed with this new arrival and certainly wasn't going to jump to attention. "Mobile One from operations team lead, are you receiving me?" he asked.

"What are you doing?" barked the major.

"My mobile patrol should have met you, so I need to find out where they are," he said, as he stood to scan the cameras.

"Excuse me, did you not hear who I am and who I need to report back to? This is a serious matter," said the major, puffing his chest out a little.

"Yes, sir. I did hear all of that, but I need to locate my men, so you will have to wait a moment."

Then he spoke into his radio. "Operations to any mobile patrol who can check on Mobile One at the entrance."

The radio was silent, and then the security supervisor heard, "Hey Operations. This is Hugo. I can do a check. Perhaps something's wrong with the comms. Stand by, I will update you." He clicked his comms unit again. "Hugo to QRF, Hugo to QRF. Are you receiving us? Over."

"This is QRF. We are receiving you loud and clear. Over."

"QRF, can you see anything on the cameras of the mobile patrols? Over."

"That would be a negative. Do you need us to move to your location? Over."

"That would be a negative. I'll make a sweep and update you and operations shortly. Hugo out."

As the security supervisor stood watching the cameras, Hugo came into the operations room.

"Hey, any sign of your mobile patrols?" he asked.

"Nothing, Hugo. This doesn't seem right."

Major Smyth, realising that Hugo was in the room, jutted out his chin and said, "Ah Hugo, about time. I am Major Smyth, and I am in charge now. We need to get something straight." He slid his left hand in a cross-draw motion into the inside pocket of his jacket and moved to square himself up between the two operators.

As he did this, Hugo said, "You're in charge, are you? I think not."

It was then, with consummate speed and professionalism, that Hugo brought up his silenced pistol and shot Major Smyth in the face.

The security supervisor, who was standing facing the cameras, began to turn, but he was shot in the back of the head and fell onto the control panel. He was dead in an instant. Hugo dragged the body off the control panel and switched off all the cameras, then stepped over the body of Major Smyth, who was now lying on the floor with his business card in his hand.

Peter, waiting in the interview room, thought he heard something that sounded like a short thumping sound. Then he heard it again. He got up and tried the door, but of course, it didn't open. He knocked and shouted, "Hey! Is anybody there? What's going on?"

As he craned his neck and placed his ear on the door, he heard what sounded like a fight.

"Get off me," a voice screamed.

It was clear Chloe was being attacked and dragged from her interview room. Peter heard her trying to resist. There was a male voice giving commands to shut up and get moving.

Peter banged on the door and shouted, "Chloe! What's going on, Chloe?"

"Peter, help me," pleaded Chloe.

"Shut up and get moving," said the voice.

Then there was quiet. Peter strained to listen and heard nothing. He banged on the door again and shouted for anyone to come and help him.

Hugo took Chloe out of the safe house and threw her into one of the vehicles. Her hands were bound and her head hooded. He shot two rounds into the other vehicles' engines through the radiators. "Tyres can be changed, but if the engine's gone, they're going nowhere," he muttered. Then he headed out the back gate, in the opposite direction that the QRF team would be approaching.

CHAPTER 40

ONE MINUTE OUT FROM SAFE HOUSE ORANGE ALPHA

"QRF leader to the group, we are one mike out."

Abigail had remained at Location Orange Alpha despite being recommended to leave. "Why aren't you going with them to the house?" she asked Devon and the Matron.

Devon's expression was focused. "They don't need unnecessary add-ons like me or the Matron. They've been trained to sweep and secure the place, and we would just get in the way. Once it's secured, we'll go. Matron, I think your special skills might be needed, so have your gear ready," said Devon.

"Copy that," answered the Matron.

The QRF drove straight through the gates, sending wood and metal splintering across the courtyard. They then entered the safe house simultaneously, their objective to secure the premises and regroup in the control room. This tactic had been rehearsed repeatedly to ensure fluidity and to avoid a blue-on-blue. With two units heading for the same point, understanding the process was key.

"Team one making entry."

"Team two making entry."

Once inside, they moved from room to room. Unless they encountered anyone alive, they simply moved on and headed for the next room. The only thing that would halt their progress was a hostile, which they would probably dispatch, then quickly move on.

If anyone was found alive, they would be secured and a guard placed with them.

Peter heard them coming down the corridor. He quickly moved to the back of the small room, standing with his hands up.

The door burst open and two men entered, shouting, "Face the wall! Do it now!"

Peter quickly turned around and instinctively placed his hands on the small of his back, ready for handcuffing.

Peter then heard, "Cover on." An operator had moved to cover him while his colleague placed the cuffs on him. He knew that if he showed any sign of aggression or threat, the covering operator would eliminate that threat. The two of them would simply leave him where he fell and move on.

One of the operators stood in the doorway, watching where his colleague was moving with his gun on aim. Positioned thus, he could watch Peter, support the team ahead if needed, and engage a rear attack if it came to that.

It was four minutes before the radio crackled into life and the QRF team leader said, "Safe house secure, stand by for update."

The cameras were then being brought up again. The team

at Orange Alpha could see the vehicles on-site, the smashed gate, and Peter lying on the floor, being guarded by the on-scene operator.

"Update to group, break."

"The four mobile security team members have been located and are confirmed deceased, break."

"Major Smyth and the security supervisor also dead in the operations room, break."

"Both inquisitors are in the lunchroom and confirmed deceased, break."

"Chloe and Hugo are not on-site. Peter has been found alive and is under our control. QRF out."

There was a stunned silence.

Abigail turned to Devon. "Go with the Matron and collect Peter. Take him to The Venue immediately and place him in our protective custody. Leave half the QRF team at the safe house to secure the building before bringing in the police. The other half will escort you and Peter. Peter must arrive in one piece."

"Understood, ma'am," said Devon, and along with the Matron, he made to leave, but not before Abigail gave further direction. She seemed distant, even a little emotional, as she said, "I'm assuming the vehicle Hugo took has a GPS?"

"Yes, ma'am. I'd have to check which car is missing. I'll have the team at The Venue track it for us. I can't imagine they will use it for long, but it would give us a starting point."

"Yes, indeed. Thank you, and keep me posted."

Abigail then turned to her group. "Take me to the safe house."

Halifax said, "I'm not sure that is wise, ma'am. We should go to your office."

Abigail, with a loud and distinctly emotional overtone, said, "I don't care what's wise. Take me to the safe house, or I will drive myself."

"Yes, ma'am."

On arrival, Devon found Peter still sitting on the ground with the QRF operator.

"Peter, we're going to stand you up. Are you going to cause me problems?" asked Devon.

"No," said Peter.

Devon and the operator got Peter to his feet.

"Where's Chloe?" asked Peter.

"We don't know," said Devon.

"I heard her fighting them as she was taken. She was alive when she left," he said.

As they stood in the corridor, Abigail came into view, and everyone went quiet. Not seeming to register Peter's presence, she flatly asked the operator where the lunchroom was.

"Head down this corridor and through the operations room. It's on the right when you come out the other side, ma'am."

"Thank you. Devon. Get Peter out of here now. I will join you later at The Venue."

CHAPTER 41

LAND ROVER, EN ROUTE TO THE VENUE

"Where are we going, and what are you going to do about Chloe?" asked Peter.

The Matron, who was sitting in the back with him, told him to lean forward. She removed the plastic handcuffs.

"If you make a move against us, I will kill you. Understand?" she said.

Peter could see the determination on Devon and the Matron's faces. Even though he'd no intention of being a pain in the arse, he decided to be on his best behaviour. He sat facing forward with his hands on his thighs to make sure the Matron could see them clearly.

"We think Chloe's been taken by Hugo. He killed everyone at the safe house except you."

"We're trying to track his vehicle as a start point to locating them. We're currently en route to The Venue, which is Abigail's headquarters. It'll be your place of protective custody." Then, fixing him a stare, she said, "We're all a little exhausted and on edge, so I would suggest you sit back and enjoy the ride."

Devon, who was driving, said, "Did anything come up in the interview that we should know about?"

"No, nothing contentious," said Peter.

"I've called operations at The Venue to get transcripts. We can have a look when we get there," Devon replied.

"Are you sure it was Hugo who took Chloe?" asked Peter.

"He's the only one unaccounted for, and he had the time and the access to do it. The only thing I can't figure out is the motive. I've worked with him for a number of years, and I wouldn't even know where to start fathoming it. Once we have you secured Peter, I'm going to do everything to find him," said Devon.

"You and me both," said the Matron, who, rather than watching Peter, was staring out the window, her fists clenched.

CHAPTER 42

SAFE HOUSE ORANGE

Abigail headed into the operations room and surveyed the scene before stepping over Major Smyth and then the security supervisor.

The QRF had divided themselves to provide continuity of cover and sight-lines of each other. As she made her way to the lunchroom, Abigail could see one of them, carbine in hand, standing at the entrance. She looked at him, and as she arrived at the door, her gaze lingered, as if she feared looking in and was steeling her resolve. She turned, and there were the two inquisitors. Sarah had been sitting facing the door and had been the first to see Hugo enter. She'd been shot in the face. The force had sent her backward, tipping the chair over. She had landed awkwardly on the floor.

Marcus had turned to see his attacker and had been shot behind his right ear, causing the side of his head to split open.

He had fallen forward onto the table, and from a distance, it looked like he could be asleep.

Abigail walked over to where he lay and gently touched his head.

Halifax appeared in the doorway and stopped.

He asked the guard to leave and secure the corridor. Following him until he was out of Abigail's sight, he softly said, "That's her son. I didn't know he'd be here. Give us a minute, and I'll give you a shout when we're done."

"Of course. Take your time. I'll make sure you're covered."

Abigail stroked Marcus's hair, then stood, quietly looking at him, his head on the table. "Have the police been called?" she asked without looking away from her son.

"Yes, ma'am, but we can keep them out of here. Please, take your time," Halifax said.

"Thank you, but we both knew the risks of this line of work. My husband died some years ago, and he would not have liked Marcus joining the service. My husband always thought it was a little too sneaky for his liking. Don't get me wrong, he was proud of me and would often be my moral barometer in the darkness, but he didn't like the cloak-and-dagger stuff. Oh, look, Marcus is wearing my husband's watch." She licked her thumb and gently rubbed the blood off the face of the watch. It was a classic old wind-up Omega with what looked like the original brown leather strap.

"It belonged to my husband's father and his father before him. It's made its way through World War One and World War Two, and even spent some time on the streets of Northern Ireland. My husband was a captain in the army for a while before he became sick and we lost him. Would you speak with the police and ask that the watch and Marcus's belongings come to me when they're done? I know they'll have to seize everything for evidence, but after they're finished, it would be nice to have them back."

"Yes, I'll make sure of that, ma'am," said Halifax, feeling a little awkward as he stood outside the door, out of sight.

She gently touched Marcus's head again, then made to leave. "I need five minutes to myself. I shall meet you by the vehicle."

"Of course, ma'am," Halifax replied. He was left standing in the corridor as she opened the door, letting the sunlight flood in.

He then used his comms. "Principal needs five minutes alone and will meet us by the vehicle. Watch her on the cameras. Be ready to go."

He received the copy from each team member, then looked back at Sarah and Marcus's lifeless bodies.

Abigail stood, knowing she was on camera, and simply closed her eyes, letting the sun warm her face. It seemed like only seconds had passed when she felt her cell phone vibrate in her pocket.

She pulled it out. Helena.

"Hello, Helena, I assume you are at Orange Alpha."

"Yes, I am. Where are you? There are only a couple of security people here."

"I'm on my way. I'll update you when I get there. I'll be five minutes."

"Okay, speak soon."

Abigail then scrolled through her contacts and dialled the number.

"Yes, hello, Abigail. How is it going?" asked Sir Goodlove.

"I need you to come to The Venue," she said abruptly. "It is urgent. I'll be bringing Helena with me. She'll be in the picture soon. This isn't a secure line, but I'll be back at Orange Alpha in ten minutes. I'll brief you and Helena then."

"Okay, should I be preparing for the rain here, Abigail?" said Sir Goodlove.

"I would stand by for a monsoon."

"Okay, I'll be ready in ten. I shall get the helicopter crew moving. After your update, I'll head to The Venue—I'll be there within the hour," said Sir Goodlove before hanging up.

CHAPTER 43

SAFE HOUSE ORANGE ALPHA

Abigail's Land Rover swung in as Helena stood outside. Helena saw her and smiled. It was the smile of trying to be nice but with the undertone of, *What's going on?*

"Helena, Sir Goodlove will be online at any moment on our secure channel. Let's go inside, and I'll brief you both."

Helena knew the routine. Without argument, she followed her inside.

Abigail's people ushered them into a conference room and set about linking up to Sir Goodlove, then stood to the side, looking at the ground, arms folded.

Helena took a seat and remained quiet.

The video feed came on, and Sir Goodlove appeared on the screen.

"Hello again, ladies. Can you please bear with me one moment?" He had his phone to his ear and could be heard

saying, *Yes, have the helicopter ready for me as soon as possible . . .
The Venue.* "Okay, sorry about that. Abigail, over to you."

Abigail composed herself. "About thirty minutes ago,
Hugo, one of our Special Forces personnel who was at the safe
house, went rogue and killed the entire security detail, Major
Smyth, and our two inquisitors, Marcus and Sarah. He then
kidnapped Chloe, leaving Peter alive in one of the interview
rooms. Peter is currently being escorted to The Venue, as it's
a secure location, for further interview. We're finding out
whether the car Hugo is using has a tracker. I know they won't
be with the vehicle by the time we pick it up, but it'll give us a
start point."

There was a brief silence before Sir Goodlove said, "Abigail,
did you say the inquisitor who had been killed was Marcus?"

Abigail looked away quickly, and with a heavy inhale
replied, "Yes, Sir Goodlove, I did. It was Marcus."

Helena looked puzzled. "Am I missing something?"

Before Sir Goodlove could speak, Abigail said, quite
matter-of-factly, "Marcus is my son, Helena. That is why Sir
Goodlove asked."

Helena then noticed the blood on her hands and at once,
Abigail's distant, almost robotic demeanour made sense.
"Abigail, I am so sorry."

"Likewise, Abigail. If you want to hand this over to me, I
will take the reins," said Sir Goodlove.

"No, Sir Goodlove, and thank you, Helena, but I will
remain. I must see this to the end now."

"Okay, well, I suggest we all meet at The Venue as soon
as possible to get briefed on what we know. Helena, might I
suggest you direct your chaps coming from Germany and our
guy Andrew to The Venue? Oh, and Helena, I know this was

going to be kept in-house, but might I suggest Michael, who is representing the director of the CIA, be in on our next briefing?" said Goodlove, taking over the coordination of matters to allow Abigail a moment to breathe.

Helena agreed. She walked around the table and placed her hand on Abigail's shoulder. Abigail, without looking up, patted her hand in response. "Thank you," she murmured, "but no more, please. I can't do sympathy right now." She looked up, smiling weakly, pain etched on her brave façade.

Sir Goodlove quietly broke in. "I shall see you soon, Abigail," he said, and signed off.

Abigail stood, looking at the floor, trying to compartmentalise her thoughts. She had to put her grief on hold for now and sort this mess out. For Marcus and all the other innocent people, other people's sons and daughters, who had been murdered.

She then realised that Halifax had entered and was carrying a packet of baby wipes. He handed them to Abigail. "For your hands, ma'am."

Abigail looked at her son's blood on her hands. "Thank you, Halifax." She cleaned herself up—Halifax noticed her carefully folding and placing one of the bloodstained wipes in her pocket. He closed the door and returned to her. Reaching inside his jacket pocket, he produced the Omega watch with the brown leather strap. He'd cleaned it up.

"I thought you should have this, ma'am. Otherwise, the police will have it for months, plus, you know how easily evidence can go missing."

"You shouldn't have taken it, Halifax." Abigail held the watch, caressing its face with her thumb.

"Don't worry, ma'am. It was me who interfered with a

crime scene, not you. You can blame me if they come asking."

Abigail allowed her stoicism to give way a little as she placed her hand on Halifax's upper arm and squeezed it. She looked at him softly. "Thank you, Halifax. It means a lot. Now, get me to The Venue so we can catch these bastards."

"Yes, ma'am."

CHAPTER 44

CABIN AT THE BASE OF RAINBOW
MOUNTAIN, BRITISH COLUMBIA

Carl, Alicia, Augustus, Johannes, and Hanna had spent the night talking and laughing about nothing and everything. The beer had flowed. It had seemed to have been the first night in a long time where they'd been able to relax and be themselves.

In the morning, Carl was up first and made breakfast. When everyone was at the table, he began the briefing. "Okay, I've loaded my vehicle, and I plan to leave at 0700 hours. The roads from here to Calgary are limited, and I don't want to run the risk of us being seen together. I want you to decide between you who's leaving and when. Put at least one hour between your departures. We are not to contact each other unless there's an emergency until we reach Calgary. Pack your vehicles carefully so firearms are out of sight, and don't be tempted to have a sidearm on your person—you don't want a routine traffic stop to compromise us. With that in mind, make sure your vehicle has valid licence plates and you have all the correct insurance documents. Make sure all the headlights and brake lights are working too. No drawing attention to yourselves and getting stopped for something stupid, so definitely no speeding. Use cruise control if it helps. Any questions?"

No one did, so they ate, cleaned up, then said goodbye to Carl. They helped each other check their vehicles and got ready to depart.

Prior to leaving, Carl hiked into the trees and produced his wallet. Inside was a SIM that he inserted into a disposable cell phone.

As before, there was only one number, and he called it. No response. He tried again.

The voice answered. "Yes."

"We are all here and on our way," said Carl.

"I have a couple of people who will be joining you. They are going to be travelling from England very soon," said the voice.

"Who are these people and why are they joining us?" demanded Carl.

"I am not going to say their names. They are loyal to me and our cause. I want them there to help you and make sure you succeed. Forward as One, my friend," said the voice.

"Forward as One," echoed Carl and hung up.

Carl wasn't happy that unknown people were joining his team, but he trusted Benjamin and would only tell the team on arrival in Calgary. He removed the SIM and threw it, along with the phone, into a nearby river.

CHAPTER 45

LARGE BRIEFING ROOM, THE VENUE

The security detail at The Venue had been advised that a number of people were on their way.

Sir Goodlove arrived by helicopter and was shown to the briefing room, where Abigail and Helena were waiting. They greeted each other, and Sir Goodlove asked to speak with Abigail privately.

Helena didn't need to be in the room to understand what was being said. Through the glass walls, she could clearly see Sir Goodlove discussing Abigail's son and offering what Helena only imagined was support and the opportunity, again, to walk away.

They soon left the small office and as they re-entered the briefing room, others were beginning to arrive, and the large screens were coming to life.

Abigail came over to Helena and said, "He may be an

arse, but sometimes, he does reveal his good qualities. He told me that when this is over, he'll ensure I get some serious time away at the government's expense." These words made Abigail smile.

Helena leaned in and said, "Why don't you come and see me? Oh, and if we get our hands on Hugo before your lot do, I can arrange for him to be located at one of our black op sites. You can torture him for so long that he will think it is a career."

Abigail blushed a little, and Helena said, "I'm not kidding. Those CIA people are a little unhinged. I'm just glad they're on our side."

Abigail looked around to see Sir Goodlove was now present, along with Jessica and, on her insistence, Shaukey. She spotted Devon and the Matron and two MI6 analysts, Patterson and Hobbs.

When the screens flashed up, there was Michael from Langley. Again, on Jessica's request, Twyla and Lars had been brought in.

Abigail began the proceedings.

"Right, everyone, we're all here as it has been decided by myself, Sir Goodlove, and Helena of the NSA that all parties needed to be updated. Sir Goodlove, why don't you start us off with why you're here?"

"Okay," Sir Goodlove began, "so some of you already know this, but for those of you who don't, a while back, information, which was believed to be reliable, was received that the British Intelligence Services—we don't know which one— had a mole. Of course, this poses a problem, as a mole in a large organisation can be anyone, from the mailroom guy to the top dog. Therefore, you can't have anyone from within conducting the investigation, not even the head. This is where

I came in, because even Abigail here, along with everyone else at MI6, was under suspicion until she could be ruled out. Which, she has now," he added with a brief smile in Abigail's direction. "So, I, as an outsider who could not be the mole, was appointed to conduct the investigation and was made head of MI6 as a cover for what I was really doing, much to the chagrin of Abigail." His smile to her this time was apologetic. She nodded in acknowledgement.

The intelligence was deemed reliable, and we were forced to look at everyone, and I mean everyone. During our operation, we identified that the mole was empathetic to the needs and wants of the Islamist extremists, and also that they had a lover. We identified that this lover was Chloe."

Sir Goodlove let that last comment sink in.

"You may be familiar with the phrase, *Keep your friends close but your enemies closer.* Well, we orchestrated her recruitment based on that and for a while, gave her free rein while we watched her. In the end, we felt a little more prompting might be in order, so we sent her to Algeria to test her operational capabilities, but more importantly, her loyalty. She'd been briefed by Abigail to meet a source who we believed was going to pass us the name of the mole. The source did this, and Chloe, as instructed, sent the name in a message to Abigail. Whomever the message was addressed to would be the mole." He looked around the room. "Chloe named Abigail as the mole."

Again, Sir Goodlove let that sink in.

"It should be noted that Abigail has been cleared, so we felt this was a hostile act from Chloe. As a result, Abigail authorised for Chloe to be detained and interrogated." He paused for a moment to take a sip of water. "Now, on to Peter. He had originally been brought in, rather like me, because he was not of the intelligence world, and we knew he couldn't be connected to the mole. He was briefed, in part, regarding the mole, our reservations about Chloe, and the purpose of the operation we were sending him on. But unfortunately, he became rather fond of Chloe, and after passing on the instruction for her to go to the safe house after the meeting with the source, he figured out that she wasn't going there for tea and cake and that essentially, he'd sent her off for a beating. So, he decided to enter the safe house, and on freeing Chloe, killed two guards. Going on this behaviour, it seems very likely he must have known the name Chloe passed on. One of the guards he killed was an undercover American agent, and Helena is here, as Peter will need to speak with the Americans once this has been concluded. After their escape, he and Chloe went on the run and made contact with one of their former trainers, Jen, here, although most of us know her as the Matron." The Matron nodded in response.

"She, in turn, contacted her supervisor, Devon, who is sitting next to her. They were taken to a safe house with all the usual measures in place, and we were all then informed. Abigail, why don't you pick it up from here?"

"Yes, Sir Goodlove. Once we knew they were secure, we informed Helena and coordinated that our teams would meet at the Safe House QRF location known as Orange Alpha. While at this location, we believe that one of our Special Forces operators known as Hugo killed everyone there except Peter and Chloe. He left Peter and took Chloe, against her will. At this time, we don't have any information as to their whereabouts or indeed, Chloe's status."

Abigail then looked at the screens and said, "Michael, perhaps give us your role in this."

"Of course, Abigail. Thank you. I was brought in from the Rangers to work with the director of the CIA to investigate the ease with which some of the recent attacks across Europe were happening. When I received the brief on the North Africa incident involving Chloe and Peter, we decided we needed to be more engaged, and not just because one of our agents had been killed. It was concerning that one of our best-placed assets had been killed, but the director and I felt there was more to it. That's why we pulled in Jessica and Shaukey's team. They were selected as they have either been out of the operational sphere or had not been directly engaged for some time— the most 'out-of-the-loop' personnel we could find who had the right skillsets, if you like."

"Thank you, Michael," said Abigail. "So that is where we are. This is the time for comments, questions, or concerns, ladies and gentlemen."

Most people said nothing, but in the background, two guys were talking in what seemed to be an intense conversation.

"Would you like to join the rest of the group, gentlemen?" said Abigail.

The MI6 officers looked up, a little embarrassed, as everyone stared back.

Andrew leaned forward. "Abigail, this is Patterson and Hobbs. They work for me. They were asked to look through the intelligence, particularly surrounding Chloe. I'm sure, since they've interrupted, that they must have something enlightening to share. Don't you, gentlemen?"

Andrew was now staring at them, hoping they actually did have something to say.

Nervously, they stood, clearly not enjoying being the centre of attention.

"Yes, Andrew, we think we do. We've prepared a presenta-tion, if that's okay?" said Patterson, dropping his folder and staring down at it, not knowing whether he should pick it up.

Abigail said, "Please, gentlemen, we're all interested. Let's take five minutes to stretch our legs, and you can get your-selves ready."

The two men then bustled up to the front, logged on to the computer, and waited for it to fire up.

Andrew approached them. "This better be good, fellas."

"We think it is, Andrew. Yes, I think you'll like it," said Hobbs.

Andrew loved the analysts in MI6. They were brilliant, but when it came to social skills, they were fun to watch. Privately, he called them the Big Bang Theorists.

A short while later, everyone was back in the room, Jessica and Shaukey commenting on the elegant white china tea and coffee cups.

"This is fancy," said Shaukey.

"Ah, I love the British. They are so refined," said Jessica, doing a little curtsey, which made Shaukey smile.

Devon joined them, greeting Jessica and Shaukey before introducing the Matron.

The Matron smiled wryly at Jessica. "And where's my curtsey?"

Jessica laughed. "I only do those for Shaukey."

Shaukey stiffened up and, looking at Devon, said, "Sorry to hear what happened at the safe house and to your people. Rest assured, we'll do whatever we can to make sure that your man is caught. We'll gladly hand him over to you."

Devon gave a little grin. "That's very kind, but if you get the opportunity, feel free to kill him —it will save me the time and paperwork."

Shaukey nodded. "Sounds like a plan."

The PowerPoint presentation had been fired up and was now on the large centre screen. There had been some issues with screen-sharing for those in Langley, but now it seemed to be working.

Patterson got up first and began the presentation.

"Hello, everyone. My name is Patterson, and this is Hobbs, and we're analysts based here at The Venue. To give our American colleagues some context, we are the Twyla and Lars equivalents for MI6."

Hobbs hit the remote, and a large image came on the screen of a railway carriage. In the colour image, you could see a man walking down the central aisle. A woman sat in one of the seats, looking out the window.

Patterson went on, "So, to give us a start point, Andrew had us look into every facet of Chloe's life. We've looked at bank accounts, social media, her university days. We covertly interviewed her friends, searched her apartment—the list goes on. But nothing ever came up.

"Chloe had attended a meeting prior to leaving for Algeria, so we looked up the CCTV coverage from leaving the meeting to the moment she arrived back at the training camp. Thankfully," he said with just a hint of dryness, "here in the UK, as we are a free and open society, you can't go anywhere without someone watching you. It was easy to get the footage. She had a work-issue cell phone, so we tracked her route and married the two together. Much of what we unearthed was just her walking through streets, getting from one place to another, nothing of interest. Then we got to this image of her on the train. The lady in the picture, if you haven't recognised her, is Chloe. As you can see, she's speaking on a cell phone. At this time, her issued cell phone was not active. We did a spectral search, and there were six cell phones active on the train at the date and time of this image. All the numbers have been traced and verified. Except one."

Patterson paused for a moment and drank some water. "The unidentified number was routed through a communications hub in Pakistan. I am going to let Hobbs explain this part, as he is our technical person."

Hobbs moved to the front of the table and got the next slide up. It showed a map of the world with varying lines going to and from Pakistan.

"Okay, so there are SIM cards out there that give protection from being traced. They're predominantly produced out of Pakistan, actually not far from where Mr. bin Laden was found by our wonderful Americans here." Hobbs smiled awkwardly and gave almost a half-bow towards Shaukey.

Shaukey, with a large smile, said, "You're more than welcome. A Delta operator will always take the credit for those Navy SEAL pretty boys."

Hobbs laughed. "Quite right."

Sir Goodlove then said, "If you don't mind, we're on a timeline here."

"Yes, sir, sorry, sir," said Hobbs. "When you use these SIM cards, it routes your call in an encrypted fashion through the hub in Pakistan. It will then send the number, for example, to a tower in India and then back to the hub. This process goes on almost instantaneously through probably six or seven countries. It makes it incredibly difficult to trace. Even if you walked into the hub, you would be faced with probably hundreds of computer towers. You would have to search each one to determine which tower was used and then decipher the route." Hobbs sat back down and handed over to Patterson.

"As we said, we tracked down the sixth number, but it didn't give us anything to work with," said Patterson, bringing up the image of Chloe in the carriage again.

"Here, Chloe is seen to end the call and walk to the area between the carriages. She throws the SIM and cell separately out of the window. We did consider searching in the area where she threw the items, but as I said, it wouldn't give us any avenues moving forward. We then decided to track down the man you can see walking through the carriage, who we can see looking at Chloe."

In the video, the man is walking through the carriage as the train approaches a short platform, which means he needs to move to the next carriage.

"Patterson, would you mind explaining, for our American partners, what a short platform is?" said Sir Goodlove.

"Yes, of course. Some train platforms are quite historic and were built when trains were a lot shorter. When modern-day trains arrive at the platform, they don't fit. So, you will hear an announcement that you will need to leave the train from carriages four through to eight, for example. Interestingly, if you go to the train station in Folkestone Central, Kent, the platform is enormous. It was designed to accommodate the troop trains bringing those to fight in World War One," said Patterson, before realising again that he needed to move on.

"Anyway, we traced this gentleman, as he used an ATM on the platform. Through his bank, we obtained the location where he lived, then sent two Special Branch officers to his house to question him about this moment. The man works in the city in corporate security at the Lloyds building and has no traces or concerns. He's a former police officer and was able to remember some elements of this moment because it had flagged up with him as strange. When we showed him the image, he remembered it well. According to the officer, his wife started asking questions —did he know this woman—and the man got quite irritated that she was quizzing him. He said that he'd looked across at Chloe because as he walked past, he'd distinctly heard her say, 'Forward as One,' then hang up her phone. He said she then went to stand in the area adjoining the carriages. He thought she was going to move due to the short platform, but she didn't. He then exited the train, and as it left, he noticed Chloe opening the window, but he has no recollection if she threw anything out of it."

Abigail shifted in her seat and asked, "What did he do after that?"

"He went to the nearest florist and bought his wife flowers, which we have confirmed. In fact, we showed him the CCTV images. He then went home, and after a couple of hours, he took his wife out for dinner. His bank records have confirmed this as well."

Hobbs spoke up. "We ran this guy through our databases, and we even got our colleagues at Langley to do the same. There is nothing on him. Just a solid police officer who became disenchanted with his own force, so he left to try something different. We do not consider him to be involved in any of this."

Devon said, "Yes, but we didn't think Hugo was involved, and we know how that turned out."

"Okay, thank you, Devon. We shall keep this person in mind. Please go on, Patterson," said Sir Goodlove.

"Yes, sir. I'm going to hand over to Hobbs again for the next part, as this was really his element."

Hobbs stood up again. "So, the phrase 'Forward as One.'

Not massively unique, but not completely unsearchable. I decided to contact GCHQ, our listening station, and managed to secure an hour of search time."

"That would explain it," said Sir Goodlove. "I got a call from the head of GCHQ and the Home Secretary asking why their supercomputer was diverted from other operations for an hour. I'm sure I know the answer, but Andrew, as head of this group, did you request permission for this?"

Andrew looked at Patterson and Hobbs and said, "No, sir, but it may be on my desk waiting for my signature, since I've been away."

"I doubt that, Andrew, but I appreciate you looking after your people. Hobbs, you understand that this computer is a multi-million-pound asset, and every minute of its use is accounted for. How did you get this search done? I am intrigued," said Sir Goodlove.

Hobbs and Patterson were looking quite uncomfortable, and then Hobbs said, "Er, I went to university with the facilitator and programmer for that department. And well, we're also on a World of Warcraft team, sir."

"World of Warcraft? What's that?" asked Helena.

Hobbs turned to Helena and explained that it was an online game. He and his friend were on a team called Lucifer Had a Heart Stone and went on missions together to fight Orcs. Hobbs then went a little off-track and explained how good they were at the game, and that he even had his own level-ten battle ostrich.

Jessica had to look down into her lap to hide her amusement.

Shaukey leaned in and said to Jessica, "I love these guys."

"Thank you for explaining that to me," said Helena with a wry smile.

"Anyway, gentlemen. We can discuss the misuse or indeed unauthorised use of the country's most expensive counterterrorism intelligence asset later. How about you tell us what you found?" said Abigail.

Hobbs and Patterson looked a little flustered, but Hobbs asked for the next slide, cleared his throat, and started to speak again. "We could use the words in the phrase on their own, but that would bring back a huge quantity of data. So, we decided to target a two-week window using the exact phrase, and we set specific geographical locations. We selected North Africa, due to the recent operation; Europe, encompassing the UK; America, including Canada; and finally, South America."

"Can I ask why South America? That seems somewhat out of focus for us," asked Abigail.

"That will become clear later, ma'am," said Patterson.

Abigail just nodded.

"When we ran the search, it came back with exact hits in Northern Alberta and British Columbia, Canada; Washington and Massachusetts in America; the UK; and South America, we believe in or around Argentina. A bit more digging enabled us to discount Massachusetts—it came from a rowing team that uses this phrase as a team motto."

Hobbs paused for a moment, then said, "Now, please bear with us for this next part. We were monitoring global intelligence reports as we normally do, and I had just read a report about a subject known as Khaleed Zaher travelling from Edmonton to Buenos Aires. Khaleed is a student at Grant MacEwan University and has a loose association with a target who carried out a recent terrorist attack in Edmonton. They were students at the same university, took a class together, and have the same faith. We happened to be watching the news from around the world when we saw that the daughter of a high-profile doctor, who happens to be a nurse in Buenos Aires, died in a vehicle accident. It's reported that she drove her vehicle into a lake under the influence of drugs.

"The boyfriend and four of his friends have not been seen since. They're currently of interest and wanted for questioning. The family and friends of the nurse are adamant that she didn't use drugs and have been on the news appealing for answers. Now, in the report about the man from Edmonton, the Argentinian intelligence service said that he travelled to Buenos Aires. Staff at a top hotel said they believe he met up with the five missing friends. This can't be confirmed, but the staff are quite sure.

"The considered leader of these five friends is known as Carl, and he was the boyfriend of the now-deceased nurse. Carl and his family are somewhat well known in Buenos Aires, as they purport that his grandfather, a former Nazi, was killed by the team hunting Eichmann. This has never been denied or confirmed. Carl now runs his grandfather's tailoring business, which is well established, and he looks after a number of prominent figures, including organised crime figures and politicians.

"We did have a hit with the phrase 'Forward as One' on the day after Khaleed left South America. This would lead us to think that someone else in Argentina is linked to Chloe through this phrase."

Sir Goodlove interjected, "So, we have someone from Edmonton who has a loose connection to a terrorist who travelled to Buenos Aires, probably for educational purposes. They may or may not have been in contact with five locals who have a connection to a former deceased Nazi. I can't imagine there is anyone in Argentina who doesn't have a Nazi in the closet. At the moment, gentlemen, I would rather sign off on the report saying Saddam Hussein had weapons of mass destruction."

"Yes, sir, I quite agree, but please, we will get there," said Patterson.

Hobbs resumed. "So we asked our man in South America to head there and speak with local police and see what he could find out. He didn't find a great deal, but he was allowed into Carl's apartment. The police had done their search and not found anything. However, when our man was searching through Carl's desk, he found, on a piece of paper, an imprint from the page above. He took it to our experts, and with a little treatment, they found a grocery list, some doodles, and at the bottom of the page the phrase 'The Greatest Show on Earth.'" He looked around at the puzzled, expectant faces. "The Calgary Stampede is known as the Greatest Show on Earth, and its opening parade is in thirty-six hours." He let them take this in, then said, "Oh, and Calgary is three hours south of Edmonton.

"We have asked the Canadians and the Americans to help, and we've been able to identify that one member of the group known as Hanna, entered Canada three days ago via the Vancouver airport under a false name. She rented a vehicle and left the area. We are now circulating images of the rest of the group to see if we can get their travel plans identified.

"It should be noted that the last hit we had on the search we did with GCHQ on the phrase 'Forward as One' was just after Hanna entered Canada. It was run in British Columbia, where Vancouver is located."

As everyone sat quietly, there was a knock at the door, and

it was gently edged open. It was one of the operations staff. "Ma'am, a message for you."

"Is it to do with this briefing?" asked Abigail.

"Yes, ma'am."

"Okay, come in and update everyone."

"Yes, ma'am. We have just been advised that Hugo's vehicle has been located and is empty. It was found near a private airfield, and Special Branch has determined that the occupants walked on foot about a mile to the airfield.

"The vehicle has been held by forensics, but they did say there was blood on the back seats, presumably where Chloe would have been held. The hood she was wearing when she was removed from the safe house was also found in the vehicle.

"Special Branch has been to the airfield, and there have been several flights today. With the time frame and descriptions given, we have two possibilities. One has been chartered to the south of France and the other to Red Deer, which when we Googled it, is located in Alberta, Canada."

"That's about one hour and thirty minutes from Edmonton," said Hobbs. "It's the midway point between Edmonton and Calgary."

The man looked a little baffled. "Er, well, that's all I've got, ma'am."

"Thank you," said Abigail, and the man left.

Sir Goodlove sat quietly for a moment. After a short time, he said, "Okay, unless someone has some other startling piece of information, I believe that we need to focus our attention on this Stampede thing in Calgary. I recommend I remain in the UK. Abigail, you travel to Calgary and work with the local law enforcement and CSIS—that's the Canadian Secret Intelligence Service."

Abigail smiled. She knew what it stood for. And she also knew this was Sir Goodlove's way of green-lighting her to get Hugo. "Yes, I agree," she said. "Helena, I recommend that you come to Calgary with us and bring your crew, headed up by Jessica and accompanied by Andrew. We can use the CSIS office in Calgary to set up shop."

"Agreed. Michael, will you bring the director up to speed on this?" said Helena.

"Yes, Helena. I think, under the circumstances, I will request CIA assets to be deployed and tasked to try to assist. I'm going to assume that you and Abigail will be joint lead on this," said Michael.

"Yes, we will, but we will bring in our CSIS equivalent to make sure we don't ruffle any feathers," remarked Helena as she made some notes.

Sir Goodlove spoke directly to Abigail. "I am going to brief the prime minister and COBRA. Can I ask what your strategy will be?"

Abigail sat quietly for just a moment, and then, leaning forward, she placed her hands on the table. Interlacing her fingers, she said, "I am going to assume that due to the parade and drain on resources, we will get a limited response from the Calgary Police Service. We will update them, but on the intelligence we have, I doubt they will contemplate, even for a moment, cancelling the parade.

"When we arrive, we will divide and conquer. Helena, I would like Jessica and her group to focus on the five Argentinians. I get the impression that this Khaleed will be with them, or certainly close by. You will join her, if that's okay."

"Yes, of course," answered Helena.

"Sir Goodlove, would you be able to speak with the

Edmonton Police and their Special Branch and get them to locate Khaleed? You can give them my contact details if that makes things easier," said Abigail.

"Yes, I shall do that once I have updated CSIS that you are all incoming," said Sir Goodlove.

"Regarding Chloe," began Abigail. "She is still one of ours, and I am surprised she hasn't been killed. It's still not clear where her loyalties lie, possibly she doesn't even know, so we need to keep the options open with her and definitely treat her with prejudice. We do need to find her, though—Peter might be useful for that. I suggest we take him to Calgary with us. Devon and the Matron, along with Peter, can work on locating her. Thoughts, anyone?"

"I agree she must have something they need or indeed want, or we'd have found her dead at that safe house of yours with all the others. Michael, I know we're going to mobilise some assets, but could we get a little work done with regards to their missing operator, Hugo?" asked Helena.

Michael merely nodded, then Lars spoke up. "If Sir Goodlove and Abigail are in agreement, could Hobbs and Patterson send us what they have on Chloe? We can look it over again."

"Sounds good to me. I'll get that organised, unless you see a reason not to, Abigail?" said Sir Goodlove.

"It can't hurt at this stage. Thank you," said Abigail.

"I want everyone ready to leave in an hour. Each group will make its way to Calgary, and I'll have CSIS meet us at the other end. We don't have a presence in Calgary, so we'll be reliant on them for logistics," said Sir Goodlove.

"Agreed," said Helena, who got up from her seat, picked up her trusty briefcase, and headed for the door. As she passed Jessica and Shaukey, she said, "I want you moving with Andrew within the hour. I'll meet you in Calgary."

The room emptied, and the video links were disconnected. Andrew passed Patterson and Hobbs. "Good job, gentlemen."

"Sorry about the GCHQ computer. I hope it doesn't cause you too much trouble," said Hobbs.

"It's okay. If this turns into what I think it will, I am sure all sins will be forgiven."

"Do you think it's serious?" asked Hobbs.

"I do. There's something about all of this that still isn't clear, and that worries me," said Andrew.

"Can I ask you something, Andrew?" said Patterson.

"Of course."

"Why doesn't everyone travel together? Everyone seems to head off on their own, and then we have to get them together again. It seems a little disjointed."

Andrew smiled and said, "A little before your time, in 1994, there was a secret meeting up in Scotland. Twenty-five senior members of the intelligence community from police to military to MI5 were put into one Chinook helicopter. Seventeen minutes into their flight, while enveloped in thick fog, they crashed into a mountain. No survivors. It was a devastating loss, so from that day forward, key figures have never travelled together. The risk of a total loss like that is too much. Remember during an operation, if one man goes down, the world will adapt and move forward. It is only when the job's done that there's time to look back at where they fell."

He continued, "I want you both on standby. I know the Americans are working on it, but the more detail we can get on these Argentinians, the better. I think they will lead us to Khaleed and maybe Chloe. Perhaps work with Twyla and Lars so we're all on the same page."

"Yes, Andrew," Hobbs and Patterson replied together.

And then the room was empty.

CHAPTER 46

CALGARY, ALBERTA

Carl had arrived in Calgary, but prior to leaving their log cabin, the group had been given burner cell phones that would not be activated until they had reached their temporary headquarters. They knew the networks in and around Calgary would be swamped due to the influx of people, and it would be near on impossible to identify them amongst the deluge of call traffic. Safety in numbers and hiding in plain sight. After the attack, they'd destroy the phones and SIMs and simply vanish.

When Carl arrived in Calgary, he parked his truck and went for a walk. Carl liked the city—it seemed clean and modern, and people were generally in good spirits. He drew out his SLR camera and took alternating routes from their base of operations to determine which worked best for ease of movement without drawing attention. He also wanted to understand where he must lead everyone at the time of the attack.

As he walked the city's Plus 15, he saw a group of Calgary police officers. He watched them for a while and, using the large lens on his camera, took pictures. No one said a word. Then some kids asked the police officers to have their picture taken with them, and they obliged. In Argentina, if you were caught taking pictures of the police or even the police station, you'd be arrested and your camera seized. After that, Carl headed to the top of the Calgary Tower to enjoy the view and noted that through the glass floor, he had a clear sight of the final leg of the parade.

Johannes was next to arrive, and after calling Carl, they met at their base of operations, the subterranean office suite. Johannes had converted one of the larger offices into an operations room, fully equipped with video surveillance covering all access points to their floor, the corridors within it, and a few of their rooms. Johannes explained that he'd placed the repeaters on the floor, as communications were appalling. "If an unexpected visitor comes down, they'll be cut off from the outside world and probably won't discover that until it is too late. They'd need to know the correct radio channel and the right encryption to piggyback onto our channel and repeaters."

"Excellent," said Carl.

"Also, from here, there are four escape routes. One leads back into the building, one into the subterranean parking area, where our vehicles are parked, and two onto the street. I have placed cameras and sensors at these exit points so we can pick up anyone trying to gain entry."

"You have really done well here, Johannes. Good work. The others should be arriving soon, and we can make our final preparations," said Carl.

"Yes, we should all be assembled by this evening. We can

then perhaps individually spend time familiarising ourselves with the lay of the land, finding our positions, and rehearsing our movements."

CHAPTER 47

TRANS-CANADA HIGHWAY, EASTBOUND NEAR CANMORE

The Israel Defense Forces protection unit had rented three luxurious dark blue Cadillacs with tinted windows. They would alternate which car Yigal Eliezer rode in and where he would sit, usually instructing him to take his place in the back, looking almost childlike in the vast seats. Often, he would tell the protection officer to go in the back and relax so he could sit up front and talk to the driver. Noya wasn't always happy with this arrangement, but they didn't do it often, and they had practised what to do if they were attacked.

On this particular journey, Noya had joined him in the back, and an additional officer was up front in the passenger seat. "We should get to Calgary in good time this afternoon. We'll get you to your hotel, and then you can relax. Is there anything you would like to do this evening?"

Yigal considered the question for a moment, then said,

"We are heading back to Israel tomorrow evening, so tonight, I would like us all to eat dinner in my hotel room to say goodbye. We should break bread together and celebrate a good trip. Can we do that?"

"Yes, of course. We shall ask the hotel to have a table prepared in your room. In fact, let me call them now so they have time to arrange it."

"Do you think they can get it done?" said Yigal.

"The Fairmont Palliser can certainly get that done. I'm just calling out of courtesy to give them a bit of notice," said Noya.

"You are a good person, Noya," said Yigal.

Noya hung up the phone. "They said it was no problem. We are making good time, and it will only take us about an hour to get to the hotel. Is there anywhere you would like to go before we get to Calgary, or even when we're in Calgary?" asked Noya.

"No, it has been a long trip, and I am quite tired. I would like to go to the hotel and just rest. I would like your team to see Calgary, so perhaps when I am in my hotel room, you can let them go and have some time off. I may go to the spa, and I don't need everyone there with me. You should also go and enjoy the city," said Yigal, pointing at Noya.

The protection officers in the front of the vehicle both smiled. Noya, the team leader, was very good at sharing the workload amongst the staff. She ensured she gave them time away to decompress, but she rarely did the same for herself, and in Yigal's case, she was there from when he woke to when he went to bed. Only when she knew the team had him secured would she take a few hours to herself. She would go for a run if she could, but if she didn't want to leave the hotel, she would hit the stairwells and run them until exhausted. On other occasions, she would opt for the "prisoner workout" in her room.

Yigal continued, "Noya, I think it would be a good idea if we lunched before our arrival. When I was chatting with the families I met in the hotel, they mentioned a restaurant in Canmore called the Iron Goat. Do we have time to go there for lunch? My treat for you and the team," said Yigal.

"Of course, sir. I would need to call them and see if they could accommodate us," said Noya.

"Would we all be able to eat together?" asked Yigal.

"No, sir. We would need to have the team deployed, but we could have half the team eat and then switch," said Noya.

"You worry too much. Who would kill a little old Jewish man like me?" said Yigal, smiling at the protection officer in the front seat, who had turned to look at both of them. "But you are in charge, Noya, so you do what you think is best. I would like the last couple of days to be relaxing for us all."

The protection officer in the front had decided to call the Iron Goat and was heard asking if they would accept a party of eleven in two sittings in the next ten minutes. He got a yes, and as they were the lead vehicle, they instructed the others to follow.

The protection unit loved Yigal, not only because he was kind and compassionate, but also because of his legacy of being an amazing politician. As an Auschwitz survivor, after the war, he'd fought hard to bring justice for all those who had perished in the camps.

They exited the Trans-Canada Highway and were soon at the restaurant. They were seated outside on the patio, where they could enjoy a breathtaking view of the Rocky Mountains and the Three Sisters mountain range.

The protection force understood that Yigal was not a typical politician. They had all worked for those who would buy them gifts as a thank-you or take them out for dinner, then submit their expenses, and the state of Israel would foot the bill. But they knew Yigal would never do this.

There was snow on the mountaintops and a chill in the air—Yigal needed a blanket to cover his legs to keep him warm. Onlookers smiled at the most cared-for and looked-after grandfather in the world.

CHAPTER 48

INTERVIEW ROOM, THE VENUE

Peter had been placed in an interview room since his arrival and was still wearing the tracksuit and sneakers he'd been given at the safe house. The door glided open, and there stood Devon and the Matron.

"Has there been any news on Chloe?" was his first question.

"Yes, there has. She was seen boarding a private jet with someone we assume was Hugo, about one mile away from where Hugo's vehicle was found. There was blood in the back of the car, which we believe is Chloe's, and also the hood she was wearing when she was taken from the safe house. Oh, and before you ask, the video surveillance was down, so we don't have anything to show what condition she was in," said Devon.

"So, what's the plan?" asked Peter.

"Before we get to that, I need to ask you if Chloe made any mention of Canada, Calgary, or something called the

Stampede?" asked Devon.

Peter thought for a moment. "Doesn't ring a bell with me. Is that where they think she is?"

"We believe an attack is planned to take place at the Stampede parade. You, me, and the Matron are going to travel to Calgary to locate and secure Chloe."

The Matron then stepped forward. "Before we go, I want you to understand our position regarding Chloe. It's still not clear what her agenda is or where her allegiances lie. For this reason, we must at the outset withhold prejudice, but the moment she compromises the safety of myself or anyone on this operation, I won't hesitate to kill her."

The Matron's expression was now emotionless and focused directly on Peter. "And if, because of your emotional attachment to Chloe, you compromise the safety of myself or this team, I won't hesitate to kill you either. Understand?"

Peter replied, "I get it. Don't worry."

"I hope you do," said Devon. "The stakes surrounding this mission are high, and feelings need to be put to the side. I would like to find Chloe and discover that she has been used to misdirect us all. If this is not the case, and you hesitate or do something that puts anyone at risk, you will be dropped without a thought."

"I said I get it. Chloe has been used by whomever is pulling the strings. I want to find her and clear her name. But don't worry, if she is working for the wrong side, I won't get in your way." said Peter.

Devon exited briefly, then reappeared with a large bag. "Clothes—your kind neighbour let one of our men into your house, and we've had them couriered here, special delivery, cheaper and quicker than taking you shopping. Find something else to wear—you look ridiculous in that."

The Matron then produced a handgun with two additional magazines. "It's loaded and made ready. Put it on your belt and keep it in the holster unless you're going to use it. Do not tuck it into your waistband. This isn't a movie. We can't have you out there with your dick in your hands."

"We'll wait outside. You have ten minutes," said Devon.

CHAPTER 49

HANGAR 2, RAF BRIZE NORTON, ENGLAND

Helena was first to arrive. Her small private jet was fuelled and ready to go. She was on the phone with Michael in Langley, asking him what assets would be available when she arrived. He explained they had no resources in the country, but they were on their way now.

She boarded, along with everyone else, who were carrying bags and equipment, and took a spacious leather seat. She ended her call, then called the Canadian Secret Intelligence Service. Each region of Canada has its own director, and the one for Alberta was based out of Edmonton.

A man named Robert Courtenay answered, "Hello? How can I help you?"

"Robert, it's Helena from the NSA. I'm on my way to Calgary with a few of my people, and we could do with some local assistance."

"Ah yes, we got a call from Sir Goodlove. I'm getting my people moving, and we're trying to get information on this Khaleed man. He's been on our radar because of his association with Abdulahi Sharif. The university is shut down for the summer, but we're doing what we can. The Edmonton Police Special Branch is also helping us," said Robert.

"But can you support us locally in Calgary?" asked Helena.

"Yes, of course. I should be there in four hours. We have an operations room in the Eighth Avenue Plaza in the city centre. We're linked in to the camera feed, plus we have access to the cameras from the Calgary Police RTOC—Real Time Operations Centre—as well as their radio systems, so with any luck, we can listen in, too."

"That's excellent, but isn't that going to be a nightmare with the Stampede?" asked Helena.

"Did you know that Paris has an almost exact duplicate of itself running under the city? There are streets big enough for vehicles, useable sidewalks, and roadways. You could traverse the entire city underground if you needed to," said Robert.

"Okay, interesting. But that doesn't really answer my question," said Helena.

"Calgary has a similar system, but it only covers the city centre and about ten blocks in every direction. You can go anywhere in the city using the tunnels. We have taken control of the area under our building and turned it into a bunker, with all the necessary tech and home comforts. Your guys can get wherever they need to without having to navigate the parade or the crowds," said Robert.

Surprised, Helena replied, "I had no idea, and that will be very helpful. Okay, we'll be there in the early hours tomorrow. I'm going to try to grab some sleep now. Thanks again, and see you tomorrow."

"It's the least we could do. Have a good sleep, and see you soon."

*

HANGAR 4, RAF BRIZE NORTON, ENGLAND, UK

Jessica's team rolled into the RAF base, and a young gentleman in a green Land Rover waved for them to follow him. The rain had now started in earnest, and the young RAF corporal wasn't going to get out and do the usual meet-and-greet.

The wipers swished on full speed as the driver squinted through the windscreen, following the tail-lights of the car in front. Finally, they arrived at their hangar. The plane looked like a commercial airliner, with the colourings on the side denoting the RAF.

The Land Rover stopped and, now sheltered, the young man leapt out and came to the driver's window.

The driver pointed at Jessica. "She's the boss. You can update her, please."

"Yes, of course," said the young man, who darted around the front of the vehicle to Jessica's window.

He then gave instructions for unloading and parking the vehicles and asked if Jessica had any questions.

"No, that's fine. Thank you."

"You're welcome, and have a safe trip," said the young man, who then jogged back to his vehicle.

Jessica got out, patting one hand on the top of her head, the universal military signal for On Me.

When everyone had gathered around, she repeated the soldier's instructions. "Once onboard, we need to get to work. Okay, let's go." She turned to Shaukey. "Can you grab my bags?

I'm going to speak to the crew."

"Yes, ma'am," said Shaukey.

On the plane, Jessica discovered it was indeed a commercial aircraft, but the rear was arranged as an office. As the group boarded, she directed the analysts to this area to get organised.

"How long 'til we set off?" Jessica asked the crew, who replied they were ready to go as soon as they got the green light from her.

The captain confirmed that the flight time to Calgary was eight hours.

Andrew had appeared, now in jeans, a shirt, and a sports jacket.

"Ah, the casual version," smirked Jessica.

"Why, thank you. I thought I might blend in a little better. I'll get my stuff on board, then come and help with the rest of the loading." He headed up the stairs.

After a flurry of activity at the back of the plane, Shaukey called out, "Jessica, we're good to go."

"Okay. Once we're airborne, we'll have a planning meeting," said Jessica.

The Delta operators then appeared. "Hey, guys. The aircrew say no loaded weapons on the plane, which I don't think is unreasonable. Shaukey, make sure everyone is good to go. You can keep your sidearms with you—they can be loaded, but not made ready."

"Sounds good," said Shaukey. "Okay, gents, you heard the boss lady. Let's get these vehicles squared away and make our guns flight-ready. Come on, let's go!"

Shortly after, they were cruising out of the hangar and into the rain that was now hammering down. Jessica sat by herself in a window seat and looked out on the miserable June day.

Just an hour earlier, it had been a beautiful summer day.

As Jessica gazed out of the window, half-listening to the captain's safety instructions, she saw a vehicle pull up to a small jet, one of those with the stairs inset into the door itself. She then spotted the occupants, three of them, exit the car and make for the plane.

She recognised the Matron and Devon, and as Peter appeared, she whispered, "There you are, Mr. Special Branch."

She watched as long as she could until her plane turned and made its way to the runway.

*

HANGAR 5, RAF BRIZE NORTON, ENGLAND, UK

Peter, the Matron, and Devon boarded the plane. With only three of them, they had plenty of space.

"Are we expecting anyone else?" asked the co-pilot.

"No," Devon answered.

"Okay, we're all here then," the co-pilot said, and almost immediately, the plane started to move and the co-pilot brought up the door. Then, using the intercom, he went through the safety procedures, including the rules for weapons.

There was then a universal un-holstering of weapons, and Peter noticed Devon watching him like a hawk. He made his weapon safe and, after re-holstering it, sat back and shut his eyes. *They really don't trust me. I'm going to have to keep my head on a swivel when we get to Calgary.*

*

HANGAR 12, RAF BRIZE NORTON, ENGLAND, UK

As head of MI6, Abigail had a jet standing by 24-7. It was big enough to comfortably hold eight, but it was normally just her and perhaps her assistant.

"Just the two of you again, ma'am?" asked a crew member.

Abigail was on the phone, so her assistant answered, "Yes, just us. Thank you."

As the plane taxied to the runway, the crew member instructed them to take their seats and ready themselves for a rough take-off.

Rather like Jessica's plane, this one also had an office, and Abigail was already busy at the desk. While her assistant took their seat, she stayed where she was. Her chair was on runners, which could be locked, and using a handle, she secured it and checked her seatbelt.

It was quite clear that the seat at the desk could move when needed, but during take-off and landing, it could be locked in place. Abigail had obviously spent many flights at her desk, because the cabin crew member smiled and left Abigail to it.

CHAPTER 50

TRUCK STOP, AIRDRIE

Alicia had arrived in Calgary, but she didn't go to meet Carl and Johannes. She had arranged to meet the contact from Alaska who was bringing the M134 Miniguns.

There was an industrial area on the outskirts of the city of Airdrie, twenty minutes north of Calgary. The large semi-truck was carrying equipment used for oil and gas production and extraction. Calgary was a large oil and gas city, so if the truck was stopped, the inventory wouldn't raise any alarms.

The M134s and ammunition were packed inside two hard cases hidden amongst the semi-truck's cargo. Alicia was concerned as to how she would get them to her room. With all the activity at the Stampede, they wouldn't look out of place, but she didn't want to take a chance. She decided to make those journeys at night-time when there was less chance of being seen.

The two men from Alaska parked the semi-truck in a long line of other trucks. They were all facing the same way, and the rear of the truck could be accessed using a service road. The two-lane service road was bordered by a high fence that was heavily overgrown with trees and bushes. This meant that, when standing in the trailer, you couldn't be seen unless you were standing directly behind the truck itself on the service road. Alicia liked this.

The two men were not the usual neo-Nazi type. No skinheads, bomber jackets, or obvious swastika tattoos. They had the air of military about them, and they were both most certainly armed.

Alicia talked to the one who was clearly in charge, and the other man positioned himself to cover the meeting and watch Alicia—a tactic known by the police as "cover contact," where one officer does the talking and the other provides safety cover.

The man said, "You can call me the Alaskan, and this is my friend Billy. What do we call you?"

"You can call me whatever you like, Mr. Alaskan. Now open the cases so I can inspect what we asked for," said Alicia.

"Suit yourself," said the Alaskan who opened the four cases.

In the darkened semi-truck trailer, Alicia pulled out a flashlight and inspected the weapons and ammunition.

"Know what you're looking at, sweetheart?" asked the Alaskan, smiling, which seemed to amuse the other man.

"How about I take it out and give you a demonstration," said Alicia, without turning to look at them. A few minutes later, she ordered, "This all looks good. Let's get it loaded into my vehicle."

"Easy, sweetheart. First, where's our money?" said the Alaskan.

"Yes, of course." Alicia drew out her cell phone, then called a number and spoke in fluent Austrian to whoever was on the other end. She didn't have to speak Austrian, but the two from Alaska wouldn't know it wasn't German and would just love it.

"The money has been transferred?" asked Alicia.

The Alaskan walked away from Alicia, leaving her with Billy, and made a call. After a short period, he was back, saying everything was good to go. He put out his hand. "It's good doing business with you."

Alicia shook the hand of the Alaskan and then Billy. They were smiling and laughing, obviously excited at making the deal and getting their money.

Alicia disappeared and arrived back with her F-150. She'd gone to the trouble of renting a vehicle with a topper that covered the rear cargo area. She asked the two men to help her move the boxes into the truck, which they agreed to do.

The F-150 was backed onto the rear of the semi-truck, and even with the height difference, the cases were slid into the truck bed and secured. The two Alaskans were inside the semi-truck and pushed them across before walking back to the other end and wheeling out the next box. When Alicia was happy the boxes were secured, she went to the back of the F-150's loading area. As she came back to the tail of his truck, she was in a half-squat position due to the height and space inside.

"Thank you, gentlemen. You have been most helpful."

"You're welcome. Now, you go give those cowboys hell," said the Alaskan.

"Excuse me? What do you mean?" asked Alicia, looking a little concerned.

"Don't treat us like idiots. You don't ask for something like this unless you're going to make a statement, and we know the

Stampede starts tomorrow. Don't worry, sister, we figured it out when we were driving down here," said Billy, speaking for the first time.

"Did you tell anyone about your discussion?" asked Alicia, looking down at the bed of the truck in contemplation.

"Of course not. We aren't stupid," replied Billy, who was getting braver.

Alicia climbed down from the truck and closed the tailgate on the topper. She used the keys to lock the back of the truck and then placed them inside her jacket pocket. She looked carefully to the left and right to make sure no one was around. As she removed her hand again, she produced her suppressed sidearm. Turning carefully, she raised the gun up at the two men. Aiming from below, Alicia shot the Alaskan under the chin, causing the top of his head to open up like a fountain. Billy was trying to go for his weapon, backing into the truck, but he only made it one step before Alicia shot him in the chest. He fell to the ground, and Alicia moved to his left to get a better angle. Then she shot Billy in the head.

"Amateurs," she muttered to herself.

She placed her gun out of sight and moved the F-150 forward a little, then returned to the semi-truck and closed the doors.

CHAPTER 51

JESSICA'S PLANE, SOMEWHERE OVER THE ATLANTIC OCEAN

Jessica and her team had settled in to the flight, and most people were either sleeping or relaxing. One of her group had established communications and been speaking with Helena about her contact with Robert and CSIS.

Then Jessica had a videoconference with Twyla and Lars to find out about any updates they may have.

"I'm glad CSIS were able to provide us with a base. I wasn't looking forward to integrating ourselves with the city or the police," said Jessica.

"Agreed," said Shaukey. "I've confirmed we'll only have our Delta group on the ground. There isn't time to get any more to Calgary. I plan to put myself in the operations room, then split my four guys into pairs so they can deploy as needed."

"What about having CSIS get some JTF 2?" asked Jessica.

"Maybe, but my guys can cover it. If need be, I can ask

the Calgary Police Tactical Unit to support us. I worked with them before, and they are incredibly effective. It would be an easier option for us," said Shaukey.

Jessica then turned to the screens and asked Lars and Twyla what they had.

Lars spoke. "About four weeks ago, there was a break-in at a US military testing facility in Alaska. A number of weapons were stolen, and it was thought that a right-wing extremist group had carried out the theft, or at least had someone carry it out for them.

"The ATF, working with the FBI, traced the weapons and the perpetrators to a warehouse in Anchorage about two days after the theft. They raided the place and recovered pretty much everything that was stolen."

"How on earth did they find the weapons so quickly?" asked Shaukey.

"I believe it was source information. Considering what they told us, I am going with that hypothesis," said Twyla.

"Okay, what did they tell us? What wasn't recovered, as I feel that is relevant?" asked Jessica.

Lars answered, "Some handguns, some C8 rifles, and two M134s. With ammunition."

The M134s caused a few eyebrows to rise.

"Just to make everyone aware, an M134 is a Minigun that can shoot two to six thousand rounds per minute. Twenty-five thousand rounds were also stolen with the Miniguns. Each gun. So, fifty thousand in total," said Lars.

He adjusted his notes in front of him and continued, "Now, this is the interesting part. The military base the Miniguns were stolen from is a facility used for testing. They send military personnel, weapons, vehicles, and technical equipment to this base to be tested in cold weather environments before they're deployed. The two stolen M134s were unique, as they had an integrated, computerised system that would allow them to be activated and controlled remotely. They wanted the system to be tested under freezing conditions. According to the FBI, it worked well. It can be controlled from your cell phone, or you can program the weapons for specific dates and times for them to become active. When activated, the built-in software of the Miniguns detects motion and will shoot at anything that moves.

"The FBI and ATF told us they had further information that these two weapons in particular were en route to somewhere in Canada. Their source has no idea where exactly and who in the group took them. They're trying to determine who may have them. They did say that the group in Alaska is quite large, so this may take some time."

Jessica and Shaukey looked at each other, and Jessica spoke first. "These guns could be placed somewhere on the parade route and activated when it's in full swing. With all those people, it would be a massacre."

"Agreed," said Shaukey. "Maybe they would cancel the parade if we told them this information."

"Helena had already considered that, but her contact in CSIS mentioned that the threat wasn't specific enough to justify canceling the parade. However, they have increased security measures and are conducting thorough searches of attendees. Additionally, more special branch and counterterrorism tactical assets are being deployed," said Twyla.

"Okay, well, there's work to do. I want the images of the five Argentinians given to the Calgary Police Services Special Branch. We need to quietly speak to hotel managers, business owners, and office corporate security and see if any of them have secured an area where these weapons could be placed. They can start with the parade route and work their way outwards from there. Shaukey, when we get to Calgary, I want your team to look for these guns. Andrew and I will focus on Khaleed. Agreed?" said Jessica.

Shaukey nodded and said, "I'll let my guys sleep and update them later. If there isn't anything else, I'm going to get my head down, too."

"Sure, go ahead. I won't be far behind you," replied Jessica. She looked up at the screen. "Twyla and Lars, please update Helena and Abigail. Andrew, is there anything else you think we should be telling Abigail at this time?"

Andrew thought for a moment, then said, "No, nothing at this point. I confirmed before we left that we don't have any assets on the ground, but I agree with Shaukey that we should use the Calgary Police Tactical Unit if needed."

"Okay, ladies and gents, we'll be on the ground in Calgary in about six hours, so I suggest we all try to get some rest. Tomorrow's going to be a long day."

CHAPTER 52

FAIRMONT PALLISER, CALGARY

Noya had sent one vehicle ahead in preparation for their arrival. They were greeted by the advance team, who guided them directly into the underground parkade.

The vehicle stopped by the elevators, and Yigal and Noya were met by another protection officer, who had the elevator ready for them. They exited on their floor, where the remaining members of the advance team were waiting, and were ushered into the already secure room. It was a very large suite that looked out over the main highway, and Yigal could see the barriers already in place for the parade.

It was about 3:00 p.m. Yigal said he wanted to rest and that everyone from the team should meet at 8:00 p.m. in his room for dinner.

Noya said that would be fine, and after ensuring the team had secured Yigal in his room, she decided it was time for a workout. She quickly got changed and made her way to the basement, where they had a good gym available. She did a circuit with some of her team, and an hour later, she was back in her room, showering and getting ready for the evening.

If his staff wasn't deploying in the evening, Yigal insisted they could wear jeans and polo shirts instead of business suits.

Noya stated that she was going to walk the route to their morning appointment. It ran from the east side of the hotel and then branched off north. The Plus 15 crossed over the streets, and since the walls were glass, it gave a good view of the traffic below.

Noya didn't like that, from the brightly lit streets, you would move into a building through heavy doors and into what seemed like complete darkness. At almost every Plus 15, there were stairs or an escalator to take you to the street. She decided she would move a vehicle early in the morning to the Calgary Telus Convention Centre opposite Olympic Plaza, leaving the remaining two at the Palliser.

If they were compromised at the convention centre, the team would extract from there. If they were attacked en route to or from the convention centre, it would be a decision as to where to go. Noya had gone onto YouTube and watched footage of the parade from previous years and decided that trying to extract Yigal from the street was not an option.

She walked behind the Calgary Tower and then north to the convention centre. The staff there were amazing and went out of their way to show Noya around and to the spot where the plaque was going to be unveiled. Noya spent a good hour on her reconnaissance and was happy with her plans. She got back to Yigal's just as everyone was about to sit down.

When she entered the room, the team, including Yigal,

stood up. She was the only woman amongst them, and all the men were wearing a kippah. She gestured with her hand for them to sit, except for the two men who had escorted her in, who made their way back out to guard the door.

"Could we just once have everyone together, Noya? Please? For me?" asked Yigal.

All eyes turned to Noya, and she said, "I shall secure the door, and we can have one hour together. I have placed a motion sensor camera outside, so if anyone comes onto the floor, it will alert us. Each member of my team can have a single small glass of wine."

"Thank you, Noya," said Yigal.

That hour together was the most relaxed anyone had been on the trip. They laughed, joked, and told stories about their families, their children, and what they were looking forward to when they got back to Israel.

When dinner was finished, Yigal stood up, and the group fell silent. "I wanted to say thank you to all of you for keeping me safe on this little adventure of ours to Canada. When I look at all your young faces, it reminds me of my friends before the war and the hope we all had. The things we do today echo in our lives forever. When I look at you, I know that when you are as old as me, you will have a sense of pride in who you have become. L'chaim."

Everyone in the group stood up and, lifting their drinks, said together, "L'chaim."

"Now, my youthful friends, it is time for this man's bedtime." Yigal went into his room and closed the door behind him.

"Okay, everyone. Let's get into our night routine. I shall be back at 11:00 p.m. for the last check-in, and then it is time to rest up," said Noya.

CHAPTER 53

CALGARY AIRPORT

There were a number of hangars on the outer edges of the Calgary airport that could accommodate large aircraft. CSIS had ensured that the planes arriving from England were directed into them, along with the waiting vehicles and staff.

Helena arrived first at just after 5:00 a.m. and was immediately informed that Robert was on his way and she was to be taken straight to the operations room.

"What about the others? Do you know?" asked Helena.

"They'll be here within an hour. We want to make sure we get you into the operations room before the police finish shutting the city down," said the CSIS member.

Helena and her team climbed into the SUVs. After her gear was loaded, they headed downtown.

Jessica, Abigail, and Peter's planes landed in quick succession, and they opted to travel in convoy to Calgary.

Since there was no general communication on their plane, Peter, the Matron, and Devon were updated as they stood in the hangar. They seemed a lot happier with the arrangement made with CSIS. They were also informed that the Calgary Police Service Special Branch had started making discreet enquiries about the group of Argentinians.

As they were getting organised, Abigail called out to Andrew, "I want you to ride with me. I need to talk to you."

Without hesitation, he walked from his designated vehicle and climbed into the back of Abigail's SUV.

Once they were on their way, Andrew turned to Abigail. "What do you need to speak to me about?"

"Oh, nothing really. I just wanted the company and to ask if there was anything said on the plane worth knowing."

"No, ma'am. It sounds like Helena has been in contact with your CSIS counterpart, so we shouldn't have any jurisdiction issues. The ops hub is really well equipped, and it's integrated into the city's underground Plus 15 network."

"Oh, yes, that," said Abigail. "I hear you can get anywhere in Calgary without being on street level. It could come in handy if the parade shuts the city down like they say it will." Andrew, I do consider that there is more to this situation than meets the eye. Whoever we're dealing with seems to be keeping one step ahead of us. We need to focus our attention on the parade and locating this Khaleed and the M134s. But I wonder how much of this is just misdirection," said Abigail.

"With all due respect, ma'am, you're a seasoned spy, which makes you suspicious of everything. If it is a diversion, it seems like a lot of unnecessary work. I mean, set a car bomb off, or just threaten that there is one. That'd be a lot easier," said Andrew.

Abigail sighed. "You're probably right, but we need to be careful, and I don't want any more surprises. Also, try to keep an eye on Peter, the Matron, and Devon. I am suspicious of them, particularly Peter. Lastly, the word is 'experienced', not 'seasoned.' I'm not that old."

"Agreed, ma'am. Will do. Experienced it is."

CHAPTER 54

UNDERGROUND PARKADE, EIGHTH AVENUE PLACE

When the large convoy arrived, a CSIS officer greeted them all.

"Good morning, ladies and gentlemen. Your colleague Helena is here and has already been taken up to the operations floor. There's another subterranean floor above this one, which contains your living quarters, meeting rooms, and so on. The functioning office floor includes meeting rooms, a gym, accommodation for sleeping, a conference room, a kitchen, and more. Operations are on the tenth floor, and we will take you all there now in stages. There are three elevators, so we'll help some of you get organised on the floor above. The rest of you are going straight to the tenth floor. We have about four hours before the parade starts and the city is locked down. Any questions?"

Everyone moved in silence, like a well-oiled machine, and the CSIS officers started to introduce themselves to the new arrivals corralling kit and equipment.

Jessica told Shaukey to take his men to the floor above and get settled in. She would take the analysts up to the operations room.

Shaukey was impressed by the subterranean floor. As people were moving their equipment into one of the staging areas, Helena could be seen in a soundproof, probably bulletproof, glass conference room, speaking on the phone. There was a large oval-shaped desk in the middle and a number of leather office chairs evenly spaced around it. Helena saw Shaukey, and with her free hand, beckoned him to come in. Shaukey nodded in acknowledgment and, after dumping some kit, joined her.

"Can you just hold on a second?" asked Helena, placing the phone on her shoulder. "Is everyone here now?"

"Yes, we are all here and getting operational, ma'am. Any updates?"

"No, nothing of significance. My CSIS colleague, Robert, is still working on the Khaleed angle. I understand that the Calgary Police Special Branch has the images of the five Argentinians and is trying to identify where these Miniguns may be. Is that right?" asked Helena.

"Yes, ma'am. If there isn't anything else, I'll carry on," said Shaukey.

"No, nothing else from me. I'll catch up with you later," said Helena.

As he left, he asked the CSIS officer, "Why's there another door in there? It doesn't look like you can get to it from the outside."

"There are lots of them in this building—they lead to the underground roadway or pathway system. When this area was designed, they were put in place as emergency exits. You can come in that way, but you would have to navigate through the passageways outside first, and of course have the right swipe card," said the CSIS officer.

Shaukey smiled. "You've covered all bases. Very impressive."

"Yes, we have. Thank you."

It reminded Shaukey of the fully functional subterranean operational floors at the Pentagon. There was a marine warrant officer who had responsibility for them. He was the most efficient and organised man Shaukey had ever seen. He never seemed to sleep and could have anything you needed with what seemed like a simple phone call.

He'd been at the Pentagon during the attacks of 9/11. When the plane hit, he felt the vibration through the building, and it wasn't long before some of the injured started coming down the stairs. Shaukey and the marine warrant officer had gone back up and found more injured staff, who they picked up and carried down to the makeshift triage area. They must have brought at least twenty-five people each down about five floors, the cries and whimpers of victims echoing on the concrete walls of the smoke-filled stairwells. Sometimes, as they went to pick someone up, their charred skin would slide off, but they'd grab them anyway, trying to ignore their sickening screams of agony as their skin fell away, exposing raw nerves. Shaukey went to lift a Navy officer, then looked to see his arm had been severed and was still on the floor. He gathered it up and took it down with him.

The story wasn't common knowledge, as a lot of staff didn't want to be interviewed or even identified due to the nature of their work. Shaukey, the marine warrant officer, and other staff members received recognition for their bravery from the director of the Pentagon in a closed-door presentation.

After the presentation, the marine warrant officer pulled Shaukey aside and gave him a custom-made Velcro patch. The date 9/11 was embroidered on it, and if you looked closely, there was a little mole peeking its head out. He handed Shaukey the patch with a discreet nod. No words were needed— Shaukey understood. He'd accrued a number of patches throughout his time with the military, but he always placed this unique Pentagon patch on his operational body armour. When his world was starting to become a little unglued, it was a gentle reminder of what they were working towards.

*

Meanwhile, Helena was updating Abigail that Robert Courtenay, the CSIS contact, was on his way.

"His guys are trying to track down this Khaleed character. He'll call if he gets anything," said Helena.

"Sounds good. We need to catch a break on this mission, so let's keep our fingers crossed," Abigail replied.

CHAPTER 55

STUDENT ACCOMMODATION, UNIVERSITY OF CALGARY

There was a carnival atmosphere at the University of Calgary campus, with students throwing pop-up parties and the whole accommodation block being taken over with Stampede fever.

"Good morning, Khaleed. How are you doing today? I didn't recognise you," his professor said as the student sat down. The last time he'd seen Khaleed, he'd had long, unkempt hair and a beard. He hadn't really liked it, and he'd only grown it to annoy the police. His friends would laugh as they said he looked more and more like a member of the Taliban every day. But today, his hair was cut with a short, tidy back and sides, and the beard was gone.

"Good, thank you. Yes, I thought it was about time I tidied up a little. I even have a cowboy hat for the parade. How are you doing this morning?" answered Khaleed.

"Yee-haw, Khaleed! I'm glad you're embracing the whole

experience. I'm curious to know if you've heard from Professor Huber. She was meant to join us this morning, but we can't reach her," said the lecturer.

"No, I haven't. We last spoke at the university just after I got back from my trip," said Khaleed.

"Okay. Maybe she's on her way."

"Yes, perhaps," said Khaleed.

"We're going to have breakfast and rally everyone together. Then we'll head over to the truck and get ready." Smiling, he leaned in to Khaleed and whispered, "I am glad to see you didn't overindulge like the others did last night."

"I have a big responsibility driving the truck today. I want to be clearheaded for what is ahead of me. Perhaps tonight I'll have an extra beer to celebrate," said Khaleed.

"And I'll raise a beer with you, Khaleed, that's for sure. Now, go enjoy your breakfast—we leave in one hour."

CHAPTER 56

ARGENTINIANS' SUBTERRANEAN OPERATIONAL AREA

Carl and his four comrades stood in the meeting room of their rented office floor. Not that they knew it, but the layout bore a striking resemblance to that of their pursuers', just across town, with its glass rooms and escape doors.

"The time is upon us, brothers and sisters. We have come so far, and we are now going to change history. Alicia, are we ready with the M134s?"

"Yes, I have them, and late last night, I positioned them. I will be in the Plus 15, and when I get the signal, I shall activate the guns. If our timing is correct, the Oilman will be in place," said Alicia.

"Excellent work. Augustus, any updates?" asked Carl.

"I know that our target is here and has his own protection, led by a female. They are still scheduled to be at their appearance at 10:00 a.m. Another item of note is that a British man was interested in Caeli's death. He asked the local police to look around your apartment, Carl," said Augustus.

"Yes, I know about that. Benjamin updated me and also told me a team of counterterrorism specialists are on their way to Calgary. If they're good—and I think they are—they are probably already here," said Carl.

"Should we be concerned?" said Johannes, sounding alarmed.

"Don't worry, I had anticipated this, and Benjamin will keep us updated. Also, we cannot say 'Forward as One' again. . . ." Carl paused, distracted by something beyond the glass.

They all turned to see Chloe being escorted by Hugo to the operations room. Stone-faced, Chloe merely glanced at the five friends. Hugo gave them an almost indistinguishable nod and kept walking.

"Who is that?" said Hanna.

"Benjamin wanted them here today. They are not our concern—we need to be ready. I want us to go over the plan again. Grab a coffee and something to eat, and be back here in ten minutes," said Carl.

Then he made his way to where Chloe was being held.

Chloe was standing at the far end, looking dishevelled. Carl could see blood on her face and arm. She looked sleep-deprived.

"Benjamin told me you were coming. They didn't give me any names, but they asked me to get you cleaned up. There are some clothes in that bag. The bathroom is that way and it has one shower."

He turned to Hugo. "We'll be leaving in about two hours, so please factor that in if you need us for anything."

"My friends and I are having a briefing before making our

preparations. If you need anything, come to me. Go to no one else—just me," ordered Carl.

"Yes, sir," said Hugo.

Carl returned to his meeting.

CHAPTER 57

TENTH-FLOOR CSIS OPERATIONS ROOM

The windowless operations room was a hive of activity as the CSIS staff mingled with Jessica's analysts, synchronising their systems and data.

Twyla and Lars had been brought up on video links. Hobbs and Patterson were also online.

"Okay, what have you got?" asked Helena.

"We've identified three members of the group entering Canada. They are travelling under false identities, but we have confirmed Carl, Hanna, and Augustus. That leaves one member called Johannes and another called Alicia," Lars said as one of the CSIS analysts brought up the five photos of the Argentinians taken from their passport applications.

"These images have been passed to Calgary Police Special Branch, and they are making enquiries to find out if they've been spotted in the city. Before anyone asks, yes, they do have cameras in the city, but they're limited, and there's no facial recognition. We're doing this the old-fashioned way, boots-on-the-ground style," said Twyla.

One of the CSIS analysts said, "If they're here, Special Branch will find them. We've used them before. They're very good."

"Seems like a needle in a haystack, but I like your confidence," said Jessica.

Abigail looked at Hobbs and Patterson. "Anything from you two?"

"Not regarding the Argentinians—we've been working with Twyla and Lars, so we have the same intelligence as they do. But we did find out more about the two planes that left the private airfield in the UK, the one we think Chloe and Hugo may have used. The plane leaving to the south of France was carrying a gentleman and his mistress, heading out for a naughty weekend, so no joy there. But the plane to Red Deer landed, and the staff said that a male and female got off and left in an unmarked vehicle. They said that the female was very quiet, didn't make eye contact with anyone, and appeared to need help getting into the vehicle. The RCMP Special Branch is trying to identify the vehicle and where it went. So far, they have it leaving Red Deer on a major highway that could take them either north or south," said Hobbs.

"I'm going to work with the hypothesis that it was Chloe, and she's been taken to Calgary," said Abigail.

"I agree," said Helena. "I don't believe our plans need to change at this stage—" She broke off, as her phone started ringing. Looking at the screen, she said, "It's Robert from CSIS. I'll take it in the conference room."

She entered the room as the others watched the camera

feeds of the growing crowds in Calgary. The police were taking their positions along the route, and the parade marshals had arrived.

"We need a break soon. This thing is about to start, and we're no further forward," said Peter.

"I am sure something will come up," said the Matron.

Helena returned. "Okay, I spoke with Robert, who's on his way from Edmonton. He tells me they have found a professor who knows where Khaleed may be, and they're speaking to her now. Also, the truck they're using for the parade is a basic semi-truck with a solid black truck unit. It will be pulling a flatbed behind it, and they're trying to obtain contact details for a university staff member here, so we can speak with them."

"Any chance we can get a list of parade participants and what order they're in?" asked Devon.

A CSIS analyst shouted across the room. "Yes, we're asking for that. I'll keep you posted."

Devon thanked him.

Andrew glanced at Abigail. "Penny for them, ma'am."

"If you were going to use Miniguns, how would you do it?" asked Abigail.

Peter watched the Special Forces personnel drawing on their skills and experience as they considered this question. One of the Delta operators said, "I used one of these guns in Afghanistan —it had to be in a mounted position because moving it was challenging. It weighs a ton, even without the ammo. For this gig, I'd say they're going to be in a fixed position. And sorry, guys, but my gut's telling me they're going to be remotely activated. Setting a timer wouldn't be as reliable because if there's any kind of delay, the guns'll go off and miss their targets."

"Agreed," said Devon. "I'd have them situated at the most densely populated part of the parade and set to activate thirty to sixty seconds apart. When the first gun goes off, people run from where the rounds are landing straight into the firing line of the second gun."

The Matron, looking at the cameras, said, "I'd choose the area in and around the Calgary Tower. The attackers will be after the highest casualty rate, but also an iconic location so that it becomes synonymous with the attack. Every time it's mentioned in the future, people will remember it, especially now that this kind of thing gets instantly broadcast around the world by every news outlet and plastered all over social media."

The group didn't disagree, and when they looked at the TV screens, they did indeed see a large collection of people all around the Calgary Tower.

A CSIS analyst then called out, "Okay, it's started. The front of the parade will get to the tower in sixty minutes."

CHAPTER 58

CSIS OPERATIONS ROOM

Everyone had migrated into the next-door briefing room to get away from the noise of phones and the distraction of screens; the analysts needed some quiet to work. Desperate for a coffee, Jessica had offered to make everyone a drink, so that she could have one herself, just the way she liked it, and she was busy at the hot-drink-making station. She passed a cup to one of the Delta operators, who gratefully took a sip, but then said, "Eugh, no sugar!"

Rolling her eyes, Jessica threw a packet of sugar across the table. It was a terrible throw, and as the operator lurched to his right, sending his coffee flying, Helena's beloved briefcase crashed off the table, its contents spilling everywhere.

"Ah, shit," said Jessica as she put her coffee down and rounded the table. "No girls-can't-throw jokes, please."

"I am saying nothing," said the Delta operator, who was

now happily pouring sugar into his coffee.

"Too easy, Jessica, but please let me know if you plan to throw any grenades so I can politely get out of the way." Shaukey laughed.

Helena had been on her phone at the other end of the room, and on seeing her briefcase clatter to the ground, she rushed over, but Jessica had already rounded the table and gestured to Helena that she was fine to pick everything up. She gathered up the paperwork and shuffled it into a neater bundle. The briefcase still lay on the floor, splayed open, and Jessica took it, making sure the flap was flipped over so she could push everything back in. She paused slightly as she guided the paper inside, making sure not to damage anything.

Helena stood right behind Jessica, hand outstretched to take the bag. Still on the phone, she smiled, mouthed "Thank you," and retreated to her previous position.

Jessica nodded, retrieved her coffee, and sat down.

"Hey, you okay?" asked the Matron.

"Yes, of course. Miles away. Sorry," replied Jessica.

Lars, Twyla, Hobbs, and Patterson continued their work, occasionally conferring with one another but mostly tapping furiously at their keyboards, gazing at their screens, then tapping again. Everyone else was in hiatus mode, having those pointless conversations when nervously waiting for something.

As Helena ended her call, Jessica said, "What's the latest?"

"Oh, nothing really," replied Helena. "Nothing we don't already know." She then picked up her briefcase. "My liaison from CSIS is almost here—I'd like you to meet him, Jessica. I may have to head back to Washington to coordinate things, so it'll be useful to have you as a direct liaison. Let's go meet him in the underground conference room."

"Sounds good. Should I bring Shaukey as well?" said Jessica.

"I would rather have him and his team here in case they need to move quickly. It'll only be a quick briefing, as I am sure Robert will want to be up here," said Helena.

"Sounds good," said Jessica before turning to Shaukey, "I won't be long."

"Okay, have fun," said Shaukey.

It only took a few moments for the elevator to reach the subterranean operations floor, where they both headed to the boardroom.

CHAPTER 59

SUBTERRANEAN BOARDROOM

Helena entered, holding the door for Jessica, who asked, "When is Robert going to be here?" before hearing the door lock behind her. When she turned, Helena was pointing a gun at her face.

"What's going on?"

"Please don't act stupid. I know you saw it," hissed Helena.

"I don't know what you mean."

Helena, with breathtaking speed, moved forward and hit Jessica in the face with her gun. Jessica cried out and reeled backward. When she pulled her hand away from her face, she could see blood.

Calmly, Helena repeated, "You saw it, didn't you?"

"Yes, yes, I saw it," said Jessica, covering her face.

"I'm listening," said Helena.

"When I picked up your briefcase, I saw a very faint

imprint on the inside of the lid. It read '*Deinceps ut Unus*.' My Latin's not great, but I know that *unus* is one. I put two and two together. *Deinceps* means forward."

"Very good, little Jessica. Please sit down before you fall down," said Helena.

Jessica pulled out one of the leather conference chairs and sat down. Helena pulled a handkerchief from her pocket and threw it across the table to Jessica, who applied it to her head.

"Now, with your weak hand, please take out your sidearm. Don't be foolish and try something, or I'll kill you without hesitation," said Helena, moving to the other side of the table.

Jessica, using her non-dominant hand and fingertips, pulled out her weapon. After placing it on the table, she slid it across to Helena.

"Good. Now, keep the pressure on that cut, but please, place your other hand on the table."

When Jessica had done this, Helena sat down opposite her. She kept the gun pointed at Jessica but rested it on the table.

"Isn't this the part where you tell me what's going on?" asked Jessica.

"No, it isn't. But I will tell you, however, who I am and why I picked you. You see, I could tell you were on the verge of desperation, being stuck at Langley. I needed someone who'd be so grateful for the opportunity to get back out there and show the world they could do well that they wouldn't question why they'd been selected. I knew you wouldn't bother me with prying questions like others might. Don't get me wrong, I know you're very good at what you do, but demanding your involvement really pissed a lot of people off. I used that to my advantage too—their annoyance at me rocking the boat diverted them from focusing on why I picked you. Basic psychology." Helena sat back in her chair.

"That's just great, but it doesn't really answer the questions 'why' and 'who are you really?'" said Jessica, who seemed to have stopped the bleeding and put her hand down on her lap.

"Hands on the table, Jessica," said Helena.

"Of course," said Jessica, bringing up her other hand and placing it, palm down, on the table.

"Have you ever heard of a man called Heinrich Müller?"

"No, should I?"

"Maybe," said Helena, pausing before she continued. "Heinrich Müller was the head of intelligence for the Third Reich during Hitler's reign. He was there right up to the very end. There's a rumour that he walked out of the bunker and disappeared. There was also talk of his body being found in a mass grave in Berlin, but this was never confirmed. He was hunted like all the other Nazis, and there were stories that he'd been seen in Argentina, Chile, Scandinavia, and even England, I think."

"Okay, fascinating, but what's your point?" said Jessica, getting irritated.

"Don't overestimate your position here. I can simply kill you now if you want," said Helena.

Jessica knew she had to play for time. "Sorry. Please go on."

"The true story is that Müller betrayed the Führer and his country. He lost courage and started working with the allies, helping them to enter Hitler's bunker and capture the Führer."

"I thought Adolf Hitler killed himself and was then set on fire with his wife. I can't remember her name?" asked Jessica.

Helena smiled. "Eva—and she was indeed shot and burned, but not with the Führer. He was taken away by allied soldiers, and a double was put in his place. But that's another story," she added quickly.

"Müller was taken to England and then to the United States. He was a brilliant intelligence officer and an amazing strategist. He helped with the development of what we might call the modern CIA and all intelligence agencies around the world."

"How has this never come to light?" asked Jessica, looking shocked.

"It has never come to light," Helena said, repeating Jessica's words, "because very powerful people have kept this history a secret. Imagine the world knowing that Great Britain and the United States smuggled the head of Nazi intelligence out of Berlin and employed him until his death. It would be an outrage, and the damage widespread."

"Yes, I can imagine, but the world would be more shocked that Adolf Hitler was alive at the end of the war. The Israelis would be incensed, for starters," said Jessica.

"They would indeed, but who do you think he was handed over to?" smiled Helena.

"You're saying the Israelis had Adolf Hitler? Why wasn't he put on trial like Eichmann?"

"As I said, that's another story, and you'd have to ask them, as I don't know," said Helena. "When Müller had served his purpose, they sent him to some far-flung corner of the world under a new name. He lived in Egypt right under the noses of the Israelis. It was agreed with the new Israeli state that Müller wouldn't be touched, and the truth about Adolf Hitler would be hidden from the world."

"It was there that he met his wife—my grandmother," said Helena, pausing for a moment.

"You're the granddaughter of Heinrich Müller?" asked Jessica, eyes wide.

"I am indeed. My grandfather, in his later years, would tell my mother the story of his betrayal and how he'd worked for the Americans and the British. He was proud of what he had done, but even as a young girl, my mother thought he was a traitor and grew to hate him. Before he died, he gave her an envelope with some instructions inside. He told her to open it only after his death or if there were an emergency. When he died, the Americans and British faded away and acted almost as if his wife and my mother didn't exist. They continued paying his pitiful pension, but my grandmother lost her house and lived in squalor.

"My grandmother was a shattered woman, and she died a few years after my grandfather, of what I think was a broken heart. My mother was only nineteen and had nothing, and our family had disowned her. My mother didn't know what to do, so she decided to open the envelope. It contained a list of people she could contact if she ever needed help. They were my grandfather's handlers when he was in Egypt, and she discovered that one of them was still at the American Embassy. So, one day, she walked in and demanded to speak to him. She told him who she was and that she needed help. This aging spy felt sorry for her and contacted Langley. A week later, she was picked up, and with nothing but a suitcase, she was taken to the UK. She was granted a place at Oxford University and given a new identity, and she started a new life as Sabine Miller. They had asked her what name she wanted, so she kept her first name and asked for Miller. She thought they would say no, as it was too close to Müller, but they didn't blink. She was given dual citizenship for Great Britain and the United States—thankfully that was also bestowed upon me when I was born—and her life began.

"In those early years at Oxford, she learned how great the Nazi party had been. She understood that if it hadn't been for her father, the Third Reich would have been the greatest power in the world. She vowed she would make it great again," said Helena.

"So you joined the NSA and worked quietly, making your rise. Mother must have been so proud. The apple doesn't fall far from the tree!" snarled Jessica.

"Indeed, I did, she was, and no it doesn't. I thought about joining the CIA, but I didn't think they'd allow that. So I contacted the NSA, and they didn't hesitate. Either they didn't do their research and discover where my political loyalties might really lie, or they took me on out of allegiance to my grandfather."

"Right. So, what happens now?" asked Jessica.

"It is time for me to make my exit and let today's events unfold," said Helena.

"You're going to let a terrorist attack take place? Hundreds of people will be killed. How can you let this happen?" asked Jessica.

"There's always sacrifice in the quest for greatness. This will mark a new chapter and fuel those who want to see Germany be great again," said Helena.

"A terrorist attack by Islamists is nothing new. You're delusional," said Jessica.

Helena simply smiled.

CHAPTER 60

FIVE MINUTES EARLIER, CSIS OPERATIONS ROOM

The group was still sitting in the briefing room, with people sporadically wandering in and out, speaking with the analysts, and looking at the camera feeds. They hadn't yet identified the Edmonton university student's semi-truck, and getting the list from the parade organisers was proving a challenge. It was then that the elevator opened and out walked a gentleman, accompanied by his aide and a close-protection officer.

"Hello, I'm Robert Courtenay from CSIS. I'm looking for Helena."

Abigail went to greet him. "I'm Abigail and I represent MI6. But Helena has gone to meet you downstairs with one of her team members."

"Oh, I spoke with her, and she told me to come straight up here. Perhaps our wires got crossed."

Abigail pondered for a moment and said, "That's not like

Helena. Andrew, please go down and ask Helena to come up here immediately. Robert, any luck with the professor in Edmonton and locating Khaleed?"

Robert looked a little confused. "The professor was found dead this morning in her apartment. She'd been strangled. I told Helena an hour ago."

Abigail again gestured towards Andrew, saying, "Now, please, Andrew. I recommend you take a weapon."

"Yes, ma'am," said Andrew, and he made for a hasty exit.

"Is something wrong?" asked Robert.

"Let's hope not," said Abigail.

"Andrew, I'm coming with you," said Shaukey.

CHAPTER 61

THE SUBTERRANEAN BOARDROOM

Helena stopped talking when she saw the elevator light come on and people get out.

"This must be the cavalry coming to save the day," she said.

She didn't look away from Jessica, but she could see that two people were moving towards the conference room—one to the door, trying to get in, and the other disappearing out of sight. Jessica turned to see it was Shaukey trying to get the door open. The swipe card wasn't working, and when he tried the handle, it didn't budge.

Andrew had moved around the outside of the office and positioned himself behind Helena, his gun raised and aimed through the glass at the back of Helena's head.

Even with the soundproofing, Helena and Jessica could hear them shouting. Shaukey was now using his body weight to try to break open the door. Realising it wasn't going to give, he considered his options. Shaukey, now looking at Jessica, observed the injury to her face and the blood on her clothes.

Jessica looked into Shaukey's eyes, and as she smiled, the tears welled in her eyes and . . . *Clack*.

It was a single shot that struck Jessica in the side of her face.

She was forced backward off the chair and sent clattering to the floor as the side of her head sprayed across the glass wall. Almost instantaneously, there was the sound of two large cracks, as Andrew fired twice at Helena.

Shaukey was now shouting, "No, no, no!" He hit the door with all his weight, but it wouldn't give.

Helena stood and picked up her briefcase. She turned and smiled at Shaukey, who was now staring at her with a look of determined hatred. She strolled over to the two marks in the glass and, using her index finger, gently tapped, emphasising the bulletproof effectiveness. She smiled and casually walked to the other end of the room, opened the second door, and without looking back, made her escape.

Shaukey ran into his team's accommodation, reappeared with a breaching shotgun, and loaded the specialised rounds. Holding it at an angle, he shot three times before the lock eventually gave. Andrew was one step behind and made for the opposite side of the desk where Jessica lay, sprawled out. His sidearm was raised, and he moved towards the door. He checked it using his access card and called back without turning his head. Locked.

Shaukey moved to Jessica and gently rolled her onto her back. He knew the moment she'd been shot that she was dead, but he hoped that by some miracle, she'd survived and they could get her help.

Her head was disfigured but still recognisable to Shaukey.

He carefully brushed her hair off her face and stroked her cheek, "Don't worry, I'll make this right."

He looked up. "Andrew, we need to let everyone know."

"What about Jessica?" asked Andrew, still covering the door.

"Gone. We have to refocus. Let's go."

In the elevator, Andrew remained silent. He knew Shaukey's emotions were raw, and this wasn't the time or place to grieve. In their world, you couldn't allow emotions to run on their own. When the job was done and everybody was safe, then you could mourn and balance the scales.

CHAPTER 62

CSIS OPERATIONS ROOM

Everyone was standing as Andrew and Shaukey returned to the operations room.

Abigail looked at them both and even though she knew the answer, found herself asking, "Where are Helena and Jessica?"

"Jessica is dead. Helena shot her. We watched her do it. Safe to say, Helena's the mole," said Andrew.

Shaukey, although focused, was somewhat absent, and Abigail could see the blood on his hand—he must have touched her after she'd been shot.

Abigail looked down at the ground and folded her arms across her chest. She took a deep breath, then looking up, said, "Right, ladies and gentlemen, we need to assume that all the information Helena provided to us has been shit. I want everyone to go over everything we have and verify its origin and validity. Our mission still stands, and our objectives are the same. Can we please make sure that Helena's swipe card is deactivated? I don't want her creeping up behind us."

One of the CSIS analysts called out, "Already done. We have some external cameras in the subterranean roadway system. She was picked up by a black SUV."

"I want the feed cut to Twyla and Lars and put up in the boardroom. Also, cut the feed to Hobbs and Patterson, and put them through to the boardroom only. Get Michael from the CIA and Sir Goodlove online now. I want Shaukey and his team, Andrew, and Mr. Courtenay in the room as well."

They all filed in, and the last man, Andrew, shut the door.

Abigail waited for Michael and Sir Goodlove to come online.

"Gentlemen, I am providing you a priority-one update with eyes-only access, understand?" said Abigail.

"Understood. What have you got?" asked Michael.

"Go ahead, Abigail," said Sir Goodlove.

"Helena was just seen killing a CIA officer, Jessica. We have confirmed she provided false intelligence to misdirect this operation. I am confirming she is the mole. Michael, I need you to speak with the NSA director, have all her access removed, and inform all relevant parties within your organisation. We have enough assets on the ground, so Michael, we're going to send you what we have, and I would like you to focus on Helena. Can you do that?"

A little taken aback, Michael blew air out of his mouth. "Okay, this is going to be a big day. Send us what you have."

"Excellent, thank you," replied Abigail before continuing. "Sir Goodlove, please ensure that we update the necessary people. We need to search through the intelligence Helena provided. I think this will change the narrative on Chloe, so please factor that in to your efforts. Hobbs and Patterson are fully up to speed—I recommend using them."

"Will do, and let me know if you need anything else. As soon as I finish here, I will speak with Hobbs and Patterson," said Sir Goodlove.

"Twyla and Lars, I am sorry for the loss of your colleague, but I need you to be in the game now. This is a time for honesty, so if you need to step out, then do it," said Abigail.

Lars was visibly upset. Twyla had left her workstation and joined him.

"We're good. We'll start backtracking on all Helena's intel. If anything comes up, we'll let you know," said Twyla, putting her arm around Lars.

"Okay, good. Let's make sure whatever Helena hoped would happen today doesn't. Then we can go after her. Okay, cut the feeds," said Abigail, and Andrew had the camera feeds switched off.

"Gentlemen, I want you to know that when this is over, I will make sure Helena pays for what she has done. But right here and now, I need you to be on point and not distracted. Am I clear?" said Abigail, looking at all of them one at a time before stopping her gaze on Shaukey.

"I'm good to go, ma'am, and my team is solid," he said.

"Good, now let's get back out there and see what we can find," said Abigail, gesturing that everyone leave.

"So as the professor is dead, do we have other means for locating Khaleed?"

"Edmonton Special Branch are working on that now," replied Robert.

"Okay, what about the vehicle? Helena said it was a basic black truck unit pulling a flat open trailer," said Abigail.

"She didn't get that from me, as we don't have information on that," said Robert.

Abigail gazed through the open door into the main ops area. As she watched everyone rushing around, she hoped they were as good as they were cracked up to be. They needed something, and fast.

CHAPTER 63

STAGING AREA FOR THE STAMPEDE PARADE

Khaleed unlocked the cab of his truck and when inside, checked on the grenades, body armour, and weapons. He took a deep breath and watched the hive of activity around him. Not only were his fellow students getting onto the truck, but all the other participants were getting ready. There was a buzz of excitement around the staging area. People with clipboards were shouting at the groups, telling them how long they had left before it was time to move off.

As Khaleed waited patiently, his passenger door swung open, and one of his classmates climbed in. He recognised her from their social studies group. She'd once told him she thought it was awful that the police kept harassing him. She didn't think he was dangerous, and the police had no right to keep questioning him. Khaleed appreciated her saying that to him but thought it was mostly motivated by her not liking the police and wanting to be seen as an anti-racist. Regardless, he acknowledged the vote of confidence.

As she took a seat, Khaleed saw she was dressed in the typical Stampede outfit—a pink-and-white plaid sleeveless shirt, tied in a knot just above the belly-button. It showed off her toned stomach, and her full breasts were cresting out of the shirt. She also had on tiny denim shorts or "Daisy Dukes" as they were known, a pair of white cowboy boots, and a pink cowboy hat. She was very attractive with her long blonde hair tied in two pigtails.

"Hello, Khaleed. I thought I'd ride up front with you and keep you company." She smiled.

"Oh, okay. But aren't you supposed to be with the others?" asked Khaleed.

"Kind of—I was going to, but then I saw how handsome you are with your new look." She slid across the seats towards him and whispered in his ear. "When this is all done, perhaps you and I can go enjoy the Stampede." She used her tongue to gently tease his earlobe into her mouth and then sucked on it.

"That sounds like a good idea to me, but you need to let me concentrate on driving. I wouldn't want to crash," said Khaleed, smiling at her.

She pulled away, looked up at him, and then kissed him. Winking, she said, "We wouldn't want you to get all distracted now, would we?"

"Okay, let's get moving," shouted a marshal.

Khaleed saw the truck in front start to roll forward.

"Let's go, Khaleed. We can pick this up later," said the young lady.

Khaleed smiled, started the vehicle, and moved forward, following the truck in front. *I will indeed pick this up later. Here we go.*

CHAPTER 64

CSIS OPERATIONS ROOM

"Okay, we might have something," shouted the CSIS analyst. "One of the Calgary Police Special Branch detectives said that he spoke to a woman at an apartment building near the Calgary Tower. She thinks she saw a woman matching Alicia's description. She had a truck in the parking garage of her apartment building and was seen taking two large plastic cases out of her truck and heading for the elevators. No luggage, just the large cases. This was around midnight this morning as the eyewitness was returning from her shift at work. The detective has checked the parking garage, and the truck is already gone. There are a number of holiday-let apartments in the building, and we're working on identifying them."

"That's a little thin, don't you think?" asked Robert from CSIS.

"Anorexic, but we have nothing else," said Abigail.

"Shaukey, take two of your men and head to this apartment building. If we get any room numbers, we'll let you know. We'll keep the other two here in case another location is identified —with two guns, there could well be. Happy with that?" asked Abigail.

"Absolutely. Beats standing around. My team will be known as Delta One, and if my other guys deploy, they'll be Delta Two," said Shaukey, and he set about organising his men and gear.

CHAPTER 65

YIGAL BEN-ELIEZER'S HOTEL SUITE

Noya came into Yigal's room. He was standing at the window, enjoying the beautiful sunshine and watching the excited parade crowd.

"Good morning, sir. Are you enjoying the sights?" she asked.

"I am certainly enjoying being up here, watching everything going on down there. I'm not sure when the parade starts, but it must be soon," he answered.

"Yes, sir. It has already started, but it will be a while before it gets here. We're near the end of the parade route. We are going to leave in about an hour, if that's okay with you," said Noya.

"Yes, that will be fine," said Yigal.

Noya had already walked the route this morning, and nothing had really changed, apart from more people being in the Plus 15 walkway system. There was also a much heavier police presence. Her group had been up early, moving vehicles and staging themselves for the plaque unveiling. Noya was comfortable that she had everything in place.

"Come, Noya, sit with me, and we can have a morning coffee together. We'll be going home soon. You must be excited to see your family," said Yigal.

Noya poured herself a coffee and took a place next to Yigal at the window.

The crowds were all in good spirits, and children were dancing to music that blared from speaker systems. Police officers were dancing with them, having their pictures taken. Other officers were mounted on motorbikes, lights blazing, going back and forth along the parade route, occasionally shuttling cowboy-hatted people around, waving at everyone enjoying the event.

"I don't normally call home until we're back in Israel. But I did call my mother, and she got all excited, thinking I was back already. I told her I was returning late today, so I would go and see her tomorrow. She said she was going to invite everyone over for dinner, but I said she didn't have to do that," said Noya.

Yigal smiled broadly. "Good luck trying to change the mind of a Jewish mother. She will invite everyone, and if they don't come, she will make them feel guilty and never let them forget it."

Noya was now laughing, "That is true. She got upset with me once that I hadn't been over for lunch for two weeks, even though she knew I was in America working," explained Noya. Then she pitched her voice higher and said, "You don't love your mother anymore, is that it? After I gave birth to you and raised you, this is how you treat me?"

"She will be happy to see you tomorrow," said Yigal. He could see the emotion on her face when she spoke of her mother.

"Yes, she will, sir," said Noya, who for once seemed relaxed.

The pair fell into an easy, comfortable silence, enjoying a rare moment of leisure as they watched the goings-on and drank their coffee.

CHAPTER 66

CSIS OPERATIONS BUILDING

Shaukey and two Delta operators went into the subterranean basement and stopped in their staging area, grabbing a couple of backpacks and their carbines. The weapons had collapsible stocks so they were a little easier to hide under a jacket.

As they entered the floor, Shaukey made every effort to not look at Jessica's body, which still lay on the conference room floor. As they exited, an operator carrying a folded American flag headed for the conference room. Shaukey stopped to watch as he unfolded it and laid it over Jessica. Without a word, he exited and gave Shaukey a nod of acknowledgement. Shaukey nodded back. Then they headed out and, using the map they'd been provided with, navigated the underground street system towards the apartment building.

They came up on the back side of the building, where the detective was waiting for them. Delta One were taken to the glass atrium, where another detective was still talking to the lady who had recognised Alicia. It turned out she was a nurse, and after arriving home from her shift, she liked to have a few minutes to herself in her car, to decompress before going into her apartment. She was doing exactly this when she saw Alicia come out and head into the elevator with the cases.

"Are you sure this is the woman you saw?" asked the detective.

"Yes, I believe so. There are a few Airbnb apartments in the building, so it is not unusual to see people we don't know coming and going," said the nurse. "Oh, and the elevator she got into stopped on the fourth floor. I do remember that."

"Delta One to Control," said Shaukey into his radio.

"Delta One, go ahead," said a CSIS analyst.

"Witnesses say the person may have exited on the fourth floor, if that helps."

"It does. There are holiday apartments on multiple floors, but only two on the fourth."

Shaukey ended the communication, then turned to the detectives and nurse. "Excellent work, and thank you for your help." Then to his men, he said, "Okay, fellas, we're going up to look around."

"Do you need our help at all?" asked the detective.

"Appreciate that, but we should be good," said Shaukey.

As Delta One headed out of the atrium and up the stairs, the radio crackled into life.

"Control to Delta One."

"Go ahead, Control."

"We've had an update that Alicia may have been seen in the Fairmont Palliser, which is kitty-corner to where you are. Delta Two is deploying to the hotel to identify if it was indeed

Alicia, and if so, which room she may be in."

"Roger that. Keep me updated," said Shaukey.

Delta One reached the fourth floor and gently eased the door open. One of the team members had eyes on the corridor.

"Control to Delta One."

"Go ahead, Control."

"The holiday lets on that floor are 4A and 4B, copy?"

"Copy that."

The operator, keeping eyes on the corridor, said that 4A and 4B were halfway down, and the doors were facing each other. This was not ideal, but they'd have to make it work.

"We'll check 4B first. I'll keep point on 4A. One of you keep point on 4B and the other, use the fibre-optic," said Shaukey.

One of the operators slid his backpack off and removed the fibre-optic camera. Once ready, he gave the operator covering the corridor a squeeze on his shoulder, and they moved on the apartments. They covered both entrances, then they gently slid the fibre-optic cable under the door of 4B. The cable was as thin as a matchstick and went under the door quite easily. Watching the handheld display, he could see that the apartment was well-lit with natural light. There were two people, just a young couple standing on the balcony, drinking wine and enjoying the parade.

The operator removed the camera and whispered, "Negative. Move point and stack up."

The other operator moved away from his door and stacked with Shaukey.

Shaukey took from this that 4B was clear. The operator with the camera had gone under the spyhole for Apartment 4A and crouched as he again slid the cable under the door. It was very dark inside, and there was no view into the apartment. The operator adjusted the camera and identified that something had been placed close to the door to obscure any view inside. He stood and looked at Shaukey, giving him a definitive nod. Shaukey stepped out, and the operator behind him removed some lock-picking tools from his pocket.

The operator with the camera was kneeling with his carbine on the door but looking at the camera. The door lock was being manipulated, and the operator saw no movement on his screen to indicate that anyone was inside the apartment. As the door gave way, the operator picking the lock carefully held it still and slid the door-opening kit back into his pocket. Shaukey glanced down at the operator looking at the camera, who gave a shake of his head to indicate there was still no movement.

Shaukey, holding his carbine on aim with one hand, placed his other hand gently onto the door. The team knew this was the sign that they were making entry. All three of them were now on aim and looking at Shaukey.

Shaukey gave three nods and softly pushed the door open.

CHAPTER 67

RECEPTION AREA, FAIRMONT PALLISER

The two Delta Two operators were greeted at the side entrance to the hotel by one of the detectives. He escorted them inside, explaining on the way that the Palliser is part of the Fairmont chain, and during the Stampede, a lot of dignitaries stay there. Also, during the Stampede, the hotel employs private security to cover the entrance and exits and patrol the large reception area. He went on to say that one of the security employees had been in the underground parking area and seen Alicia. His description of what he saw Alicia do there was almost identical to what the nurse witnessed over at the apartments. The Palliser has identified which room Alicia had been booked into.

"Delta Two to Control."

"Go ahead, Delta Two."

"We have identified Alicia's room, and we're moving there now. Delta One, do you copy?"

There was a pause, and then the radio crackled, and there were two discernible clicks. This meant that the message had been received, but the team was unable to respond.

"Delta Two to Delta One, we copy your last. We'll provide an update as soon as we have one, out."

After about five minutes, the radio crackled to life again.

"Delta Two to the group, we have used fibre-optics under the door, and there's something obscuring the view into the room. We think a table has been flipped over to create a block."

CHAPTER 68

CSIS OPERATIONS ROOM

"Okay, the detectives at the site for Delta One have been busy. They've used video surveillance and tracked the vehicle your target was in and the building she entered. It's only two, maybe three blocks from the location of Delta One. It's The Edison. The vehicle used the underground parking. They haven't asked for video surveillance inside that building, as they wanted to speak with you guys first," said the CSIS analyst. "Peter and the Matron, I want you to head there now and make some discreet enquiries. Devon, I want you and Andrew to work together in case we get anything on Khaleed. Sound good?"

"Sounds good," said Devon.

Peter and the Matron were heading for the door when Devon approached. "I know the intelligence suggests Chloe has been played, but I still think she must be treated with prejudice. If there isn't absolute cooperation, then please don't play nice. I want you both to come back here in one piece," said Devon.

"Don't worry, we will," said Peter. As he left, the Matron gave Devon a little wink.

Devon rejoined Andrew, who said, "Would you rather have gone with them?"

"Yes, but the Matron can handle herself," said Devon.

"I have no doubt, but you seem unsure about Peter," said Andrew.

"No, I think Peter is solid, but he does have a blind spot with Chloe. He could end up getting himself killed if he isn't careful, as there are a number of things that his blind spot could make him do," said Devon.

"We shall see," said Andrew.

Robert then came over with news. "Okay, Edmonton Special Branch has determined that the truck we're looking for is a semi-truck towing a flatbed trailer. There's waist-high siding on the trailer for the safety of those on board. What's interesting is the entire main truck unit and the trailer have been given a custom paint job. The whole vehicle is painted in rainbow colours, you know, LGBTQ2S and all that. It's quite distinctive."

"That shouldn't be hard to find," said Andrew, who requested that the CCTV on the parade route be brought up onto the big screens.

They stood watching as truck after truck rolled slowly by on the various points of the parade. One of the analysts was searching through previous footage at a faster speed.

"There it is!" said Devon suddenly. "Coming to the end of Leg Two."

There, in full Technicolor, was the truck and trailer,

crawling along the route. The camera angle was elevated, and although they could see the cab unit, they couldn't make out who was inside.

"Okay, Devon and Andrew, let's get moving down to that truck and confirm Khaleed is in there. Can someone bring up Khaleed's passport image for me? Then send it out to Andrew and Devon," shouted Abigail.

"Absolutely, give me two minutes," said Lars, who was on one of the video feeds.

"What are our terms of engagement?" asked Andrew.

Robert from CSIS answered, "I don't want a young Muslim boy assassinated because we got played. The world is watching this parade, and we don't need another Jean Charles de Menezes. However, I certainly don't want a terrorist attack on our hands. If we confirm he's an imminent and real threat, then I authorise you to stop him by using deadly force. Anything to add, Abigail?"

"No, that pretty much covers it. We need to be sure, but the margins are very small indeed," replied Abigail.

Andrew and Devon's phones buzzed, and they both took in the image of Khaleed as they departed.

CHAPTER 69

THE EDISON

Peter and the Matron entered a marble, air-conditioned atrium with a large security desk manned by a bored-looking young man.

"Can I help you?" he enquired.

"Yes, we're with the Calgary Police, and we're looking for some gentlemen who may have been witness to an assault last night. Can you have a look at these pictures and let us know if you recognise them?" said Peter, showing his phone to the guard.

"Oh, of course. Was it a bad assault?" asked the young guard.

"Yes, I am afraid it was. A gentleman decided to beat up his girlfriend, and she's now in hospital," said Peter.

"That's awful. I hope you catch him," said the security guard, looking at the pictures.

It was when Johannes's picture came up that the guard said

he recognised him. "He was the one I showed around the floor he rented. He and some of his friends have been coming and going for the last couple of days. They all arrived in pick-up trucks, and they've been taking stuff in and out of the vehicles ever since."

"Do you know if they're still here?" asked Peter.

"No, I only have cameras in the parking garage, the reception area here, and parts of the exterior."

"Okay, we're going to need to go to their floor to speak with them," said Peter.

"Sure, I can take you down there," said the guard.

"Look, I've not been completely honest. They're not witnesses. We want to arrest them all for the assault. It is going to be quite dangerous, so I'd appreciate you waiting here. If you hear we might be in trouble, would you mind calling 911 and making sure our backup gets to us as quickly as possible?" said Peter, suddenly looking earnest. "Also, what do you mean 'down there?'"

The security guard stood up. "Oh, absolutely. You'll need this swipe card. It's two floors below ground-level."

"I don't want to use the elevator, as it will alert them. Which stairwell can we use?" asked Peter.

The security guard almost vaulted over the desk to show them where to go.

They went to the stairwell door. Peter turned to the security guard. "Thanks for your help. The young lady will get some justice because of your help." He gestured at his security get-up. "You should look to trade that in for a police uniform someday."

The young man's chest puffed out, and he said, "Anytime. And maybe I will."

They swiped into the stairwell, and when the door closed, they stood for a few minutes, just listening.

"I can't believe he didn't even ask to see identification," said the Matron.

Peter smiled. "Nothing like a damsel-in-distress tale to distract a wannabe knight in shining armour. And that Thin Blue Line patch he was wearing showed his sympathies with law enforcement, so a bit of fluffing in that direction clinched it."

"I can think of someone else who falls easily for that one," said the Matron with a knowing smile.

"Yeah, I guess," replied Peter, "but not completely."

He had drawn out his handgun, and they were now moving together down the stairwell, covering the angles as they went. When they reached the floor, it read "-2," and the numbering was green.

"Let me use the fibre-optic under the door, and you keep point in case anyone comes in," said the Matron.

The Matron squatted down and slid the cable under the door. She gently manoeuvred the camera around and watched the monitor. She could see movement in the distance, but it was hard to determine who was who. She could pick out some movement through the glass of the central conference room, but it was a challenge to get a decent view. It was then that she spotted Hugo walking with someone who was hooded and handcuffed. The Matron couldn't be sure, but she was convinced it was Chloe. They went past the people she had seen moving before and entered a room at the far end of the office space.

"Chloe's in there, and so is Hugo. I also think that the five Argentinians are here, but I can't be sure," she told Peter.

"Okay, what's the plan?"

"We need more help, that's for sure," said the Matron. She keyed her radio, but it just made a bonking sound that meant no signal. "Okay, I'm going back out to street level to get some support. Do not go anywhere until I return, understood?" said the Matron.

"Understood," said Peter.

The Matron carefully removed the fibre-optic cable and headed up the stairs.

*

It was perhaps thirty seconds later that Peter heard a clear scream. He knew it was Chloe. He'd been here before and contemplated the fallout again, but Peter was sure Chloe had been played and was innocent in all this. He pondered for a moment, then gently eased open the door that led onto the office floor. He could see movement on the far side of the conference room, but they didn't seem to notice him. While keeping aim, he carefully made his way round to a corridor from which he thought he'd heard the scream.

Pausing for a moment, he strained to hear the people in the room. To the left, he could hear a woman's voice. She wasn't screaming, but he heard her say, "Don't touch me!"

Peter knew it was Chloe, and she was still not going down without a fight. As he watched the corridor, a male walked across from left to right and entered the room where the voices could be heard. Peter was convinced it was Carl, but he couldn't be sure. Then he heard one of the male voices say, "Can you shut the door? I can't concentrate when all I can hear is that bitch complaining."

The door then gently clicked shut, and Peter saw his chance to move. With his gun on aim, he moved towards the room.

Once past the doorway, he shifted his aim to the room where Chloe was being held. He reached the door; there were voices inside, but for some reason, they seemed quieter, and Peter struggled to make any sense of what they were saying. He put it down to his adrenalin skyrocketing and his heart rate racing.

Hoping the door wasn't locked, he took a firm grasp of the handle.

1 . . . 2 . . . 3 . . . He depressed the handle and pushed open the door.

Hugo was sitting with his back to the door and started to turn as he heard it open. Chloe was in the chair opposite him. Her hands were pulled behind her, and she was wearing a black hood. Swiftly, Peter placed his gun on Hugo's turning head. "Don't move."

Hugo froze, and Peter then heard Chloe say, "Peter, is that you?"

"Yes, it's me. Don't worry. Stay still—I'll get you free in a minute."

Peter moved to face Hugo, his back to Chloe. Hugo did have a sidearm holstered on his belt but was smart enough not to go for it. Peter stood in front of him and, raising his weapon, aimed it at Hugo's left eye. "I might be going to jail for rescuing Chloe the first time, but I think I would get knighted if I just shot you right here and now."

Hugo looked at Peter, and a big smile spread across his face.

"What are you smiling at?" asked Peter.

"I told you when you first came to Wales that you should never turn your back on the enemy."

Peter then realised that on the table next to him were a number of TV screens with camera feeds displayed. There were various shots covering the office floor as well as the stairwell that he and the Matron had used. Peter looked at the screens, somewhat confused, "You must have seen me coming, so why . . .?"

CHAPTER 70

CSIS OPERATIONS ROOM

Andrew and Devon had been moving out of the operations building as the Matron came on the air. "Control, this is the Matron. Do you copy?"

"Go ahead. This is Control."

"We have located Chloe, Hugo, and the Argentinians. They're in The Edison on floor minus two, which is two floors below ground-level. I request assistance to my location, do you copy?"

"We copy, stand by."

The analyst looked at Abigail, waiting for a decision.

Abigail, using the radio, called Devon and Andrew. "Devon and Andrew, do you copy?"

Devon and Andrew had just walked out onto the street. Devon responded, "Go ahead."

"Devon, I want you to go and help Peter and the Matron.

Andrew, you need to move to intercept Khaleed and the truck. Robert, can you get hold of the Calgary Police Tactical Unit? We may need some support here."

"Of course. I'll do that now," said Robert.

Andrew and Devon both acknowledged their orders.

"The Matron from Abigail, do you copy?"

"Copy, Abigail, go ahead."

"Devon's on his way to you, and I am looking for additional resources. If you need to move in, then do so. We have to stop them, and saving Chloe is not the priority at this point, copy," said Abigail.

"Copy. I'm heading back down to support Peter. We lose communications down there, but we'll hold until Devon joins us," said the Matron.

CHAPTER 71

FLOOR -2, THE EDISON

Peter could feel the metal being pressed into the base of his skull. "Please don't do anything stupid, Peter. I would hate to have to kill you," said Chloe.

Peter's head went down.

Hugo stood up. "You know what, Peter? I thought you were going to shoot me. Thank God Chloe was right." Hugo took Peter's gun and searched him for other weapons.

Immediately, the door opened, and Carl came in.

"Everything okay?" asked Carl.

"Yes, we're good. You need to leave soon. Please get yourself prepared and continue with your instructions. Hugo, please go and help them. I am going to have a little chat with Peter," said Chloe.

The men left, and as they did, Chloe said, "Make sure you close the door."

When they were alone, Chloe said, "Sit down, Peter. I want you to put your hands on your lap, facing up."

Peter did this. Chloe moved over to the TV monitors and switched them off.

Without taking her eyes off him, she sat down, crossed her legs and rested her gun on her thigh with her finger on the trigger. "We've got a bit of time to spend together before I have to kill you. You must have lots of questions—perhaps I can answer some of them?"

"What's going to happen today? What's the attack?" asked Peter.

"Shut up. This is not some Hollywood movie where I tell you the grand plan and you escape and save the day. If you're going to be a fucking idiot, I'll just kill you now."

The change in Chloe was quite remarkable. She was focused, and Peter knew he would indeed be shot if he went down that road again.

"Okay, who are you really? What happened in Algeria? How did you escape the safe house in England, and how long have you and Helena been working together? How about that for starters?" He hoped this might get Chloe talking and buy him some time.

"Okay, now we are talking. I am Chloe Greene, and I did go to Cambridge. When MI6 recruited me, I saw through their pathetic ruse straight away. I knew I was only there so they could watch me and try to figure me out. So I let them. Idiots. But it's interesting you mention Helena. Why?"

"Helena killed Jessica and fled. She's left you and the rest of your little group to fend for yourselves."

"She's doing what she needs to do. What you don't understand, you pathetic little man, is that this is bigger than all of us. I sit here, part of a race that almost took over the world. If it hadn't been for Helena's traitorous grandfather, the world would now be ordered, focused, and pure." She shot a contemptuous look at Peter.

"Now, what was your second question? Oh, yes, Algeria. It wasn't until I had spoken with that dickhead Dominic that I realised the source I'd been tasked to meet might be someone I knew from my previous visits to North Africa—the name was familiar, you see. But I needed to know for sure, so I decided that you would arrive after me. That way, if we did recognise each other, I'd be able to act without you cocking it all up. If we didn't know each other, you'd have just shown up, and it would have gone as per instruction," said Chloe.

"When the source arrived, he came to the table and sat down. I knew straight away, but it took him a few seconds before he recognised me. He panicked, as I knew he would, and ran out of the café. I went after him, and thankfully, he used the exit route we had given him, so I knew where he was going. I headed him off and killed him. I cut his throat. I stole his wallet, watch, and a gold necklace, and threw it all into a nearby stream. I then cleaned the blood off me and returned to the café. I had just gotten back when you came bombing round the corner. I needed time to think of what to tell you, so I asked if we could talk elsewhere, and you were, as always, so accommodating. I knew naming Abigail would cause a little chaos. You're probably wondering why I went to the safe house."

"It did cross my mind," said Peter.

"I knew they wouldn't kill me. I was a little surprised at the level of torture, but I was even more amazed when you came charging in like Sir Galahad," said Chloe with a smile.

"It couldn't have been any better. Naming Abigail certainly put the cat amongst the pigeons, but because of what you did, they couldn't focus on the real issue. So, Peter, on behalf of the Fourth Reich and the New Order, thank you," said Chloe, placing her hand over her heart.

"To hell with you," said Peter.

"Easy now, Peter. Don't be rude or this little chat we are having will end. What was the other thing you asked about? Oh yes, the safe house. Well, on the beach, you might have noticed Hugo whisper something into my ear. What he said was, 'Forward as One.' Our motto. I hadn't known he was one of us and suspected it might be a trap. So, I waited until he acted. I knew for sure when he disarmed the cameras, came into the interview room, and of course killed my interviewer. I then made all the right noises as we walked out. It is a shame the cameras weren't working, as it would have looked quite comical seeing me scream out in pain as we both strolled through the house. When we walked to the car I slid on the hood and Hugo plastic-cuffed me for good effect.

"I took the hood and dumped it in the vehicle. It wasn't difficult to get one of my wounds opened up again to drip a little blood, which I thought would be a nice touch.

"You also asked how long Helena and I have been working together. Well, it's been a long time. When I killed the source in Algeria, Helena and I knew we needed to be more careful. Helena found out that the intelligence didn't relate to us, but from then on, we were more cautious. She and I will be together soon." Chloe sat quietly just looking at Peter with a smirk on her face.

"What's funny?" asked Peter.

"I never thought that this is where you and I would end our

adventure together."

"Were you hoping for a big musical number?" asked Peter.

"Oh, I don't know. I thought I would hear that you were spending your life in an American prison. Or perhaps you had gone to live on some remote island because you couldn't get over me."

"Don't flatter yourself. A good shower, and you're yesterday's news."

"Glad to hear it." Chloe laughed.

The door eased open a little, and Hugo leaned through the gap.

"Okay, we are good. What's the plan with Mr. Superhero here?"

"I think our time has come to an end, Peter," said Chloe, standing and moving her chair back against the wall.

Peter didn't turn, but he heard Hugo say, "You could join us, Peter."

Then a *clack-clack* sound came echoing down the corridor. The door crashed open as Hugo fell forward into the room.

Chloe had already raised her weapon, and as Hugo fell, she shot twice down the corridor. The Matron, who had been advancing towards her, fell backward and lay motionless on the floor. Peter took the opportunity and flew at Chloe. She had adjusted after shooting the Matron, and when she fired, Peter felt it whizz past the top of his head.

He grabbed the gun and, placing his forearm on her throat, drove her backwards into the wall. The force was enough to dislodge the gun, but Chloe immediately fought, and she fought hard. The fingers and thumb of her spare hand were brought to effect on Peter's face, and the fight was on. Peter let go of Chloe's now gun-free hand and Chloe used it to continue attacking Peter's face. She brought her knees up sharply and caught Peter squarely between the legs, which knocked the wind out of him, but using the close proximity, he head butted her. Although he felt her nose crack, she didn't miss a beat and continued to fight with impressive ferocity. Peter grappled and managed to throw her across the room. Her feet came off the ground as she was hurled into the table and TV monitors, which wobbled and fell. Steadying herself, she stood to face Peter. Her nose had a cut across the bridge, and blood was running down her face and onto her chest.

"Chloe, it doesn't have to end this way. We can figure this out," said Peter, wiping the blood from the scratches Chloe's nails had dealt to his face.

Looking a little defeated, Chloe smiled. "Hugo was wrong. You could never join us. You're too weak." The smile faded, and from behind her back, she produced a long-bladed knife. It reminded Peter of a commando dagger.

"Where have you been hiding that?" Peter took up a defensive stance.

"Haven't you learned anything? I'm full of surprises," replied Chloe, bringing the knife up in front of her.

The room wasn't the biggest, and Peter was scrambling to figure out his next move. He really didn't have time, as Chloe came at him, slashing furiously. The knife was moving so quickly, it made an unsettling noise as it cut through the air. Peter tried to remember some of his police training for knife attacks. He knew he needed to close the gap and wrap up the arm, but in reality, this seemed like a stupid idea. They both danced around the room, with Chloe becoming more confident and cutting down the angles for Peter's escape before finally lurching forward.

Peter took his opportunity. He went to wrap the arm, but his timing was off, and Chloe's determination caused the knife to slice into his lateral muscle. As it tore through him, he slammed his arm down, trapping Chloe's arm. She immediately flew a clenched fist into his face, targeting his nose, causing Peter's grip to falter. Her arm came out, and Peter grabbed the hand, trying to gain control while protecting his face. Then instinct took over. In a split second, he stopped protecting his face and wrapped both hands around Chloe's hand and, of course, the knife. He then used his strength to bend Chloe's wrist and guided the knife towards her chest.

Chloe stared at the knife as she tried to fight the momentum driving her backwards. She began to panic, fighting to break free. She even tried to drop the knife, but Peter made sure he kept a firm grasp on it and drove her hard into the wall, watching as the blade disappeared into her chest and feeling it crack and squeeze through bone. Chloe twitched and struggled, but Peter just drove the knife deeper. Her hands fell away and Peter drove it to the hilt, squashing her ribcage as he did.

Chloe looked up into Peter's eyes, and he saw the determination and hatred fade away, replaced by a gaze of longing and despair. As he felt her life slipping away, a tear rolled down her cheek. Her head then fell forward onto his chest, and he released his grip on the knife, cradling her head as he slowly stepped back to lower her gently to the ground. However, only her head slumped, and Peter realised he had driven the knife through her small frame and into the wall. Chloe's body now hung, impaled by the knife, with her head flopped forward, her arms by her sides, and her feet just touching the ground. Peter stepped back and took in the macabre scene as he fought to get his breathing under control.

"You're okay. Hold this dressing in place, and I'll be right back."

Peter wasn't sure who had said those words, but it was enough for him to regain a little composure. As he turned to look towards the door, Devon appeared, gun raised, looking around at the lifeless Chloe pinned to the wall, and Hugo, lying still on the floor.

Peter realised he hadn't checked to see if Hugo was dead. Devon glanced at Peter, almost as if he could read his mind. Then, without a word, Devon raised his handgun and shot Hugo twice in the head.

"Okay, that's them sorted. Now come and help me and the Matron," he said.

Peter moved into the doorway, and there was the Matron, slumped against the wall, holding a dressing to her stomach.

The first round shot by Chloe had hit her body armour, but the second had caught her just underneath it.

"What happened to Chloe?" she asked.

"Peter here killed her. Don't worry," said Devon.

"Nice work," said the Matron, looking up at Peter.

Peter moved past them and looked around. "I heard the Argentinians in a room close by. I'm going to see what I can find."

"Go with him, Devon. I am good here," said the Matron.

Devon got up, and they moved to the closest room. Devon, with his gun raised, moved into it, but it was empty. Peter could see Calgary Police outfits and other various bits and pieces that would be worn by uniformed officers. Devon then found on the table a map and realised he was looking at a plan of the Plus 15 walkway system.

Peter came over and, on examining the map, saw that

the parade route had been marked. There was an area high-lighted and a route outlined from where they were to this marked location.

"This is something to do with the attack," said Devon.

"Maybe, but the route marked here takes them away from the parade. Looking at what's in the room, I think they're dressed as police officers. Wherever they are going, I think it's going to be near this convention centre. They have a number ten marked on here. What do you think that means?" asked Peter.

"I am going to suggest ten o'clock, fifteen minutes from now," said Devon.

"We need to get there," said Peter.

"Agreed. Let's get out of here—I can get some communications up and running. I need to get word to Abigail and Robert. The Delta teams may have found the Miniguns, and I need to tell them that these things may be going off at ten. Come on, let's go."

The Matron was clearly struggling and said it would be safer to leave her where she was. She asked that the security guard call for an ambulance and bring them down to her. Peter didn't want to leave her there, but once Devon got direction from the Matron, he told Peter they should leave. Peter went back into the room where Chloe hung from the wall and armed himself with Hugo's gun and ammunition.

CHAPTER 72

CALGARY TELUS CONVENTION CENTRE

Noya and the team had gotten Yigal to the convention centre with ten minutes to spare. The walk had been easy, and when they crossed over the main highway, high above the parade, they stopped and watched the festivities. The police were everywhere, and they'd made sure spectators could not watch the parade from the Plus 15.

Yigal was a man who didn't like to just glide in, unveil a plaque, shake a few hands, get the right pictures taken, and then leave. Yigal understood that those waiting for him cared about their endeavours; he liked to talk to them and hear their stories.

They arrived, and Yigal saw the group—all about his age—sitting with their families. But despite some of them being old, they all got up. Some needed to be helped out of their chairs and wheelchairs. Yigal tried to insist they stay seated, but they all rose to greet him.

Noya's team spread themselves out and took defensive positions while she stayed with Yigal, who mingled with everyone, shaking hands, hugging, laughing, and finally managing to get them to take their seats so they could talk before he unveiled the plaque.

CHAPTER 73

LEG TWO OF THE STAMPEDE

The crowds were loud, and the warm summer air came wafting in through the open truck windows. Khaleed's passenger was leaning out, waving and smiling at all the crowds as they slowly drifted along.

Khaleed had to pay attention, as the parade would stop and start as it meandered along. As they moved to the end of Leg Two, Khaleed looked over, and all he could see was his passenger's backside in short shorts as she leaned out the window. The parade had come to a pause just as Khaleed was turning onto Leg Three, so he put the vehicle into neutral.

"Hey, are you enjoying yourself?" he shouted.

She flopped back into the truck, the biggest smile on her face, almost giddy with excitement. "I'm having so much fun."

"I have a little surprise for you," he said. Using the controls next to him, he brought up the tinted windows, and the cabin dimmed.

Khaleed reached out and, putting his hand inside her shorts, pulled the young woman towards him. She giggled and started to kiss Khaleed. The kissing became prolonged and intense—she needed to catch her breath. Pulling back, she opened her eyes to see Khaleed staring stoically back at her without a trace of emotion. Then he brought the box cutter he had in his other hand across the young woman's throat. There was a moment of panic on her face and then sheer terror. Khaleed quickly pushed her against the window as her throat opened up. She was grappling her neck, trying to process what had happened and fighting to control the bleeding.

Khaleed stared into her beautiful eyes, watched the light in her slip away and the colour drain from her face. It didn't take long before she fell, lifeless and still. She had such a petite frame that Khaleed merely folded her over so her head fell between her knees. He lowered the windows back down and waited for the parade to restart.

"Allahu Akbar," he said as the parade started to move. "Western women are whores of the devil. I have now made you pure, infidel," murmured the Oilman.

Now on Leg Three, he knew that after passing the trees on the left, he would mount the sidewalk and start his attack.

CHAPTER 74

ROOM 4A

Shaukey and the two Delta operators had moved into the room and called, "Clear." In front of the window, they found an M134 on a tripod. The tripod was substantive enough, but it also had supporting arms that reached out, bracing it to the walls. The weapon was attached to a large crate containing thousands of rounds encased in a metal belt that would be fed into the gun. Shaukey could see the control panel on the rear of the gun. Although it was illuminated, there was nothing to indicate when it would activate. He feared that if he tampered with it, it might cause the gun to start firing.

"Delta One to Control, do you copy? Over."

"This is Control. Go ahead, over."

"We have located the M134. I need assistance with the control panel to disarm it safely, over."

"Copy, send a picture," said Control.

"Delta One to Delta Two, have you made entry into the room at the Palliser? Over."

"Delta Two, that is a negative. But we have evacuated the floor, over."

"Delta One, copy. At this time, make entry and send what you have to control. If we have the same thing, it'll make life easier. Your information may provide a clue on what to do, copy Delta Two, over."

"Copy Delta One, wait out."

It was only a few moments, but it felt like an age.

Shaukey looked out of the apartment toward the Palliser, hoping he didn't see the room explode when the team made entry.

"Delta Two, we're in. I'll send Delta One and Control what we're looking at, over."

Shaukey sighed and keyed his mic. "Copy that, Delta Two, standing by, out."

CHAPTER 75

PLUS 15

Carl, Johannes, Hanna, Augustus, and Alicia were walking through the Plus 15, heading to the convention centre. Alicia paused and removed her cell phone, then placed herself near to the glass and looked down the length of the parade route. Johannes, Hanna, and Augustus moved away and headed through the next set of doors.

Carl stayed with her, "Can you see the Oilman?"

"Not yet, but I recognise the vehicles coming into view. He should be in sight soon. You should go. I will join after," said Alicia.

Carl looked at his watch, then down the long line of trucks. "As soon as the guns start, come and join us. We shall start this together, sister."

"I will. I promise," said Alicia.

CHAPTER 76

THE STAMPEDE PARADE

Andrew exited out onto the street, and the warm summer air enveloped him.

The crowds were excitedly cheering and waving at everyone going by. The sidewalks were packed, and Andrew was doing a good job of weaving his way through.

"Control from Andrew, I am on the street and heading to Leg Two. Where's the truck? Over."

"Andrew, this is Control, the vehicle is now turning onto Leg Three. Do you copy? Over."

At the next intersection, Andrew walked out onto the road. He looked down the long line of vehicles, and there it was. It was about 800 metres away, but with the sun reflecting off the garish paintwork, it was easy to pick out. The semi-truck, emblazoned with a rainbow design, was making a slow turn onto Leg Three.

Andrew had only been on the road a few moments when a police officer approached and asked him to move back onto the sidewalk. He obliged and updated the operations room that he'd seen the truck. Then he headed away from the parade route, turned in to an alleyway behind the buildings, and ran. Luckily, there were few people around, and he covered the distance quickly.

Casually rejoining the parade route, he soon got eyes on the vehicle, which had by then made the turn onto Leg Three. He observed his surroundings and could see there were trees for the first block, then the sidewalks were clear.

"Control, if he's going to make an attack, it'll be when he clears the trees on the north side. I'm in position and will intercept if needed, copy."

"Andrew, this is Abigail. You have to be sure before you intercept. I am authorising deadly use of force, but you have to be sure. Understand? Over."

"Yes, ma'am. Out."

Andrew did a reassuring check for his sidearm and watched the truck slowly nudge its way along the route. He could see the driver, but it was difficult to tell if it was indeed Khaleed. The passport image showed a man with a beard and long hair. Andrew decided to move into place. He wanted a better view of this guy.

CHAPTER 77

LEG THREE, PLUS 15

The vehicles turning onto Leg Three were about a mile away, but Alicia had seen the rainbow-painted semi-truck and trailer make the turn. She had carefully gauged the movement of the vehicles passing underneath her and knew she had to give the Oilman a little time before she activated the M134s.

She had discussed with the Oilman the consequences of activating the guns too soon. The Oilman said it wouldn't be a problem as long as he'd made the turn onto Leg Three. He would simply push his way forward and start his attack.

She gave it a few more minutes, then pressed the button, activating the M134s' control systems. Once done, she placed her phone on the floor and stamped on the screen, then picked it up and removed the SIM card. Discarding it in a nearby trash can, she proceeded through the heavy double doors at the end of the Plus 15, towards her meeting with Carl.

CHAPTER 78

FLOOR -2, THE EDISON

"Devon to Control, do you copy? Over."

"Go ahead, Devon. Over."

"Hugo and Chloe are dead, and we believe the Argentinians are dressed as Calgary police officers, break.

"We found a map in the staging area, and we don't believe they're going to attack the parade, break.

"We believe they have another target in the TELUS Convention Centre, which is scheduled for ten hundred hours. We're heading there now, over."

Robert shouted to the group in the operations room, "Do we know of any events at the TELUS Convention Centre?"

There was a pause, and then one of the analysts called out, "It's used for vendors and other trade stands during the parade, but nothing stands out. It isn't open to the public until tomorrow. So, nothing."

"Abigail to Devon, over."

"Go ahead, ma'am. Over."

"Okay, we have nothing that would indicate why they'd be going there, break," she said. "You and Peter head there and report back. We've got the Calgary Police Tactical Unit en route to us and will divert them to you, over."

"Copy that, over," Devon said.

"The Argentinians are dressed as police officers—ensure target identification. We do not want to shoot a real police officer by mistake, understand? Over," said Abigail.

"Understood, over," said Devon.

"Peter, do you copy my last?" said Abigail.

"I copy your last, Peter out."

Robert hung up the phone and said, "The Calgary Police Tactical Unit should be on scene in about eight minutes. They don't like the intelligence about the police disguises, so we shall see how this plays out."

"It gets worse and worse, doesn't it?" said Abigail.

Peter and Devon had just made their way past the back of the Calgary Tower and were now coming up to the Plus 15, where Alicia had just been standing.

"Devon to Control. We're at the last Plus 15 and are making entry into the TELUS Centre. Copy? Over."

"Copy that, Devon, and the police tactical unit will be on scene with you in about seven minutes, copy."

"Copy, over," said Devon.

They paused by the doors and did a weapons check. They had concealed carbines under their jackets, which were now being brought out and made ready. They extended the stock and ensured the gun was clear of obstruction.

"Peter, we need to be sure and fast, but we cannot shoot

an innocent police officer. Take a breath, but be decisive. Understand?" said Devon.

"I got it. Let's go," said Peter.

CHAPTER 79

ROOM 4A

Shaukey had been looking around the room, considering the situation, when the control panel glowed into life. He looked down at it. There was a timer counting down from thirty seconds.

"Delta One to Delta Two and Control. Our control panel is active and has a countdown timer for thirty seconds. Now it's twenty-five, over," said Shaukey.

"Delta Two, copy. Same here, ours was forty, now thirty-five. Any advice? Control, over."

The concern in their voices was audible as the control panels counted down.

"The Americans haven't called back. We've no guidance. Do you copy? Over," said Control.

"Copy, over," said Shaukey. He turned to his guys, saying, "Any ideas, fellas?"

"How about we smash the control panel? That might shut it down," said the Delta operator.

"It might also make it fire straight away. Shit," said Shaukey.

The M134 barrels were now coming to life and slowly starting to tick as they began to turn.

"That's not good," said one of the operators.

Shaukey slung his weapon behind his back and keyed his mic. "Delta Two, hit the deck—now!"

The two operators in the Palliser looked at each other wide-eyed and dropped to the ground. Shaukey grabbed the handles of the M134 and with all his strength started to force it against its desired path. The M134 kicked into life and the rounds from the crate started feeding their way into the weapon. The noise inside the room was deafening, and the vibration from the weapon was intense as Shaukey forced it away from the crowds below. The glass window of the apartment shattered, and as the gun spewed out bullets, the crowds below started screaming and running.

"Help me," shouted Shaukey, and one of the other operators helped Shaukey force the weapon towards the Palliser.

It was then that the second gun was coming to life and as the rounds shattered the window, Shaukey knew where to aim. Shaukey and the Delta operator forced the gun to aim into the hotel room. It was like trying to control an angry grizzly bear who was spouting fire.

It kicked and bucked, trying to get back on its original programming. Shaukey and the operator had to use all their strength. Now, with the second M134 coming to life, the crowds below were in sheer terror and running in every direction.

Abigail and Robert watched on the cameras as the

carnage unfolded. Women, children, seniors, parents, and office workers were scrambling to get away from this lead-spitting monster.

Dignitaries in the parade were being extracted by their security details, armoured SUVs appearing out of nowhere, courtesy abandoned as they were thrown inside and driven away at speed.

People in the parade were being hit, but they didn't just drop down dead. They were thrown backwards by the force of the rounds and in some cases, had limbs torn off as they were hurled onto the highway.

*

Amongst the carnage and chaos, Abigail could see the police officers pointing towards where the rounds were coming from. It had only been a few seconds since the guns had started, but law enforcement was already moving in on them.

Abigail admired their bravery and said to herself, "Calgary's finest at work."

*

Shaukey had forced his M134 across the face of the Palliser, destroying every room as he guided the weapon into position. His M134 was then aimed at its twin and quickly incapacitated it, sending metal and shrapnel in all directions. The room it had been in was now missing its entire frontage, but the gun had been stopped.

The other Delta operator with Shaukey then decided to take drastic action. He had removed his breaching shotgun and walked over to the encased ammunition feed. He fired as quickly as possible three solid slugs into the ammunition belt.

This caused the metal casing to fragment. Now the twisted metal was heading into the weapon and at speed. The action did what he had hoped and stopped the ammunition from reaching the M134, but when the fragmented metal entered the weapon, it did not go well. The weapon bucked violently and sent Shaukey and the other operator flying across the room as the main housing of the gun exploded. Metal and flame burst across the room as it spun like a crashing helicopter. Shaukey had been thrown onto a sofa that had tipped over, and he was now lying on his back with the sofa between him and the M134. As he lay, gaining his composure, he could still hear the barrel ticking but clearly slowing down.

He checked himself: some small cuts to his face and arms, but otherwise, okay.

"Delta One, are we doing okay?" he shouted.

The room was smokey, and debris was still in the air as he got up from behind the sofa. He looked around and saw his operators doing the same and giving themselves the once-over.

"That was a little intense," said one of the operators.

"Yeah, that was a wild ride. Delta Two from Delta One, unit contact, over," said Shaukey.

There was no response. Shaukey walked to where the front of the apartment used to be and looked out towards the Palliser. The entire floor had been destroyed by him strafing the gun across the building, and the room where the M134 had been now looked like a disaster zone. Shaukey's heart sank.

"Delta One to Delta Two, unit contact, over," he said bleakly. Time seemed to slow down as he squinted at the building across the street, scouring the wreckage for signs of life. This didn't look good. He was about to make one final call when he saw something—was that activity, or just rubble settling?

But a moment later, his hope was realised as a thumbs up slowly emerged from the debris. A few seconds more and the two Delta operators stood and came to the window, covered in dust and debris, clearly hurt but alive.

Then, these two men, who moments earlier had been facing death, both raised their thumbs to their Special Forces comrades, their broad grins plainly visible to Shaukey.

"Yeah, this is Delta Two. We're solid. How you doing over there? Over."

Shaukey looked back into the room. His two guys had just finished their self-checks, ensured their weapons were in working order, and gotten to their feet, brushing themselves off.

Grinning like little boys, they gave Shaukey the thumbs up.

"Delta One, we're good to go here," said Shaukey, who then started laughing.

CHAPTER 80

LEG THREE

Andrew was making his way through the crowds to get a picture of Khaleed for the operations room.

Even though he was almost a mile from the M134s, the sound was unmistakable. Everybody, including him, looked in that direction, trying to figure out what was happening. Then the first flash-bang went off, and as he turned back to look at the truck, saw that a smoke grenade had been thrown. The truck was now revving hard, and plumes of black smoke were filling the air. The crowd and those in the parade weren't quite sure whether this was part of the event, but you could see that their senses were heightened.

Khaleed was now throwing out his second flash-bang and smoke grenade. He made sure the windows had been brought back up, and reaching above him, he pulled the body armour down to cover his chest.

He could hear the students on the trailer behind him scream as he accelerated and steered towards the sidewalk. He'd placed the sidearm next to him on the seat, and he now worked through the gears.

He mounted the sidewalk. Even though the crowd was running, they weren't quick enough. Khaleed could see the terror in their eyes as they disappeared under the front of his vehicle. He could feel their bodies being crushed under the wheels, but he just continued to move forward. People were running in every direction to get away, and Khaleed swerved a little to get those who had avoided his path.

Andrew had looked back along the parade route. People weren't reacting, rather they were rooted to the spot in disbelief and fear as the truck made its way towards them.

Police officers were helping the crowd escape, and others were now starting to dump rounds into the cab of the truck, its windows shattering as the rounds found their marks, but it kept moving.

Khaleed then picked out Andrew, who was running towards him, and saw the gun in his hand. Reaching for his sidearm, he one-handedly shot at him through the windshield. This, while driving, made Khaleed inaccurate, and as he ran through the escaping crowd, Andrew could hear and see people being hit by Khaleed's indiscriminate shooting.

*

Through the mayhem, a Calgary police motorbike rider had spotted Andrew, gun in hand, moving towards the truck, and had identified that he was trying to stop the driver. They also observed that the driver was getting more accurate with each shot he was firing. They needed to do something. The police motorbike rider gunned their Suzuki V-Strom towards the truck, deftly slaloming through the fleeing crowd, covering the ground quickly and bringing the bike to a halt.

Standing astride their motorbike, feet planted firmly on the floor, they drew their sidearm.

Their aim was on target, and they drilled rounds into the windshield. The bike had all its emergency lighting activated, making it an easy target for Khaleed. Andrew saw one of its lights shatter, and its windshield flexed and splintered as rounds began to hit. But the officer didn't miss a beat and continued putting rounds into the truck.

*

Andrew decided that if he got out of this alive, he was going to buy whoever this Street Hawk Road Angel was dinner. He ran towards the front of the semi-truck and jumped up onto its large, solid bumper, landing with only one foot making good contact, but his free hand managed to grab the large radiator ornament. It took all his strength to get his other foot on the bumper and steady himself before bringing up his sidearm and aiming at Khaleed.

The semi-truck was bouncing all over the place as it navigated its way along the sidewalk. Rounds were still going into it from the police officers on scene, and people were screaming as they got hit. Andrew steadied himself; the heat from the truck's engine was incredible. He fired into the cab and was sure he'd hit Khaleed centre mass, but the truck just kept rolling.

Khaleed had been hit twice in the chest, but the body armour had done its job. He was in pain, but he was still able to keep driving. The impact of the rounds hitting him had really hurt—it had taken a moment to refocus. There was a guy on his hood; he needed to take him out.

But as he brought his gun up on aim, he was staring right at him.

And with a single shot, Andrew hit Khaleed in the head.

Khaleed died instantly and slumped against the driver's window. The vehicle began to slow, then veered left, with Andrew still standing on the bumper. It ploughed through a plate glass window and headed into a large office atrium where Andrew was thrown off and, like the shards of glass, flew spiralling through the air.

The vehicle came to a stop with the cab unit inside the building and the engine still running. Students were starting to climb off the truck. Clearly, some were injured and needed help. The police were now massing on the vehicle from both sides. They entered the building, stepping over the shattered window and fallen masonry, knowing they needed to clear the truck from one side and opting for the driver's side. On pulling the door open, Khaleed was roughly manhandled from the vehicle and landed heavily on the ground.

Seeing he was dead, the officers pushed forward into the cab itself, where they found the body of the young lady. They called the truck clear and from the other side of the vehicle, headed into the atrium to find Andrew.

At this stage, they were unsure if he were friend or foe, so they held him at gunpoint.

"Let me see your hands. Do it now," ordered the police officer.

Andrew was a little dazed. He'd landed awkwardly on his shoulder, which was most likely dislocated. But the officers shouting at him brought back his attention. He let go of his gun and raised his hands, which was hard to do when lying almost face-down and with a shoulder out of its socket.

"I am British Intelligence. Don't shoot," he called.

Dragging himself onto his backside, he pulled open his jacket to show he wasn't carrying any other weapons. He really didn't want to be forced into handcuffs, but that didn't happen. A sergeant arrived and directed the officers to keep him under control until his identity was confirmed. Calgary Police Special Branch were en route to do this.

The atrium was in pretty bad shape, but an officer grabbed a set of seats that had, until Khaleed's truck had smashed its way in, been bolted to the floor. He put them upright again, and Andrew was helped onto them. A police officer the size of a house said, "Now, just sit there until we find out who you are. If you blink in the wrong direction, I'll fold you up like a travel mat. Sound good?"

Andrew looked at this behemoth of a man. Ordinarily, he could still make him into the shape of a pretzel if he wanted to, but he was too battered and bruised, and his shoulder was very painful. Instead, he leaned back in his chair as everyone else ran around. He looked at Khaleed, sprawled out in a heap with the side of his head missing. The police were now lowering the passenger out—a petite, pretty young woman, who up until that morning, had her whole life stretched in front of her. Even amongst all the chaos and carnage, the officers were gentle. They laid her down, and one of them checked her pulse. Andrew thought it a strange thing to do but it was probably a procedural thing, or maybe they just hoped they could help.

The officer stood, shaking his head as they covered her with a blanket. They did not do this for Khaleed.

Andrew then saw the police motorcycle rider coming

towards him and called out, "Good morning. Thank you for the help out there."

"You're welcome. How you doing?"

"I've had better days—but you gave me the chance to get to the truck, and I said to myself that if I got out of this, I'd buy you dinner," said Andrew. Was that a female voice he heard? It was hard to tell through all the headgear.

His question was answered as the officer slowly removed their helmet. Blonde hair cascaded out. Striking blue eyes, dazzling smile.

"I'll hold you to that," she replied.

"It's a promise. Name the time and place," said Andrew.

She paused a moment, then took a business card from her pocket. "I heard you were British Intelligence. Do I have to call you Bond?"

Andrew smiled.

She slid the card into his pocket. "In case you do want that dinner."

"And what do I call you?" asked Andrew.

She smiled. "Well, if I'm calling you Bond, you can call me The Russian," she said, and she left.

CHAPTER 81

UNDERGROUND PARKING GARAGE, TELUS CONVENTION CENTRE

The Israel Defense Forces staff member, Victor 1, who was the assigned driver for the vehicle at the TELUS Convention Centre, sat patiently in the driver's seat and watched his surroundings.

On the in-car entertainment system, he had found the parade being broadcast and was watching it on a live TV feed. When the vehicle was stationary, the reasonably sized TV screen that rose from the centre of the dash could be activated. The driver could watch it and still monitor movement around him. But the parking garage was deathly quiet, with only the odd person coming and going.

As he sat waiting, he thought he heard a sound that didn't harmonise with the day so far. He muted the TV and wound down the window to listen. It was an odd sound, but then his eye caught the TV feed. It was clear from the erratic filming that the camera operator was running. He switched off the mute button and heard the noise of the M134—that was the sound he had heard.

He grabbed his comms unit. "Victor One, Victor One to Team Lead, do you copy? Over."

Noya was watching Yigal unveil the plaque when she keyed her mic. "This is Team Lead. Go ahead, Victor One, over."

"We have an attack taking place on the parade. A large machine gun has been deployed from a building on the route. I am unaware of anything else, but we should stand by for extraction, over."

"Copy that Victor One. Team Lead to the group, tighten up, over."

The three other team members in the room didn't need to look at Noya. They simply dressed closer to Yigal, their postures visibly changing.

Noya went to Yigal and, gently touching his elbow, said, "Sir, we need to make our way to the vehicle."

He turned to look at her and he could see by her expression it was serious. Turning to the elderly lady in the wheelchair and shaking her hand again, he said, "Noya tells me it is time to leave. I am so sorry."

The old lady smiled and said, "She looks so young. I bet her mother worries. A good man knows when to listen to a lady. Thank you for coming here today."

"Noya, what has happened?" asked Yigal.

"The parade has been attacked. That's all we know at the moment, but we would like to get you out of here," said Noya.

Her radio then crackled into life again. "Victor One to Team Lead, over."

"Go ahead, Victor One, over."

"We have a number of blacked-out SUVs coming in hot. Other dignitaries are being extracted and additional tactical responses are inbound. We should leave now, over."

"Copy that. We are en route to you, over," said Noya.

As they neared the exit leading to the underground parkade, Noya saw five Calgary Police officers coming in through the opposite end of the atrium.

"Team Lead to the group. I am going to get the Principal to Victor One, break." She continued, "Can you engage with the police and see what they want? Find out what's going on, over."

"Copy, will do, over." Two of the perimeter protection officers moved towards the approaching police officers.

*

Carl was leading the group into the atrium, and as the two security team members approached, he saw Yigal heading for the exit. He made his decision, and as he smiled at one of the protection officers, he drew his sidearm and shot him.

The other protection officer was moving, but on Carl's action, his four other friends spread out, drawing their weapons.

It didn't take a lot of time or effort for both protection officers to be taken out. Next, the group moved on to Noya, Yigal, and the only remaining protection officer. Noya heard the shots and turned to identify the threat. As she spun, she flicked her jacket out of the way and located her sidearm. She drew it from the holster, pulling Yigal behind her.

The other protection officer managed to shoot and hit Johannes, killing him instantly, but was then killed by Alicia. Carl had levelled his weapon on Noya. Even with her reaction time, she didn't stand a chance. Carl fired twice, point blank, and she fell backwards, knocking Yigal down, landing on his legs.

Carl moved quickly and stood astride Noya's body, one foot pressed heavily on her hand, securing her gun. Blood soaked her shirt and flecked her face. She was clearly in distress, struggling to breathe.

Alicia checked Johannes, then looked at Carl, who shook his head. The group moved into a coordinated protective perimeter, quickly bringing guests from the unveiling under control. If anyone attempted to be brave, they were met with quick and sharp violence.

Carl looked down at Yigal, and as their eyes met, a malevolent grin spread across his face. He brought his gun up on aim, and the room went very quiet. Carl had yearned for this moment for so long that he almost couldn't believe it was happening. As he looked down at Yigal, his thoughts raced to his mother and the emptiness she had suffered.

*

Noya knew she was dying, but she still tried to get her gun free. It was hopeless. Carl had her hand and wrist under control with his foot, and she simply didn't have the strength. Composing herself, she used her free hand to locate the knife she carried on her belt, a CRKT Shrill Fixed knife with a four-inch blade. Silently, she slid it clear of the sheath, and with as much force as she could muster, drove the knife upwards. The knife entered Carl's perineum, and his legs buckled immediately from the pain.

Noya pulled the knife clear and stabbed Carl again. This time, she hit him in the anus. The knife broke free from her grip as Carl dropped his knee onto her knife arm, pinning it to the ground. Using his free hand, he reached behind and pulled the blade out of his anus.

Augustus moved towards him, but Carl shouted, "Keep your positions! I shall deal with this."

Carl held the knife in front of him and then looked down at Noya, who was smiling back up at him. He didn't say a word. He simply flipped the knife around in his hand and drove it straight into Noya's eye.

"No, you bastard!" shouted Yigal, who struggled to get up and attack Carl.

Carl swung his arm, striking the old man—who landed on his back—then tried to stand, but the feeling of his severed muscles flexing almost made him vomit.

He raised his gun and, looking at the now distraught Yigal, said, "This is for my grandfather."

CHAPTER 82

THE CONVENTION CENTRE

Peter and Devon were approaching the final set of doors when they heard the shooting start. People had come running out and were shouting that the police were shooting everyone. The two men didn't need to make a plan—it was clearly a need-to-go-and-now situation. Peter remembered his training on active shooters: On arriving at the scene, even if solo, it was imperative to first find the person with the gun. The shooter needed to be hunted down, even if that meant stepping over the dead and injured. The objective was to kill the gunman before they got anyone else, although there was always the hope they would kill themselves instead.

Peter and Devon opened the doors, and in they went. They separated, breaking the area into two halves. Peter could see a police officer kneeling over someone while pointing a gun at an old man. He identified the people dressed in police uniforms as the Argentinians, but despite recognising them, he hesitated for just a moment. This gave Alicia enough time to get Peter in her sights. She fired twice, the first round hitting his ribcage. As he fell, spinning, he took the second round in the shoulder blade.

Devon demonstrated why he was a solid operator and killed Hanna in the blink of an eye. Peter hit the ground and saw Devon heading towards Carl. Thinking Peter was out of the picture, Alicia was now moving to intercept Devon. Peter managed to roll himself over and fired, hitting Alicia in the legs. She crumpled to the ground. He aimed again, this time shooting Alicia under her chin.

Devon then saw Augustus approaching Peter, gun levelled. He shifted away from Carl and dispatched Augustus with a double tap to the head.

Wanting to help his friends, Carl raised his gun and shot at Peter as he lay on the ground. The round struck Peter at the top of his chest, and he rolled over onto his back.

Realising that all his friends had been killed and could not be helped, Carl aimed at Yigal's head and carefully squeezed the trigger. Devon heard the sound of a suppressed weapon, but it was Carl who flew backwards as the rounds struck him.

Peter was in severe distress now, his world slipping away. Through the growing darkness, he could make out Devon moving towards him. In the background, members of the Calgary Police Tactical Unit were flooding in and heading towards Carl to make sure their shots had been effective.

Dressed in their urban tactical equipment, they seemed to glide past Peter and Devon, covering the area in a spider's web of efficiency. He could hear Devon calling out his name, but very softly, like he was far away. And then his world went dark.

CHAPTER 83

TWO AND A HALF WEEKS LATER, FOOTHILLS MEDICAL CENTRE

Peter felt that he had been lying awake with his eyes closed for quite some time. He didn't feel uncomfortable, but opening his eyes seemed like a Herculean task. He wanted to do a little internal self-assessment before attempting to move. He sensed that if he did that, it would hurt—and hurt a lot.

Eventually, he forced his eyes open and found himself in a brightly lit, windowless room. Two of the walls were floor-to-ceiling thick glass, and the area beyond was clearly allowing natural light to stream in.

He lifted his head slightly, then saw a police officer sitting at the end of his bed, reading a book.

"Hello," said Peter.

The police officer looked up. "Look who's awake. Let me go and get the medical team." He disappeared into the large area outside and spoke with another officer. Peter could see they were wearing the same uniforms worn by the tactical officers in the atrium.

It wasn't long before a nurse came scurrying in.

"How are we feeling, Peter?" she asked as she checked his monitors.

"Not bad at all. A little achy. How long have I been here?"

"Just over two weeks. Your people will be here shortly, and we've just called the doctor, who's on his way, okay?" she replied.

"Sounds good. Can I get a cup of tea, please, and something to eat?" asked Peter.

"Sure. I'll be right back with that," said the nurse. As she left, the police officer returned and sat in his chair.

"Can you tell me what happened?" Peter asked him.

"I've had to sign the Official Secrets Act, so I am not sure what I can say. Sorry," he said.

"No, no, that's fine. I understand," said Peter. "Sorry you had to be my babysitter. I know how tedious it can be."

The officer smiled. "We're all on triple time"—he rubbed his thumb across his fingertips—"*cha-ching!* The last two weeks, twelve-hour shifts. I've earned a fortune watching you sleep. You've paid for my skiing holiday, so feel free to lie there as long as you want."

Peter laughed. "I don't think that would be too difficult."

The doctor arrived, followed shortly by Andrew, complete with arm in a sling and healing cuts on his face. "Look who's decided to join us," he said.

The doctor lifted Peter's chart and asked the police officer to step outside the room while they spoke.

"Peter, I am your attending physician. My greatest concerns are your primary injuries and your three gunshot wounds.

There's one to the left side of your ribcage, one to your left shoulder blade, and one at the top of your left chest muscle. You were taken into surgery, and thankfully, it was only muscle tissue damage and broken bones. You have somehow managed to score a hat trick in avoiding vital organs getting hit. We placed you in an induced coma for a week, then allowed you to come back to us in your own time.

"Today is Wednesday, and I plan to discharge you this coming Saturday, but you need to be off intravenous support, and I want to be relatively satisfied you are functionally mobile.

"You will be given some painkillers and a course of anti-inflammatories, but you're in a bit of a mess, so it's going to take some time. I recommend only using painkillers as needed—they're quite addictive. If you can tolerate it, have an ice bath, as that will reduce the inflammation and flush out any unnecessary waste. Any questions?"

"No, that's enough for me to process at the moment. Thank you, Doctor," said Peter.

The doctor then said, "You have cuts and bruises, but generally, you're in good health. Please take it easy." He shook Peter's hand and, as quickly as he'd arrived, made his exit.

Andrew smiled, "Not the friendliest doctor, but he's been outstanding for you and your treatment."

"I don't doubt it. So, what's the update?" asked Peter.

Andrew grinned broadly, "I have been doing some Soviet liaison work while you've been sleeping, and I've been tidying up the mess we made."

"I don't want to know about the Russian stuff. What happened after I blacked out? Who was that old man the Argentinians were after?" asked Peter.

Andrew stood and said, "Peter, you're the only person who

hasn't been debriefed. I'm not trying to be an arse, but I'll be back to interview you tomorrow and hopefully, get some more puzzle pieces in place. There's a lot still at stake, and you may tell us something that changes things, understood? I understand that you want to know everything, but we need your full account before we can do that properly. Once we've processed your statement, we can give you an accurate debrief. We've secured an off-site location for Saturday, where you'll get a formal debriefing and interview. I will tell you, however, that the Americans have changed their view on you regarding their agent in Algeria. All will be revealed in due course—we have to stick to the protocols, I'm afraid. How about that?" said Andrew.

"I have so many questions, but I'd really like a cup of tea and some fresh air," said Peter, smiling.

Andrew asked the police officer to come back in and told him Peter wanted to go to the patients' private garden.

The tactical officer said that would be okay but that he needed a few minutes. He went outside and spoke to his teammates, and they started to move and make some calls.

About fifteen minutes later, the nurse returned, and Peter was carefully assisted into a wheelchair, ensuring his catheter and IV lines remained in position. He felt he could walk, but he quite enjoyed being wheeled to the garden by the nurse.

As he made his way from the private suite, he noticed at least six tactical officers moving ahead of him, securing corridors and clearing the elevator. Some were already in place when he entered the garden.

He was wheeled into the shade, and the warm, fresh air felt amazing. Andrew sat next to him on a bench, and the nurse spoke with the police officer who'd been in Peter's room.

He agreed they would bring him back to the ward when he was done.

The nurse then arrived with an English breakfast tea and a Mars bar.

Peter smiled and nodded at the Mars bar. "Thank you, it's my favourite."

"I thought it might be. When you were in and out of consciousness, you kept mumbling about Mars bars," she joked.

"At least you didn't divulge state secrets," said Andrew, laughing.

They sat together in easy silence as Peter sipped his tea and devoured his chocolate, watching the other patients in the courtyard, who were visibly perturbed at the sight of so many police surrounding him.

An hour later, the police officer came to take Peter back to his room, where, on arrival, all non-medical staff were asked to leave. The nurses pulled back the sheets and removed his gown. He was shocked to see the bruised state of his body, and using mirrors, they showed him his back, too. His dressings were then changed, and when all was done—and despite having slept for more than a fortnight—Peter fell into an exhausted slumber.

Andrew returned the next day. The nurses said he had two hours, max. Andrew said he wouldn't need that long and would be mindful not to tire Peter out. He placed a small recording device on the table, and once the police officer had left, they began. It didn't really take that long, as the only piece that was unknown to them was the conversation Peter had with Chloe.

CHAPTER 84

FOOTHILLS MEDICAL CENTRE

Peter had been given the all-clear and, with a little help, got dressed. He was handed packets of painkillers and anti-inflammatories, and they insisted that he leave the hospital in a wheelchair.

The police officer, using his radio, updated the team that they were moving to the vehicles.

"Is this really necessary?" asked Peter.

He told Peter they had been assigned to him for an unknown period. The threat of attack was still deemed high.

"Okay, if that's the case, then when we get to the doors, could you push me to the vehicle? This nurse shouldn't be put at any risk."

The nurse gently touched Peter's shoulder. "Thank you."

As they reached the doors, Peter asked them to stop, and he got up from the wheelchair. He turned and thanked the nurse before sitting back down to be pushed outside. Andrew had removed his sling and was waiting for Peter by a Range Rover, flanked front and rear by another two blacked-out SUVs. It was kept as low-key as possible, but the presence was there and palpable.

Peter was finally permitted to get out of the wheelchair. Once in the car, Andrew opened the large centre console between the seats. He then removed a handgun and three magazines. He handed them to Peter. "We're not in the clear just yet. You should have this."

Peter took the weapon and ensured it was clear, then loaded a magazine and made it ready.

Andrew handed him a holster and a magazine holder, and as Peter got himself squared away, they pulled away from the hospital. The two SUVs took up position, and they made their exit away from the hospital.

They arrived at the impressive Calgary Rugby Union club-house, entering through a side door and into a private suite that overlooked one of the rugby pitches.

The police tactical officers were all in plain clothes, but they were still quite noticeable as they formed a perimeter of the room. It was a typical stadium function room, furnished for meetings, and with comfortable leather recliners for watching the game afterwards through the large window that looked down on the pitch. Peter eyed the sandwiches and snacks that were laid out, eager to get his first taste of non-hospital food.

"This club's division-one team, the Calgary Knights, are playing in the provincial final, so we can watch that after. Remember I said after all this, we would sit in a quaint English pub and watch a game of rugby? Well, this is the best I could do," said Andrew.

"It's just what I need. Thank you, Andrew," said Peter.

"This briefing, Peter, shouldn't take long. Let's start with the nucleus of all of this: Helena."

Peter sat back in his chair with his cup of tea, ready to take it all in.

"When Helena's grandfather died, her mother, who was Egyptian, was brought to the UK and put through university at Oxford. She was clearly intelligent and worked within the British Foreign Office as an advisor to the ambassadors who worked in the Middle East. She was fluent in several languages, including Arabic, but she was considered to be emotionally detached and what some described as fanatical when it came to her work. We understand that there was a holiday romance where she fell pregnant. Helena was the product of that holiday fling and an only child. Nothing is known of Helena's father—our records show he was Middle Eastern, but we only have his first name and a scant description. In those days you had to disclose these types of contact, but this is all we have.

"Helena was just like her mother. Brilliant, linguistically talented, and driven. Staff members at the time reported that Helena and her mother were inseparable. Helena spent all her time either with her mother; with a nanny, when her mother had to work; or with a tutor, receiving private one-on-one schooling. I am making the next statement as an educated assumption: This is when Helena was indoctrinated in the same right-wing ideology as her mother. Helena went to Harvard and, after graduating, joined the NSA and quietly made her way to the position of deputy director. While in North Africa, Helena encountered a very young—we believe sixteen- or seventeen-year-old—Chloe, and what started as a friendship quickly morphed into a love affair. When we had intelligence regarding the lover, codenamed Benjamin, that Chloe was meeting, we assumed it was a male. It turns out that Benjamin was the name of her mother's childhood teddy bear, intel acquired from the case officer who managed her father. He'd recorded it when the family lived in Egypt.

"On the information provided by you, Peter, it was clear that Chloe was concerned the source they'd been instructed to meet in Algeria might recognise her from her previous visits with Helena. She orchestrated the meeting so that you wouldn't be present at the start, allowing her to deal with the source if she had to, without your knowledge. When the source arrived, they did indeed recognise each other, and Chloe knew she had to kill him. Then she quickly and quite brilliantly spun a narrative whereby the source had been very jumpy; had given the name of the mole, which was Abigail; and had fled before you had arrived. This, of course, put us all in a tailspin, and the rest is history, as they say.

"Now, we will cover Chloe's use of you. Sorry, this may sting a little," said Andrew.

"It's okay, let's hear it." Peter sighed.

"Basically, she seduced you and made you easy to manipulate. She did this so you would go along with her plans without question. This charm offensive exceeded her expectations, however, because you entered the safe house to rescue her, which was an added bonus, got her out of there, treated her wounds, and got her back to the UK."

Peter smiled. "That could have been worse. I am not sure how, but I shall take that."

"Peter, you aren't the first and won't be the last to fall victim to the honey-trap tactic. However, given what you believed to be the facts, your concerns were valid, and your actions to take

Chloe out of the safe house were justified."

Andrew then paused and allowed Peter to take it in a little.

"Yes, I was duped, and I'll never live it down," said Peter with a wry grin.

"Oh, I am sure that no one will mention it again," said Andrew, smiling. He then continued, "Everyone can raise their hand for doing something stupid in the name of romance, so you are in good company. However, it normally involves expensive divorces, not impaling them to a wall, so bravo, Peter," said Andrew, raising his coffee as if to toast Peter's achievement.

Andrew moved on. "By emphasising her right-wing 'sympathies,' shall we say, and by playing on Carl's loyalty to his grandfather, Helena cultivated a relationship with him and his family. His four Argentinian friends naturally followed on. The story is that Carl's grandfather died in Argentina during the extraction of Adolf Eichmann. The family decided, rightly or wrongly, that the Mossad had extracted information from him, then killed him. The autopsy said it was a heart attack, but the family has persistently refused to believe that.

"Yigal Ben-Eliezer is one of the men who went to Argentina and brought Eichmann back. We have spoken with the Israelis and Yigal, and they deny killing Carl's grandfather. To do such a thing would have seriously interfered with their purpose. Yigal said killing anyone so publicly a week before they were planning to leave would have been operational suicide."

He stopped speaking to allow Peter to take a minute to process what he was hearing and figure out why they were talking about Israel all of a sudden.

"Peter, that little old man in the atrium of the TELUS Centre, being attacked by Carl, was Yigal Ben-Eliezer. He's a folk hero in Israel, and they are extremely pleased with what you and Devon did that day. They would like you to fly to Israel to get a hearty thank-you from a few important people," said Andrew.

"What about the guy driving the truck in the parade? How did he get involved?" asked Peter.

"Ah, yes, Khaleed. So, there'd been a terrorist attack in Edmonton. His university classmate Abdulahi Sharif, with whom he'd had no meaningful association, had been responsible, but the police were all over Khaleed. Helena got to hear of it as she was provided with the debriefing notes, and she reached out to Khaleed. He hadn't been fully radicalised, but the harassment by the Edmonton Police Special Branch was the tipping point. Helena exploited that," said Andrew.

"What also helped," he continued, "was Khaleed's professor at the university, Alice Huber, whom Khaleed murdered. We assume that he murdered her to tie up any loose ends or after receiving instructions from Helena. She is the great-granddaughter of Irmgard Huber. Irmgard Huber, a devoted Nazi, was the chief nurse at the Hadamar killing centre and was responsible for the deaths of an estimated 15,000 people who didn't meet the criteria of the master race. We have found intelligence that Alice Huber was sympathetic to the cause and was recruited by Helena.

"Now, the next element is merely a hypothesis. During World War Two, Hitler and the Third Reich had an affiliation with, and admiration for, the Islamic world. There were even Muslim units within Hitler's army. We believe that Helena saw the killing of Yigal Ben-Elizer and the attack by Khaleed Zaher as a way to bring Islamist extremists and the right wing together. This is why there were two seemingly unrelated attacks at the same event. We think Helena used her position and influence to advance her cause, orchestrating the attacks while remaining unidentified."

"So why did she kill Jessica, and do it the manner she did?" asked Peter.

"We aren't sure about that. We assume that Helena felt that Jessica had become suspicious of her or had identified something about the impending attack, and Helena wasn't going to let anything stand in the way of that. Also, she may have wanted to shift our focus, and killing Jessica almost did that. Thankfully, we stayed on task," said Andrew.

"It should be noted that there is a joint task force involving the Americans, ourselves, the Canadians, and a number of European agencies working on locating Helena," said Andrew.

"Peter, what I have told you are the exciting parts. The rest you can read about later at your leisure. Do you have any questions?" asked Andrew.

"No, apart from what do I do next? I guess I need to check in with my chief," said Peter.

"So, Peter, I did speak with your inspector about that. You have been given six months' paid vacation starting today and you aren't expected back until you feel ready. I also understand that they have a little something for you, possibly a medal, I think. Do you have any other questions?"

"No, I think that sums it up. If I think of something, I can always ask later. Thank you, Andrew," said Peter.

Peter and Andrew grabbed some food and ensconced themselves in the very comfortable chairs looking out over the rugby pitch. It was an hour before the 2:00 p.m. game, and Peter knew that if he started drinking this early, he wouldn't last long.

"So, Peter, I've a few more things to tell you," said Andrew.

"I am intrigued. Go on."

"Firstly, as I mentioned, the Americans have taken you off their most-wanted list. They discovered that their agent, the one you killed in the garage, was working for Helena, so now they consider what you did to have been a little housekeeping for them. Their president wants to present you with an award, and they have deposited a financial thank-you into your bank account."

Andrew went on, "And as you've just been informed, the Israelis are also happy, since you saved one of their national treasures. They, too, have an award for you and have also sent funds to show their appreciation.

"I'm not going to labour the point, but the same goes for the Canadians and ourselves. So, to sum up, you are now quite wealthy and will have to get a bigger mantlepiece for all these little gongs you're about to receive. When you're back, I will make all the arrangements, so don't worry about that.

"And lastly, Peter, I have been asked to offer you a job with us. It would be similar work to what you've been doing thus far, but hopefully, a little less intense. It's been backed by Sir Goodlove and your chief."

"Oh really!" said Peter. "Can I have more details and a bit of time to think about it?"

"Of course. When you have finished your six months off, we can figure it all out. You would be good for our little group, and I strongly recommend you join us." He hesitated awkwardly for a moment, then said quietly, "There's something else I want to say, Peter. I hope you don't mind. Your wife. She would have been proud of what you've done, but I think she would want you to be happy."

"Thank you, but where did that come from?" asked Peter, a little taken aback.

"When you were in the hospital, I looked through the documents you completed when you started the course. I don't know who this Sophie is, but she must be someone special for you to put her as your next of kin. We don't get many opportunities for happiness in our line of work, so don't throw something away you might regret."

"Yes, you might be right, Andrew," said Peter, Then, changing the topic, "What does Abigail think about all this and me joining the team?"

"Ah, yes, Abigail. She went back to the UK straight after the attack. She buried her son, then resigned. She's planning to move to a cottage in Scotland or Ireland, I'm not exactly sure where, and Sir Goodlove was made the head of MI6," said Andrew.

"I didn't think Abigail would give this life up," said Peter.

"I think that after losing her husband and then her son, it was time."

Peter sighed. "Yes, you're probably right."

"After the game, we're going to stay at the Fairmont Chateau Lake Louise. The protection team from the Calgary Police Tactical Unit will be with us. We'll be there until we can be sure that you can protect yourself. You struggled just getting into that chair."

Peter laughed. "I can't deny, I am a bit of a mess. And besides, there are worse places for the protection team to hang out."

Just as the teams were running out, Andrew went off and quickly reappeared with two ice-cold pints of beer. "Cheers, Peter," he said, raising his glass.

Their pints clinked, the whistle blew, and Peter took the first sip.

The beer tasted great, and the game was exciting. The Calgary team won, making them provincial champions. As the teams congratulated and commiserated with each other and the crowds began to disperse, Peter and Andrew also departed and headed out of the city.

CHAPTER 85

FAIRMONT CHATEAU LAKE LOUISE

Peter took the time to relax, refocus, and convalesce. For the first week, he would hike to a teahouse not far from the hotel. He would arrive exhausted, wheezing, and breathless, which amused the tactical officers. As time went on, they would all run to the team room. As was natural in these types of environments, teams started to challenge each other to get the fastest time there and back.

The tactical officers won hands down, but Peter and Andrew held their own. Andrew got the second fastest time, and Peter the fifth.

On the last day, they ran the route together. It was decided they would all jump into the glacier-fed lake at the end, a very quick dip into the water before they headed back to the hotel. On the final evening before they were due to check out, Peter asked them to meet in his room. The hotel manager was there, and Andrew sat quietly in the corner.

"Guys, I couldn't have asked for a better bunch of drill sergeants to keep an eye on me and get me back into shape." There was a sprinkling of laughter and a couple of heckles from the men. Peter waited for them to quieten down, then said, "I have spoken with the various powers that be, who have agreed that as a thank-you, you will each receive an all-expenses-paid, seven-day stay here with your families."

The sergeant for the team stepped forward. "That's very kind of you, Peter, but not necessary."

"I know, but it's my choice and my money. My chief has cleared it with yours, so there we go. Take some time off and bring your partners and kids here. Everything is covered, from the food and drink to the spa. So enjoy and decompress."

After thanking Peter, one by one, the men left the room. "That was a nice gesture," said Andrew. "I'm sure they'll appreciate it."

"I hope so," said Peter.

"What about your plan for tomorrow?"

"Did you ever watch the TV show *The Long Way Round* with Ewan McGregor?" asked Peter.

"I did not."

"Well, McGregor and a friend go on this round-the-world motorcycle trip, but they end up having an accident in Calgary. They go to a motorbike store called Barnes Powersports Blackfoot. I found out it's still there—I think they got a little famous from being on the show. Anyway, I like a bit of biking myself, so I have ordered a motorbike and all the required gear, and tomorrow, I take delivery of it here. I've booked an extra night to get prepared, and then I'm going to take a little road trip. There's someone I need to see."

"Sounds fantastic," said Andrew.

In the morning, everyone ate breakfast together, and Peter watched them all head off.

Andrew pulled him aside before he left. "Peter, just to remind you, there are still people out there who might want to find you. Call me if you need anything, and keep your sidearm close." Then he climbed into his Range Rover and pulled away from the Fairmont Chateau Lake Louise. For the first time in a very long time, Peter found himself alone. He'd reflected a lot during his time at the hotel, assessing what had happened; identifying the person he'd become from the experience; and deciding what he wanted his life, moving forward, to look like. He took a deep breath and wandered back inside.

Later that afternoon, the delivery people from Barnes Powersports Blackfoot delivered the bike to the underground parking, along with bags, a jacket, helmet, gloves—everything he needed. Peter had dinner, then packed up his bike and stood back to admire his Moto Guzzi V7 Stone Centenario E5. Beautiful.

CHAPTER 86

It was another beautiful evening in the land of paradise with not a cloud in the sky and the sun, once again, radiating heat. The people who lived along the shoreline all had secluded spots—it really was their own slice of heaven. One of the residents stood with her feet curled into the sand as she watched the setting sun. Even at this time of night, the sand was hot, and burying your feet a little gave some respite.

A warm breeze drifted on the shore, causing the large linen shirt she was wearing to gently flutter in effortless resistance.

The house she stood in front of was a single-storey modern home with large windows that looked out onto the ocean. Her house was a little unique in that it had air conditioning for when it got a little too much.

At dusk, she would sit in her favourite leather chair, sip

her expensive scotch, and watch the sunset. Tonight was no different, so she walked up from the beach and strolled into her lavish living room. She poured a healthy measure into her favourite crystal glass, added some ice cubes, and took a seat.

She knew she'd have to clean up the sand dropping from her feet, but that could be done later. The leather chair sat behind one of the large glass windows, and tonight, she had them all swung open, allowing the outside world to cascade in. The chair had wide arms on which to rest her scotch glass if needed and a high back so she could rest her head and relax.

She sipped her drink and placed the glass on the arm. She felt an itch on her foot and tried to use her other foot to brush it. Strangely, it didn't seem to want to move. She tried to sit forward and look at her feet. This didn't work either, and then she realised she couldn't move the hand holding the whisky.

The man who had been hiding in the house then came up beside the chair and took the glass from the lady's hand. She could see he was wearing black surgical gloves and was pulling a chair from the kitchen behind him. He put the chair in front of the lady and sat down to face her.

"Good evening, Helena. How are you? That question is rhetorical, as I know you can't answer," said Shaukey, placing the glass on the floor. "I am going to tell you what's happening, as it will add to your anxiety and fear.

"You have been poisoned with a refined venom from a puffer fish. This remarkable stuff causes paralysis, starting with the extremities. Then it causes the lungs to dissolve internally and you to eventually drown in your own blood. The most impressive part is that you are fully conscious throughout the fifteen minutes it takes for you to die. Your body sends your heart rate through the roof, trying to fight the poison. The pain is extreme. So, as you're drowning, you will probably have a massive heart attack."

Beads of sweat formed on Helena's face. The veins across her exposed flesh were standing tall as her heart did its work.

"You're probably wondering what sadistic human beings developed this poison," said Shaukey, sitting back and enjoying the moment. "During World War Two, a group of nasty bastards that you might have heard of, the Nazis, had some people work for them at a place called Auschwitz. These people were doctors, but their commitment to the Hippocratic oath was a little lacking. Not quite content with exterminating people, they decided to torture and experiment on them using some new poisons. This particular poison took time to develop, but they didn't care, because they had the time and the Jews to test it on.

"I thought you'd appreciate the irony of being killed by something developed by your own people," said Shaukey. "Do you know how we found out about this? Yigal Ben-Eliezer's wife, Eliana, was a test subject. He mentioned it when we met with him. His wife didn't die when they were developing the poison, but it did cause her reproductive organs to slowly liquify and leak out of her orifices. She almost bled to death, but she wasn't going to let them win.

"Yigal Ben-Eliezer's wife had to steal clothes from dead Jews and cut them up into small pieces. She would then push these small pieces of rag inside her to slow the bleeding. But she never gave up, and all her fellow female inmates worked together because they wanted to live."

Helena was now beginning to struggle with her breathing. The sweat continued to run down her face, and the vein on her neck looked as if it might burst at any moment.

"You look like you are in a lot of discomfort, Helena," said Shaukey, who sat impassively, watching it all unfold.

"You probably don't have much time left, so I better say my piece. This is for everyone you have had killed or allowed to be killed. I volunteered for this so that afterwards, I could visit Jessica's grave and tell her I didn't let her down, and that we got our revenge." There was emotion in Shaukey's voice.

Helena was ash-grey, and although she was paralysed, she was starting to convulse. Blood trickled out the corner of her mouth, the veins around her eyes were bulging, and the blood vessels in the whites of her eyes started to fracture.

He had nothing else to say. His expression as he sat watching her agonising death said it all. In time, the convulsions slowed to intermittent twitches, and eventually, she fell silent.

He leaned down and whispered into Helena's ear, "Now, it is done."

He retrieved the glass and the crystal decanter containing the scotch. Once he had safely disposed of the contents, he rinsed them out, dried them, refilled the decanter, and put everything back where he'd found them.

Shaukey, wearing a short-sleeved shirt and shorts, walked outside and headed towards his motorbike. He slid on his helmet with the blacked-out visor and activated the comms inside. When his phone and helmet had connected, he dialled the number and rode away.

"Hello," said the voice.

"I have completed my homework. Heading home," said Shaukey.

"Thank you," said the voice.

Shaukey was following a coastal road, and when the call ended, he threw the phone into the ocean.

Andrew, without speaking, hung up the large speaker-phone in the middle of the table.

Michael, Twyla, and Lars nodded their acknowledgement and cut their video links from Langley.

Hobbs and Patterson got up from the table and left without saying a word.

Yigal Ben-Eliezer, who was in Mossad headquarters, stood up and thanked everyone in the room. Then he turned to the camera. "Thank you," he said, and the video link went dead.

Colonel Grieves, Devon, and the Matron shook each other's hands, then killed their video feed from the training base in Wales.

Sir Goodlove got up from the table and, heading into another room, made a call.

"Hello," said the lady who answered.

"We are all finished for the day," said Sir Goodlove.

"Thank you." The call ended.

Abigail took the SIM out of the phone and threw everything off the cliffs into the roaring ocean. She brushed her thumb across the face of the Omega watch she was wearing, took a deep breath, and turned to make her way back to her little stone cottage on the Isle of Skye.

CHAPTER 87

VICTORIA GENERAL HOSPITAL, VANCOUVER ISLAND

Sophie loved her job, but at times like this, she just felt awful. As she stood at the end of the young girl's bed, telling her family that there was yet another delay, she could see the look of heartbreak etched across their faces.

She promised this would be the last delay, but she had said this before, and the family were losing faith. Their daughter needed the surgery urgently, and delaying it again might not be a viable option for their little angel and her failing heart.

After leaving the private room, Sophie walked down the main stairs, speaking on the phone. "This is the third time we have cancelled this surgery for this young girl. We can't do it a fourth time."

The voice on the other end seemed to be in agreement and said they would find out why it had been rescheduled again. "She needs this operation, and it's our errors that have caused the delays. Think how we're going to look if she dies."

"I understand, Doctor, and we'll make things happen. I'll drive the damn valve there myself if I need to," said the voice on the phone.

"If that's what it takes, I'll come and get it," said Sophie. She was now walking through the large foyer as she ended the call and slid her phone into her pocket.

The hospital was busy, but above the noise, she heard her name being called.

She turned to see her colleagues beckoning her over. Like Sophie, they were all dressed in surgical tops, trousers, and colourful caps.

Sophie joined them, and one of the nurses asked what the verdict was.

"They told me the valve will arrive tonight," said Sophie, giving a fingers-crossed sign.

"So, it's hurry up and wait. Again," said one of the nurses, smiling cynically.

"As always." Sophie smiled.

They asked if she wanted to join them for coffee, but she said she needed some fresh air instead. Walking outside, she slid off her cap, then made her way from the main entrance to see if she could find a little peace and solitude. After a short distance, she stopped and looked around. That was better, much quieter. She closed her eyes and took a deep, calming breath, and as she opened them, she saw it, parked in a stall by the sidewalk: a V7 Stone Centenario E5.

She stared at the bike, then stepped off the sidewalk to stand next to it. She gently touched the brown leather seat, allowing her fingers to follow its contours. Her mind wandered. She was back in Italy, holding on to Peter's waist, squeezing his thigh, wanting him to go faster so they could get back to the hotel.

She felt suddenly strange, like she was being watched. Looking up, she scanned the area, anxious to know who might be looking at her. And then, barely able to believe them, her eyes fell on a familiar face. Peter, standing on the sidewalk, holding two coffees.

She still had her hand resting on the saddle of the bike as the smile that Peter loved grew across her face.

A little pause, then Peter said, "Hi."

"Hi," said Sophie.

"I got you the fanciest coffee they had." He raised the take-away cup in his left hand. "I didn't know if I should just turn up or if you would even want to see me after all this time."

Sophie stepped onto the sidewalk and into Peter's open arms, which, despite still holding the coffees, managed to pull her closer into a kiss. As their lips reacquainted, he felt a surge of happiness, mixed with pure wanting. He'd made the right decision.

At last, they broke away, looking at each other in disbelief.

"Hi," they said, once again, laughing.

"Hang on, hang on," said Peter, and he put the coffees on the ground. He then gathered her up again. "God, I missed you." He held her close, and they embraced for the longest time. Peter was transported back to the bridge in Venice as the same waves of emotion overcame him. He didn't want to let her go, and he buried his head in her neck, gently cradling the back of her head.

They leaned back again to look at each other and, seeing the tears in each other's eyes, wrapped their arms around each other once more, crying and laughing at the same time.

Eventually, they finally composed themselves. Peter

retrieved the coffees and looked across to the hospital, where he spotted a group of medics with their noses pressed against the glass, waving wildly. "Are those friends of yours?" he inquired.

Sophie looked over and saw her entire team jumping around and cheering. "Never seen them before in my life." Then the nurse she'd spoken to earlier appeared. "Is this the Motorcycle Man from Venice?"

Sophie smiled and looked at Peter. "Yes, it is."

The nurse turned to the group and gave them a thumbs up. "I am so happy for you, Sophie," she said, and then sprinted back to the hospital.

The whole group then started to clap. Peter gave a little curtsey, and catching Sophie's eye, they laughed again.

"Can I whisk you away from here?" asked Peter.

Sophie's head dropped, and she said, "I would love that. But first, I have to fix a little girl's heart."

Peter lifted her chin and kissed her softly. "And then, perhaps, you could have a go at mine?"

THE END

www.ingramcontent.com/pod-product-compliance
Lightning Source LLC
Jackson TN
JSHW080453190225
79081JS00001B/3